Praise for WOMAN WITH EYES CLOSED

"By slow and steady degrees, Matthiessen takes all the familiar elements of the standard heist thriller and transforms them into something more. Readers who might initially feel that too much time is being spent focusing on the lives and relationships of the thieves, for instance, will find themselves increasingly fascinated by the author's ability to bring all the disparate worlds of the narrative to vivid life. Just as Hobbs is drawn to Perrin ("the sound of her voice, her courage and her forlornness"), readers will be totally engrossed. A riveting and richly nuanced art-crime novel."

~*Kirkus Reviews* (starred review)

"A beautifully crafted suspense thriller of a read from cover to cover, *Woman with Eyes Closed* is especially and unreservedly recommended for community library Contemporary Mystery/ Suspense collections."

~Midwest Book Review

"Matthiessen's depictions of Sagaponack, where she grew up, are wonderfully true to life. This high stakes art thriller delivers an entertaining cast of Hamptons characters, from Russian oligarchs to art-world brats. The mob is involved and, oh, a hurricane is barreling in. The author's delivery of suspense, with a sophisticated insider's view of the social milieu, makes it a top-notch read."

~East Magazine (The East Hampton Star)

"This moderately to briskly paced novel has skillfully crafted twists and consequences that branch into emotional turns of events. Multilayered and diverse characters help paint the atmosphere, add intrigue and drama to the storyline, and drive the plot . . . *Woman with Eyes Closed* will appeal not only to fans of thrillers, suspense, and romance but also to readers curious about the culture and dynamics of the art world."

~Carmen Tenorio, *Readers' Favorite*

". . . especially for East End readers, *Woman with Eyes Closed* will longingly resonate, recalling a time before luxe buildings and big money art acquisitions came to dominate a once genuine artists' community. And the novel has—no spoiler alert—a lovely ending."

~Joan Baum, *Sag Harbor Express*

"A compelling suspense novel, *Woman with Eyes Closed* explores the contrasting lives of the wealthy living in opulence and the desperate actions of the underprivileged longing for a way out . . . [*Woman with Eyes Closed*] delves into themes of relationships, romance, trust, money, and crime, making it an intriguing read for fans of suspenseful mysteries."

~Angelique Papayannopoulos, *Readers' Favorite*

WOMAN WITH EYES CLOSED

WOMAN WITH EYES CLOSED

a novel

RUE MATTHIESSEN

Woman with Eyes Closed

Paperback ISBN: 978-1-957607-32-0
Hardcover ISBN: 978-1-957607-33-7
eBook ISBN: 978-1-957607-34-4

Cataloging-in-Publication Data is available upon request

Manufactured in the United States of America

Published by
Latah Books, Spokane, Washington
www.latahbooks.com

Art evokes the mystery without which the world would not exist.

–Rene Magritte

Being good in business is the most fascinating kind of art. Making money is art and working is art and good business is the best art.

–Andy Warhol

CHAPTER 1
FULL MOON

Rotterdam, Netherlands
July 3rd, 2012

The museum had a religious feeling at night. It was serious here, a deep seriousness that made him ashamed, like a church would if he were breaking the law, which he certainly was. Luuk felt along the pipe wrench with his fingers, his eyes scaling up the sides to the yellow brick that encircled the second story of the building. His brother Piet and Piet's girlfriend Ineke assembled into place behind him. Luuk wound up and hit the top panel of the door—a dull *thwuck.* But the glass held, a bullet-sized hole in the middle. One more good-sized swing, and it gave way, shards and irregular cubes skittering onto cement and the black granite floor inside. He crawled through, his brother crouching low and following, and Ineke last. The alarm firing—that was expected, a high-pitched whine, not very loud. They had gone over this many times—in the day when the museum was open, and on the maps of the interior that his mother had sketched out at home.

Their sneakers chirped on the polished stone floor of the cavernous entrance hall. Orange runner lights ran this way and that at their feet; they hadn't seen that during the day. For a moment, Luuk was frozen, awestruck by the fact that they had gotten through the door, by the spookiness of the lights touching the bottom of the paintings, and by the enormity of what they were going to do. Piet was frozen too, so Luuk barked at him to get moving. Piet, with a ski mask on, managed to express in a millisecond that he wasn't in need of directions or as stupid as Luuk thought he was. Luuk pointed again—Go, *Go!!* you *fool!* Piet flew up the stairs to the Van Hoensbroeck gallery, while, as per plan, Luuk started through Old Masters. Twelve portraits mounted on the chocolate brown walls of the corridor had picture lights on very dimly, as if the caretaker thought they might be lonely in the night with no one to look at them. Luuk remembered them all—Count Schimmelpenninck, Baron Van Coeverden, and Jonkheer Wladimiroff—his flashlight beam swooping over bulbous nose and stern glare, gilt filigree and cascade of gray curls.

Last night in Amsterdam they had gone over their routes again and what they would bring. Piet had had last-minute jitters and didn't want to go, but Ineke said no more delays, the time had come. The Kunsthal was nearing the close of a three-year-long renovation which had added an entrance hall and kiosks to its north side. Its susceptibility was just there for anyone at all to see. Soon it would be finished, vulnerabilities plugged up, and security upgraded, she had said, adding that of course they weren't to talk about that in the newspaper. It was absurd that the museum hadn't at least extended the hours of the security guards, but the fact was they hadn't. She had come on three separate nights to make sure. Luuk and Piet had spent a few nights nearby also, looking for signs of life behind the scaffolding and never found them.

Leonie had had shots of black coffee ready and the diagrams on the table, while Couscous the big orange cat sat half-asleep next to the sugar bowl, watching it all. On the table were three black hoodies, three flashlights, three balaclavas, and two bags for the paintings which were not very big. Piet thumped around upstairs, late as usual. Ineke had double-checked that the weather would be clear and the moon would be full. "On the one hand, more visibility," she'd said. "On the other, police stations were always busy then."

Luuk's route was to go right up the stairs at the end of the Old Masters' hall. Even though he was determined, he found that time and space refused to acknowledge his efforts. He couldn't seem to get there, just to the end of the hall. In the dim dark, he found himself having a conversation with the past, the eyes of long-dead luminaries drilling into the side of his face. Each second fattened with pressure. The old goats were holding him hostage—he couldn't get out of their grip. He suddenly felt dizzy, like some silly girl. He stopped under Van Coeverden and leaned against the wall next to him. He thought he was going to faint. *Shame on you, disgusting toad!* they screamed, sensing his vulnerability. Schimmelpenninck guffawed, his red fleshy mouth opening wide to show ancient yellow teeth.

Soon a rich one, Luuk mouthed, sucking air into his lungs. A break in the orange lights up ahead meant the stairwell entrance. There, the sign for the de Stuers gallery rose up, blurry and hot and skewed, as if the ceiling might come crashing down at any moment. Forcibly, Luuk steadied his breathing and told himself to keep his head. Unlike Piet, he was not a total novice. As young as fourteen he had spent summers breaking into the tall houses that leaned into each other in graceful rows along the Keizersgracht. He had been in this situation before, alone and in the wrong, someplace where he shouldn't have been, taking things that were not his, listening to alarms squeal and shivering in a house shut down for the winter, which was always so much colder than outside on the street. He had grown up on this kind of thing and had almost always gotten out of it. He had never been caught—he had never even been questioned. He had known enough to stagger the thefts in the neighborhood, never take anything too valuable, and never to rob houses close to each other, so as not to establish a pattern. This much greater risk didn't bear thinking of at the moment.

He took the stairs two at a time, while behind him the grandees kept on with their epithets, more distant now, ratcheted down, shouts turning to whispers and grumbles among themselves under the sound of the alarm. In the gallery, his flashlight beam disappeared into moon-thrown rectangles from the skylights. Oddly, he thought about Ineke, the way the curve of her breasts still showed under the oversize sweatshirt she was wearing last night and her shapely legs under it. What a thing to be thinking about *now.* He stuffed the flashlight into his hoodie while stepping up his pace. His own blood pounded in his ears, steady and fast, drowning out the alarm, which made the room start to spin again.

Still no sirens, no interference. Ineke had certainly done her homework. Crazy. His heart was thundering now. Ineke, Ineke, *Ineke* . . . while he tried to quell such stupid thoughts. Piet's sneakers were squeaking again on the lower level. He had either already gotten the Monets and was headed for the exit or he was doing his idiot dance, spinning and whirling around. It was possible—Piet had an overexuberance that liked to tempt fate, which complimented Ineke's weird tics, and that was the how and the why they had found each other. Luuk came to the Picasso. Ineke had said to just take that one out with the razor; it wasn't that important—but a Picasso nonetheless. With the gloves on he was clumsy and pierced the corner of the painting. Then he came to the last of the booty, a small portrait of a young woman with shoulder-length brown hair that was chosen for its size. Clippers in, scraping the wall. Thank God, or the fates, or whoever took care of things . . . *thank you* . . . but the clippers were not long enough. He heard a shattering of glass on the first level. What was Piet doing? He couldn't yell at him because they had to be silent; they were of course being taped. He remembered what Ineke had said—just rip the painting down if the clippers didn't fit. Sweat broke out on his upper lip, while the alarm continued its steady screech. Was it louder up here? Between that and his own heart, he was deafened. He placed his gloved hands on the frame and tore it from the wall. The frame broke, the canvas hanging precariously. She had allowed for that too, supplying everyone with a razor. *If the frame breaks, keep it—might be worth something.* But first he had to straighten it out on the floor, like arranging the wings of a dead bird. Razor it out, roll it up, stuff it in the bag along with the broken frame. He quickly looked around the gallery before he left, knowing he'd never see it again.

Downstairs he saw that the top section of the door had given way, leaving its frame bisecting the middle. Shards of glass were everywhere, popping and cracking under their sneakers. He heard a far-off siren. As the oldest, he'd have to be last—that was his burden. Go, go, *go!!!* he motioned, throwing his bag onto the walkway, while Ineke and Piet shimmied through. The sirens were closer now. He saw Piet up ahead, already past the scaffolding, bag flailing at his side, halfway across to the van. Luuk noticed that the parking lot contained the same two cars it had earlier, with the old farmer's van they had stolen parked in the farthest corner—the license plate blocked with newspapers because of the cameras. Wouldn't want to get *him* into trouble, Luuk thought, emerging from the scaffolding. At the last minute, Piet had worried about it and bought the tape and paper to cover up the plates.

Again, it seemed as if his feet were spinning while he made no progress, each second bulging with pressure. Piet flicked open the van's back doors, yelling to Ineke, *Go!!* as she took the driver's seat. Luuk's hands were damp in his gloves; his ears filled with their muffled shouts and the sirens, now probably within five streets. He saw that Piet—having not yet seen him—was clocking the parking lot as if Luuk could be left here to greet the police, freeing him to run away with Ineke and the paintings. Piet was all emotion, no logic. An idiot. He had no connections, especially concerning sales as delicate as these would prove to be.

Ineke saw him and gunned the van toward the entrance, the back doors swinging wide. Once in Luuk's path, she slowed but not by much, forcing him to jump for it, heart pounding so hard he thought his chest would burst. As she screeched toward the main road, the doors were still open, so he braced himself vertically inside the hurtling vehicle, holding on to one of the wooden storage units the farmer had fortunately built solid against the interior wall. Stretching as long as he could, he hooked one door with his foot, pulled it in and secured it while yelling for Piet to hold onto the paintings. The sirens were either very near or behind them, it was hard to tell which. He could hardly afford a glance to the street. Ineke was good on the straights but took the corners too fast, the old jalopy practically on two wheels, the other door still swinging. It was just a matter of getting over to the other side when the force of a turn would waft the door to him so he could catch it. As he scrambled across, a sack of potatoes fell out. Bracing himself against the closed door and the farmer's spare tire, he was very nearly dispatched to the pavement before grabbing the door's inside cubby and slamming it shut. He fell back against the potato sacks, panting, dust flouring his hair.

"The masks! The masks off! Fuck!" he coughed.

They had forgotten. Fortunately, it was still so early that it was almost dark, and no one was up to see them looking like the cast of *The Hot Rock*, bowling around the streets of Rotterdam. Piet was scanning the surroundings, his head rotating from one side to the other like a baby. The sirens sounded about the same, but after a quick scan of the streets, Luuk still didn't see anything. One of the back doors flew open again, and another sack of potatoes went. Fuck! Shit! Luuk did his Houdini treatment of the door, lashing it shut with a length of rope he found. He crawled forward and tried to hold on to the potatoes while the back of the van fishtailed onto the main road.

"Slow *down*!" he yelled to Ineke, who was angled forward like the prow of a Viking ship.

Vibrations rumbled up steadily through the bags, the property of an old codger who left his van running outside the green market in the town. Tough luck for him. Luuk popped open the hatch window, listening to the sirens warbling in and out strangely, and yes . . . receding.

"Hear that?" Ineke said.

The other two nodded.

"Just barely," said Piet. "I think it's good."

Piet lit a cigarette with gloved fingers and offered one to Luuk and Ineke. They smoked in silence, Luuk dropping his on the potatoes. It was hard to smoke with the gloves on, but they all needed something to steady their nerves.

"Savor, *savor*," Piet said. "This might be our last."

"Don't make a joke," said Luuk under his breath, his whole body still shaking. "You'll tempt the fates."

They progressed at a more moderate pace, each trying to catch their breath.

"But what about the plates?!" Ineke said suddenly, as if prodded with a fork. There were cameras all along this road that might note such an anomaly.

What slick customers they were, thought Luuk. The key thing he consoled himself with—they lived halfway across the country from here, a long way in Holland. They put on their masks and pulled over. Piet jumped out and ripped the papers off the license plates, and they all relieved themselves in the bushes.

Back on the road, Ineke ventured a little more than the speed limit, just like everyone else. Sodium lights swished over them, along with a sense of numbing shock. It had *worked.* Piet swore and slapped his knees, pulling from a flask of *Jenever* he had stashed in his jacket. All three of them were awestruck with wonder—that Ineke had come up with this idea, that they had worked on it for the last six months, and that they'd pulled it off. Not one of them had ever had a success like it. They each sipped from the flask, feeling the bone-racking night melt away, and imagined that the cops were drifting farther and farther behind in their wake. So far, very good. In about twenty minutes they'd take the park road and go onto the trail, pushing the van deep into the woods as far as it could go. Then they'd transfer the paintings, tools, bags, and balaclavas to the backpacks they'd left in the trees, eat the sandwiches they left, and roll out of the wood, one by one in a leisurely way to merge with the morning bike traffic heading west. They'd leave the bikes at the station like so many did, shuck the gloves they no longer needed into the bags, and take trains back to Amsterdam, separately. Nothing to distinguish them from the other commuters. Holland, a well-run nation of seventeen million, was still a place you could get lost in, if you knew what you were doing.

Ineke brushed back a lock of her blue-black hair, the row of chrome studs in her right ear gleaming. Luuk thought about the stud in her tongue. Lights passed over them like riffled playing cards, while the rumble of the old motor came up through the potato sacks. He felt for the paintings, the pierced Picasso light as air, the Monets in their frames. The one called *Woman with Eyes Closed* was no bigger than a magazine. Hard to believe. Piet pulled deeply from his flask and kicked his boots up on the dashboard as if he were going on holiday. The van floated creakily into the turn off the main road and then took a speed bump too fast, causing the Monets to clack together testily. Luuk kept his hand on the bag while studying Ineke's tense pale face.

* * *

"No, they weren't going to listen to the news," said Leonie. "Absolutely not. I know you want to, and so do I, but let's not spook ourselves."

Dust motes drifted around the old Südfunk radio where it sat in the bay window on a milk crate, next to an almost-as-ancient stereo.

But something had to be done, thought Luuk. Since they'd gotten back from Rotterdam, they'd been up all night.

Leonie shook her head. "There will be a bulletin. This is going to be a very big deal for Holland. You'll thank me later." She set down a tray with a pitcher of hot coffee, mugs, milk, and *appeltaart*.

Piet leaned in to the table, his boot dangerously close to one of the Monets. Ineke, loopy from exhaustion, swooped in and moved it to a corner, placing it where they could still see it. On a side table, she had the portrait of the woman pinned flat with empty glasses, next to a stack of bubble wrap sheets. The Monet and the Picasso were propped around the room, looking a bit sad. He could see her gearing up, beginning to think again. Hard. She was too much for Piet.

The air in the room was fetid, so Luuk cracked a window to the street, making sure the curtain was pulled. Shifting her attention to Luuk, Ineke asked him which one was *his* favorite. He gestured with his chin to the woman with brown hair on the table that he'd had to cut out. All he could think was of course it was the dreaming woman because she shared two "X" chromosomes with this be-studded, black-clad minx. While lighting a cigarette, he offered her one from his pack, which she took and he lit, cupping the match. Her full lips trembled a bit on the filter.

Later that morning, a dingier reality was upon them. Ineke wandered, looking at the four paintings, while Piet dozed, his boots up on the coffee table. Leonie took away the coffee things and came back with a rag. She briskly wiped away the crumbs left on the table and faced them, her hands on her hips.

"Okay, that was the job. Now we get to the marriage, and marriages are long and difficult and not thrilling—so—the hardest part." She landed a smack on Piet's boots to wake him.

Ineke curled into a corner of the sofa, the two empty blue backpacks next to her like deflated puppets.

Piet yawned and stretched. "How can this be the hard part? The deed is done."

"Because there is nothing to do," said Ineke.

"What d'you mean?"

"Just go to your school. You go and I go for my accelerated courses, and things go on like before. Today."

"But I don't want to go to school anymore."

Leonie chimed in, "Did you think you weren't going to get an education? What would Papa have thought?"

Luuk wished she hadn't opened up this subject.

"Papa would have been damn happy that we won't have to work like he did," said Piet.

Luuk shook his head. Six years younger and always showing it. Their father would hardly have believed their lives now.

"I'm not going back to school. I won't," Piet said.

Ineke inched toward him on the sofa. "It will get easier, and we have only one more year!"

"You'll get out earlier with those extra courses," Piet said, as she nestled under his arm.

"That's a long way off," said Ineke as she caressed his knee. "Don't get ahead of yourself, *schatje*."

Leonie began rolling up a joint. "Here's how it's going to go. Ineke and I will handle it. You remember that we said it, right? We have to be safe. The best way to do that is to not make any changes."

Piet continued to scowl.

She choked smoke back into her lungs for full effect. "Fuck! Do you think I want to go to work tomorrow? Lining up those girls in the windows, making sure their lipstick is on straight and the lighting is right? That they don't look like the sluts that they are? Haggling with the men over what they will get for how much and for how long?"

Luuk was shocked.

"Mom!" said Piet.

"I really shouldn't be talking this way in front of you—it's degrading. I'm not going to put sugar on it. I am also degraded. Sometimes it will come spilling out. I'm sick of it, but I'm going back. Tonight."

Luuk looked quickly between Leonie and Ineke. There was a supply chain of information. He had believed that he was somewhere behind Leonie in receiving it, but not too far behind. Now it seemed as if Ineke was guiding Leonie, telling her to act tough and go for shock value in order to convince them. Like she would.

"What are you going to do with them?" asked Piet. "I mean, who has the plan?"

"Remember, we said to leave it to us," said Leonie hastily with a strange intonation.

Piet looked imploringly at Ineke. At least he knew who was running things. "I don't completely remember that."

"Well, it was said," Ineke said, meeting his gaze, the two staring at each other almost nose to nose.

"Yeah, but last night was intense. Now I'm supposed to just go to school?" said Piet. "Luuk doesn't have to go to school."

"I'm done with school," said Luuk.

"You aren't though. You never graduated."

"Yeah, but it wasn't for me."

"It isn't for me either," said Piet. He stood up and shook himself out like a tree after a storm. His boots were heavy on the floor as he slowly walked around the works.

"Be careful!" snapped Ineke.

Piet was sullen. He looked at Luuk for help. Everyone was very much awake now, Ineke's gaze flicking around the room and landing on Leonie, waiting for her to speak.

"Okay, it has been a lot of excitement. I am not a very smart person. But I know how to wait and when it is important to wait," said Leonie.

Couscous stretched to her full length on the sofa and tested her claws, as if mulling over the importance of this statement.

"Exactly. There's a knowledge base," said Ineke, sitting up, vibrating a little, gearing up. "Don't you see? We four have the same knowledge! We four all have the updates to this exact day! But after this day, it will have to be different. It would be a very dangerous thing for us all to know everything that happens now. First, the communications are dangerous. If we meet, they could be watching. If we phone, it could be taped. Email can be hacked, and . . . okay . . . I'll just say it. That time you were in prison, Luuk."

This again. "I told you about that. I was fifteen, a juvenile. Not the same risk. Mom got a good lawyer. That's what he said."

"But *a* risk anyway."

Didn't she remember that it was only for shoplifting and that Dhr. Maijer got him off? All he had to do was fifteen hours of community service. Those cops were so puffed up, never knowing that he had done worse, *much* worse than a little shoplifting. At that point in his young life, he lost respect for the Dutch judicial system altogether.

"I told you," Luuk said. "It's taken care of."

"I don't think we should count on that, do you? You can't be certain of anything. Especially with something like this! I'm not going to go on, except to say that the entire city is going to be watching. They will take this personally."

"They won't be watching us."

"Just be as normal as possible," she retorted.

"I'll get some snacks. Everyone could use a bite," Leonie said nervously, padding off to the kitchen.

After a while, Luuk said, "Look, you can work your magic with the paintings. I'm not against it. Don't know *how* you are going to do it since you know no one and are still in high school—"

"Exactly. You don't know how. And you shouldn't know. Better for all of us."

Leonie set a platter of sliced bread and cheese on the table.

"Now we all know each other much better," said Ineke, wrapping a slice of bread around a chunk of cheese. Her manner was unruffled, though her cheeks were flushed.

Luuk should have just left that painting on the wall. Somehow everything was made worse by the violence he had done to it. But she was the one that had gone on about the Hochberg—that it was the only one of the three artists who hadn't been dead for a hundred years.

"You said that because we were only getting four paintings, we had to get them all. I couldn't have predicted what would happen—"

Ineke clapped her hand on her head. "*That* doesn't matter. What I am trying to say is that you will go out there and be hit on all sides with this story. It will be like shrapnel. But you must forget it for now, as if it never happened."

"Wait a minute," said Piet, leaning over the portrait on the table. "At least I get a picture!"

"You do not get a picture!" Leonie scolded, grabbing his shirt.

"No funny stuff," said Ineke, holding out her hand for his phone, which she then pocketed, along with Luuk's.

Luuk went to stand next to his brother, for once in solidarity with him. Before the works were borne away, they should at least get to wallow. Yesterday they were one petty crook and another in the making, sharing a heavily mortgaged house with a mother who was like a teenager herself in some ways. Leonie spent so much energy guarding her few small pleasures she hadn't graduated to big concepts like this one. She just went along, happy enough to scrape enough together for a birthday cake, champagne now and then, a Sunday at secondhand shops or a trip to the country. And then along came Ineke and this idea.

Luuk took full stock of the girl as she leaned over the coffee table and coolly tucked one of his last cigarettes behind her ear.

"I think you overestimate the power of the internet," he ventured.

"How so?" she asked, clicking her stud against her back teeth.

"I'm guessing you are going to try to sell them there."

"Not denying or confirming," she said, grabbing the bubble wrap.

The dispute was pointless—he was not going to win against the two of them.

Each painting no more than sixty centimeters wide, small enough to transport easily, and prestigious enough to command a lot of attention in what Ineke had called the shadow markets. Luuk had disliked Hochberg, but Ineke had assigned that one to him. He remembered first seeing the small portrait from their "prep" visits to the Kunsthal—just a youngish woman with her eyes closed. And now it was here, held down by shot glasses, the subject indifferent to her new surroundings. No, it wasn't the worst of the lot by Hochberg, not by a long stretch. No bleary eyes, no bulbous veiny noses. No penises like deflated balloons. The woman looked like someone resting her eyes by closing them in the daytime. She might even have been a little bit pretty, but this artist would never have shown that. She looked like Leonie when she had her tea in the orchard under a tree, back at their farm when his father was still alive.

"I'll be down at the employment office in the morning, registering for a job," Luuk said, just to play along. "Then I'll probably be at the Parrot later. All the usual boring stuff."

CHAPTER 2
THE SHACK BY THE SEA

Sagaponack
July 13th, 2012
10 days after the heist

Perrin Clayton lived in a modern beach house in a village called Sagaponack, a two-hour drive from Manhattan. The area was called the Hamptons, yet many locals, including Perrin, called it the East End, meaning the eastern tip of Long Island. It consisted of five villages mostly strung together by one central road. Every summer the population increased four-fold. The main road, bordered by the sea and the bay on three sides, offered no exit for the overspill of traffic from the city. Once people were on that road, they were committed unless they wanted to battle back through the traffic in the other direction. No one did, of course. So in the summer, the pressure became intense.

Most wanted to stay as long as possible anyway because it was beautiful. Farmland had been preserved and was still being farmed. Due to conservation, the look of the old villages was more or less as it had been a hundred years before. The ocean beaches were wide and well-kept, bordered by old dunes on one side and the Atlantic on the other. On weekends when the weather was warm, the upper crust of New York City's financial, political, and cultural sectors came out to their houses, and the people who aspired to their milieus followed. There were charity events and auctions, art fairs and music festivals. There were parties orchestrated like movie productions, and bonfire cookouts and drum circles on the beaches. There were crowds of people known as "day trippers" that came from the island's middle shank (crisscrossed with freeways and sprawling apartment complexes called *Fairview* or *Greenfields* that had nothing to do with nice views or green fields). There were weddings, bar and bat mitzvahs. Bar scenes in the small villages spilled out over sidewalks, prompting neighbors to complain. Car accidents, sometimes deadly, tripled in number. During "the season," Perrin could practically feel the spit of land she called home sinking under the weight of the luxury cars, the Hummers, the party tents, the pop-up stores, the massive houses and the hordes of people.

By August the island was simmering and exhausted. Some summer workers had jumped ship early, leaving local businesses short-handed. Snaky lines of cars jammed the main road. People hadn't had the fun they wanted or did have the fun they wanted and were paying the price. Frustrations of every kind permeated the salty soft air. The sea lapped listlessly at the shore, the birds on the wires were ho-hum, and the overgrown deer population slept in the woods, black noses tucked delicately into their flanks. When Labor Day finally arrived, gleeful locals put up homemade signs that read, "495 this way ➔"

Perrin was one of those locals, though not a "real" local. Real locals descended from the pioneer families who came out to clear the scrub oak woodlands for farming or lived on the beach in shacks, haul seining for fish three hundred years ago. Real locals generally complained, a lot. "Summer people, Summer not," read the bumper stickers. Perrin thought that to wish for the East End to be like it was thirty years before was a waste of time. How lucky they all were to live in a place of such beauty. In the summer especially, it could be jarring—the traffic, the rudeness, the entitlement that seemed to get worse every year. And sometimes she felt as though it wasn't hers anymore. But wasn't that what people often felt about their childhoods? There had always been something "real" going on, something genuine and eternal that had disappeared.

For better or worse, Perrin knew no other home. Her father, George Clayton, an artist, had moved to the East End in the late-forties. At eighty-six, he now lived in a drafty ranch house down the road from Perrin, and she worried about him constantly. His wife, her mother Iris, had died four years ago, and he was now alone most of the time. Iris, a painter as well, had hardly been a domestic goddess, but she did keep him company and keep their house in some kind of order. It looked a mess, but at least she was another brain semi-focused on the task of knowing where things were and making sure the electricity bill was paid. George wasn't good at domestic things, except for baking any kind of pie, and he did make a very nice clam chowder when clams were bountiful.

Long before Perrin was born, George, later joined by (thirteen years younger) Iris, was among the first handfuls of artists who came from the city, exchanging their tenement apartments and illegal industrial spaces for cheap barns and farmhouses and shacks on the beach. And the light—they talked about the light. A story was bandied around, spoken of in interviews and cocktail parties. The reason for this unusual light was that the great long island lay in an expanse of water that dwarfed it entirely. The ocean worked like a clarifying lens for the sun, bestowing the egg yolk-y summers, rich tawny autumns, metallic winters, and springs the delicate hue of straw that the artists depended on. No one knew whether the theory was true or not, but why not say it? It sounded good.

In the early days, the work of the artists was considered outrageous, awful, unintelligible. People loved it. People hated it. In the wake of the Second World War, a new frontier was opening up; American artists were finding the freedom to create in the language of the interior self. They were challenging Europe's preeminence in the *avant-garde.* The work was charged and messy; it reverberated all across the globe. An epic spewing out of a long-held breath, it was specifically post-war experience, which then expanded into *all* experience. George and Iris were on the crest of this wave, though George had had much more recognition. In those days the work flowed from his brush onto his canvas with an alacrity that now eluded him, at least according to the critics.

Just now Perrin sat with her feet up on her deck railing that overlooked a misty sea, wondering if George was actually going to show up. Recently, he had become more punctual, but it didn't matter so much because she'd be here all day. She heard her husband of two years, Jack, come in from his studio, the screen door slamming behind him. She made a mental note that she must get that fixed. And that he didn't intend to slam the door; it just slammed of its own accord.

He stopped just short of the deck. "I need the samples," he said. "You got the list from William?"

This was an announcement as much as an inquiry. Yes, she said, she'd order them. Perrin had thought William wasn't going to work out. He was from the Indian reservation and had no experience with the internet which was an elemental part of managing anything now.

"Hey—dinner list—Babe—"

"Mmmmm?" Perrin feigned distraction, watching a surfer paddle out to the break.

He peered at his phone. "Hope you haven't called anyone. It's kind of the same old, same old—and Chaz will be out," he said, referring to the owner of the Bloodstone Group, his rep, who would be staying at his house in Bridgehampton.

Perrin stirred her tea. After two years of marriage, these dinners had become a bit of a chore, but important nonetheless. Lately, when people were coming, she had gotten into the habit of biting a chip off a Xanax, while Jack got himself something from the bar. In terms of mixing things up, she didn't know where to begin. There was a criterion—a criterion that had been delivered into their house and into their lives when she'd married Jack. George, herself, the neighbors less so—they all had had to adjust. Changes had happened fast, some of them pretty big—like tearing down the shack that she had grown up in on this very spot, and building the big glass box they lived in now.

Jack picked up the paper. "Anything on the Kunsthal thing?"

"I don't think they have anything. The museum has just admitted that the thieves got in through a side door with some kind of tool, and that the thieves were inexperienced and young. Can you believe it?"

"Crazy," said Jack. "Doesn't make them look very good. The museum, I mean. What does George say? He'd hear something. He knew Hochberg, right?"

"They were friends; they admired each other's work. George once went to an opening of his in London, and Hochberg came here too, way back when." Back when George and his friend were on par, before her father fell behind.

The sun's twinkle poked through the dissolving mist, a few surfers getting up here and there. Having run out of couples, she riffled through her mental Rolodex.

There was her book group and her yoga group. Maybe this time she'd invite a single friend from one of those. Though somehow that was considered uninteresting unless the friend was accomplished, lived for their work, had a fat resume, and was not in real estate like so many now were. Single was also fine if they were attractive—but young—younger than her, not full-blown women. (Weirdly, if she weren't attached to Jack, she wouldn't have invited herself. At thirty-five, she was too old.) If they were single and male, however, it didn't really matter the age. An eligible solvent or insolvent male could stand on his own. But she had no male friends to choose from. Jack didn't like her to have male friends, though he was subtle about it. Gay was okay.

She sipped her tea and thought about the days of jug wine, a few blankets, and the beach—when everybody was just who they were and that was that. Were those days really so far away? Yes, they were. The low-stakes era had faded away. Though many around here had had a hard time parting with it, they had welcomed the skyrocketing real estate values.

"I think you're going to have to be open-minded . . . about the dinner," Perrin said, unsure that he had heard her, half-hoping that he hadn't.

"How open-minded?"

"I have a photographer friend from yoga, Gia. An interesting, outspoken girl. Has shown in a lot of places. She's Italian, actually."

"Really? Don't get many Italians here."

"She came on a program to NYU and fell in love with the city. She's got a show at Calliope right now."

"Hmmm—impressive."

That meant that she had his okay. Perrin felt a rush from that small success. She got up and put the kettle on to boil. She was looking forward to the evening. The word "outspoken" hardly covered Gia.

"I had to call George yesterday," Jack said, hoisting the dumbbells he kept in the bottom of the bookcase. "Had to ask him to come pick up those paintings. I'm sorry."

Perrin stuck her head out of the kitchen. "I talked to him on Sunday, and he said he needed to bring a few more over here!"

"I had to turn that around. I need the space for the rocket materials. It's lots of boxes." Holding the dumbbells with one hand, he pushed his tortoiseshell glasses up. This was a constant ever since he'd traded out his trusty wire rims for the fashionable fifties look.

Originally, her father had given them the shack and this property as a wedding present. The land was worth a fortune, but George said he wanted to keep it in the family and, of course, the taxes had gotten so high they'd be doing him a favor. At the time, Perrin had thought it was a good idea and had helped him relocate. George had had only one wish for his new home—that he would be able to bike down to the ocean in ten minutes or less, or drive there in three. He did not think pragmatically. At all. He bought a leaky ranch house, which she deeply regretted. It was now filled to the rafters with his art works, aisles running mazelike all through it from room to room—a hazard for an old man. But

George didn't think of himself as old. Age was immaterial to him.

"Jack, what about a new house for him? And sell that dump he lives in. That would solve all problems. I went out with a broker last week. Nothing fancy. Something that doesn't flood, with decent storage space. The broker said it's a good time to buy."

Jack, curling the weight to his shoulder, grunted, "They all say it's a good time to buy. Any salesperson says it. *Uhhhh!*" His words were strangled with his effort, a vein bulging on his bicep. "I don't want you to come in today—the fumes—not good for your fertility."

The dumbbells went back in—*clunk thunk.* He hovered, out of breath. "George has a good thing. He should slow down now anyway, or he's going to hurt himself. You're so beautiful. I could paint you right now, Cinnamon."

"You don't paint anymore," said Perrin. Portraits, *people*—that was the hardest thing. He had never been very good at it and so had always been envious of people like George, who were.

"It's true. And the critics hate me for it. Maybe I should do a show to balance the scales." He turned to her. "Let's have George to the dinner. Everyone is going to want to know about the Kunsthal theft."

"I—"

There was a muffled pop from the front of the house. "Not *again*!" Perrin exclaimed, running down the stairs to the patio, where a large black bird fluttered and hopped.

"Damn," Jack cursed from behind her. "Damn, damn, *damn!*"

"Don't!" said Perrin. "Don't get too close!"

She stayed back, softly cooing to the bird in what she hoped was its own language.

"That's a crow. They don't coo. Pigeons coo," said Jack wearily.

It kept trying to alight upon the air, its beady eye watching them both carefully, shifting between them. Up it would go with a hop, try to get airborne, and crash back down again.

"Can you get a box and paper towel?" Perrin asked. "I'll stay and hope he calms down."

The last one had been in a similar stunned condition. After it stopped eating the worms and water she brought it, she had taken it to the wildlife center, where they told her it had no chance.

"You staying is hardly going to make it calm down," she heard Jack say as he went to find a box.

But she felt she had no choice. It was the only thing to do.

He handed her a box—it was small but would do for the moment.

"Move slow," said Perrin. "I need you to get William, so we can corral him into the box."

"Okay, I have work though."

"Jack, we aren't going to leave him to die in the dunes . . . like the others," she added, trying to keep the sarcasm out of her voice. It was this house—this *house.* It was a solid glass block. The architect had insisted they do the walls and floors in glass block like a modern townhouse in say, Dubai. It wasn't a completely clear glass block. It was called "Veil," and it was treated to let the light through but not the sound. On the beach side, the bedroom windows were almost floor to ceiling, which Perrin abhorred. From inside it was like a doll's house. You could see up and through to any room, the undersides of furniture, feet, a roving vacuum cleaner, a floating rug, clothes on the floor, and you could see where anybody was as long as they weren't in bed or in the bath. When they crossed, you'd see their ghostly figure pass over the squares, and sometimes footprint shadows, except for areas where tunnels of mechanicals were stored. All was changed by whatever the light was doing. In cloudy weather with all the lights off, the ceilings turned a sort of gray, a reflection of the ocean, the sand, and the sky. Perrin could not have called it a color. Colors had a point where the mixture of hues and tones came to a conclusion. This was more a strange infinity.

After a number of tries, Jack and William moving like Kabuki figures, they succeeded in getting the bird into the box.

"Crows are bastards," Jack said.

"Why do you say that?" she asked.

"That sound they make, to begin with. Groups of crows are called murders."

William found a bigger box in the storage room and brought a piece of old screen. Together, doubling and stapling the screen, they fashioned an aerated top for the box. A screw jar top with water and pieces of apple went inside. With a towel, Perrin gently slid the bird into its new home.

Perrin looked at the arrangement and said, "This is a better house than the last one had."

"What happened to the last one?" asked William, sweeping his long black hair into a ponytail.

"I don't know," she sighed, feeling her hopes deflate when thinking of its fate. They said it was a song sparrow, a juvenile. It wasn't as hardy as this crow appeared to be.

"Here it is," said Jack, looking at his phone. "Crows are scavengers and will feed on carrion, as well as take small animals such as lambs, eggs, and baby birds. Historically, crows would have been seen near battlefields, medieval hospitals, cemeteries, or the gallows waiting for a chance to pick over dead bodies. This association with death resulted in the development of superstitions and folklore, that led to the term *a murder of crows*."

The crow, from the corner of the box, cocked its head and fixed him with a puzzled eye. Perrin fancied that it wondered what Jack's point was.

"Why do you think this is happening more now?" asked Jack. "Change in the wind?"

"It's a simple matter of decals or drapes, or both!" said Perrin.

"I don't think Moretti would be happy with that," he said, referring to his friend Max, the architect who'd designed the house. "It would ruin the look."

"Birds have a hard enough time as it is," she said, peering into the box. "This is the third one this year." The crow crouched lower, a strip of sun tracing its blue-black feathers. With a sense of the surreal, she thought forward to years and years of bird deaths. How many would there be in her lifetime? And of what species?

"It isn't so bad in winter," said Jack, putting his hand on her shoulder.

William picked up the box. "Where to?"

"You can leave it here," said Jack, "where its home is, outside."

"It has to be up on the deck, so I can look after it," said Perrin.

"Alright," said Jack. "But I'd rather not have it be a subject at the dinner."

After the crow was relocated, Jack got the weights from the bottom of the bookcase and resumed his workout. "You didn't say anything about my new nickname for you."

"Cinnamon?"

"Because you're sweet but not fattening."

She felt guilty for never liking what he came up with. He'd had many nicknames for her: *Foomfy, Baby, Bombalicious*. None of them caught on. And now, *Cinnamon*. It was ridiculous. She tucked it away in her little purse of gripes that shouldn't matter so much.

From the deck she could see that William had set up on the bit of lawn between the house and the dune. He was finishing canvases for himself. Gesso dripped from the brush, sometimes onto the grass. His shoulders were lovely and smooth, a rich red-brown.

"You're ogling William," said Jack.

"I'm not. Though he is nice to look at."

Jack straightened his spine and sighed, "I don't paint anymore. Maybe I should go back to that."

"Do you think so?"

"Sometimes I think I've gotten too plastic, too far removed from the original thing."

"But you never really did the original thing. And what do you care what people say?"

"I shouldn't read the critics. Then I wouldn't care."

Perrin's eye caught on William again. He had four canvases done, propped up on lawn chairs to dry. "Critics are always suspicious of success, especially if it endures."

Jack's face reddened with the effort of the weights, his breath meting out in short bursts. "If you say so!"

"I do say so. It's better to have made it."

Perrin had seen a lot in this vein. If she understood anything, it was the art world—that enigmatic engine that marked down artists in bold and then forgot about them. George had had his biggest run before she was born. He began teaching in the city and then met a student, her mother Iris, with whom he fell in love. His career had foundered because he had stopped producing very much, though it wasn't Iris's fault.

Jack stopped straining at the weights and put them back into the bookcase, *clunk thunk*. "I've got to get to work. The day is half-gone already."

While she was comfortable with being a reassuring bulwark of history for Jack, she felt guilty at having appeased him. They were sitting on top of the best investment George had ever made.

"I think we can buy George a house," she said. "He's got a show coming up. In fact, I know what's in the bank, liquid, and I'm sure we can do it."

"Yes, well, you never know when the party is going to end. And it's always a good idea to keep a certain amount of liquidity as a hedge. What exactly is the problem, anyway?"

"His basement flooded last week—I did say that. He's got an elaborate system of sawhorses to keep the works out of the water, but as you know, he has no more room!"

Jack paused, pushing his glasses up on his nose. "I'll think about it." He turned the side of his face to her, distracted by his phone. "I've got to get going." He left, the screen door slamming again.

Perrin remembered her childhood home on this very spot. Though the bar was well-stocked and they never ran out of cigarettes, there often wasn't enough food. She remembered the jug wine, *Gallo,* too big to fit in the garbage, so empties were lined up on the deck, a few encrusted with candle stubs and drippings from the long nights.

The sea was all aglitter now, surfers floating about like bowling pins near the break. It was a shame about George's career, though she'd never asked him how he felt about it. She guessed that her father simply preferred the company of artists and his young wife to working. It was easier to tune into the muses in the shack by the sea, smoke pot and talk about art, than to create it. Before Perrin was born, Iris convinced him to cut out the hard booze and drink only wine because he got too wild. Their group was supportive of each other, and kind in their criticism of each other—it was agreed that everyone was doing good work. But by the time the seventies drew to a close, they were attuned to their own ruin, almost relishing it, the wind off the sea whistling on the roof of the shack and rattling its windows.

Perrin felt a daydream about William coming on and shooed it away.

CHAPTER 3
CATCH THE SUN

Sagaponack
July 15th, 2012
12 days after the heist

Onshore wind, blue sky, fat and silver-tinged clouds barely moving. George Clayton popped on the emergency brake of his van and surveyed the boxy structure in the dunes and the massive wedge next to it—Jack's studio. He had never liked the house, but he coveted that studio. It was any artist's dream—spacious, climate-controlled, and full of the ocean's luminescence. Jack had been able to get around every building code there was to build it, and people in the town did not like him for it. Thirty feet tall, it had a wall of high windows at the top looking out over the beach, and on the other side, the potato fields, or anyway what was left of the potato fields.

Now the Jack machine cranked full bore. George had to credit him—he had been smart. He had managed to reach beyond the tight sphere of the New York art world into the global market. Early on, he had done big pieces, large investments, and had gotten more forward-thinking galleries to show them. They were outlandish, shocking, not in "good taste." One was a replica of a football trophy his brother had won, thirty feet tall. Another was a bottle of fabric softener in solid chrome. Another was a Gumby figure, fifty feet tall, pink, with a set of pink toy-style genitalia, bumps like golf balls on either side of a broom handle penis. Critics had appreciated the irreverence and the echo of Warhol. That series had been the beginning of everything.

Now Jack was disdained by more educated buyers (who bought him anyway), and he was surrounded by sycophants. George knew he worried that all the tacky adulation and money would kill his perfect instincts. George believed he had good reason to worry, at least a little. The worry might prevent him from buying into his own myth. A lot of George's early artist friends had done just that, and it was the beginning of the end for them. But Jack's was the market of the people, not critics. His works were in many international airports and the lobbies of major hotels. In the last few years, he'd had blockbuster shows at the old Whitney, Guggenheim Bilbao, and the Tate. The public loved it, buying tchotchke-sized replicas of his giant bunnies and Gumby figures. "Merch" it was called. Keychain Jack, George called him, but not to his face.

George looked around, scanning the dune for Perrin, who had said she'd be back from her run about now. He turned, and there she was, flushed from her exertions. No sneakers—she liked to go barefoot on the beach. Perrin, wild child of the dunes. In the field behind her, one of the Aldrich kids was guiding a rear boom sprayer in the northernmost corner.

"Dad, let William move them out—ok?"

"Absolutely not," said George. The last thing he would accept was that *Playgirl* centerfold handling his paintings.

Perrin stamped her foot. "Dad!!"

He looked toward the studio. "Is he here?"

"Yeah, working."

George could see that it was Jed, Aldrich's eldest pulling the tractor along, looking back to make sure the rows were straight.

Perrin handed him a bottle of water. He sipped at it a little. She didn't think he hydrated enough.

Inside the studio, Jack—wearing what looked to be a butcher's apron—was pulling a face mask on. He did a double take at George in the doorway. He was surprised, but then he always looked a little surprised. Boxes of fabrication materials and pink and blue color forecasting panels were stacked along the wall of windows.

Behind Jack was the wooden frame of the rocket ship. It was twenty-five feet tall at least, with two ladders resting on its sides. Jack and William were working on sheeted casts that looked to be wings of an appropriate size to fit onto the main. With simian ease, William flew up one of the ladders, took measurements with a laser device, and tapped them into his phone. Art was no longer earth-bound. It was Space Age, evidenced by Jack's soon-to-be candy-colored rocket ship and the airplane hangar it was in. Not finding his stack in the corner where he'd left it, he looked around.

"Behind the bathroom door," said Jack, looking up from his clipboard. "Sorry. Truly sorry, George."

There were about seven in all, and smaller than George remembered. He riffled through the stack, reflecting that he just as easily could cart them to the dump and the world would go on turning. He had done them when his studio was four houses down the dune. Farmer Aldrich's father had moved an old train station building there in 1922. It had unusually high ceilings and fantastic light, and George had had it for a pittance. Just recently it, too, had been knocked down. A ridiculously outsized cottage had been put in its place.

"Can you believe this smell?" asked Jack.

"They gotta spray," said George. "You should be glad to be on this side of the wind today. The houses on the other side of the field are getting it much worse."

"We're going to see if they'll go organic," said Jack, his voice swallowed into the cavernous space.

"Who organic?" said George, edging around the structure, taking care not to bang anything.

"Aldrich. William is handing out flyers at the post office next week, and I've got an environmental lawyer in the city who is interested in taking the case pro bono."

George balanced the painting on his boot. "Do you have any idea how expensive it is to go organic?"

"Yes," said Jack. "There's a huge market, for that field at least."

"That's for smaller farms, Jack. You aren't going to get anywhere with Aldrich. He farms a hundred acres. You will just piss him off. Don't forget, he didn't make a fuss about all of this," George added, waving to their surroundings.

"Why should he care? I've raised his property values by thirty percent at least."

"And his taxes," said George.

"I have a few tricks up my sleeve," Jack said.

George looked up at the rocket. "I like it," he said, thinking that honestly, he did like it, though liking it was painful.

Jack lit up. "I'm thinking about camouflage—orange and pink, or pink and blue. What do you think?"

"I would never presume to guide you."

"Camo. So the work is—theoretically at least—hidden. We can't see it, we don't control it . . . the rocket goes into space, and BLAAAH!!!"

"I liked it even before the explanation," said George, jimmying his painting over the threshold.

"Dad, please, William can do it," Perrin said. "That's what he's here for."

"William is on the rocket," George said with a tone of finality.

George hated looking at old work. He hated dealing with it, but it would be worse having someone else deal with it. After a few trips, he surveyed the topmost one, which was about circles. It was junk—dusty cracked images from thirty years ago. Who had he been then? A completely different person, doing oil paintings of plates, tires, the full moon, a coffee cup, Iris's breasts, or another woman's breasts—anything he found round and interesting. Its only worth was as a journal of himself—an artifact from a past he could barely remember. A drop of sweat dripped from his chin, his boots scratched in the gravel that he and Iris had put down, softened under the dirt that had migrated from the field.

March, march, march. Perrin's blonde hair was ruffled into whorls, her runner's bloom already subsided. She was so hammered down. No light in her eye, and only thirty-five. The last time he saw her completely happy was during that period in N.Y.C., when she had that studio shared with friends from art school. Nothing all that interesting developed, but there was still plenty of time.

"Perry, I'm gonna finish this myself," he said, hitching his shoulders and walking more quickly. Empty space on his kitchen counters remained—if the new work for the show didn't go, he could stack them across since they were fairly uniform—which would leave enough space to make a sandwich. He was being edged out of his house by his own unsold work, which would be funny if it were not him.

He fetched another one, only three left. Perrin was still somewhere behind him. He didn't want to face her. He could feel her restlessness and his own frustration—there was no hiding from either. Separately they could bear it; together they were finished. Her emptiness would come together with his and become an abyss. And he had to survive—that was the bottom line. And so did she.

But there she stayed, just in the corner of his vision. His eyes swept the jammed interior of the van. The reality would surely be softer if he could get rid of one or two. eBay? He'd have a time packing them, though he might get a decent amount because the market—that all-important higher power—knew that his time on planet Earth was getting short.

He turned around and said, "Saw you in the paper," not above a certain pride that his daughter was in the society pages, though as a rule he hated that kind of class worship.

Perrin saw his conflict at once. "It's all gotten pretty stupid, Dad."

"Guy down the dune in the old train station—European?" he asked. Euro-trash types usually liked his stuff, especially when they could meet him. He delivered on a certain sort of rugged individualism that was right up their alley.

"Russian."

"Russian!" Plucking his bandana from his belt loop, he mopped his brow. Together they stared at the winged, shingled monster that had taken over where his old studio had been.

"That was the train depot, remember? It had no central heating. I had it for thirty dollars a month." In winter he worked wearing two sweatshirts, workman's boots, a hat and fingerless gloves, while she sat on the floor next to the stove, with her pad and crayons. "Remember when you came to work with me?"

"How could I forget," she murmured.

"You made such nice pictures, Perry. I still have them," he ventured.

"You do?"

"You'll have them back one day. And you can see them anytime," he said, stuffing his sentimentality away, along with his bandana. It wasn't a good idea to always harp on the past.

They watched as a red Hummer bumped down the dirt road and turned into the driveway of the new mansion.

"They've built in too close," he said. "A good storm will take off the front half."

"Chaz knows him," said Perrin. "Hard to tell what he does, but he has an interest in art."

"What type of thing?"

"Old Masters. Chaz said he bought a Van Gogh in Paris. He bought a small, early one—*Beach at Scheveningen,* I think it was called. It was in that trove that was discovered in the family's attic that was passed around for decades in a box. Remember?"

"Yes! Have you seen it? There was sand in the paint!"

"Only on the internet. I haven't even met the guy yet. And we *can't talk* about it. He's secretive, and I wasn't supposed to say anything. If word gets out, Chaz will kill me."

"Maybe he thinks he'll be judged. Which, of course, he would be. He'd also be admired for something like that. Everyone would be interested."

"That might be the problem," said Perrin. "Word around town is he's a criminal of some kind—but Chaz won't, or can't, say."

"Listen, if all the criminals were weeded out of the art scene, the whole thing would grind to a halt," said George.

She laughed as George thought how Perrin was turning out to be the best thing he had ever done, the most lasting. And though she was terrific, he could hardly believe it had come to that.

"But why do they think he's a criminal?" George asked.

"Russian and rich, really rich, I guess," said Perrin.

Together they watched a stocky woman in a maid's outfit come out and begin unloading the Hummer. She stacked two twelve-packs in her arms and made for the wooden walkway up to the house.

"Tell him you know a local artist that's selling cheap, with art-consulting services thrown into the bargain," George said.

"You might be able to tell him yourself. He's going to have some sort of bash."

"How long did it take him to put that up?"

"About eight months. There were workmen at it day and night. Floodlights—we had to sleep with masks on. Jack was going to call the town but never did."

"Unbelievable."

"Dad, I feel so bad about this."

"What?"

"Your house!" she cried.

"You know, I don't care that much," he said. "There's a twinge, but it was going to fall down if you didn't knock it down."

"No, I mean your house *now*."

"It's fine."

"It is not," she retorted.

"Too bad about the Kunsthal," he said, changing the subject. "*Woman with Eyes Closed*, along with the rest. Only one, and not a famous one, but still."

"I saw a photo of it. It is lovely. She looks as if she's dreaming."

"She was a young friend of Hochberg's. I met her when I was there. She has since died, I heard."

"How sad! Do you think they can get it back?"

"Possibly. Sometimes they do."

"Wow—I hope so. I've got a crow now," she said.

"Another bird?" In the beginning, Perrin put up black tape on the windows, but Jack took it down. Ruined the design, the transparency, he said. She'd tried drapes and stickers; he took it all down. Jack seemed to want to share his dirty socks with the world. *Consume me,* he pleaded. Maybe churning out his factory-made artworks had done it, and there remained a germ of an unexpressed soul.

"Dad, we can't have you living like that!"

"What? I've lived there for four years. Why all the fuss now? It isn't your fault—it's nobody's fault. What's the guy's name?" asked George.

"What guy?" she said.

"Where my studio used to be."

"Oh—Glasgow."

"What kind of Russian is named Glasgow?"

"I don't know!" she laughed again.

"Do you think you can get me an invite to the bash?"

"Just come with us. It'll be fine. You can tell him the story about the studio—that is, if he can understand you."

They looked down the dune as the Hummer pulled away from the house and a cloud of dust sailed away over the field. What would they call this one? *Tara? Monticello?* Down at the local bar, people referred to Jack and Perrin's house as *the Napoleon.* People on the beach regularly stopped and looked at it, and it was interesting at night, like a clear, lit-up Rubik's cube. But birds regularly splattered themselves on it.

"Glasgow . . . doesn't sound Russian . . ." George continued with what he hoped was the right amount of warmth. He didn't want to go overboard. He never could quite get the hang of a daughter, yet he had no sons with which to compare the experience. He had only this one child, a girl, who, despite her confident pose, was wan in some way that he couldn't put a name to. He grabbed her hand. "How are things?"

Not accustomed to the attention, she dug her toe into the dirt.

"It's all going to work out, Perry," he said, squeezing her hand, his blue eyes crinkling as he smiled. Jed Aldrich bumped around the top of the row and was now aiming towards the sea. "Remember when you were sweet on him?"

"Yeah, he was a good kid," she said, feeling the sun warm on her back.

"Ya gotta tell Jack not to bother with the masks. This early in the season he's just fertilizing." He lifted his nose to the wind. "I can smell it."

Jed was down at the bottom of the row, his hand off the big wheel waving before he had to make the turn. He had turned off the jets for their benefit. Perrin waved back, thinking she was glad she wasn't married to Jed Aldrich, stuck in the town and resistant to new ideas. George had some kind of romantic thing about it.

"Do you remember when you thought you could catch the sun?" George asked.

Perrin was puzzled. Was she ever that young?

He pointed at the dune. "It was a game you played. Well, at the time you were very serious about it."

When she was five, he'd try hard to see it just as she did, one who completely trusted her own perceptions. It was an optical illusion, where the setting sun looked like a red ball atop the dunes. A red ball that she wanted to catch. So up on the sand mountain they'd go, the sun moving with them, now bouncing along the top, now filigreed by beach grass, now whole again, then fragmented, always moving but stopping when they did, maddeningly close. He'd follow her up and down, right with her, her boots chugging away in the sand, hair flying out behind her. "I can catch it, I can!" she'd shout, so sure of herself. Until, exhausted, she'd flop down on her back.

"What do you mean?" she asked.

His deep blue eyes met hers. "Let's call it a riddle. See if you can figure it out. Perfect conditions right now," he said.

Behind her, the big red ball would be just touching the Marram grass. The sun at the tips of your fingers. Who was to say it couldn't be done?

CHAPTER 4
YOU REALLY GOT ME

Amsterdam
July 18th, 2012
15 days after the heist

With her stiff-kneed gait, Leonie crossed the living room. She set down upon the coffee table a bucket full of ice that cradled two bottles of *Veuve Clicquot*, the orange label. A significant splash out, Luuk thought, but a few bottles of *Dom* might have been more to the point. (After all, weren't they rich now?) He kicked himself for having such selfish thoughts about his mother's lack of sophistication and possible lack of funds. And for being the sort of drug-dealing sleazeball that worked in the clubs and knew the prices of the bottles he had either been treated to or stolen.

Couscous, basking in the sunny bay window, gave two quick licks to her shoulder and resumed her slow-eyed inspection of the scene. The big TV near the pocket doors to the kitchen had the sound off. Leonie's dusty potpourri with faded buds and no smell was in the center of the coffee table, as it had been for seven years. A few magazines hung about and—obscuring Ineke's face as she read—a *De Telegraaf*. According to what Leonie had just told him in the kitchen, Ineke had been there all day. Though—as per her very own rules—she was supposed to be in school with Piet. The cover of *De Telegraaf* showed a freeze frame of the three of them in the museum's doorway. The headline shouted, *Kunsthal Director Kaarle DeVries Gives Press Conference.* Luuk was beginning to hate the headlines.

He turned to Leonie's old record player, shooing Couscous off the top. Right under it, the seventies-style cabinet from their old farm held Leonie's massive collection of vinyl. It was a good thing she never threw anything out.

"Happy occasion?" Luuk tossed over his shoulder.

Ineke peered over the paper, and Leonie's thin, pink-frosted lips creased into a smile. She reached forward to jostle the champagne in the ice. "Yes, Piet will be here soon," she said. "Put something on," she added.

Luuk was sure she'd been into the *Jenever* already.

"Okay—listen," Ineke looked up at him sternly, her cute, grown-out Mohawk flopping to one side. "Authorities are perplexed. Some think this was the work of amateurs, *very young* amateurs, and others say we could only be pros. The police have announced that the third thief is female. I wonder why they think we're young." She dropped the paper to her lap. "And how do they know I'm female?"

How indeed, thought Luuk.

"From the films, probably," said Leonie. "The young move differently."

Ineke crawled over to perch on the arm of the biggest chair, the one that Piet always sat in. "It *is* a good day, Luuk. How about something to relax?"

"What would that be?"

"Uh . . . punk—Sex Pistols or Sonic Youth."

"Yeah?" asked Luuk, dragging his fingers along the record spines, not really liking either of those bands, and absolutely sure that Leonie didn't like them.

He dropped the needle into the groove to the sound of prickles and pops. The Dutch/American band Van Halen was his pick. Their first and best album, he announced, before settling back on the mushy old sofa. He could feel the terrain of blown-out springs all along his backside. It was a relief to be home, yet the atmosphere was thick. He wished Piet would hurry up. Though it had been agreed that Ineke had the connections (she wouldn't say what they were) and would handle everything, it was about time now that they should have an idea and get their share.

He fished a smoke from his pack of Marlboro while noticing the ashtray full of stubs of Leonie's hand-rolled cigarettes. Leonie was rolling up another. Luuk feared for her life, she smoked so much. But who could blame her, constantly worrying about them all. He could tell that she liked the music; it was helping her to unwind. After all, the best rock was from her generation, and that was her album. What happened after that, he could not say.

As they sat waiting, plural rock guitars emanated from the giant, antique speakers. Right after the heist, Ineke and then Leonie said they all must stick to their usual patterns. Piet must go to school because it would look odd if he suddenly didn't. Ineke, not following her own program, had opted to hide out here today. When she met Luuk at the door, she announced she was tired and maybe a little sick. She then slipped across the street to her apartment to grab her backpack in case her father noticed whether or not it was there when he got home. Very likely he hadn't. He barely knew she was alive.

As per the plan, last night Luuk had done his usual, selling coke at the *Blue Parrot* until the early morning hours. He had made around five hundred euros and dropped off Doguru's fifty percent on his way home. Nothing, in fact, was all that different, but for the face of his mother who looked like a cat who had just swallowed a canary.

Missile-like exhalations from Leonie halved the sunlight in the room. Eddie Van Halen's "Eruption" began with an explosive drum triplet that sounded like stumbling and falling down a steep staircase, but in a good way—accompanied by Leonie's expert smoke rings that fit one inside the other. Ineke sat very still, as if encased in sound. When Luuk first knew her, he thought she could have been a guidance counselor at his old school, if his guidance counselor had been a sexy punk with blue hair, coolly laying out pitfalls and options on the path ahead. Ineke lived across the street in what Luuk could confidently call a worse situation. She grew up rattling around their shabby apartment mostly alone because Mr. Visscher worked crazy hours and Mrs. Visscher had been gone so long no one remembered her. Mr. Visscher might even have had another family, Leonie had once suggested, just by assessing the comings and goings. But one thing Mr. Visscher had done for his daughter was buy her a good computer, believing it would prepare his girl for life. If only he knew how much.

"This music is fantastic," Ineke said, grinning as much as she ever did.

Luuk felt a bit smug. A few weeks before, he had tried to impress her with the record player, one of the few left in Amsterdam in 2012 by his reckoning. She had ignored him and finally snapped at him. No, she did not care about any old record player. Hah. Like hell she didn't.

"Eruption," really just a guitar solo, took off, gritty depths ascending to feather-like heights before sailing back down to earthy, bubbling bottoms. Ineke unnerved him, peering at him through a curl of smoke. She seemed to be saying that to have perpetrated a crime together was an intimate thing, more intimate than the other thing—and that the heist had in fact brought them together in a new way. Peaks and valleys of the music went gliding around their silent heads, her eyes narrowing and considering him, he staring right back at her until it was unbearable and the last chord wrung itself out and faded away.

Couscous fled from the window and darted across the room as Piet came blasting through the front door.

"Quiet, Piet, quiet!" said Ineke, jumping up. "We don't want the whole street to hear!"

"I can't help it!" Piet said, throwing his bike leathers in the corner.

Leonie popped the cork on one of the bottles and poured out the *Veuve* into the four waiting glasses.

"Time for a toast!" exclaimed Leonie.

Strangely, Luuk didn't feel like drinking. He was already buzzing, almost too much.

Piet opened his arms wide. "Can you believe it? It's been two weeks, and we've just been going on as usual, as if nothing happened! What is the matter with this fucking country!"

"Hey-hey-hey!" Ineke said, grabbing Piet's shoulders and pressing him down into the armchair.

"How *easy* that was!" he exclaimed, laughing as she tried to push him down. "Eighty *million*!"

"It isn't going to come to that much!" she said with a tone that expressed that maybe it would, in fact, come to that much. She curled herself back onto the chair, as if to lure him back there.

But Piet was up, dancing—whirling around with his head thrown back to "Jamie's Crying." It was a thing he did. Luuk wished he could contain himself.

Leonie laughed, clapping her hands. "You are like Zorba!"

Luke had heard that one too. Now Piet would ask, *Who is Zorba?*

"Who is Zorba?" said Piet, pulling Ineke up to him, his hand fitting neatly into the small of her back.

"A crazy Greek!" Leonie said, clapping in time to the music, her eyes aflame. "And a handsome man, Mr. Anthony Quinn," she yelled, topping off her champagne.

She was going off. Last week, she had actually hinted to Luuk that he should steal Ineke from his brother because Piet wasn't tough enough for her. Leonie blurted out odd challenges in the middle of the week when hitting the bottle after work. For her, the middle of the week was the weekend because she worked nights and weekends at the Yab Yum brothel, a job that was beneath her. Two drinks or a half-bottle of wine on a Wednesday, and she was clobbered. No tolerance at all.

He watched Ineke and Piet dance around the room, dipping

and diving, almost as if they were meant for each other. Sometimes Leonie had to be protected from her own ideas, and mostly, he was the one to do it. *He* was her favorite because he felt this way. And how, really, was he supposed to partake of the riches that Leonie had drunkenly suggested? If he did, he'd lose control. In the waning light, Ineke winked at him from over Piet's shoulder.

Leonie raised her glass. "To the day, which is still far away, when we can all go back to Oosterwolde, at least for a visit."

"To Oosterwolde!" Luuk toasted, wondering what all the build-up was about.

Ineke reached for her glass. "To Oosterwolde! What is Oosterwolde?"

"Where we lived before this," said Leonie, her glass clinking with Luuk's.

"I wonder what it's like now," said Piet.

"Probably just the same," said Leonie. "Farms and farmers in a beautiful place. Fresh eggs from the hen, and gouda from the cow!" She was a little winded.

With the needle bumping on the record's last track, Leonie asked for something a bit more quiet. Luuk riffled through the cabinet, not finding anything he liked that was quiet. He didn't *want* to be mellow. Leonie hauled her voluminous white bag from the floor. She extracted four stacks of cash secured with rubber bands and held them in her lap.

So, this was what it was all about. The stacks were only about five centimeters high while sporting five hundred euro notes on top.

"Yes! We have something to celebrate!" continued Leonie, setting the stacks in four points around the potpourri.

Ineke met Luuk's gaze again and said, "Things have been happening behind the scenes, as you can see."

Luuk nodded at the table. "Okay. But that doesn't look like much."

Piet had lunged in and was already counting his.

"You haven't even counted it!" said Ineke.

Luuk felt about five years old, when his aunt played at whether or not he deserved an extra piece of candy. But he was not five years old.

"They phased out the thousand euro note, and I'm guessing you put the biggest notes on top, and that those are all fives and hundreds—probably a third five and the rest hundreds. Which makes it no more than sixty thousand. You are going to have to tell me something."

Ineke bypassed him. "You can't bank it. You have to sit on it—"

"What was sold?" interrupted Luuk.

Ineke snapped, "Of course we can't tell you that!"

Luuk picked up the remote and turned up the TV; the story was again on the news. The Monets, one after another—*Bridge Paintings,* they were called—and then the Picasso—*Tête d'Arlequin,* that one was called. The portrait of the woman with brown hair and the dreamy look was on the screen. The one that he had had to razor out of the broken frame. Luuk had been a little sorry to read that the young woman had died not long after the painting was finished. The artist had died too, but he was old. It was tough luck. And Luuk had had tough luck too. Like when their father was killed in a thresher accident when he was only thirteen.

"What is this *we*?" Luuk asked. "I thought that my mother was not going to be involved in any way."

"She isn't. I haven't told her anything. But obviously she did know when it happened. And provided moral support, like the mother I do not have."

"Oh, okay," he said. *Jesus.*

Leonie rearranged the three remaining packets of cash in the middle of the table, as if to better display their attractive properties. At her job at the strip club, she handled lots of cash, so this deference was odd.

Luuk pressed on. "Where is the rest of it?"

"You haven't even looked at how much is there!" Ineke said, pushing his stack toward him, making sure their hands touched.

Piet flopped back in the big chair. "Sixty-five thousand. Luuk, chill the fuck out."

"Each, obviously," Ineke added.

Leonie was prim.

As the oldest, Luuk felt keenly the rough time Leonie had had. After the accident, she was forced to sell the homestead that had been in her family for four generations. They came to Amsterdam and bought this house. She had gotten it cheap. A man had been murdered there the year before, a fact that would have spooked most people. Luuk remembered Leonie finding out from a neighbor and coolly reducing her offer by twenty-five percent, her mouth set in a determined line. She was not superstitious; she did not believe in ghosts. She liked it because it was the only real house for blocks around—everything else was chopped up for apartments. If she could get it for less, even better. It had a plot of land with a little wood in back and a root cellar where she stored potatoes, turnips, and carrots like people did years ago. It had a wood-burning stove they could use if money for gas ran out. It was big enough to rent rooms if it came to that. Most important, said Leonie, was the patch of ground facing west for a garden. If the end came, if the money dried up and the stores all closed, they'd still have a living.

"Right," said Ineke, as if to underline what had already been said.

This girl. The image on the TV changed again, to the Picasso puppet, then the first Monet, and then the second Monet, then back to the woman again, cycling over and over like spokes on a wheel. He had laid eyes on them all for only about five minutes before they were swept away that morning.

Ineke fell back onto the chair arm and nuzzled into Piet's neck. All while giving Luuk a sly look. She timed it just as Leonie was pouring out the rest of the *Veuve*. If only Leonie knew what a vixen this girl was, she might not have put so much faith in her.

Leonie turned the TV off. "It's no good to keep watching." She extracted rolling papers and a bag of sticky weed from her bag. "Luuk, I have little knowledge of how this goes. But you must have known this wasn't going to happen all at once. This is money for living, for a house, for a car. You can't put it in a bank. If you went into a bank or a dealer with even this much, you would be red-flagged. If you are going to get a car or a bike, you have to get a stolen one."

It was much harder to argue with Leonie. He combed through his hair back to front and tossed his long bangs back to stop himself from pointing out that most of that speech would be obvious to anyone who wasn't stupid.

The question of where the rest of the money *was*, and *which* of the paintings had been sold, galled him in a way that he hadn't expected when he signed on for this adventure. One of them? All of them? Probably the Monets first.

"Patience," intoned Ineke, while Couscous hopped up onto her lap.

Only Piet seemed not to care, riffling through his pile gleefully.

Leonie motioned with her head to Piet, indicating that Piet was the wild card they had to control. That was another thing that hadn't changed—Piet had always been the wild card. Though Piet was the one with the clean record. Luuk could not claim the same.

"Piet, you can't, *you can't* be foolish with it. Put most of it in your mattress," said Ineke with a snort.

"That's right," said Leonie with an affirming nod, lighting the joint and passing it to Luuk. "This will make us all feel better."

Piet turned up the stereo again, grinning ear to ear. At the first few chords of "You Really Got Me," he scooped Ineke off her chair arm perch and spun her around. Together, they danced and screamed, *Please, don't ever set me free, I always want to be by your side . . .*

Ineke didn't know the words well, but it was simple enough, thought Luuk, trying not to smile as she stumbled along. What a circus. Piet reached over and turned it up more, head banging to the sound . . . *You-really-got-me, you-really-got-me* . . . his arm-spiraling-air-guitar at the solo. Ineke dragged deeply on the joint. When

Piet's back was turned, she flicked her tongue stud at Luuk, sending a bolt of fire all over his body.

How incognito she had been last summer when starting up with Piet. To begin with, how did she mark *them* for friends? He wondered how, in her weird way, she knew that she'd fit in here. She just slipped into their house and their lives, shadow-like. She didn't really think of Leonie as a mother—no. She thought of Leonie as an equal, because that worked for her.

Unhappy Ineke. Druggy, tattooed, pierced, fuck-anybody Ineke. And then there was the other stuff.

A girl of seventeen, who did everything she could to hide her waxen beauty behind bad haircuts and baggy clothes. She had been the enigma of the neighborhood as soon as she was able to walk. A straight "A" student at the top of her class, she seemed to drop out of life sometimes, though was physically still there. Periodically, she froze, as if her words couldn't catch up with her thoughts. She wasn't at all concerned about what people thought about it. In their neighborhood, she had always been considered a bit mad, not the friend career-type parents would want for their kid. When she wasn't out drinking beer with the black jackets in the park, she was on her computer cooking up schemes, as well as immersing herself in the art book collection Mr. Visscher had in the living room. She had an uncanny ability to shut all of her surroundings out. It was a blessing, as well as her possible downfall.

CHAPTER 5
REALITY TELEVISION

Sagaponack
July 25th, 2012
22 days after the heist

Perrin set five fat white candles on her kitchen counter and set to work digging the wax out of a candelabra she had missed from last time. With her thick blonde hair, brown eyes and coltish figure, she looked the part of a savvy Sagaponack hostess, but for a sheen of sweat on her forehead and upper lip.

She threw the wax shavings into the trash and slid open the window over the sink. The ocean breeze leapt through, ruffling her thin cotton blouse. It was one of those beautiful nights that were almost a sure thing in July. In the lower-right corner of the window the sky was expanding red, pink, and gold with white clouds here and there like spilled popcorn. She wished she could paint it, or gather enough confidence to even think about painting it. What was it that George said? You can never paint one of these incredible sunsets; it would just look cheap—I've tried. The essence of it, yes, he said—you might paint *that.* How it makes you feel, *yes*. Lately, she reflected, she had not felt up to the task of trying to paint anything. Her efforts in her studio, the last that she had made, felt so small.

She rustled in her bag for her compact and checked her makeup. Lately, she had begun to cling to distancing phrases like *never complain, never explain,* trying that on for size. Was she going to be that type? A Jackie O of the art world? Like Onassis, Jack made money, just piles and piles of it. She'd never want for anything again. It was kind of like how Onassis made money, snoozing fat and tan on the deck of his yacht, an empty highball glass in his hand.

Mascara clumpy in one spot, she found her tiny mascara comb in the bottom of the bag and teased a dried mass into some sort of a better state. Did Jackie really love Onassis? Or did she just love the sort of life he provided her? Well—his money had provided the extra security she needed, Perrin remembered reading a long time ago. The fact comforted her until she questioned why she felt she had to model herself on Jackie O, a brainy, anorexic socialite who happened to marry a president. When Perrin was still a teenager, Jackie O's daughter lived about eight houses down the dune, and sometimes she and her mother would walk slowly by their house, arm in arm, talking, stopping from time to time, their heads leaning toward each other in quiet conversation. The sight filled Perrin with a deep longing she didn't understand. Then much later, Jackie O's son's plane went down and every news outlet in the world was camped in the potato field for weeks. Jackie O's daughter no longer felt comfortable here, sold her house to a movie star, and left.

But Perrin wasn't Jackie O or her daughter. She was not of that milieu. Jackie O was born just one town over into a rarified world of clubs and private schools and outrageously expensive vacations and went on to the White House. Perrin grew up in a fisherman's shack and went to the little Red School House in the town. She went to high school locally and then to Hunter College. After years of bouncing around in the city, acting and waitressing to support herself, she got herself into the School of Visual Arts, where she met Jack. She had landed back here in a state, many would say, of relative splendor. She clicked the compact shut and reached up on tiptoe to grab her Xanax scrip from the top cabinet, where it was hidden behind a jar of beans. She extracted one pink pill and bit the end off it, carefully depositing the remainder for next time.

A rustle of voices carried over from the deck, while she busied herself with a platter of crudité, tapenade, cheese, and olives. The double-death vegan cupcakes she had made earlier were still warm to the touch. She opened a pack of cocktail napkins and shimmied them into a spiral, a trick she'd learned from her catering days. They were pretty like that, she thought, placing them on the tapas platter. Housekeeper Dolores would be here soon and would take care of everything else, which—along with the warm creep of the Xanax—was a kind of relief.

She came out into the living room and was surprised to see that her own recent effort on canvas had been lifted by Jack from her studio and put on display on the mantle piece. Acrylic, a still life of wilted June roses, fairly impressionistic. She didn't like it. It wasn't ready. He turned to her smiling and shrugged. He was trying, she thought.

* * *

The fiery red ball at the horizon was now a third gone, leaving a sky of painterly violence. Their guests were silent for a bit as they watched the sun descend from the one protrusion Max had allowed—a white deck that rested on wooden supports in the sand.

"A de Kooning of a sky," said Chaz Bloodstone, hunched over the railing, wearing his usual white button-down and jeans.

"No, a Turner—but more foreboding than a Turner," said Joseph Seth, Chaz's main publicist, the sun picking up the dark metallic blue of his sharp collar.

"Turner in a bad mood," said Max Moretti, a largish man in a tailored suit of beige linen.

"None of those," said George.

Perrin saw that George hadn't changed out of his paint-splattered clothes. He was wearing shorts, his expired sweat socks cascading from the top of his boots.

Jack jumped in. "I think—"

"Can't paint this," George said. "I dare you to try."

There was a bit of a silence as people weighed options. Was this a joke? A real challenge? In the middle?

Liz Kiss, Perrin's studio-mate from school, said, "But really, isn't it anyone's choice? I mean, what they *want* to paint?"

George cocked his head as if considering that and then went on. "No one can paint that. Well. It would end up looking like something in a doctor's office in Polynesia."

Max laughed, his hefty shoulders shaking. "I agree! But how wonderful to see the real thing."

"So true," said Liz's boyfriend Wyatt.

"I think someone should try," interjected Joseph.

"Something in a doctor's office in Polynesia might be excellent," said Jack. "How would we know?"

"People have tried," said George, shaking his head. "It's just corny and over the top."

"I'm going to take a stab at it," said Jack, popping an olive into his mouth. "If anyone can do it, it would be me."

From outside came a loud squawk. Though Perrin had put a towel over the box, the crow, now named Agatha, had woken up. The guests migrated to Agatha's corner of the deck, and Perrin lifted the towel gingerly. Liz was entranced, as Perrin knew she would be. Agatha waddled unevenly over into the corner and cawed loudly.

"What happened?" asked Wyatt.

"We found her outside on the patio," said Perrin, "and she couldn't fly. Jed Aldrich, you know the guy who owns the farm, said we should feed her and get a wide box and take off the top from time to time, to see if she can launch. He said we'd have a friend for life."

"You'd have a friend, alright," laughed George. "Tapping at

your window morning, noon, and night once they know there's food."

"Well, I wouldn't care," said Perrin, filling the jar lid with water from the spigot.

Agatha hopped and cawed again.

Later, when Perrin thought about it, she realized that Jack didn't want people to know why the bird was injured because he thought it made him look bad. He cared about aesthetics, as she did, but so much more than she did. To not just simply put up drapes and stop this seemed cruel, along with not bailing out George, just because he had made a bad decision. There were people who enjoyed punishing a lack of common sense when they could easily help. That peculiar quirk of human nature, and the possibility that Jack was in some way one of those people, had lately taken up permanent residence in her mind.

From behind the group, Jack said, "How do you know it's female?"

"I don't," she said, while everyone gathered closer. "And there's almost no way to tell. Jed said this is a fish crow. Because of the sound it makes—like a regular crow but with a cold, saying, no—*uh-uh! I'm not a regular crow.* And also because it's here, where you don't find regular crows. Fish crows come to the beach to scavenge, and sometimes they'll go after eggs in ground nests."

"Ugghh," said Liz, while Wyatt lent a soothing hand to her back.

Max shook his head. "That's life."

As if to emphasize the point, Agatha cawed again, her nasal *uh-uh, uh-uh!* She then seemed to turn off to her audience and hunkered down in her corner.

"I like that sound," said Chaz, his woolly blond head bowed over the box. "As if she is refusing something, with panache. *Uh-uh.* Like a sort of Diana Vreeland type, putting the kibosh on the choice of a hat."

Joseph giggled his strange giggle. Liz leaned into Wyatt, resting her head on his shoulder.

And the amazing thing is, she's still alive, Perrin thought, deep inside herself. She noticed the lines of worry gathering on Jack's face, as if the crow presented some sort of threat. And that last piece of it. He would probably try later tonight. The thing that she had once liked, sort of, and had grown to hate. It was all tied in together with this house. She found herself feeling sick about him, sorry for him, and frightened of him as he rattled his fingers on his pant leg.

She said, "This really is bedtime for Agatha" and covered the box.

Inside, Jack was shaking up some gimlets, and everybody wanted lots of fresh lime. Perrin poked her head into the kitchen door to ask Dolores to cut more while thinking of her own brief, disastrous stint in the city as a bartender. The bell rang, and a few moments later Gia alighted from the top staircase.

In the center of the art and sculptures and tall bookcases, she twirled around and exclaimed, "What a cool cool place! I've always wondered about it!"

"I know!" said Liz through the open bookcase that bisected the room, her brown curls pinned in an updo, her face radiant from a day in the sun. "Perrin, I've never seen your house at this hour—it's splendid!"

And it was. Perrin had gotten out Iris's Peruvian plates and the silver from George's mother. She had picked wildflowers from her garden and made a curving line of them on the table. Dolores brought out the tapas, the salads and baskets of bread, ice buckets with mineral water and wine, and linen napkins, freshly ironed that afternoon. All of the earthy old things looked lovely on the glass table, and the house fairly glowed.

Max was talking about a new restaurant he had discovered near his place in Williamsburg. Next to him on the sofa, Chaz took up enough room for two, his legs splayed wide. Chaz had done well for Jack, selling almost exclusively to the roster of buyers in his rolodex and to vetted referrals, whom he could depend upon not to sell into the secondary market. What was good for Jack was good for Chaz and vice versa.

George was at the fireplace, looking curiously at Perrin's painting. He turned to her. "Yours?"

"Yes," said Perrin, embarrassed. She wished that she had had the presence of mind to put it away.

"It has po," said George.

"Po?" asked Perrin.

"Potential. You have a kind of sureness, a sense. Do a series."

"Oh, Dad . . ." she said, trailing off.

"No, I'm serious. Set aside a few hours a day—just a few hours a day. Is it tangible? No. Not yet. But so what? It has to be brought out. Forget about all this extraneous bullshit," he said with a wave of his hand.

This was another new aspect since Iris had died. George seemed to know her better than she knew herself—well of course he did. Through the noise in her head and the chatter in the room, Perrin was drawn into her father's gaze, his focus, his sureness about things. He could have been a great teacher, better than any teacher she had actually had. If only he could have mustered the patience.

Gia was suddenly there, the green of her sweater setting off her ginger curls. "I like it," she said, nodding to the painting, throwing a wink at Perrin, somehow knowing that it was hers. Silver bracelets a-jingle, she shot out her hand. "Mr. Clayton, it's an honor to meet you. I'm a big fan."

George's eyebrows shot up. "I'm touched! That's lovely. Thank you."

"Agatha?" asked Chaz, bemusedly nosing into the conversation. Everyone loved to hear what George had to say.

"Agatha, yes. Just . . . somehow . . . the bird is Agatha," said Perrin, noticing the glasses that needed filling. *Max, George, Gia . . .* she was never able to relax at one of these things and stop catering. It was nice though, that George was hitting it off with Gia.

Not wanting to break into the buffet stock, Perrin hopped for the basement cooler three flights down to get two more bottles and brought them up to the kitchen. As she was unloading them into the fridge, Jack poked his head in.

"Who is this girl?"

Not wanting him to be overheard, she motioned him deeper into the kitchen, where Dolores was fanning carrot sticks around a plate.

"Who is the girl with the red hair?" Jack asked.

Perrin guided him to the corner, as far away from Dolores as possible.

"That's Gia, from my yoga class. I told you about her. A photographer—she has a show at Calliope."

"She is tone deaf. No one is interested in adopting the kittens she found at the railroad trestle."

She studied his face, trying to find happy Jack, original Jack, with a twinkle in his eye. Jack who paused from time to time and was satisfied. "You said you wanted different people."

"Maybe not this different."

"Kittens? She has a soft spot. What's wrong with that?"

"Something about it. She says she has three cats already." He stole a glance at the living room. "Will you get out there? She's onto Max now."

"If you saw the kittens, *you'd* probably adopt them," said Perrin, smiling at him, humoring him. "If you weren't allergic."

"So true! I love cats! It's okay for me. But a single woman shouldn't be obsessed with cats. It's unattractive."

Perrin was annoyed that Gia needed to be perceived as attractive. Also annoyed that cats were considered unattractive. Did Gia have to be attractive? Couldn't she just exist? Anyway, she *was* attractive, cats or no cats.

Jack reached around her to pick up a bottle of salad dressing on the tray. "Hey, I thought we were doing vegan for Chaz."

"Yeah, we are, mostly," said Perrin, having worked on the meal all afternoon. She found vegan to be an incredible time suck. "Thai peanut noodles, jicama and French lentil salad, a green salad, the cupcakes . . ."

He nuzzled into her neck, and the familiar clean smell of him, layered with linen and lime cordial, filled her nostrils.

"But there are eggs in this, Babe."

"Okay, we'll put out the oil and vinegar."

"Make sure to tell him," Jack said, giving her waist another squeeze. Art tycoons could not be seen to be concerned with things like salad dressing, though they might care a lot.

He whispered into her ear, supposedly so Dolores couldn't hear, "I'd like you to shave . . . or wax, or whatever they do. The Brazilian thing."

Perrin tensed up. "What?"

He gripped her waist a little tighter. "I'd like you naked."

Why this question now, she wondered, with Dolores a few steps away. But it wasn't really a mystery—she knew why. At first it had been mild, then more and more and then unstoppable, like water swirling down a drain. If she were honest with him about her shock at having arrived at such a pattern, she'd have to explain the make-out sessions in crowded nightclubs when they first knew each other. And the rest—in the subway with people around, in the back of cabs, and sunbathing topless on the beach when his friends were there, catching them catching glances at her. *It made you hot, Perrin,* he'd say. *Distinctly hot.*

"What do you mean—naked? I've been naked with you," she said, flushing a deep rose red.

"Perrin, I'm *serious.* I'm making myself vulnerable to you," he said, his breath hot on her neck. "Isn't that what you want?"

He leaned into her, running his hands all over her backside. She'd read about this . . . waxing. Everything, everywhere. It was a new thing that college-age women were doing. It sounded excruciating. "Did I say that?"

The vein at his temple bulged, and his blue eyes were lightly circled with sweat. Along with everything else, he now wanted her shorn of hair, as if she had never had any at all. He wanted her to be a pre-pubescent girl. He wanted it because everyone else was doing it.

Dolores flipped the water on needlessly and began bustling around.

"Where's this coming from?" Perrin asked.

"I'm being a sensitive guy, showing you my feelings." He stuck his knee between her legs, nudging them apart.

"Jack!" she gasped.

Dolores crashed a dish into the sink, which only served to increase Jack's focus and the pressure of his knee.

"So will you?" he persisted.

"How many drinks have you had?"

He pressed his knee in harder, his eyes narrowing as if to pierce her very soul. Amid the crackle of conversation from the living room, whoops of laughter fractured the air. With effort, she broke away and smoothed her dress, her breath light and fast.

"I think you had better cool it," she said.

* * *

In the corner of the sky, there remained a pink glow, and the red windsock George had given them was like a jumping bean. A dark wind was sweeping into the house, flurrying papers and knocking an ostrich egg off the bookcase. Perrin could hear bits of conversation floating from the dining area. Liz, after putting back the egg, was extolling the virtues of Brooklyn. Joseph was explaining to Max why he'd never live there. "Can't do the commute. Never going to happen."

George held his glass out to Jack and said, "I'll have just the wine."

Perrin was glad that George was sticking to his rule while noticing the bones of his shoulders through his old T-shirt.

Jack turned from the drinks table with a small tray of gimlets, his smile expectant.

Perrin stepped up, "I'll have one," she said, touching his arm lightly and reflexively.

At the table, Wyatt drummed his fingers on Liz's knee. "Perrin! Golden girl! Where are you?"

Max chimed in, "But Joseph, you wouldn't have to leave—it's

all going to be in Brooklyn in a few years. Manhattan will be a ghost town of financial offices and empty condo towers."

"And museums. Not for me. I will never leave Manhattan. Never. Brooklyn is such a sprawl. And so ugly—most of it. What about you, Jack?" asked Joseph.

"Well, I'm going to have to. Have to have the space." He flashed his quick smile—*vulgar facts of the matter*. He squeezed a lime over the shaker, juice dripping from his red fist. Could he have explained himself? Did he not need to because it worked so well?

"Brooklyn's finished," interjected Gia.

There was a lull as Gia sat down, and everyone dug into their salad and absorbed this, weighing options.

Chaz was sweating as usual, though it was not hot. He mopped his brow with his white handkerchief. "Listen, Jack. Maybe you can just buy a building in Harlem."

Gia scratched into her tight red curls. "How great to have the choice." She looked around with starry-eyed irritation.

Perrin remembered when she herself was struggling along in the city. She thought about what all of this luxury would have looked like to her then.

"I think you're doing pretty well, Gia," Perrin assured her, passing the bread along.

George said, "Hey, Jack, are you aware what they call this place down at Gandolph's?"

"Oh yeah . . . yeah," Gia murmured through a mouthful of food, "I heard that . . ."

"What?" said Jack.

Joseph pulled on his sparkly collar, eyes darting back and forth between them.

"This very house. *The Napoleon*," said George, with a twinkle in his eye.

Everyone laughed, Jack without any mirth. He mouthed, *The Napoleon*? to Perrin.

She shrugged, not minding that someone was making fun of it.

Jack said to Perrin, "Did you hear this?"

"No," said Perrin, truthfully.

"You should be flattered," George said to Jack. "What's the line? 'It doesn't matter what people call you unless they call you pigeon pie and eat you up.'"

"What is that?"

"Well, it's funny, Jack."

"Oh, yeah. I get it. Don't know what pigeons have to do with it, though."

"Evelyn Waugh, I think," said George.

"Never heard of her," said Jack.

"At Gandolph's they wouldn't know good design if they tripped over it, as you Americans say," said Max, tipping back his glass.

"Well," said George, "you've made a statement here in the dunes. Better, maybe, than something boring. Maybe in ten or twenty years people will appreciate it."

Gia semi-whispered to Perrin, "I love your dad!"

George, emboldened, continued, "Unlike that guy where my studio used to be . . . what a stupid house."

"Oh, I don't know about that," said Chaz, a tart smile crossing his face. "It just needs a little weathering. All of these houses look terrible at first."

"Not this house," said Max, waving a forkful of noodles. "It was beautiful from the first."

"Big party there coming up," said Jack. "I'm curious—"

"He has an interest in art," said Chaz. "Sort of a hoarder though. You won't see any of it there. All the living areas are wainscot panels, probably rosewood. All of it, even the bathrooms."

"Hate rosewood," said Joseph. "Sorta cheapy Chinese. I know I'm not supposed to say that."

Liz, who was an interior decorator, said, "It has to be done a certain way," while taking a spoonful of the lentils.

Perrin's eyes narrowed as she thought of the two inches of water in George's basement and the moldy smell of his house.

"What's going on with the Kunsthal?" she asked. "Any latest news?"

"Well, I watched that press conference," said Joseph. "DeVries actually suggested that the Abbiate Foundation was behind it, for the insurance. That's a stretch."

"The Rotterdam robbers," said Chaz. "That was over a month ago. Those idiots just might have gotten away with it."

"George knew Hochberg," said Jack. "What's the story of the painting?"

"You know how he worked, right?" asked George.

"I don't," said Wyatt.

"Basically, he only would paint people who were a part of his life—well, except for the Queen. He did paint her, and never diverted from his method, never strayed, even with her."

"What was that?" asked Max.

"He'd have them sit for hours and hours at a time. And the sittings numbered into, sometimes, the hundreds. Maybe friends and family were the most tolerant of his grueling schedule."

"I loved that painting," said Gia. "But, of course, I could only see it on the internet."

"*Woman with Eyes Closed*, it was called," said Perrin.

"Wonder why he called it that?" asked Joseph.

"Well, her eyes are closed," said Perrin, smiling.

"Gotcha! Haven't seen it. The Monets, though . . ."

"I was there in London when he was painting that," said George. "I met the woman—Julia. She was in her thirties, with two small children. You've read that she has since died. Well, I can tell you that the children are still pretty young."

"That's SO sad," said Liz, her curls trembling.

"What was the Kunsthal doing with it?" asked Max.

"They loaned it to them. The painting was on loan from the family, and not a very wealthy family," said George.

"It had to have been insured. At least there's that," said Jack, topping off everyone's water and wine. He looked at George and said, "*The Napoleon?*" with a sort of laughing irritation.

"Gandolph's. Don't blame me," said George.

I have another name for it," said Gia, leaning forward. "Perrin and Jackcam. Do you know that at night you can see everything in here?"

"Everything?" said Jack, like a geezer uncle hiding a quarter up his sleeve.

"I can't believe a major museum wouldn't have better security!" said Perrin.

"It was under renovation," Chaz said. "Not an excuse, though."

Perrin leaned forward and said, "Four works—the two Monets, one Picasso, and the Hochberg—gone into the black of night. Isn't it incredible?"

Gears began to shift while everyone commented on how terrible it had been, and how really bizarre that these three kids in balaclavas had been able to so easily rob a major museum of four major paintings.

But Liz persisted. "Max told them they couldn't have shades even if they wanted them!"

Max shrugged. "Shades would ruin the effect. Jack and Perrin are both nice looking—who cares who sees?"

"Lights off, nobody sees," said Jack.

"What about lights on!" cried Liz, her wine glass meeting the table with a click.

"Then everyone sees," said Jack, super cool, in that genuine animation character voice only he could do.

They all laughed again, Perrin as if it was the funniest thing she had ever heard. George wasn't laughing though.

Gia's voice traveled over everyone else's. "But isn't that where it's all headed?"

"What do you mean?" asked Joseph.

Perrin did a quick mental accounting of who at the table might have been on the beach a few weeks ago. Joseph and Chaz, no. Liz, no. Wyatt, possible because of that smirk. Gia, well, she had just said as much. Perrin shrunk into herself, wishing that she were living in the seventeenth century where a glimpse of an ankle was considered shocking. When two unmarried people could cause a scandal just by going for a walk together.

"In the culture," Gia continued. "Everything out in the open. Good and bad. Black and white. Everything so real. We don't even need the artist anymore. It's just, *Oooof!!* One beeg reality show."

"Well—" interjected Joseph.

"That's what it is now! I like there to be meaning, something delicate. I don't want to be—*come se dice*—a fly on the wall—"

"That's kind of a thing of the past," said Joseph.

Gia inhaled sharply through her nose and began to populate her plate with precise piles of lentils. She wasn't high, thought Perrin, but what was she?

Gia turned to Perrin and suddenly asked, "May I photograph the house, with you two in it? At dusk when it is perfect light—it would be beautiful. Just on the deck, or in front . . ."

Jack looked at Perrin. *Why not?*

Chaz said, "You should do a whole series—you could probably get a book out of it. Of course, only if Jack agreed . . ."

"Oh no, I couldn't do that," said Gia, pulling her mohair wrap tighter around herself. "Absolutely not."

Around her, rivulets of small talk dried up.

"Why not?" asked Chaz, mopping his brow again.

"Because then I drink—how do you say—the Kool-Aid," she said with a short cough like a cat with a hairball.

"What do you mean?" Jack asked, pushing his glasses up on his nose.

Gia said, "If I photograph you, they'll just be my photographs. But a book will be . . . I'm not sure, but I think I will endorse you. And I'm not sure what I think about you. I like your house. But your artwork . . . I am still with thoughts, I am not *pulled.* I'm thinking, can I live with it—do I respect it?"

"Art having to be painful, art having to be *vile*—that's over," said Joseph. That was one of his main points about Jack's work—it was fun, it made people smile. "People say that about Jack all the time. He inspires happy feelings. What's wrong with that?"

Gia went on, her brow furrowing with concentration. "I will try for the words . . . I wouldn't want to have to live with *every* piece of art that I respect. But there have to be reasons—in the work—that make it unfriendly or too difficult. Your work is not hard in that way, it isn't *painful* of the times. And it isn't only a decoration either. So then my question—what does it say? How does it fit with me? How do I feel about it? Can I live with it? I'm not sure I could live with anything you've made."

"And very likely you never will," said Chaz, looking around for a quashing consensus.

Perrin twisted her napkin on her lap as if to snuff out this conversation. It was too, *too* much. Yet, in another way, she felt a sort of glee, like taking a crystal sculpture and smashing it to pieces.

Another wind came rocking through. "Wow!" they all gasped, as it blew out the candles on the bookcase.

Perrin laughed with delight, surprising herself. Wyatt looked at her curiously.

"Uh-*huh!*" said George, as the sea wind swirled around the table, lifting the corners of napkins and ruffling everyone's hair. George nodded in a sort of reverie, while between the wildflowers the wind blew the votive flames sideways. Perrin's canvas blew off the mantle piece and clunked onto the floor.

With a pious air, Jack got up, picked up the canvas, and shelved it. He re-lit the candles, saying sometimes it's just a blast and then over for a while—a statement that he knew wasn't true.

Another blast, and the candles blew out once more.

"Here we go, here we go, *hoooo!*" said George, laughing like some deranged Buddha.

He was getting goofy on the wine, thought Perrin, yet she knew why he was laughing. But just what did he think was so great? Did he know what was going on? Had he understood what they were saying? She desperately hoped he hadn't and was high enough right now that he wouldn't remember anything tomorrow.

Jack got up to close the sliding doors.

"Oh no—no," said Perrin, jumping up. To her, the wind off the sea had a personality. This one was a rowdy friend and was going to go on all night. She was not going to let it go. She opened the doors again, and the wind came coursing through.

"Fuck the candles," she said, sitting down.

There was a leaden pause. Joseph looked at Perrin as if he'd never met her before. Chaz's eyebrows shot up. Jack's smile was gone. George was beginning to tune out. Liz looked at the floor, trying to think of something to say. Max chuckled and excused himself.

Perrin looked around, invigorated. *Let's go,* she was thinking. It was catching. Everyone was sort of holding their breath, waiting. *Let's go.*

Liz leaned forward and said, "I think Jack's work is cheerful! I can see why people like it. We've had enough doom and gloom."

With a schoolmaster's enunciation, Joseph said, "Jack's work bypasses the old question of whether or not it can be *lived with.* It's much *bigger* than that. It's a conduit, an expression of the culture—so if one person can't "live with it," it doesn't detract from its validity."

Perrin recognized that from the catalog.

Gia bypassed Joseph and said to Jack, "So tell me . . . how does it happen?"

"What?"

"Your process, the work." She seemed in earnest, but it was hard to tell.

"I get a feeling, and then it sticks with me, and then it fleshes out," Jack said, his blue eyes pooling with sincerity. He loved this kind of question. "It used to be a more inward journey at first. Now I'm involved in a more objective art."

Perrin noticed that these were also Joseph's words, straight from a catalog. She refilled her wine glass. Oh, to get through this night. And mainly it was Jack, all the rage and determination that he wouldn't admit.

"Art is a window, a dialogue. That's what he's doing," Joseph said. "That's its importance. That's always been its importance. Now it's just better defined, more pure."

Jack spoke with studied calm. "To answer your question, Gia, ideas just come to me. A lot of it is staying open, not being judgmental. There's a phase . . . an image will come to me, and stay with me, and then I have to figure out how to express it."

Dolores, still a bit flustered, put the double-death cupcakes and whipped cream next to Perrin. Surprised at her own razor vision, Perrin found herself seeing down through all the layers. The troops were assembling, Jack was staying, for the moment, unruffled. Max passed on the cupcakes and eased his bulk back onto his chair. Joseph was stiff, Wyatt and Liz were rapt. George had gone silent. Maybe he was waiting for the next blast of wind.

To everyone's amazement, Gia kept going. "But these are toys, just beeg toys. They are only a little part of life. They are full of nothing, no matter how much the cost is to make. And they . . . they talk down to people . . . make them idiots, *figure brutti.*"

Perrin had never heard anyone talk to Jack like this. She took a cupcake and a big dollop of cream.

Gia went on. "Beeg beautiful toys—the worldview of a child. Children are little morons; they like cartoons and loud colors. Why do we want to be like them?"

Jack's smile trembled. He was cracking, just a little. No, he didn't have a clear vision he was pursuing back in New York, and that had been fine with her. Instead, he was precisely attuned to his surroundings. He was a shapeshifter, and some might have called him shallow even then. But that was why she had loved him. After growing up with a cantankerous painter who was an outsider most of his life—much of it his own doing—the future with Jack had seemed full of light. Levity and good fortune had followed him through the door of that first studio on Houston and had stayed with him all the way. Even if he had to strain a little more to hang on to it.

Joseph pulled at his sparkly collar. "You can't argue with his reception. The world loves him. To the tune of a lot of money. A LOT of money. If you don't like that, take it up with the world."

"I will take it up with the world," said Gia, forming her lentil salad into a new pile. "There's a way that I see. Artists are mirrors, social commentators. Artists are like politicians now. They think too much about the audience. The world mirrors itself, looks in a mirror. Then we are all so much the same. Like to look at your . . . *ombelico*." Gia pulled up her sweater and pointed to her belly button. "*Sempre, sempre*—who cares? What is the point of saying this or that if it is the cheapest thing and then just repeat back to you? Repeat, repeat. What is lost? Leaders. No one is a leader, no one is firm. Art is lost. Human is lost. No one says this is IT. I'm not a reflection . . . I'm telling you instead, *this* is who I am."

Jack, sitting back in his chair, spoke quietly and earnestly. "Someone like de Kooning or Pollock did it by being elusive, removed, distant. They knew, or pretended to know, something that was unavailable, that only they had access to, like the Wizard of Oz. They were veiled and authoritarian, like an authoritarian God. Their work was ugly and hard to understand. I never wanted to be that. I was never interested in the big mystery. I wanted to invite people into the work at *their* level instead of holding it away, shrouding it in secrecy. What I'm saying is, look, *you* are it. It isn't wrong to be like a child, to return to that. It isn't wrong to feel sexual. It isn't wrong to love bright colors. Not everything that's meaningful is dark and unclear. What I'm trying to say is: These are the original things that you liked. That's what everybody liked. That's how I'm a conduit. That's how I *feel*. I love people. I don't mind average, non-critical people. The people that I came from weren't artists. They weren't intellectual. They were ordinary. They had a little furniture store in the town. I never wanted to forget that. I find a certain divinity there."

Perrin was touched by this speech, and so was everyone else. It was the real Jack.

Jack said to Gia, "I want you to do the photographs."

"You do?" said Gia.

"Yes, you, and no one else. Doesn't have to be a book," he added, with gentlemanly dash. "Just a few. My studio. You'll find it interesting."

Deft, thought Perrin. Only she could see the sheen of sweat on his upper lip. Inwardly, she wondered if Gia had anything left to say and half-wished she did. The wind came rocking through again, sending napkins off the table and *The New York Times* airborne. Chaz grabbed the paper out of the air with a crunch.

"Perfect example, Perrin—the Rotterdam robbers," said Gia, while Perrin's attention snapped back to the table. "They always go for the Old Masters—why?" asked Gia.

"So sad," said Wyatt, reaching for the mineral water.

"Limited supply," said Joseph.

"The first question is why those four?" asked Max. "They weren't distinctive."

"They weren't even very good," said Chaz.

"Isn't the answer simply *money*?" asked Liz in her lilting voice.

A few people nodded, but most stared. Perrin, having not had money historically, observed that when people had a lot of it, they wanted to eliminate it as a reason.

Gia touched Liz on the arm. "You're right. They were chosen because they were valuable and small."

"They were buffoons," said Chaz. Forgetting he was vegan, he took another cupcake and half the whipped cream. "A pipe wrench! One of them froze at the end of a corridor, like he was having an anxiety attack."

"Not so bumbling though," said Max, sipping his wine. "They're getting away with it, aren't they?"

"With the art register, they can't be sold," said Jack.

Liz, her pretty eyes wide, asked, "Why would they steal them if they can't sell them—I mean why go to all that trouble?"

Chaz leaned forward. "Sometimes criminals want them—just like you or me. The Monets are instantly recognizable, of course. They're impressive, even though there are quite a lot in the Bridge series. The Hochberg, I can take it or leave it, and the Picasso was minor. But they can be used as collateral for drug deals, ransoms—"

"But it isn't always about money," said Joseph. "Some people become obsessive about an artist, or a particular work, and will hire a pro to steal it. Not the case here, obviously."

"Nobody poor can do that," said Gia, grabbing everyone's attention again.

"What is your point?" said Chaz.

"That money is ruining art. All of the money is making it cheap. Art is the artist, the subject and the people who see it. For example, Hochberg paints a portrait of his friend and then is a memorial. Right? She's gone. Now the painting is gone. Now is lost to everyone. Its value is nothing, we can see. The thieves will be able to sell it for something, but now it's gone."

Liz put her hand on her heart. "But it isn't gone. We don't know yet."

"I don't know what *you* are talking about, but I say limited supply," said Chaz, popping in the rest of the cupcake. "That's the key."

Gia lowered her eyes at Liz, as if she were talking to a child. "But it is, Liz—whether or not they find it. The personal is gone. It's a thing, a meaningless thing."

Liz slumped. "Oh, don't say that. I can't *bear* it. I feel so sorry for the kids."

Wyatt put his hand on hers. "That's totally in the abstract. The loss is to the public, and to the family of the woman, of course. At that level. If it has to be *explained* woman-terminal-disease-friend what have you, that isn't really a part of it as a work, is it?"

"You are wrong, completely wrong, *amico*. The public, the cops, the museums, the insurance company, the family . . . it is a commodity now. Even if they get it back, it's ruined. Too big. Too much. The personal is gone."

George snapped out of his doze and tuned into the conversation.

"Too big? No such thing," said Jack, pushing his glasses up. "Everyone wants to go big. They just don't want to admit it. I was always upfront about it. The more eyes on my work the better."

Gia added, "No, no, no, it's a *feeling*. The thing from the soul. We are too far away."

George nodded sagely. He was a little bit in love with Gia and trying not to show it.

Chaz wiped chocolate from the sides of his mouth. "Okay, now *that's* adorable. From what?"

Gia inhaled again through her sharp nose. "If you want to talk about *markets,* thieves hardly ever go for the new stuff. Even they know the value is . . ." she shrugged, ". . . they are always making more."

Chaz threw his napkin on the table and rolled his eyes.

"Markets make everybody at the lowest level, people know it," Gia continued. "Even if that painting is found, the family of that woman will never have it in their house unless they are rich. If they aren't rich, they will have to sell it. People know something about art before the mid-century. People are wise. They know that it was serious—Hochberg is like that, though he is from a later period. He took months and months to make a single painting, as George said. Markets have gotten too fast and shallow. Nobody past the abstract expressionists—maybe a small group—are going to last. That era was the last. People are going to wake up having paid so much for this or that and say, *what the fuck*, why did I do that, why did I buy this stupid thing? Now I want to sell it. And the world will have moved on."

Jack doubled over in mock pain. "Ouch!"

"You've had too much education. It will wear off," said Chaz. "Where do you show your photographs?"

* * *

As always at night, the sound of the waves came closer, and the wind persevered. Jack squared his shoulders and pinched a dribble of cold candle wax between his fingers. People poked at their cupcakes, trying to turn the conversation back to lighter subjects. Tomorrow would be Sunday. There was a dim watchfulness that something more of interest might drop, something they could add to the weekend's conversational fodder, coupled with a fear that there might actually *be* more and the night would never end. Perrin studied every aspect of their new friend. Her tight green wrap, her worn jeans, her voluminous red hair, her lazy, cat-like movements. It was as if a door had opened for Perrin—indeed, Gia had blown the roof off *The Napoleon*.

Gia asked for a glass of Cointreau, and Jack jumped to get it for her. The condemnation wouldn't have been as severe if Gia weren't a fellow artist *and* a young woman who, in any parallel universe Perrin could think of, would defer to Jack. This fiery girl was more troubled by Jack's success than a problem she had with him. Yet this was criticism of the most intimate kind. In Perrin and Jack's world, questioning the meaning of the work was always personal.

As people collected their things to go, Perrin could see Jack felt it keenly. Gia got a warm goodbye from George. Max was curious about Gandolph's and promised to meet Liz and Wyatt there next weekend. Chaz gave Gia his number and said he'd stop by her show. Joseph was staying at Chaz's house in the village, and so they left together.

After Joseph disappeared down the staircase, Jack turned to Perrin, his smile collapsing like a waterfall. In the hard light, she could see the bags under his eyes. He blinked slowly.

"Fuck the candles?"

"Yes, well . . ." she stammered, "the wind was so refreshing."

She put the oil and vinegar back on the condiments tray.

Helping to clear the table, he said, "You're a bit crazy. Like you want things to go crazy . . . be crazy. I could tell you were enjoying all of that—with Gia."

He looked so exhausted, Perrin thought. It can't have been easy to hear a point of view that ran counter to everything he was doing. An opinion not unlike the critics who disdained him. Only Gia wasn't a critic. She was a fellow artist who had no problem delivering—face to face—what amounted to a condemnation. And so casually, seemingly not understanding the power of her words.

"She's just an opinionated person. It isn't the end of the world. And yes, I do like the wind off the sea."

"You and your father are nuts. I get no credit for all that I've done for you."

She felt a stab of guilt because she didn't feel grateful. Lately, she had strained to remember the happiness of the early years, to fill up her vacancy of feeling and talk herself out of the constant sense of being in the wrong place. As if remembering, which she did so well, would return her to the person she used to be.

He wanted her to come up the transparent stairs to bed. She stalled again, saying she would make tea first. She went to the kitchen, picking up the tray of condiments on the way, and flipped on the burner.

The living room, now bathed in blue frost, showed the big rectangle of the bed. She looked up, watching Jack's blurred footsteps go into the bathroom, one after the other, right-left-right. Now he was brushing his teeth. Water on, water off. Water on, water off. Right-left-right again to bedside table. Sit on bed. Off with socks, feet on floor while flossing. She turned off the lights inside and went out on the deck. Lifting the screen lid from the box, she looked in. It appeared that Agatha was sleeping.

"Hey, Agatha," she cooed. "I'm trying not to think of you as a pet. You can't be, much as you seem to like cat food and grapes. This is the wrong place for you. You are a wild creature."

The crow looked up from the bottom of the box and shuffled with a lopsided gait to the other corner. Its sides rose and fell with its quickened breath, and it opened its beak as if to caw, but no sound came out. Perrin feared that Agatha would not survive. What would she do then? Agatha must survive. Perrin sat down and closed her eyes, hearing the bird's claws on the box.

Opening her eyes again, she watched little fluttering squiggles and amoeba shapes in the night air—just an optical illusion. She wished she were more like them, not in a body at all. Twenty minutes of misery for a month of peace. Her diaphragm was hidden behind a box of Brillo under the sink. Blocking the door to her womb was as close as she could get to having a private room, a dark place where no one could see, where there was no audience. If an innocent child could be held away, then part of herself could too. The sea air soothed her, the delicious dark wrapped around her like a cocoon. Oh, to slip into it now . . . what she wouldn't give.

CHAPTER 6

A FEELING CAN BE AS IMPORTANT AS A FACT

Amsterdam
August 1st, 2012
29 days after the heist

Often, Luuk would go into the Centrum and sit in a cafe on the *Herengracht*, watching people for hours, shrugging off the irritated wait staff who wanted him to order another drink. Even though he had fifty-five thousand euros in his sock drawer from a few weeks ago, he was still repeating this pattern. And surprisingly, his old, crummy life was a comfort to him, though it wasn't exactly the same.

Last night he'd done a run at the Blue Parrot. And as he had done before many times, when he didn't feel like making the long trek home, he had slept under the *Prinsengracht*, on that little patch of grass. At mid-morning, his favorite place was almost empty. Unshaven and bleary-eyed, he ran a hand over his hair to smooth it and took a seat in the corner of the terrace. That wasn't any different from before either; Ineke and Leonie would be pleased. Later today, he'd drop by Doguru's and pay back the advance.

He ordered a coffee and asked for an ashtray. It looked to him as though things were calming down. The Kunsthal was no longer claiming the headlines. Across the street at a news kiosk, he was just able to see that the story had been moved to a side column, headed by a freeze frame of himself kneeling over the Hochberg. He thought about buying a paper but felt if he touched one his hands would catch fire. And what did he want one for? A souvenir? Yes, he reflected, he did want a souvenir. So far it was the perfect crime; not many could lay claim to that.

Same as always, he had chosen a table far from the kitchen. They tended to overlook this one, and he could be left in peace for a while. As a river of people streamed by, he closed his eyes and listened, picking up snatches of conversation, accents and attitudes. No one in this neighborhood older than twenty-two went to clubs every night like he did. They were all professionals or students. They went buzzing by with their pastel shopping bags, their chirping phones, their endless plans. He tried to pick up the differences, the things that had always separated him from them.

He had started selling marijuana and coke as soon as he was too big to wiggle into unlocked windows on the *Keizersgracht*. Never heroin. It was against his principles to sell a drug that could kill. Of course, he did a little coke on the side, but what he was really interested in was the profits. At first it was fun. He liked going out every night, and these girls—rich foreigners especially—liked him. He'd gotten to the point where he knew before they had opened their wallets to pay him. Because of his profession and his dark good looks, they saw him as dangerous, but not too dangerous. He would take advantage—they expected him to—as part of their walk on the wild side. It was the ruder-the-better-the-happier-the-girl. Well, not every time, but most of the time. He'd feel like an exotic specimen, a curio, fodder for some giggly story. It baffled him because he was really not that bad and from Holland.

He set his pack of Marlboro next to the ashtray. Everything was the same, except he had about him a taint of a dark sort of miracle—something he owned, something he loved, a future that sparkled instead of loomed. That sparkle only bubbled up when he was alone and giving free rein to his imagination. He caught the eye of a pretty blonde rounding the corner, her arm tucked into the arm of her boyfriend, chattering happily. Sometimes they didn't mean what they said, or were laughing at what they didn't find funny. He could tell by the tone of voice. This one didn't, just got away with it because of her blue eyes. These people were not natural wonders; they had fashioned themselves. They had learned a style, and he could learn it too. Maybe he had even become a little bit more cultured, having had one hundred and ten million euros worth of art pass through his hands just a month ago.

His phone whistled a text alert. It was Leonie, checking to see if he was all right and wanting him to pick up eggs and milk on his way home. He texted her back, *OK* and *YES*.

He ordered a split of champagne—that would keep the waiter off his back. He tapped out a cigarette and half-closed his eyes. In streams of light chatter, he heard vacation plans for Africa, a bit about a divorce and having the wrong lawyer, and snatches of conversation centering around the Kunsthal. He did feel a bit sorry for them, how personally they seemed to take it. And then thought that he himself would've taken it personally too if he wasn't guilty as hell. Oh, the "bozos" in charge of security . . . "The horror" of the theft . . . Hadn't they learned from the time before? There was the usual undercurrent of enjoyment, the appreciation of each terrible detail, questioning it, questioning again, speculating . . . *was there hope*? Then the respectful awe . . . *things happened.* Then something about organic turnip puree, how good it was. He chuckled silently, holding a match to his cigarette. He hated turnips. Leonie grew them in the summer and kept up a steady supply of them in her cooking all winter long, utilizing her beloved root cellar. He hoped that would change, that soon he'd be able to move out and have his own family—a wife who would cook what he wanted. He tried to picture Ineke in the role. A wife was someone who perhaps held a modest job and did the housework. A wife was never bigger than her husband in any way. A wife was supportive, adoring, and maternal. Ineke was none of those things, and half-crazy besides.

There was that officious, almost staged lecture—the *job,* she had called it. She had gotten a VPN for her computer, and they would need to do that also if they were in. Also, they'd all have to use burner phones exclusively. She wanted them to know that it would be a total crapshoot, and if they didn't make it, there would be a heavy price. No, no, no—when it was all said and done, she didn't want to talk anybody into *anything*, she would *not.* At the time, Luuk respected this because he felt the same, especially about Leonie. It was then that he decided in favor. He stubbed his cigarette out. School was almost out, Piet was home, and he hadn't seen Ineke in weeks. It was odd how well she had known what to say in regard to his thoughts. He had decided early on that he wouldn't try to influence Leonie, that it was her decision to make.

He watched a tourist boat churn down the canal without really seeing it. His head hurt. Once Leonie decided about the Kunsthal, she didn't waver at all. She said that even if they had no buyer at first, it wouldn't matter. If the paintings were worth that much, eventually there would have to be. She said that to get a quarter, or even a tenth, of these numbers would be more money than anyone in their family had ever seen in one place going back to the fourteenth century when they were land barons, before the Viscount de Bus screwed and gambled it all away. As the day approached, she came alive in a way he'd never seen before. Color came to her cheeks, and a bright spark to her eye, as if the clock had turned back to when she was much younger. He remembered thinking that his mother's tastes were not as dignified as he thought they should be. Basically, a farmer, though from a good old family—and now a criminal? His father's ashes would roil in the urn.

Across the street, a man grabbed a *De Telegraaf,* dropping coins into the hand of the vendor. The man stood looking at it, transfixed for a moment or two. He then came striding fast across the street to his bike which was locked to an iron railing right next to Luuk. He went about folding the paper neatly and strapping it to his briefcase and then securing the whole thing to his bike rack. Blank-faced, the man fixed upon Luuk as if he had been thinking of something else—but then he thought that he had seen Luuk before—that if Luuk *wasn't* one of the thieves he looked like someone *capable* of such a vile and scurrilous thing. The man hated him, just like the creeps in the Old Masters' hall. He scowled and snapped the strap onto the paper before pedaling off.

Suddenly, Luuk's cigarette tasted bad and the water along the canal was scummy and sickly brown. Four paintings out there like wild cards, deciding his fate. As Ineke had predicted, the story had been broadcast all over the world. He didn't have a computer and tried to avoid television as much as possible, but the neighborhood around the house had warehouse stores and for weeks the videotapes had been everywhere. Dozens of flatscreen TVs dancing with the images of himself razoring out the portrait of that woman, and of Piet shattering the already broken door on the way out. Passersby were riveted by these images. He felt exposed and that he must stop and look too for as long as he could stand it, or seem furtive and out of step. Cops and civilians both had become hawk-eyed. What sanctimonious fools they were, with the actual burglar right there breathing the same air as them! People were such hypocrites, puffed up with righteousness when most of them, given half a chance, were just as bad. He shored himself up with the thought that, theoretically, he could buy and sell the bastard with the bike a thousand times over.

The waiter gave him a hostile look because he was drinking slowly and his ashtray again needed servicing. Alert to anyone striding purposefully towards him, Luuk watched the swirl of people around him. A policeman on a bike pedaled along the canal, but with a diffuse quality to his movements. Luuk thought about Ineke, that weird, faraway look in her eyes she sometimes had. The past week had tested his patience mightily. It wasn't so much that he had expected instant results; he knew that was unrealistic. It was the drip drip drip of the days, one after another. It was the plainly dressed fellow who fell into step behind him as he left the Parrot last night. It was the police cars that sidled down the streets around the house with greater regularity than they used to.

The sun crested a building and spilled onto him, while a few passersby took note of his morning cocktail. He surveyed the table: white paint worn off in places, crumpled napkin, empty bottle and one glass, ashtray with five butts. A smartly dressed woman all in black hurried by and looked at him without registering him at all, which was worse than the disdain from the bike fucker. He could hardly believe he was only twenty-five, he felt so old. Patting his pockets, he found a few euros for the bus. He wondered how it was that at the end of the day he had agreed that this blue-haired punk and his own mother, an old woman with some hard years on her, would walk off with one hundred and ten million euros worth of paintings, making him into a blind participant. It was like owing money on a house that he might never live in. As lousy as he felt, he knew he was going to have to get the situation in hand.

The vendor clipped the twine on more newspapers and stacked them in front of his kiosk. The cop turned back and was meandering toward him. Another man plucked a fresh paper from the stack, reading while he dropped change into the vendor's hand. Luuk signaled the waiter and shoved the ashtray to the edge of the table.

* * *

Back at the house, he was sorry to see Ineke sitting primly on the sofa in the living room; he had hoped to speak to Leonie alone. Also, he could not keep playing these dumb games. If he wanted to know more at the end of this day than he knew now, he'd have to stay strong against Ineke and just go for it. He noticed, too, that she was dressed more conservatively, in clothes that looked like she had just cut the tags off them.

Leonie was in the kitchen fixing up something. He went in and got the tray of *appeltaart* and coffee she had prepared, with a decanter of *Jenever* alongside and a few glasses. A pitcher of milk steamed next to the potpourri. The TV was on in the corner as the head of the Art Ministry was being interviewed.

"Shhh-shhhh . . ." said Ineke, leaning toward the TV, listening closely. Piet was frowning. Ineke turned her attention back to Piet. ". . . not suddenly," she said, "just gradually. You know the way people move on sometimes? That is what this will be. We couldn't do it right after, of course." Ineke made a move to hold Piet's hand, but he pulled it away.

Couscous sidled up to Luuk's leg and purred loudly. She ground her head against him, as if trying to shove him onto the old sofa.

Ineke looked up, meeting Luuk's gaze. "Things have been happening behind the scenes, as you can see."

Luuk took in his brother's mood, and four stacks of euros on top of the record player.

"You'll be happy," intoned Ineke with flat sarcasm. While Piet sulked, she watched Luuk's movements intently. Couscous hopped up onto her lap.

"Really, though, it isn't us—it's me you are talking to, right?" Piet said to Ineke. "I'll be *happy?* How can you say that?"

"You didn't think we were going to carry on like before?" Ineke asked him. "It's impossible!"

Piet spoke through his teeth. "You are so . . . *so*—"

"It isn't that bad though. It's all going to come right in the end. We just have to wait."

Leonie nodded, handing out pieces of *appeltaart*, Luuk's favorite.

"I don't care about the money," said Piet, his nose getting red. "This really sucks."

"It won't be forever—I mean *forever* forever," Ineke continued, brushing Couscous off her lap with a touch of impatience. "It might seem like a long time though, to us, of course."

Piet's eyes welled with tears, and he brushed at them furiously.

"What is going *on*?" asked Luuk.

"I told him that he can be the one to do it. He can save face in this way." Her voice became more quiet. "I mean at school."

Luuk sat down, and Leonie pushed the tray towards him. "I still don't know what you are talking about," he said.

"Well, it doesn't affect you directly," said Ineke, "though it is all of us. Piet and I were known as spending time together. But people move on. It isn't unusual. For us to *remain* close is a bad idea. So we change gradually, right?"

Luuk pulled the sugar bowl to himself and dug his spoon in. Piet sniffled. Luuk kicked his boot, hoping he would compose himself.

"I'm sorry you are upset. I am upset too," she said, grabbing Piet's hand again.

"Gradual? What about you?" Luuk said. "You've gone from Shirley Manson to Reese Witherspoon in one week."

Leonie chuckled, and Piet laughed through his tears. "Yeah! What's going on with that?"

"I didn't think it was that noticeable," said Ineke. "I just didn't want to stand out. So much."

Luuk took note again of Ineke's conservative look. Mohawk clipped back, pearl earrings. Blue jeans, a cardigan sweater, trainers. Eye makeup much softer. Shell pink lipstick. Still sexy as hell.

Leonie collected the four stacks of cash and doled them out. She then extracted rolling papers and tobacco from her bag. "It's the same money as before and the same rules, of course. You'll thank me later," she said, sounding suspiciously like Ineke.

"You can be the one to do it," Ineke said to Piet. "We'll have a big fight in the cafeteria tomorrow. You can pour a drink on my head. It will be good for you, and I won't mind."

"Okay," said Piet, his brown curls shaking.

"All the girls will come running. And you still have the bike, right? You'll forget me in a week."

"No, I won't."

Ineke slung her arm around his shoulder. "You will, and one day, later on, who knows?"

"What about your make-up courses?" said Piet, his eyes welling up again.

"Now that I have turned eighteen," Ineke said, staring off at the wall, "they are going to let me just do lessons and a test. And presto, I'll be done!"

"I knew this was going to happen," said Piet, flopping back onto the sofa, looking gutted. Couscous' head butted his arm as if to distract him.

The sound of the art minister's interview cut through the silence. ". . . equally by other nations: France, Spain, and Great Britain. No one in Europe is untouched, directly or indirectly—"

"Aren't you sick of hearing about it? Turn it off!" yelled Piet, pouring himself a glass of *Jenever*.

"No," Ineke said. "We have to stay on top of it."

"The Monets, right?" Luuk asked, cleaning crumbs of *appeltaart* from his plate with his finger as if he wasn't that concerned.

"We aren't saying," said Leonie, filling her cup with hot milk and coffee.

"We aren't, especially now," said Ineke, looking him straight in the eye.

"Why especially not now?" asked Luuk, a prickly sensation underneath his skin.

"You've seen them?" asked Ineke, eyebrows raised.

"Seen who?" asked Luuk, as Couscous chose his lap next.

"The cops, the presence. It's a change," said Ineke. "Can't quite say what it is. I did think about that neighborhood watch thing they began last year. But this is different. I feel as though this street, this house is being watched."

"What about your place? Is that being watched?" asked Luuk, trying to figure out his angle.

"I don't know. But I go outside, and the hairs on the back of my neck start to rise."

Leonie lit the joint. "Me too. We do have to take steps."

"Maybe you are just more afraid to go about normally now," said Luuk, knowing full well what she was talking about. Over the last month, his earlier arrest had glanced through his mind often enough. It was as if the very air around him had tightened.

"And also, it could be just general worry," said Leonie, pouring herself a dram of *Jenever*, looking at it appreciatively. She was getting floaty, entering that dangerous stage where any subject became kaleidoscopic.

Reflexively, Luuk smoothed the cat's back with his big hand.

Piet grabbed his packet. Instead of rubber bands, each one was contained by a paper sleeve. He ripped it open and started counting.

Leonie spit a stream of smoke into the air. "I have felt it, and usually I want to pay attention to feelings. A feeling can be as important as a fact. But then I have my common sense too. Out of all the kids in Amsterdam, how can they make a connection to us? That record is sealed."

"There *is* the remote possibility that some sort of evidence was left, somewhere. Though we were so careful," said Ineke, shaking her head.

"Exactly *how* were we careful, Ineke?" Luuk said. "And especially, how were *you* careful?"

"Well, the gloves, the masks—you know, not touching anything on the bikes, in the van . . ."

"Even if there were," said Leonie, "we hired a good lawyer. He was only fifteen."

"Did they take a swab?" Ineke asked Luuk, while Piet was busy counting.

"A swab?"

"Yes." She stuck her finger on the inside of her cheek and rubbed it around with a nasty, jeering look.

Luuk wanted to hit her. "Looks like you've had a swab," he retorted. "Lots of them."

"Stop it, you two," said Leonie. "It doesn't matter. Guus Maijer was the best. Just keep going about your business."

Luuk was barely able to restrain an encroaching sense of disgust. "I barely remember. It was ten years ago. Shouldn't we have had that conversation before all of this?"

"We did have that conversation," said Ineke coolly.

"Not with me," said Luuk, shaking his head. "What—"

"Don't go out and spend that," Leonie said to Piet who was riffling through the cash. "I just wanted you to know that it's yours. We can't spend a lot of money right now."

"But that's tiddlywinks, Mom," Luuk said. And immediately regretted it.

"Such a big man!" Leonie barked at Luuk, a scary glint in her eye. "All you've ever done is crime, so how can you know the value of money? You didn't even finish school!"

"Mom—"

"What's the matter with you? We all can't know everything. It just makes it more dangerous! We agreed!"

"No, *you* agreed! You and Ineke! And now, with all of us feeling we are being watched, maybe it's time for a change of plan. Maybe you can't handle it on your own. Maybe you're in over your head."

Ineke shook her head slowly, as if he were a most pathetic creature.

"Me? *Me?*" said Leonie. "When your father died, he had more debts than Dorrit. We barely got out of Oosterwolde with our skin on. You did know that, didn't you?"

"Yes and no," said Luuk, when in fact it was mostly no.

Piet was rapt. He was too young to have been aware of any of this.

"Then I set us up here. No, it isn't very grand . . ." she waved a hand at the living room. "But it is a roof over your head."

Luuk tapped out a cigarette, his breath getting shallow. "And I help you out, don't forget—"

"Your gym membership is out, right?" Leonie said. "Take some of that and bring it up to date! No one will question it. You are always more calm after a workout."

Leonie's beady eyes squinted at him. Oh, how he hated that look. Her condemnation was made infinitely worse by the fact that now she couldn't see him well without her glasses.

"I'm calm," said Luuk, watching as Ineke mentally left the room.

The conversation was running aground. Even Couscous knew—she jumped down off his lap, her paws hitting the floor with a thud.

Leonie turned to the others and announced, "His workout. Then he can be more beautiful and calm. All is right with the world when my twenty-five-year-old man feels pretty."

Ineke laughed, her tongue stud flashing. Piet snorted. Ineke shot Luuk a daggers look. She felt that she had just racked up some points because Leonie liked to be a funny character more than almost anything else in the world. But Leonie's humor was the default of the powerless. Only Luuk knew how deep that went.

Totally unmanned, he had no comeback. Leonie had had her moment, and she was right—he was ridiculous, a preening monkey. Just yesterday he'd bought himself new jeans and a black T-shirt of the softest cotton that he was looking forward to wearing. Piet was finishing school, which he hadn't been able to pull off. Ineke, with her new soft haircut and prissy attitude, was untouchable.

And just a few hours ago, alone at the café, the future had looked so much more inviting. He remembered those kids dancing by, shopping bags swinging on their arms, giving their nanny trouble. He had begun to think that his own children, if he had children, would have to outgrow him completely. Even though one day they might be able to brag about how their dad pulled off one of the biggest museum heists in Europe and had gotten away with it. By then, if they were lucky, they'd be in America or Switzerland and no one would believe them, as they would be the sort that went to excellent schools and talked about turnips with reverence and could laugh on cue.

"You should have told me," Piet said to Ineke.

"Told you what?"

"How this was going to turn out."

"I didn't know. I'm sorry, *schatje*."

Piet stood up and felt for his keys in his pocket.

Luuk shook his head. "No, Piet, no." Piet was stronger than him, towering over him in his boots. Luuk wished this entire worthless day would just come to an end.

Ineke hopped up, brushing Couscous' fur from her jeans. She looked up at Piet and ruffled his hair. He looked like he was melting and exploding all at once. She instantly became more serious. "You are *not* going riding now, Piet," she said.

"Piet, no," said Leonie. "Never ride when you are upset or drunk—that's the rule."

"I don't care," he said. He took a few bills from the table and stuffed them into his pocket. He grabbed his bike leathers from the corner.

"Piet!" said Leonie. "Stop!"

He leaned in close to Ineke's face. "You never told me that this was going to happen!! You *lied*!!"

She went pale.

Finally, thought Luuk, something was unsettling her, and it was his baby brother.

"I thought it would have been obvious how things would play out!" said Ineke, alarmed.

Piet contemplated her, his eyes filled with tears of rage. It was as if he were transforming, becoming harder and tougher from one breath to the next. "You might not have planned each thing, but you knew deep inside. You knew. You were just using me."

Piet took his stack of cash and threw it at them, the banknotes fluttering down over coffee cups and *appeltaart* crumbs, phones and cigarette butts. "I don't give a *shit* about this! I really don't!"

"Oh, *don't blow up, Piet!*" Ineke ran after him and held still in the front hall. "Don't slam the door, *don't slam the door!*" she cried.

They all braced themselves, as Piet banged the front door so hard all the windows rattled, and he disappeared into the afternoon.

CHAPTER 7

WATERLOO BRIDGE AT SUNSET, PINK EFFECT

New York City
August 1st, 2012
29 days after the heist

Englishman Kit Hobbs, thirty-seven years old, had pale, slightly flushed skin that hadn't seen much sun, and dark fashionably spiky hair. If he were on business in London, he'd wear a crisp shirt with a silk tie. Sometimes he'd venture a light-pink shirt, which worked well on him. Glancing at him on the street, you would have thought what he wanted you to think: "Quantitative analyst on lunch break meeting girlfriend from rival hedge fund" or "Test pilot on weekend spree." His face would divulge none of what he was thinking, except for his eyes, and that he could not control. They were dark blue, watchful, and prone to dreaming. You wouldn't have noticed his limp unless you were very observant because he hid it well. If he decided it would suit him to have a limp, you'd see it.

Other than that, he wasn't a very practiced spy. Kit, who was a serious fellow from Edmonton, had tried to do everything right. He'd been a scholarship student at Royal Holloway in maths. After graduation, he started in sales with a finance firm, a job that he soon detested, though it paid his bills. Then on to the service. He believed in the service, he believed in England, and he was a fan of Churchill (except on India). But he'd had terrible luck. In the short time of his employ, he had been on three stakeouts, and the last one had gone extremely badly.

Three months later, the opportunity to fly first-class to New York, where he'd never been, had come as a complete surprise. He had been assigned to an operation called *Viridian,* which sought to restore a number of stolen artworks. Kit had no background in art. As he sunk into his sumptuous seat on the plane, he reflected that *Viridian* was an international op—and so soon—in what had been a short career. Upon his first flute of very good champagne, he wondered if *Viridian* might have been the service compensating him for their major screw-up, or a plea of some kind that he not drop out and write a book about them one day. He quickly dismissed the thought as ridiculous—he'd go to jail immediately, and the service didn't do compensation (unless after many years, and maybe not even then), and they certainly didn't do pleas. But the fact remained that he had something on them.

Landing at JFK in a state of mild puzzlement, he had gotten a cab to what was called the West Village, in the lower third of Manhattan. He had gone directly to a place on St. Mark's that his boss Martin Green had told him about. Perfect for the "young fogey" clothes he would need, said Martin, suggesting khakis and at least four worn shirts in plaid and bland colors like (dingy) white and faded light blue. Well, that wasn't hard. While rummaging through piles of funny-smelling clothes, he practiced the moniker he had been given. *Christopher Pinsmail*—Oxford graduate, specialty in the Renaissance. *Christopher Pinsmail*—married but separated. *Christopher Pinsmail*—representing an art collector from Milan, who needed to remain anonymous. *Christopher Pinsmail* would have to be on a side job, skewing more towards an academic type rather than an art world whiz. Kit slipped into the khakis he had found in the back, leaving on his white undershirt which showed unbecomingly under one of the shirts. Standing at the full-length mirror, he held up a pair of nerdy-looking brogues—fortunately in his size—eleven. Stroke of luck right there, he said to himself. There was no one around. He looked himself dead in the eye and said, *Hello, Chris, pleased to meet you . . .* in his crisp accent. How in the world was he going to pull this off?

As per protocol, they wouldn't tell him reasons, because reasons were a dangerous distraction. He was merely to stick to a part and be briefed as needed. One of the stolen works was by a British artist (he hadn't known even that much). That painting, *Woman with Eyes Closed,* and the other three stolen works had possibly made their way to New York, to some beachside town. All he had was pictures of each work in a folder. Less risky, they said. His connection was gallery owner Chaz Bloodstone, who was a friend of his boss Martin's wife. While shucking the khakis, Kit wondered how it was that Martin had pulled an unwitting friend of his wife's into an operation and hoped that it wasn't going to be another problem. Martin, an art lover and collector, had described the job to Kit with an unusual degree of savor. "In New York, you're going to have to learn the names of these artists and a lot more," he had said in his London office. "And he's Mr. Bloodstone to you, at least at first."

About forty, Chaz's fleshy face was deeply tanned from his weekends on Long Island, and his faded blue eyes hooded from his ample appetites. *You only go around once,* said Chaz. He kept a white handkerchief about his person to mop the beads of sweat that continually popped out on his brow—because it was August, he explained over a steaming dish of coq au vin that night. As the evening went on, Kit thought Chaz wasn't quite as easygoing as he seemed. He wanted to know, he *wanted to know,* everything about Kit's life. On the plane, Kit had slipped off his wedding ring and put it in his computer case because *Chris Pinsmail* was separated. Martin's idea was that it could be useful to have the interest of the ladies, but with options built in. If Kit were honest with himself, which he wasn't always, he'd have to acknowledge that his wife back in London would care about the singleton approach if she knew, but he'd never tell her.

Kit was intimidated by his new friend's nosiness until he realized that the man was obsessed with other people's relationships. Kit just said that he and his wife were taking a break of six months and changed the subject. The conversation circled around—Wimbledon, tennis stars Andy Murray and Roger Federer, Obama, the Newtown school shooting, the London Riots, gun laws in the UK vs. the U.S. Kit managed to avoid the Renaissance, which he knew little about beyond inhaling as much of *Painting & Experience in Fifteenth-Century Italy* as he could on the plane before leaving it on a chair at the airport.

The next night, in his jovial way, Chaz convinced Kit to ditch his beige and gray hotel and stay in an extra room in his loft downtown. Chaz welcomed Kit into his home with open arms, and Kit found himself wishing he didn't like Chaz as much as he did. It was unprofessional. He had the run of the place while Chaz was out, and all he had to do was feed a lonely cat named "Cat" and run some laundry. These were pleasant things to do when jetlagged, padding about a new place with the fuzzy otherworldliness of a different time zone, shooting updates to Martin now and then. He was so grateful, he even went the extra bit and changed the poor cat's disgusting litter.

On the third day, Chaz took him to a Japanese restaurant around the corner from the loft and asked about Kit's Milanese "buyer."

"Well, what're they after?" asked Chaz.

"Old Masters—or at least in the style of Old Masters," said Kit, thinking of that most recent piece, the woman dreaming, that he liked. It wasn't really old, but it seemed to be.

"Going for the crackle, are they?" Chaz said, eyebrows raised, slurping his miso soup.

Not knowing what he meant, Kit nodded.

"Tough and pricey. Christie's, Sotheby's. Check out Acquavella too. They're not an auction house, so you wouldn't have to wait.

Anybody with anything good is going to sell it through them. Unless it's private. I can ask around. Better to go private and cut out the bigger commissions."

"They're open-minded," Kit said, as he'd been coached to. To his relief, Chaz didn't want an art history lesson.

"I thought your guy or woman, whatever . . . never mind," said Chaz, shaking his head. "Nothing like that right now that I can think of. How long do you have?"

"Depends . . . Meanwhile, I'd like to get a picture of what's going on *here*. All levels. Don't know when I'll be able to get back. This is an unusual kind of thing for me."

Chaz extracted a pen from his bag and, poising it over the back of a menu, asked, "Sticking to Manhattan or going further afield?"

"Just give me the comprehensive tour."

During the next four days, Kit absorbed every scrap the town had to offer, sometimes with Chaz, sometimes without him. It had been a crash course. Monet and Picasso, of course, but Hochberg had a following here too. Chaz had first directed him to the uptown galleries like Gagosian and Skarstedt, and of course, his own, Bloodstone. Then the downtown circuit, the edgier stuff. The museums, the Metropolitan, the Guggenheim, the Whitney, MoMA, and the Frick. Old Masters, Impressionism, Cubism, Dada, the Surrealists—Kit absorbed it all, feeling exhausted and sated by the end of each day, and the next morning, hungry for more. Sitting in front of these mammoth works done so long ago had been purifying, somehow putting his own problems into perspective. At MoMA, he discovered that one of the works stolen in Rotterdam, *Waterloo Bridge 1901,* had a cousin called *Waterloo Bridge at Sunset, Pink Effect.* It had been painted in 1903, just two years later. He sat in front of it for an hour, resting his aching leg, letting its blues, pinks, and yellows meld into a virtual place in his mind. *Pink Effect* was almost a different bridge in the same spot. It was delicate and strange; even the faint smokestacks in the background were evocative. It replenished him, made him feel at home and understood, a sharp contrast to the life he had left behind.

When he got home from work, Chaz liked having a buddy to do the town with. He seemed to know at least five people everywhere they went, and one night, Kit ended up not quite alone at Chaz's loft. Chaz, amused, thought this was normal for Kit, and Kit let him think that, though he'd never been unfaithful once in his life. Only, it so happened that a good-looking, chiseled dancer from a place called Queens, with an accent that was oddly British but not British, ran a finger down his back at a bar, and that was it. He slipped into her embrace as easily as walking through a revolving door, as easily as the entire world could be blown up in an interval of two seconds, as indeed it had been three long months before. No, he wasn't the same since then—yet he himself wasn't aware of the difference. He was merely stepping in and out of different spaces in time, putting bricks of his former self together here and there in piles that were remotely recognizable. The dancer was just part of the reconstruction. Seeming to understand this, she slipped out of the loft in the early morning hours.

"What's with the limp, man?" Chaz asked the next morning as they headed out for coffee.

"Car accident," Kit lied. "Broken in three places." His head hurt dreadfully, and his leg was firing up. There was that nosiness particular to Americans. They'd ask you almost anything. No manners at all.

"Ouch," said Chaz.

Yes, thought Kit. *Ouch.* Only it wasn't a car accident at all. It was much, much worse, because the whole mess could have been avoided.

In London, he and a colleague, Meredith, had been surveilling a mid-level Russian criminal, Demyan Egorov, at the Taj Hotel. They had spent their days monitoring the front of the hotel with two small wide-angle cameras. There were also cameras in Egorov's four rooms inside. Their screen was split eight ways, and because it was impossible for them to watch everything, the cameras to the front and back of the van were being monitored at headquarters. When things got active in the rooms and in around the van, it could be difficult to stay on top of it. To compensate, they all had to rewind and fast-forward the video when things were quiet in case something was missed. The people backing them up at headquarters were supposed to be experts at this.

Sometimes he and Meredith talked. They talked about the Saudis at the hotel, who were the fifth-richest family in the world. The men wore long white robes and keffiyeh headdresses and seemed to go about business mainly. The women, mostly on off-the-hook shopping expeditions, were covered from head to toe (except for pampered feet in expensive sandals) with dark beautiful eyes peeking out from their niqabs. Kit and Meredith joked that the family looked sophisticated enough to have their own surveillance team—maybe from the blue van up the street. Meredith had had an inkling about the blue van. That fateful day, it had been parked for hours, ahead of a long black limousine that belonged to Egorov's cousin. She mentioned it several times and even walked up to see that the driver and passenger seats were empty, with a curtain behind that blocked off the interior. Like any surveillance van, she said, like *their* van.

She had pestered him—shouldn't they just approach? Kit, not having seniority, pondered what action he could take. Couldn't they let them know they were clearing the area, she asked. Didn't they have the authority? They did not, so together, they contacted control. Could be a hooker doing business, said control. In *Mayfair,* asked Kit, somewhat naively. Yes, they said, in Mayfair. Well, look, here's the hotel, Kit said. Maybe a hubby getting out on the sly. Some people like that kind of thing, thinking of that actor fellow who got caught in Hollywood in the nineties with a transvestite. Something about shoes. Kit joked with Meredith because he didn't want her to worry. They had no cause for entry because no law was broken, he said.

Needing to relieve himself, he had left the van, closing the slider behind him with a click. He had a spot in an alleyway he liked to use. On his way, he brushed shoulders with one of the Saudi daughters with kohl-rimmed eyes. He had always found it hard to smile at a mostly covered woman. It wasn't just that the culture was so different (that was attractive) and that they were largely forbidden to him and he to them (even more attractive), it was that it was almost impossible to tell if they were smiling back. Unless they had the sort of eyes that met his, that told a story—or at least opened a book to the first page. She was like that, coming from the corner as he was walking to the alley. He could not have called her flirtatious; she was more somber than that. He would never forget her.

In the corner of his eye, he saw the blue van pull away from the curb, not in a rush at all. He would never have recalled its slow progress were it not for what happened after it reached the corner and slunk through a red light. A force knocked him to his knees; red and hot-orange with jagged spikes went through him. His untucked T-shirt billowed out from below. He was enveloped in a gray and white cloud and deafened but for a piercing high tone, while pieces of their van hit the pavement in chunks. Around him, tissues and cups, newspapers and Styrofoam food containers blew about drunkenly. Shouts and screams sounded far away, then close, then far away again. The screeching went on, both inside his head and all around. His knees thundered with pain. Sirens poked through—an ambulance, the police. He slumped over on his side, the world askew. The pain worked through him, demanding his attention, focusing him, gathering into his left thigh. He felt there and found his hand wet and slippery. For a moment he wondered if he might roll down the pavement because it was no longer flat under him. He felt terribly alone. He was a bug, pinned to an angled then completely vertical surface. He tumbled into a wall of black and was cast out into space.

He and Meredith and the Saudi girl, Mayla Khalife, were not the targets; they were merely in the way. The bomb was intended for their mark, Egorov, mistakenly believed to be in the limousine in front.

Four days later, he regained consciousness, first hearing Susannah speaking, and then, days later, seeing her crisp outline against the window in the ward. Martin visited and told him that Meredith, Khalife, and the driver of the limousine had died. The bombs had detonated from a garbage can in between the limousine and their van. It was found on the tape—a hooded figure exited the van with two bulky packages and dropped them in. The people back at control, whose job it was to monitor the front and back cameras, had missed it. For a long time, Kit lay in the hospital dreaming and feverish, feeling the bomb's thud on his back, the red-hot fire and the numb crack of his knees on the pavement. Shrapnel had ripped through his left leg. On its tirade through his head, the bomb had taken a piece of his hearing. The world had been reorganized for the sake of one mistake, and three people had died.

"How much?" asked Chaz, calling him back into the present.

"How much what?"

Chaz fumbled for his keys to the loft. "I was just asking what the budget is for your buyer."

"Oh—sorry, preoccupied." On the narrow sidewalk, people swirled and pooled around Kit, most a head shorter than him. He felt queasy, as if he had fallen into a deranged child's Lego creation. A rest would help, and later he'd text Martin about progress.

"Kit, I know a great massage person out at my country house. Help you with that leg."

"Is it that obvious?"

"It was a long night, and the floors at the Met will kill you."

"I'll be fine, I'm sure. All I need is some ice and my trusty painkillers." Kit patted his jacket pocket.

Alighting from the elevator to Chaz's loft, Kit again noticed the mingled smells of stale booze and candle wax. Grimy windows wrapped around the big, dusty space; industrial-sized fans swished at the heavy air. The little used galley kitchen moldered away in the corner, behind which a hallway led to Chaz's quarters.

"Where was this accident?" asked Chaz, tossing his keys on a side table.

Kit took a beat. There *was* a reason, in case this came up—

custom-made for him in the *Viridian* file. Only he couldn't remember what it was.

"Country road in Ireland," he said. "They're very narrow, unlike here."

"You've never been out to the country here, have you?"

"No. I haven't been here at all," Kit said, his leg beginning to buzz.

"How do you know then?"

"Judging by everything else, I guessed they must be bigger. Do you have ice?"

"Of course I have ice," Chaz said, finding a plastic bag to put it in. "Also a bag of frozen peas," he said, handing that to Kit.

As they puttered around, there ensued a companionable debate about how calculations about road size were made, and how to set up the automatic cat feeder that Chaz hadn't been able to figure out.

"Wouldn't want to leave you here in this weather. Going to get *hot.* I'm going out to the country on Saturday. You can stay here or come out to my house. My house isn't very big but does the job."

"That would be great—yes—the country," said Kit, careful not to seem too enthusiastic. "Don't worry about lodgings—I'm not picky."

"We'll take Jane—there will be a party," said Chaz.

"Jane?" asked Kit, believing Chaz to be single.

"My baby, my one and only—you'll see, she's sleeping across the street right now," said Chaz.

"Who's giving the party?" Kit asked casually, not letting him go.

"A Russian guy. House on the beach. Should be good. All the main players will be there."

"Great! Hey, thanks, man," Kit said, mirroring Chaz's way of speaking, watching him disappear into the rabbit warren behind the kitchen. When Chaz didn't feel like going into work, he conducted affairs and made calls from this apartment, and there was no one to tell him he couldn't. What a life. Kit pulled a glass and a pint of bourbon from the bar.

His room was a cubicle in the corner with a twin bed, into which he collapsed. Cat had decided to join him and planted herself along his side, purring wildly. He slapped the frozen peas on his shin, and the ice on his knee, and pulled the whole thing tight with a bathrobe belt he'd found drifting around the living room. Chaz was right, it was getting hot. Looking up, he noticed the space between the top of his flimsy walls and the ceiling. No, he wasn't picky, this was just fine. And so quiet. Cat was happy. The ice felt nice and cool. Shifting on the creaky bed, he popped half an Oxy and swallowed it with a gulp of bourbon. Susannah was probably just getting home from the museum and would like to get a text, so he sent her one. For the moment, his drug supply was good enough to keep the pain under control. There was the NIH bottle Susannah had filled for him. Then, in the side pocket of his bag, another four bottles he had procured with forged scrips at an Indian pharmacy in Southall before he left. Altogether, they'd last a month, maybe less, depending. Then he'd have to figure something out. His phone buzzed; it was that dancer from the other night. He had tried to give her every indication that he wouldn't be around long. There was that funny line he had heard in a song somewhere: *When your phone don't ring, it'll be me.* He put the phone on silent and texted Martin: *Out to the country tomorrow, a place called Sagaponack. Will attend a party at a Russian's house this weekend.*

Outside of the cubicle, Chaz's air conditioner came to life, vibrated, and settled to a hum. Kit's leg pulsed and throbbed. His dosage had to be right, but also the pain dialed up and down with his mood. Or maybe it was that he cared about the pain to varying degrees depending on his mood. He didn't know, and soon it wouldn't matter.

He picked up the thin file for *Viridian* and leafed through the pictures of the artwork and the names again. Martin didn't like the artist Hochberg, but Kit was taken with the portrait of what seemed to be an ordinary woman. Brown shoulder-length hair, florid cheeks. Not very young, not very old. Average in every regard, like someone he might have stood behind at the grocery store, who loaded things into a bag. What wasn't ordinary was her expression, which was a mix of someone having a pleasant, intensely private daydream while at the same time conscious of sitting for a painting.

Kit sifted through the others, a scrambled harlequin by Picasso, painted two years before he died, a blurb said. It was ugly. He had only needed to see what it looked like and try to get it back. Then the two Monet bridge paintings, which were Martin's favorites. After the hour he had spent with *Waterloo Bridge, Pink Effect,* Kit understood a little better why Martin felt that way. He remembered what he had told him about the portrait. The subject was a friend of the artist, and she had a terminal illness—a mother of two. *You're going to have to learn the names, and artists, and a lot more . . .*

So far, Kit had found his weeklong immersion in the New York art world surprisingly diverting. And to add to his luck, Chaz was a good connection and trusting. Some people are suspicious, and some believe what's in front of them. Chaz was the latter. But, of course, Kit wasn't after Chaz. If he had been, Chaz might have more to worry about.

He balanced *Woman with Eyes Closed* on his fingertips. He thought her face peaceful—that the painter's brush touched her skin as lightly as a butterfly wing. And yet she was dying. She, the person in this painting, felt more mortal than he had ever felt, even with the accident. He had *woken up,* essentially safe from danger, with the rest of his life ahead of him. And yes, he had felt sorry for himself, and sometimes he had cried, but never admitted that to a living soul.

That's one of the tamer ones. Hochberg had a penchant for realistic, one might say grotesque detail. Nudes, every pore and hair. He was the grandson of the great psychoanalyst by the same name. Not to my taste, but neither is psychoanalysis . . .

As if in disagreement with Martin, Kit ran a finger over the paint strokes that had created her brown hair.

. . . he was one of the last great portraitists, so they say. Before all of this conceptual nonsense took over. There are merits, though I find him rather merciless . . .

Kit wondered what her name really had been. And at the same time, he knew her name. He nodded, feeling the narcotic take its little golden hammers to his pain. Before the accident, these sorts of things hadn't been as real—the places his mind would go. Yes, she was a Nathalie, or a Felicia, possibly a Felicity. Tallish, not too thin. The type of person who wore those thin Indian caftans and maybe drawstring pants. Pastels, colors. She made jewelry—no, she was a potter. She had a house in Islington, with a studio that caught the afternoon light. Originally, she'd wanted three children, but she couldn't give up her workspace for the extra room. So she had only two. Her kiln was in an outbuilding. Her kitchen was ramshackle, looking out over a garden. She grew her own herbs and lettuce and had her parents for dinner often. She made her own pasta, and she had painted the house herself, though she could afford painters. She liked to engage with things, materials, people—she resisted an intellectual life, a life of concepts. She liked dirt under her nails, and paint. She had a row of orange and pink Gerber daisies in summer, stuck incongruously among the meadow rue and baptisia. When she bought the house, she rented a jackhammer and took the concrete out in the back of the garden herself. She liked tools—her kids had given her a circular saw for Christmas. Sometimes she got tired of all the handicrafts, the effort. Her back hurt, her hands hurt. But it was the principle of the thing. She was no longer married. She was on her own. Kit pictured himself living with her, not necessarily her lover, but maybe, very definitely her lover. He tried it a few ways. He couldn't see her with someone like him. He was too straightlaced, boring even. But maybe she was the type who would take pity and let him into her world. Yes . . . she might be. The kids were grown and gone, and she was glad she had hung on to the studio—she often said. She liked to glaze the pots in the afternoon when the light was perfect. She'd notice every step of its change as it marched across the crook of her ceiling: April, September, and winter's metal chill. He watched her in the morning kitchen, making coffee and marketing lists, calling friends for a weekend party, a giant

Wisteria vine crazing the kitchen window, in bloom now. In the amount of time it took him to fall asleep, she had hung up the phone and left the list on the counter.

The next thing he knew, it was morning.

CHAPTER 8
SAW YOUR SHOW, LOVED THE DOG

Sagaponack
August 6th, 2012
34 days after the heist

A few days later, Kit was riding along next to a farm field in the Eldorado convertible that Chaz called "Jane." Every minute or two, the saggy shocks of the car bottomed out. The car was thirty years old, got ten miles to the gallon, and was prone to fires. It was Chaz's pride and joy. He could probably afford much better, so Kit wondered aloud why this white whale of a car.

"Makes for good stories . . ." Chaz yelled over the engine's loose roar.

"Difficult, though, on roads like this?" Kit replied. But not all that much better on the highway, he thought. Last night, while driving "out from the city" with the top down, Kit could have sworn the body of the car was going to float right off the wheels.

". . . and women like impractical cars the way men like high heels," Chaz continued. "Who can explain it?"

Who could indeed. He could see the dirt road go by through a hole in the floor. Shocks creaking, the big white boat bounced, sending Kit's government-issued briefcase airborne. Filled with art magazines to give it heft, it had a hidden camera in the handle and a microphone in the lock. Kit cut a glance at it, doubting that this was the kind of place where anyone brought a briefcase.

"So what is your budget for this guy?" asked Chaz.

"Can't tell you that, mate." A Briticism like that usually worked. In America, he had found that his Englishness would protect him to a degree. Here, with his accent, they believed one was smart and had interesting things to say. Then the women would turn to him as if waking up from a long sleep, which presented its own problems.

His phone vibrated with a text. It was Martin. *A party is the perfect foil. Plant it where it has a clear view of the main room.*

Early this morning, Kit had paced around in Chaz's backyard, giving Martin a progress report. He intimated as best he could that he needed to know more—*much* more. Martin consulted with the others and got back to say the Russian with the beach house was probably the guy they wanted. That the Russian's name, unless they had it wrong, was Grigory Kusnetsov, aka Glasgow, a known criminal. And that it was in Glasgow's house, in a basement bunker of some kind, that the stolen paintings were supposed to have been seen. A former housekeeper of his, since fired, was the source of the tip.

The car listed along, Chaz humming with the radio. Kit looked at his phone again—Kusnetsov, aka Glasgow. He had heard that name before. Why did he call himself the name of a Scottish city? If he remembered correctly—and his memory was not as reliable as it once was—Kusnetsov had been a presence in London. On-the-ground intelligence gathering in Russia had been reduced since the Cold War, and some of that battle was moving online. But Martin had to have something more on him than a tip from his housekeeper.

"You don't need a briefcase at a party, do you?" said Chaz.

"Got my toothbrush, you know," joked Kit.

"Planning on spending the night?"

Kit laughed it off. He'd lag in the car with his phone and a smoke, and by the time he got into the house, Chaz would be completely distracted.

"I get the feeling you aren't telling me everything," said Chaz.

"Your feeling is correct," said Kit, laughing again.

He had decided that for the most part, he wasn't going to bring Chaz in. Chaz liked to play the expert on everything and everybody—the guy who had his "ear to the ground" as he had put it. Chaz was a braggart in a sort of lovable way, and a gossip, but he was insubstantial. He had met Glasgow once months ago. He knew nothing about him beyond the Van Gogh Glasgow was purported to have bought in Paris.

As they pummeled down the dusty path between farm fields, the ocean glittered beyond. Sagaponack—the name meant *land of big clams* in Indian, Chaz said. It reminded Kit of Italy, the late day sun throwing a color somewhere between gold and rose across the countryside, illuminating every clump of dirt and hopping bird. With the mad money Martin had said was out here, they could have at least paved the roads, although it wouldn't have been as pretty.

"This is going to be a real rat fuck," said Chaz, passing a red Hummer on its way out. Chaz pulled up and parked parallel along a large field. The country road was packed tight with jeeps, luxury SUVs, and a few pickup trucks.

Kit wondered what a rat fuck was and decided not to ask. He'd have to judge for himself. He felt for the foil pack of pills in his front pocket, because the pain minions were beginning to march.

* * *

The house was a cottage-style, wider than it was tall, with wings reaching into the delicate dunes, and two outsized chimneys jutting into the sky. Inside, it was darker than he imagined a seaside house would be. Another stroke of luck. The great room had wood paneling, a floor-to-ceiling bookcase on two sides, and four waiters who stood at the doors like sentinels with trays of champagne. It was very loud. He plucked one flute off and downed it while noticing that there were no paintings on the walls. Even the kitchen had wood paneling, which was extremely odd. He had never seen anything like it. A few attractive girls were draped upon the sofas. Kit thought they might be too young for a party like this. He went up and said hello to one of them while slipping the briefcase into a dark corner of the bookshelf as if he owned the place. Happily, the girl was not very alert. He bid her goodbye.

Through his damaged ears, the party sounded like a waterfall. The club where he met the dancer the other night had had the same distinct effect. He went around with Chaz, who again seemed to know everyone. It was so loud that names were difficult to discern. People seemed to be inside the waterfall, their voices joined together in a rush until they were introduced, whereupon they popped out at him like frogs. Chaz introduced Liz, an interior decorator, and Wyatt, who did something in finance. Second champagne gone, he wondered where the bar was. Then a wild-looking girl with a lot of red hair climbed into his view.

"Gia!" yelled Chaz, while Kit yelled hello, his hand locked in hers.

Strong grip for a girl. Mingled smells of perfume, wood varnish, salt, and watery booze assaulted his nostrils pleasantly. He could only think to ask when the house was built, yelling this question into Chaz's ear.

"Uh, probably finished a few years ago," warbled Chaz. "He pissed a lot of people off."

"Why?"

"Because it isn't to code," yelled Chaz. "Been in all the papers. Big fight."

Kit could barely hear his own words as they came out. "What do the neighbors think?"

"They've all done shit too, so they really can't point a finger."

"Crikey."

Four double doors opened to a copious deck, an open bar, and a so-called infinity pool, its moniker robbed of all meaning by the setting. Behind it stretched the wide glittering sea, and above it a soaring blue sky that did in fact go on forever. It was so lovely that Kit sucked in a breath. Land and sea seemed bigger here than in England, and more inviting because the line between them wasn't demarcated by cliffs or stone beaches.

Chaz barely glanced at the water. "There are two levels out here—well, three. People at this level come in by plane, they never go into the village, they hire lawyers from the city to back up a local team so they can grease the wheels to get whatever they want done—the house, the party permit, the benefit. This guy really has a low profile. Hardly ever here . . . no one knows much about him. Some dicey stuff . . . there are rumors. Some dealers I know wouldn't do business with him. I would not. He wouldn't have any interest in my artists, so the problem isn't mine. I am friendly with him, though."

"What artists does he like?"

"I think his taste tends to Old Masters, European type of stuff."

"And what about the others?"

Chaz looked at him curiously. "Well, he can't force them to sell to him. Dealers are protective of their artists, as you very well know."

"The other levels," corrected Kit, grateful there was something handy in his brain to refer to.

"Oh—people like me, who just come out for the season. The locals can be clannish. There are some writers and software people, retirees, some year-rounders, artists like Jack Triplett—he's about four houses down."

"Could that be the place I passed on my walk last night?"

"You couldn't miss it," said Chaz, "if they were home."

Kit remembered the luminescent box in the dunes, the third floor glowing like the bridge on a cruise ship. Just below it sat a woman in silhouette on the deck, her knees pulled up to her chest.

"Don't laugh. It was designed by Max Moretti," said Chaz.

"Oh, I'm not laughing," said Kit.

The red-haired girl was at the bar outside. She was wearing a green linen dress—quite attractive in a Milly Theale sort of way. Her accent pegged her as Northern Italian, as did her coloring. He was surprised to see his usual tipple in the long row of bottles.

"Glenmorangie with a splash of water," he said to the bartender, while Chaz's glance darted back and forth between Kit and Gia.

"Have you heard?" Gia asked Chaz. "Two of the Dutch thieves have been caught!"

Chaz's eyes popped open. "Wow! How long ago was that?"

Gia looked at her phone. "It says this morning . . . not the third one, though."

"Where was the arrest?" asked Kit, keeping his tone casual.

"In Amsterdam."

"Can't believe they have my drink," Kit said, toasting his new acquaintances. The news would have broken internationally at the same time, so Martin would have to be finding out now.

"I would have taken you for a whiskey neat type," said Chaz.

"Ahh, this is Scotch. You can't drink it neat without disorienting your taste buds. It would be a waste," Kit said, hoping this would establish him as an aficionado of at least one thing.

"I'll try it next time," said Chaz, with the pleased look of an international someone.

"I wonder if they can get them back," mused Gia, looking at her phone. "It says: *speculation, misinformation, and even some mudslinging abound.* Then a list of the four paintings—Monet, Picasso, Hochberg. Then it says: *this list is a eulogy, not an obituary . . .*"

"We'll have to see," said Chaz. "I'm not optimistic. The pipe wrench is pretty crude. And how connected could they be?"

"It was a long time to find them," said Gia. "They had to be good at covering their tracks in some manner."

"Or maybe the Dutch police aren't very good," said Chaz.

"They're pretty good," said Kit.

Chaz sipped largely at his drink. "There was a French thief, Breitwieser was the name. Did it for love—"

"Hah!" said Gia incredulously.

"No," said Chaz, "he really did. Stole hundreds of works, *hundreds*, traveling all over Europe with his girlfriend. Small paintings, silver pieces, ivory carvings, all 16th and 17th century. He stashed them in the attic of his house in France. His mother's house. Pieter Brueghel the Younger, Corneille de Lyon, Willem Van Aelst . . ."

Gia was rapt. "Where can I find out more?"

"There's a documentary," said Chaz. "Breitwieser was the name."

"What happened to them?" asked Kit.

"Well, this is the sad part—" Chaz said, surprising Kit by how he warmed to the subject.

Gia groaned, "Oh no, I *did* hear about this . . ."

"—they were at his mother's house in France. He kept the lighting low and just looked at them. Like a mini-museum in the attic. When she heard he had been arrested in Lucerne, she destroyed many of them. Shredded with scissors, dumped in the Rhône-Rhine Canal, into her garbage disposal, and burned. First, she said she did it because she was angry at him, and then she changed that to, 'I did it to destroy the evidence against him.' Of course, that didn't look as bad."

"*Molto pazzo*," said Gia.

"Yes, very," Kit chimed in.

"I am sure that no one would ever do *that* over the garbage called art today," said Gia.

"I *know* how you feel," said Chaz succinctly, "which is why I told you that story."

"Sorry," Gia said sheepishly.

Sensing some tension there, Kit addressed Gia. "So how do you know the elusive Mr. Glasgow?"

Gia shook a red tendril from her pale forehead. "I think it's Glasgow—Glasgow only."

"Here I am in the man's house, and I haven't yet been introduced." His phone buzzed in his pocket. Martin.

"He's right over there," she said, pointing to a conversational cluster by the pool. "These houses just are empty most of the year, it's a shame."

"Why is it?" asked Kit, having never heard such disdain from a guest to their host.

"Many people have no place to live in this country. The poverty . . . some of these big houses are empty. They're investments, or places to stash stuff, or cash—*chi lo sa*."

"Who knows," Kit translated. "Which one is he? Baldie?"

"Yeah. What a peeg. You're shocked I said that. I don't know him. But I'll introduce you as if I do. He's with some people I know, so it won't be awkward."

"Right-o. We'll be a team," he said, getting his drink refreshed, curling his shoulder into the space above hers in that way that women usually liked. This one didn't notice; she was too feisty. His accent had no effect either. Strange. Anyway, he was married. He was *married*. What was he thinking?

"Nice shoes!" she exclaimed as they walked over.

Glasgow was muscular and on the short side, with chunky cheeks and a bald head flushed pink. Wide nostrils, violent terrain of acne scars on upper arms and face. Otherwise, his skin was the tallowed hue that only the Urals could produce. Adidas sandals, Bermuda shorts, and an impossibly white Tommy Hilfiger T-shirt, sleeves rolled up Brando-style. Ever hopeful, all wrong. At the moment, he was gazing up into the face of a pretty blonde. She was about five-nine, her hair in a tight braid and surprisingly brown, black-fringed eyes.

"What's your name again?" asked the Milly Theale girl under her breath as they approached the group.

"Christopher, Chris Pinsmail, and yours?" he asked, the ringing in his ears worsening. Glasgow was now five feet away from him.

"Gia," she said, adding, "Your name is kind of a BBC name, isn't it? I watched a lot of the BBC when I was learning English."

"You speak very well," said Kit with automatic politeness, his phone buzzing again.

He felt time expanding, each second big as the sea. Up close like this, Glasgow had an exaggerated quality of futility; he was a sad sack. He seemed harmless, and people can seem harmless; sometimes the more harmless they seem, the worse they are. The danger being that it is all the same to them. At the moment, he was playing the role of host, showing them the bar, motioning to a stack of beach towels in the corner of the deck. "Take a swim, it's beautiful! We're here all day!" he exclaimed. No one moved or said a word. It was like a freak show. The people here were not his friends. What were they all doing here, then? Kit's leg started to pulse. The pain always had a precursor, a series of beats before the full-on ache began.

He stalled, whispering to Gia, "So sorry, still haven't got your name."

"*Gia*," she said impatiently.

He met Jack Triplett, whose show at the Whitney he had gone to see. In it, there was an enormous red and gold dog, as tall as a two-story house. He also remembered some sculpted flowers in vases made of eternal-looking materials that he liked.

"Saw your show, loved the dog," Kit said, which was true, though the rest of it pretty much went right by him.

He sipped at the Scotch, which helped turn the ringing in his ear down a notch again. Perrin-beautiful-girl was with Triplett. Kit shook her hand, an absurd way to greet one so lovely. He met an older gentleman in an expensive but old light-blue linen suit, who Perrin introduced as her father, George Clayton. Kit remembered the name—he had a few pieces in one of the museums that Kit had liked—and complimented Clayton on his work. Glasgow was besotted with Perrin, his puppyish stare fixed on her face. She had a wedding ring on, though Triplett did not. Kit noticed Triplett's possessive grip on her elbow.

"Amazing place," he said to Glasgow. It was amazing, for its lack of taste and its efforts to be something it could never be. It was a spanking new movie set inspired by the Savoy that had somehow ended up in the dunes of New York. He half-expected Laurence

Olivier and Vivien Leigh to come trotting down the stairs. Only, they'd be made of cardboard, like movie standees.

"Here we are with all of these artists, but where's the art on *your* walls?" Kit asked Glasgow with as much jocularity as he could manage.

"Well, my designer did this crazy wood paneling," said Glasgow. "So—no place to put it!"

Kit noticed Glasgow's fingers clenched white around his highball glass. He didn't enjoy big parties, so why was he having one?

"What you have here is a virtual collection," said George, tugging at his wine.

Glasgow looked confused.

"Well," said George, "there's word around town that you are a collector, yet there's no art displayed. Your guests have come to see you, and also, if we are being honest, they've come to see it. Having none on the walls is kind of a statement. I think it's terrific."

"What's your name again?" asked Glasgow.

"George Clayton."

"An honor to meet you, Mr. Clayton," said Glasgow, bowing like a recent charm school grad.

"Thank you," said George. "Just George is fine. In fact—this building is where my studio used to be. It was an old train station they moved here to this very spot."

Perrin smiled tolerantly. Clearly, she knew this story.

"I like very much what you say, George," said Gia, as if to fill up the gap.

George continued, "Do you know when I had a big opening I was supposed to attend, I'd go in disguise and eavesdrop. It was all valid to me. Even if they hated it, I ate it up, every word. Jack would understand that—art is as much an exchange of ideas as an exchange of objects."

Gia tipped her head back and laughed with delight.

The Scotch was kicking in like tumblers in a lock, and Kit

jumped in chummily. "Mr. Glasgow, do you have *any* idea what he's talking about? Surely, I don't."

"Ha-ha, ha ha ha . . ." Glasgow blubbered, unwilling and perhaps unable to commit to any level of understanding.

George continued, "Artists are always looking for an unquantifiable essence—a scene, a form, a person. But somehow people and their daily concerns can get in the way of that, don't you find? Great doctors have no empathy; some very good artists make shitty parents." George cut a glance at Perrin.

Everyone laughed except for Glasgow.

Jack interjected, "I'm going to be a *great* dad."

"Sure, you will," said Chaz.

Perrin's smile tightened, while George's stare briefly lit upon Jack. No love lost between these two, thought Kit.

"What I need is a wife to look after these things," said Glasgow, his eyes cutting to Perrin.

"She's married, sport—so where do you keep it all?" Kit continued lightly.

Glasgow narrowed his eyes as if the question was audacious. "A little here, a little there, mostly in Europe. I don't really have much . . ."

Liar. Through the crisping effect of the second Scotch, a portrait of Glasgow fell together. He might be the black sheep in the *Bratva* nest. He was the one who would never really succeed. Maybe he was sloppy in his business dealings—spoiled. Or he was a rat and had been sent packing. His personal fastidiousness was a cover for his screw-ups. He was well-funded. He was looking for a mate, that's why he had thrown this party. But he lacked intuition. Otherwise, he wouldn't have bothered with this crowd. None of these women would go for him.

"What I can't believe is these damn birds," said Glasgow, looking around as if he had just gotten there the night before.

Which he might have, thought Kit. He didn't really look at home.

Gia stepped up. "You mean the piping plover?"

"Yes, those things. I spend nineteen million on a house, and half the dune is fenced, and half the beach is fenced by the EPA. I can't even use my own land."

"Uhh—s'not yours, no matter what you paid for the house," said Gia.

"Yes, it's mine."

"All of the beaches are owned by the government. They cannot be privately owned."

Glasgow threw back his head and laughed. "I'll tell you what, Miss Red Hairs. I'd like to get my BB gun for those birds one morning."

Kit drained his drink—and a blowhard. Not wise.

"But don't tell anyone I said that," added Glasgow. "You aren't with the press, are you?"

"No," said Gia, "but I walk by the nesting sites almost every morning. And now you've threatened some poor struggling birds. I'd tell anyone that."

Kit hoped that this Gia would know when to stop.

"I'll check those sites," she added, standing her ground.

"Hey, what about me? I'm trying to find a wife. I had a modeling agency come to do a shoot last week, and the best light was right where the nests were. I would have taken the fence out, but the girls were worried about it, and the photographer was some kind of pansy."

"At least they had some sense," said George, visibly backpedaling.

"But—don't you get it? *I'm* trying to mate. *They're* trying to mate, and so am I."

George laughed and so did Chaz.

Kit repressed a smile. Perrin's brown eyes alighted for a fraction upon his, which caused him to wonder whether either one of them would be limited by their domestic situations.

Kit quickly threw in and said to Glasgow, "Are you here all summer?"

Glasgow ignored him. "Hey, you know some of the people around here feel the same. I saw on one guy's car, *piping plover tastes like chicken!* It was a local guy! *Tastes like chicken* . . . hah hah ha ha ha . . . ha ha . . ."

"Those people are idiots," said Gia, glaring.

There were a few embarrassed titters, Jack among them. George was looking for an out. But not Perrin, whose glance had steadied upon Kit as if to say, *can you believe this?*

For a moment, all the other guests melded into the crowd in this preposterous movie set of a house. He wondered if he could trust himself—his hearing coming and going. He tried to catch her again, and did. Shy and quick, but not quick enough. An instant of black-fringed eye and blonde tress. The second time their eyes met, Pinsmail emerged. Oh yes. Pinsmail, the character he'd been seeking, unfurled his talons like a hawk. He was Pinsmail and could do no wrong.

Mr. Clayton handed Glasgow a napkin with what looked to be a number penned on it and snuck away. Jack was smiling tightly, figuring a way out for himself. Chaz had gone back to the bar with Gia. Beyond the tan slope of Perrin's shoulder, Kit caught glimpses of the sea. Such splendor in the vicinity of this troll was sickening.

Glasgow put a hand on Perrin's arm. "Don't want to annoy my beautiful new neighbor. I'm going to ask you to do a special mission. Nobody gets full access to my house, but I trust anyone who cares about those stupid birds." He pulled her aside to whisper something in her ear. With a pursed face of distaste, she listened.

* * *

The DJ had started. Upstairs. The party had kicked off, and there was the confidence, no, the assurance, of—what? Chris Pinsmail was a bit of a lush. Pinsmail had taken a wrong turn . . . he took a wrong turn, yes, that was why. The loo, of course. Kit was wasted, but Pinsmail had it all in hand. One of the waiters had said it was down here. What? The *bathroom*, what a cumbersome *word. Thump thump thump* up on the deck—that's what they called it. Deck. Another dreadful word. A *deck* was on a *ship.* Pinsmail to the rescue of the language. *Thumpa thumpa thumpa*, the whole thing gathering speed under the pitch of a disco diva so shrill she sounded like a rabbit in dying throes. Everyone as nearly deaf as he, eardrums pounded into leather. Excellent. At the point when they couldn't trust themselves, he could really move. Pinsmail would do . . . whatever needed to be done. Down here, it was nice and cool. He had to keep his mind straight.

He felt along the corner of the corridor, the sheetrock, behind the paintings—there must be a chink somewhere, a secret door, a set of controls. How could the basement just end? His hands groped along a cool refusing wall. The footprint of the house had to be bigger than this by quite a lot. There were a few framed Disney posters, with only sheetrock behind them. Where was the rest of it? Nothing—only two corridors and a wine cellar. It was hard to tell how quiet a person would be coming down these halls. Heels? Yes. Waiter shoes? NO. Would he hear a door slam? Probably, coming through as a sort of thud, like a body hitting the floor. As if in retaliation for this thought, the ringing in his ears dialed up. Cryptic, now quite deaf Pinsmail.

He thought of that girl.

Booze managed to shake loose things at the bottom, things that he had avoided thinking about. The dancer from Queens, the Milly Theale girl, and now shy Perrin swept away the clumsy fact that he was married. *He was married.* Yes, of course, he was! At an extreme angle past the tip of this island, then almost a straight shot over four thousand miles of ocean to London—there his wife sat or was busy. He had no interest in which it was.

A friend had suggested that, with no clear way to revive his marriage, Kit could blame himself. *Look, you're a wreck, so take the opportunity,* he posed. The friend had assumed their childlessness was Susannah's fault, while the tests had shown she was in fact alight with fertility. Another piece of London scuttlebutt that was completely untrue. Look, the friend said, the accident—bombing, whatever, helps you enormously. *Get out now . . . I am not the man I was,* or *I am not the man you thought I was . . . were . . . whatever.* Take your pick. Make it your fault. If you don't take this opportunity, you'll regret it for the rest of your life. It couldn't be any more perfect. Kit leaned against the wall, feeling the coolness on his hot face. *Accch* . . . Susannah. He did want children; he just didn't want them now or soon. Would he ever? He felt an enormous pull from her, an emptiness he could never fill.

And here was Perrin. Poured gold. Unusual brown-eyed blonde. Perfectly, lightly tanned. Two rose spots on her cheeks. A yellow lock escaping again. A short dress, a long golden leg, ears seashells creamy and pink and gold. Lioness eyes, deep-set, looking out at him. A smile that flashed fire, slightly snaggle-toothed as he remembered from upstairs. A utilitarian quality about her body, not delicate or small-boned. A peasant quality, nothing like a fashion model. Lots of curves and muscle. Not starved at all. A grand weight of a girl. A comfortable, pretty girl. He could picture her lying on top of him—their feet would meet, and the crown of her head would come up to his nose. A long-limbed thoroughbred of a girl, English in her way. Like someone he had known at school. But over here—splashy, *new,* her dress all emerald and blue scrolls. Perrin of the sea, her tan legs poured into gold strappy sandals. The skin above the knee darker, downy, dappled with short golden hairs.

She looked at him indignantly. "What are you doing down here?"

"Shtaff told me this was where the loo was."

She did not believe him, that much he could tell.

"I'm here getting champagne," she said. "I don't know what you are doing."

He followed her into the wine cellar, trying to think of some sort of plan. Scab-colored brick arched over hundreds of bottles in wooden cradles. What to say? She seemed as if she knew where she was going. He wondered if the wider picture would be relevant to her.

"Do you know this place?"

"I've never been down here," she said, all business-like.

"Don't you hate this guy?"

"I'm going to report him to the EPA if Gia doesn't," she said as she extracted two bottles of Dom Perignon from a cooler.

"There's worse than that," he said, eyeballing the bottles in her hands. She was willing to please Glasgow.

"I'm curious to see if he lets anything else slip," she retorted.

Oof—mind reader. A good sign, though not in every way to his advantage. "Funny, you never protested up there. I never would have been able to tell that you disapproved of him. That much."

"I'm his neighbor. Don't get on the bad side of neighbors . . ."

"Yes but—"

"We get people like that out here in the summer all the time. The population quadruples, and people come from all over the world. They think they can do whatever they like. He made a stupid statement about an endangered bird, and now we're going to watch him."

"Are you and . . . Jheee—"

"Gia?"

"Yes. Are you close?"

"Not really. I might be able to pick up more because . . . well . . ."

"He likes you. Smart thinking," Kit said, shaking his head and smiling. She was adorable. But he had to keep his head.

"You are up to something sneaky," she said thoughtfully, gazing into his face, "and you are drunk."

"You might be interested to know what I know," he said, trying to gauge her trustworthiness. Best not to pile it all on at once.

"I'm not sure if I want to know," she said.

He watched her hesitate. Like many rich women, she was comfortable with her innocence and reluctant to let it go. Pinsmail, confident in his abilities, didn't care much whether it was this bird or another (although this one would be fun), birds in general, or criminals and birds. Pinsmail saw her as good raw material that might be molded. Whatever was not there, he felt he could create. "You have no idea—"

Above them a door slammed. *Thunk.*

"—you are going to have to kiss me," he said while removing the two bottles from her hands and encircling her waist. Another cue from the movies, only now he was Bogart—to hell with Laurence Olivier.

To his surprise, she kissed him back, her eyes serious and lovely.

Some minutes later—he couldn't tell how long—one of Glasgow's waiters squeezed by. "Never mind me," the waiter said, inching by, his footsteps a shuffle on the sandy floor. It was hard to tell whether he was coming or going. They were in a fabricated space all their own, Perrin fighting the urge to lose herself completely.

"Wait," he said, kissing her again, while Pinsmail lurked in the shadows, egging him on. She responded, arching her back. Her lips were impossibly soft. He felt all along the back of the mermaid dress with one hand, the other trying to hold onto the two bottles of champagne. He leaned her to the side, attempting to shelve at least one of the bottles on the wine rack. It went crashing down to the floor.

"Oh no!" she cried, hopping back, brushing champagne and broken glass off her front.

Pinsmail deserted him utterly. "Staff will deal with it; we don't have time to waste."

Perrin felt champagne leaking between her toes. This was the first time in a long time that she had kissed another man. She took off one sandal to shake it out while trying to balance on the other one—knowing she looked good that way—the thought bouncing through her head absurdly. What had just happened? She had often fantasized about such a moment, though it wasn't like this at all. This was all skewed, but then of course this was *real*, unlike her nocturnal imaginings in the extra room under the house pilings, where she went to sleep alone sometimes, the flimsy door locked tight, her feelings buoyed by what she knew best, the sound of the sea coming through the window, the sounds she herself made muffled by the water's rush. It was the one room in that house she liked, a hiding place that was like a cell, albeit with great acoustics. Her fantasy was always of a person who wanted to be hidden away too, with her, in the deep dark, like two owls in a tree hollow. (When, in the light of day, she thought about her tree hollow fantasy, she told herself that she was ridiculous and out of step. Owls and tree hollows were for weak, frightened people who had plaster gnomes in their gardens and could not face reality. And that she could not be.)

Suddenly, she remembered what she was supposed to be doing. "What do you mean, I have no idea?" She looked at Christopher more carefully, again noticing that he was drunk, but holding it moderately well.

"He's part of an international crime ring. A 'higher-up' guy. Bad, bad stuff . . . drugs . . ." Realizing that language was deserting him, he stopped.

"No kidding?" she asked hesitantly.

"Do you really want to know?"

"I do." She didn't really. She was afraid.

"Can't you just take my word for it?" said Kit. He didn't want to go into details, and anyway, he had so few of them. Inwardly, he cursed Martin, who had given up trying to reach him.

"Why do I need to? I just met you an hour ago. Why *would* I?"

Christopher stood there, watching her, gathering her hand into his, which was somehow as intimate as his kiss. The image she had before of Glasgow flashed in her mind—macho, tacky, a grabber. Before, he had been a harmless cartoon. Now brewing like a storm upstairs, waiting for his champagne. Her blood rose with intense dislike. She'd have to deliver the champagne. She'd have to smile. Her head was spinning as she tried to step into the next few minutes.

Breathe, said Christopher Pinsmail. *Just breathe.* He squeezed her hand.

Behind him, orderly rows of wine gleamed. Along with the fear, a mad promise hung in the air. She looked around at the low vaulted ceiling, the weird, fakey color of the brick, heard the *thunka thunk thunk* of the music. This was a world that was foreign. Like the city, it was compressed—jarring, ugly, rhythmic—fun. This was where you got lost. Like walking a plank, the murky brown East River rolling at your feet. This wasn't home. There were no rules, no plan to follow, like flying too fast down to FDR at night, kissing someone you didn't know. Like city lights spinning above your head in Sheep Meadow. No one could be trusted, unless they *could* be, in which case the trust ran deep because no one was tethered, like trapeze artists they weren't, and had to trust the grip of the other one.

Her hands were wet from the champagne. What was this life if it wasn't taking a dare and not getting hung up. She reached up under his sweater and wiped them on his shirt, gripping his sides on the way down, just to see if he was real. He was. Oh Lord. Patched elbows, rumpled khakis, clean-smelling. Geeky shoes like an English schoolmaster. Weird package T-shirt. No one shopped for him, she thought, eyeballing the neckline. Unless he bought that himself and had just made a bad call.

"C'mon . . . we've got to go," said Christopher. He reached around her into the cooler, got another bottle, and arranged the two bottles against the small of her back. She could feel them there, weighty and cold.

She looked into his face, trying to read him. "What the hell am I supposed to do?"

"Just be nice to him. That's all. It's easy—could not be easier, in fact."

Perrin tried to toughen up, while Christopher's voice, soft and sonorous, was somehow the only thing. If only she could continue to listen to it and forget about all this other stuff.

"We need time that we don't have," he said. "We have to get upstairs—one at a time."

"You're married," she said, noticing his ring.

"Separated—but so are you—married."

"I think you better explain."

His smile twisted a little. "I'll meet you on the beach in front of your house tomorrow night."

"You don't know where I live," she retorted, hovering somewhere between wanting to seem sensible and actually being sensible.

"I do. I'll be there at eight. Call me Chris."

"*How* do you know?"

"I just do," said Kit.

Perrin was thinking of the kiss again, redolent of whiskey and ice.

"Meet me," he said, turning to go, as if it were a foregone conclusion that she would be there.

CHAPTER 9
ASK ME ANYTHING

Sagaponack
August 20th, 2012
48 days after the heist

The sky was draped, distantly, with scarlet and blue, and a ribbon of gold at the horizon. Christopher was supposed to be out here, somewhere. Like the other times they'd met over the last few weeks, he'd said eight. He seemed to like that hour, and a beautiful hour it was, as well as a place of hiding. It was the moment, dusky and obscure, that pitched into the cover of night. Of course he liked it. She was surprised at how eagerly she was waiting for him, like some besotted schoolgirl, her feelings going completely out of control.

In sharp contrast were her many reasons for resisting him. First of all, Jack. Was she really going to blow everything up now? Was Chris going to be just a fling? Or was he going to be real, and did she even want him to be real? She knew little about him except that he was into art, and he was playing some kind of a game. In accordance with the game, not entirely hating his objective, she had let him into her world. Sticking her toe, then her foot in, feeling the water's salty tickle, she braced herself for the smooth words he would say. The ocean was chaotic tonight, which had the opposite effect of slowing her thoughts down.

As a kid she was known for being physically brave. She liked to hurl herself at the elements, stacking up her own strength against them, playing all day on the beach with her friends and into the night if there was a bonfire.

One day, green-gray waves came boiling down the coast; they were told that a hurricane was on the way. Pre-hurricane water was often warm, warmer than it looked, and for Perrin and her schoolmate Jed Aldrich, it was irresistible. The local surfers were all in the water down the beach, so why not them? They jumped in. The sea and sky were almost the same color, the rain coming down in spattering sheets. They rode the swells, not noticing how fast the water was taking them down the coast. She stayed close to Jed, grabbing enough air when she could and diving deep when the waves were at odds and smashing up white water. There were patches of calm laced with foam where they floated on their backs in slow circles, Perrin holding her mouth open for the freshwater drops, counting them as she caught them. It was like a roller coaster ride, but better because there were no constraints and no limits to anything. She was in the grip of a wild, loving embrace, believing that the sea would not betray her.

After a little bit, she noticed she had drifted. She was farther out, and the houses along the shore were unfamiliar. Jed was farther away, not smiling and whooping like before. He was pointing toward the shore. She could see that he was having trouble getting in, and she realized that she must be in trouble too. The ocean was stirred up, bouncing in different directions as if warring with itself. Usually, that was only a surface effect, while underlying rhythms remained predictable and constant. But this was an angry, chaotic sea all the way to the sea floor. Deep down beneath her feet, it was pulling her out. She felt as powerless as a piece of driftwood. She tried diving toward shore, but the undertow was too great. She tried to get closer to Jed, but there were hundreds of feet between them. At a certain point, she could no longer hear him yelling, and the rain was driving her down into the water. Her heart began to beat double-time.

She drifted to where she thought she could see a bunch of surfers not far offshore. By this time, she had lost Jed completely and was finding it hard to keep her head up. Waves were coming from all sides, sometimes breaking over her head. Wearing a red bathing suit, she trained all her focus on trying not to panic, not to fight too hard and exhaust herself, but keep herself buoyant like a red ball in the waves. If she kept on yelling and waving, someone was bound to see her.

The black dots of the surfers were borne up and down, up and down by the waves. Perrin kicked toward them with everything she had while still being borne away. She thought of her parents, how awful it would be for them if they lost her. She waved frantically at the surfers and mustered her waning strength to shout above the wind. To her profound relief, one finally waved back, and then one by one they were all waving and yelling to her. She felt a rush of hope; at least someone knew, even if they were so far away. A few minutes later, a lifeguard pulled up alongside and dragged her onto the back of his jet ski. She clung to his back, exhausted and cold. He took her a little farther out where they found Jed, and she helped pull him aboard, her fingers wrinkled and pale.

The police let her mother know they were at the station. Iris picked them up on her way back from the store. Six packed grocery bags in the back seat, with Jed and Perrin squished together in the front. The other mothers thought Iris negligent because Perrin was allowed to run on the beach unsupervised. Iris called them "clucking hens." She never worried, or not that Perrin knew about, because Iris would never admit worrying. Perrin was constantly embarrassed by Iris, on the deck of the shack with her Pall Malls, like a homeless person in all weather. Her mother claimed to have been damaged by all the constrictions that had been foisted on her by America and the Episcopalian Church. She wanted to look out on the wide horizon of the sea because it was there she "really lived." Perrin lived there too, said Iris, with the "commitment of a child," the most beautiful and pure state of being. That day in the car, she said, "What a pair of lunatics" in her amused flat tone, lighting a cigarette. She winked at them and promised Jed that she wouldn't tell his parents if he wouldn't. She lifted her hand to brush the hair from her eyes and looked the children over as if they were part of the haul from the grocery store, just another errand. However, Perrin knew that her mother's bravado was just a pose. Iris was so intimidated by the dangerous business of living that she flew in the face of it, as if that would make her lucky.

Iris hadn't been overly fond of Jack, and though Jack had put up with her, he thought Iris a self-indulgent alcoholic. Iris would have appreciated the challenge of Christopher and his willingness to learn. He had a subtle admiration, that slightly feminine quality that made an artist, or at least an aficionado of art. Last week, while Jack was in the city, Perrin had taken him to meet Agatha, who now had a big shallow cage on the deck. It was a short visit with the crow because, of course, Chris could not be seen outside.

On that sunny day, she swept him through the house—avoiding the master bedroom—and up to her semi-neglected studio. Together in the sun-blasted room, they riffled through her old work, and her current project, a series of large charcoals of Agatha. The impressionistic still life of roses that George had liked was on an easel. Surprising herself, she had begun to work on that lately. Chris had poked around, absorbing every detail—the work, the cans of brushes and easel, the sea view a head turn away. He was entranced with her and her paintings. Silhouetted in the steady light of the glass block, he loved it all with an innocence that rubbed off on her, and lifted the shadowy veil she had been living under.

She found herself putting the brakes on just as fast. Iris would've wanted Perrin to put her fears away and seize this adventure. Especially on the subject of a man, any man, Iris would have played the expert. One of her mother's favorite things to say was *never turn down a lover, no matter what.* A maxim from her early Paris days, she claimed to have learned it there, and had lived by it thereafter, sometimes to her own detriment. Iris would have found Christopher strange but attractive. Very attractive. She would have loved his otherworldly, slightly formal English air. She wouldn't have questioned him—the whole idea of him, with his mellow gaze, his voice, his tattered blue sweater, and his inscrutable nature.

But Perrin did. Mainly, she wondered, how could she possibly help him? What was he thinking? He loved her so passionately, it was as if his life were on the line. How could she inspire such a thing? And what did he want from her? Sometimes she thought she could see wheels turn behind his eyes.

It had something to do with the Rotterdam heist, and Glasgow—she had gleaned that much. Just the other day, he said that Glasgow had one or all of those paintings from Holland, which now seemed *quite incredible*—and that they might be inside the house that she was now standing in front of—Glasgow's house.

The blue rectangle of his phone bounced toward her on the beach. "Chris!" she exclaimed.

"Let's walk a bit," he said, touching her arm lightly. "We can come back here."

"Do you swim?" she asked.

"Yes, but I don't have a bathing suit," he said.

Perrin motioned to the darkening sky. "Hardly matters," she said.

He stopped. "Really, you want to go in now?"

"I'm teasing you. But maybe I do, later."

"What about Jack?" he asked, at the moment when she most ardently wanted to forget about Jack and let this fantasy keep rolling.

"He's in his studio with his assistant," she said, pointing to a row of lit rectangles above the dunes. "You see those windows up high?"

"Yes."

"He'll be there until midnight at least."

"Works a lot?"

"All the time."

"But why—why is your house dark?" he asked.

"Because then the birds won't hit it. I never leave the lights on when I go out."

"Ahhhh . . ." said Kit. "Do birds often hit it?"

"That bird you met, Agatha, she was the last one. Sometimes they're just stunned, and sometimes they break a wing and I have to take them to wildlife rescue. And sometimes they die."

"So there's a reason one's house shouldn't be all windows," Kit ventured.

"There are many," said Perrin firmly.

"How's Agatha?" he asked as they resumed walking.

"She's okay. She likes the new cage. Soon I'll take off the top portion and see if she can fly. But she's doing better than I thought she would."

"I can't get over how gorgeous it is, the stars . . ." he said. "And you are . . ." he spun her to him, his long arms encircling her.

Kissing her neck, he was still saying something . . . what? It didn't really matter what. It was his voice. It was like pearls, if pearls had a sound.

"You can't even see me," she said.

"Don't need to see you. I've got you absolutely committed to memory. Every. Single. Inch," he said, gathering her up to him.

"What about you? What are you doing here?"

He held her away. "I'm here to buy art!"

"No, you aren't," she retorted.

"Why do you say that?" he asked, a knowing smile curling his words.

"Well, let's just say I've never met an art buyer like you. And I've met a bunch."

"Whatever can you mean . . ." he said, leaning to kiss her again.

"I think you know what I mean," she said, loving his touch, wondering if this was all going to be over soon. She tried to think back to before she had kissed him in the wine cellar, before they'd said a word to each other. But she couldn't locate the original Chris in her mind, and that was just a few weeks ago. A Cubist work, Chris was a Cubist work. All in pieces, as if he'd been thrown into the air and had come down in a different form from the original.

She smoothed the back of his neck to soften her words. "You don't know much about art to begin with. And although it's been fun . . . have you bought any? Art?"

"No. Got Chaz on it. My client—well, I can't talk about them."

"You have a feel for it, though . . ." she said, while realizing she could no longer see him. They were talking past each other, Chris persisting with the ruse.

"I'm more an academic type," said Kit. "Old world stuff. Have people talked about me?"

"No—well, no one has seen you much since the party, and you've made sure to keep it that way. Meeting out here, with me, night after night. Kind of odd for an art buyer, don't you think?"

"Possibly. But I'm an odd fellow," he whispered, leaning close. "Haven't you figured that out yet?"

"You don't make a habit of kissing women you just met in basements, do you? You certainly aren't going after those paintings on your own."

"Ahh . . . no."

"Then you must be a spy."

"You were pretty hard to resist," he said.

"So, are you? A spy?"

"Are you good at secrets?" he asked.

"I am an expert at secrets," she said with surprising conviction.

"I'm an agent, you can say."

"Same thing though, right?"

"If you like."

"I'm on the outside looking in, and it's what *you* say you are that matters," she said.

"Funny. I feel like I'm on the outside looking in on this whole scene. And I've been meaning to ask—how do you feel knowing what you now know about him," he said, stopping in front of Glasgow's again and pocketing his phone.

On the left side of the building, a room lit up—in what Perrin guessed was the kitchen. A woman, possibly a housekeeper, brought something to the sink.

"It's horrible. But Chris, this is all beside the point now, isn't it?"

"Yes, they did get the thieves, only two of them. They aren't talking, and the third thief has not been caught. I've got a camera in there now," he said, gesturing to Glasgow's, "with a view of the living room."

"Okay . . . and?"

"We have the intel on the paintings from a Valeria Lopez who was his housekeeper. By any chance, do you know her?"

Perrin said she had never heard of the woman. Someone lit up the pool, a blue shimmering rectangle that rested half on the dune and half on the deck. "The summer people get their help through an agency. Who is she?"

"She was with him in July, here. Romantically. They had a disagreement of some kind, and she was fired. She called the police to say that she knew major works of art when she saw them, and she *did* see them in his basement. Now she's gone back to Colombia, and we can't find her."

"Do you do this kind of thing a lot?"

"Yes, but it's different every time," he said, slipping an arm around her waist, "and I'll tell you a funny little thing. Lopez was especially offended that he thought he had to explain the Monets to her at the time. She had been an art history major at university. It's all in the transcript."

"That's hysterical," she murmured, thinking of Glasgow making such a miscalculation. One that might not have served him well. Behind Chris, Glasgow's house slowly lit up, while that same woman swept something from the edge of the deck.

"Since last night I've been at Chaz's, monitoring through the camera I told you about. It's quite boring. Glasgow sits around, orders up pizza, lords it over his employees—they all talk behind his back."

"But this tip is just something that was said, right? He's never been convicted of anything—otherwise we'd know."

"Well, you see, that's the thing. He's insulated by his position in a crime family in another country. He's about thirty-five, not active. But he was for years running drugs in Amsterdam, London, Berlin and was responsible for many, many deaths. You must know it's the smaller fish that get arrested."

"I've heard that—"

"Look, have you ever done any acting?"

"Some."

The fist inside his chest unclenched a little. "Of course, you're an actress . . . I knew it."

"I'm not an actress, only a few classes," she said firmly. Her teacher at HB said actors were like paper players in a shoebox, and every night when the theatre went silent, they folded. Anybody in the world could then lift the lid off the box and see that no matter how great the performance or how they were moved, the players—the very best—had no selves. They were paper dolls, wilted on the floor of a shoebox.

"Anyway," she said, "acting isn't that great. I'd rather paint."

"Why?"

"Acting removes you from yourself. It can blur your identity so much that you don't have one anymore."

"It's a skill like any other."

"*You* seem to be pretty good at it."

"Me? Pshaw . . . I've never done it."

"Huh—what about when you kissed me in the cellar?"

"I'm a professional. That's different. I do what's necessary to further my goal. That's my *job.* It just so happens that it can be extremely pleasurable."

She scoffed at him. He pulled her briskly around and kissed her, running his hands down her back. She melted and came alive all at once in his tight embrace and felt so hungry for him she thought she'd go mad.

His voice was soft and persuasive. "Why do you stay, *why*?"

"I don't know," she cried into his shoulder. "I think—I just can't face tearing everything up again, and I don't want to hurt him."

"It isn't easy. I'm in the same situation myself, to be honest."

Perrin chuckled. "Oh, we're being honest now, are we?"

"Yes," he said, pulling her in close again. "It's clear that your marriage is unhappy . . . well, to me. I was able to see it because I'm trained to see it."

Perrin hesitated. "What else have you seen?"

Wrapped in each other's arms, they watched the moonrise for a few moments. "Don't worry about it," he finally said.

"Why would I be here on the beach with you if things were good." Oh, how had she gotten herself into this mess? If she were smart, she'd walk home now, turn on the lights, and see to Agatha.

"Made sense at the time?"

"Yes. It did."

"It still does, for now. It's good cover. And you have me behind you." He turned to face her. "We can get him. We *can.* You and me. There's no shame in it. Just call it what it is—power. Power is power. Can't be picky. It's what you do with it, how you use it. If we get anything back, even *one*, we can bust his family's entire operation wide open. Think of it!"

"I have thought of it," she said, feigning a toughness she did not feel. The moon's silver light scattered over the water, twinkling. All she could think of was her power over him. That was more interesting. Feeling him struggle between his various motivations . . . thinking about it, about him. All the different layers, what he wanted to accomplish, how he thought he'd go about it—how he was trying to work on her and how tangled up he was getting.

"I'd be bait, Chris. That's what this is."

"Bait implies passivity. You are anything but passive. It's more subtle than that. I'm sure you can be very persuasive in a myriad of different ways . . . and I know you can think on your feet."

She was silent.

"Look, this isn't about how you *see* yourself. It's about what you can *do.* What you are *good at.* That's how you make a mark. Unless being a rich housewife is enough for you—"

"*What?* That's not me! We were poor when I was growing up!"

"But that's what you are *now*. Why not be more?"

Perrin turned to go, but he grabbed her arm. "Ask me," he said, holding on tightly.

"What?"

"Ask me anything, anything at all."

"How about let's start with your real name."

"I can't tell you that yet, but I promise I will once we are through this. I promise."

"What is wrong with your marriage, and what is her name?"

"Fiona. I don't love her anymore. I didn't really know that when I left England, but I know it now."

"I'm not going to just march over there. That's insane. If I showed up at his door, he'd have just one idea about me."

"Look, you'll have to feel it out—look for opportunity, create it." He wound his fingers through her hair and twisted it tight, sending chills all over her body. "I wouldn't want you to do anything you aren't comfortable with—at least to a reasonable degree given the nature of what I ask."

She pulled away, still wanting to challenge him for the sake of not deeply regretting this whole thing one day. "But Chris, you're the one who said he is a thug."

He checked himself. "But I don't think of him as a predator. Legally, he can't hold you there—you can just leave."

"Hardly matters to him, though—what's *legal!*"

"Psychology, it's all psychology. You can control him with it. I knew an operative who was held all night long by a couple of really bad actors. She had an amazing touch—she survived because she talked to them, she pretended to empathize with them . . ." Too far over the mark. *Damn.*

"It sounds familiar, Chris."

He took a long breath before replying. "But isn't that always true? Don't we present ourselves in a certain way that often doesn't have anything to do with who we really are?"

Perrin felt caught between two extremes: her life which no longer made much sense, and this man who had found out almost everything about her in two weeks.

She sank into his copious embrace, finding herself no longer down the beach from her house, but in a garden at the very beginning of things. She could hardly put her finger on the memory—it was more a bodily sensation, an imprint, coming and going. She felt sorry for him and felt that she could help him by letting him kiss her, by letting him believe that his recruitment effort was working. There wasn't much to lose in only that; in the end, she didn't have to do what he wanted. There was only right now, his breath close into her ear. He must feel something, he must. It wasn't just about the paintings, the theft, and helping him—it was about them together. He was fascinating, dark and light-infused, electric. What more was there in that place he dwelled? It was as if a door had opened, one she never knew existed. It was irresistible to just walk through it. Away, away—just her and him. Deep and rich and so like a dream—impermanent, shifting rooms leading one to the next and the next, foreign and familiar, in glass and leaf-filtered light.

CHAPTER 10
BURN THIS LETTER

Amsterdam, Bijlmerbajes Prison
August 27th, 2012
55 days after the heist

They had no TV or internet here, so Luuk had heard about it on his roommate's radio. He had then gone to the library and found that Leonie was featured on the front page of every single newspaper in the Holland section. When the librarian wasn't looking, he had nicked two of them, today's and yesterday's. He felt that as Leonie Berkhof's real-life son, he deserved to have them.

He let the papers drop into his lap and stared at the pistachio walls of the visitor's room. It was a hair that had been found in the van they'd ditched in the woods. One hair found in the van, *one*, had managed to land him back here three weeks ago. His lawyer had not yet explained how that could have happened, though he'd been patiently waiting. And now this. What had his mother done?

She was late, probably visiting Piet first in the other tower. He pulled his bangs from his forehead and scraped them back. Was this color supposed to be cheerful? It was an insult, making him feel more depressed than when he had woken up this morning. A guard loomed at him from the corner behind his chair. He remembered that there was a certain type that worked in these places. Most of them were worse than the criminals, who at least had some sort of reason for whatever they had done. The guards, generally, were provocative and mean all day long and got paid for it, and that was the fact of the matter.

Poor Piet. Despite his bravado, he had never been in such a place. Luuk had seen him only once since their capture—he was in the C tower and had a different exercise yard. The idiots running the cells were directed by the slightly more intelligent idiots in the management office, and their grand goal was to keep them separate. However, the plan had failed because on the first day Piet's card was misprinted, and he was sent to the B tower dining room. Luuk had grabbed his arm and hissed in his ear, *remember Mom—don't talk*, just because he thought he should. But now . . . what a mess.

He bent his gaze to the front page of *De Telegraaf*.

NATION SWOONS: PRECIOUS WORKS FROM KUNSTHAL FEARED BURNED

Underneath it, a picture of Leonie, her worried face a blur as she ran past reporters in front of their house.

August 26th, 2012 *Amsterdam*

In the matter of the July 1st theft of four works from the Kunsthal museum, investigations had led to the home of the Berkhof family on August 2nd, where Luuk Berkhof, 25, unemployed, and Piet Berkhof, 19, a student, were arrested. It is now believed that Leonie Berkhof, 51, an employee of the Yab Yum club, had possibly burned the stolen works before or after the arrest. Police discovered recently burned wood and canvas fragments and old nails in her stove. A DNA test was ordered for the contents of the furnace, which can take as long as three months. The value of the stolen works has been estimated at one hundred million euros.

On the next page, there was a cartoon that if he lived to be a hundred, he would never forget—a peasant woman with a stick broom dancing around a bonfire, with the Mona Lisa stuck on top of it, and the word *Next*? The whole thing was inexplicable. Why would Leonie *do* this? It made so little sense that his head was spinning with the effort to understand. Because even if the evidence was destroyed, they'd still be guilty. In fact, more guilty. His whole body felt riddled with a sort of disgust, his skin crawling. For a moment, the flimsiness of which told him it would not last, he felt united in a national sorrow, as well as being the reason for it. He pulled at a hangnail, stewing in apologetic remorse. If he had known where the paintings were, he might have returned them, anonymously, of course. His problem and Holland's problem solved at the same time. No chance of that now. He was stuck in here, Ineke was playing everyone, his mother had lost her mind, and his family was a national disgrace.

On the opposite page, there was a frame of Ineke from the museum tape, her face hidden behind her balaclava. *Who Is Mystery Woman?* the headline shouted. Good question. It went on to say that, as per the digital analysis, the third thief was female and young, and that the police were making a public appeal for her whereabouts.

"Which is your favorite?" he remembered asking her the day of the heist.

"I almost don't want to say. If I say, then this whole thing is real. And if it's real, it's unbelievable . . . but—it would be that one, absolutely," she had said, her hand brushing his as she pointed to one of the Monets, the bluer, lighter one.

"Why?"

"Because it's like a piece of heaven you can get lost in."

His stomach growled. All of that nonsense seemed so very long ago. Lunch was almost finished. Even though the food here was abysmal, he really didn't want to go hungry.

He was just about to give up when the guard buzzed the door to the visiting room open, and there was Leonie, carrying her big white purse and a sandwich bag, looking smaller than he had ever remembered.

She reached over the partition, the papery feel of her fingers soft on his face.

"My Luukie . . . you don't look well."

"I'm okay," he said, pulling his bangs back again. "How's Piet?"

"He's thin, his eyes are too big. It is breaking my heart."

The guard inspected the bags and the sandwich, which she handed to him. She sat down and looked over at the next visitor's booth, empty, also a vomitous green, with a plexiglass partition so nothing could be hidden.

"He got lice, so his hair is short now," she continued. "The medicated shampoo they have here isn't working. You should call him."

"I will. I did a few days ago. The line is long at the phone—"

"This place . . . *Occcch* . . ."

"It isn't your fault," he said, feeling the irony of his words.

"You're tougher, Luuk. I wish you could be together." She looked down at her folded hands. "What have I done to my boys . . ."

"Don't worry, Mom."

"You'll make yourself bald if you keep pulling on your hair like that. I can see a little patch there. Just cut it. You'll look more innocent without all that hair."

He ignored her, saying, "I asked at dinner last week—this is definitely not bugged. It's against the law. They can't listen, couple of old timers said, so we can talk freely."

But still they sat in silence, each wondering how much they could ask the other. He was embarrassed for her, that cartoon fixed in his mind. The overhead light shone down on the gray stripe where her hair was growing in. One of her few vanities was that she never liked any gray and usually touched it up herself every few weeks. He felt caught in a new intimacy, one that he never wanted, and was hardly appropriate for a mother and son. He felt it would be wrong to ask her flat out what had happened.

Her eyes drifted to the paper he held in his lap.

"How's Couscous?" he quickly asked.

"She's fine. Sits in the window looking out most of the day. We watch TV together."

"Mom—"

"All I could think about was that the police were after you. They had Piet. As I told you, they knew about the nightclub connection. They had their own channels."

"I know, but—"

"I paid Gus Maijer a fortune! *Occch*! All of this going on, watching and waiting, while we were just going about our normal days!"

"I know about that part."

Her restless fingers were brown with nicotine. "Maijer is dead. A heart attack three years ago. Did you know that part? The new lawyer I have said that the usual way they do things was thrown out! Because of the seriousness of the crime."

"*What?*"

"Yes, dead of a heart attack three years ago. Didn't leave useful records that might have helped us either. He was only fifty-eight," she said, her eyes full of agony. "I'm sorry, I'm so sorry . . ."

"He tried to soften the hardness that he knew was in his face. "But, Mom, didn't you make it worse?"

"After you left for the club, Piet texted me to warn you. I didn't want to call you, or text. I didn't know what to do. I was waiting—*alone*. When you have kids and they are in danger, we'll talk again and see what you say. I was just so sick of the worry! The pressure! I thought that if they had *nothing* . . ."

"But where had you kept them?"

"In the attic. Would have been fine if they hadn't made that connection to you."

"Ok, great. Make *me* feel guilty," he said, slumping lower in his chair.

"I don't want to make you feel guilty. We didn't think it through. And Guus was recommended by that counselor, so I used him. I realize now that those kinds of things are a racket. They just keep each other going with referrals. They don't know any more than you or I would just opening up the phone book."

"You had them up there all the time?"

"Yes."

"Where did that money come from then?"

Leonie leaned forward. "She sold one."

"Which one?"

"This is more than you need to know."

Luuk, knowing how stubborn she was, put the subject aside. "What about her?"

Leonie whispered, "She's gone. After the last meeting in July. You saw her."

"You haven't heard from her?"

She reached into her bag. "I brought you some real cigarettes. Not that shit that I smoke." Out came her tobacco, rolling papers, a makeup kit, a comb, a fat blue wallet with receipts sticking out of it, and a carton of Marlboro that she must have had on the bottom. She pushed it under the partition.

"Only one time," she whispered.

"Did she . . . ?"

"Set me up? Yes. Very well."

"How well?"

"One hundred fifty thousand well."

"Still not very much. You didn't put it in the bank."

"Of course not!" she snapped. "I did buy Krugerrands and silver."

"Why?"

"Because I like them and they're easy to hide. Dogs are trained to sniff money, you know, not metal."

Luuk groaned. He wondered where the criminality started in this family. Did it start with him? Or her? Was it just pressure? Or was it something they had always carried with them, like a bad gene?

"Do you think they'll be back through?" he asked, meaning the police.

"I have no idea," she snorted.

"That's still a fraction."

"It will hold us. She'll come through."

"Where did she go?"

"No. No details. She knows how to lay low. The police have been over there, and nothing happened. Her father happened to be home one time. He thought the whole thing was bringing the neighborhood down. He came over and spoke to me in a nasty way. But I told him that they were looking all over the city, and that he was not special."

Luuk sat back in his orange chair, "Mom—"

"I could not explain. I wanted it all to go away. I do not have a friend except the new lawyer, Benny Bakker. And I've hired him, so he has to be my friend. Well, Gwen, that old nut from work. But she is just a gossip. It's a wonder that I still have a job, even at the Yab Yum. All of these people judging me—do they not know that I go to work at night almost every day now? I'm not living a luxury life! I tell them, *'Considered Innocent Until Proven Guilty.'* That is the law."

"I can't believe you're still working."

"Of course I am. Benny Bakker says I should be working. Otherwise, it looks bad."

Luuk laughed bitterly. "Wow! *Looks bad.* I don't understand. What am I sitting in here for if you are still working?"

"Luukie. You know how I am—frugal. Always putting away something for a rainy day."

"It isn't a rainy day *now?*"

"No, not the worst that it could be. I've taken some for the lawyers, and that is all that we need right now. The rest is well-hidden. I got you a good lawyer. And Piet. They said that you will get out in about four years. Just take it. Don't talk and take it. It's all going to be okay."

At the sound of four years of his life wasting away in this place, his eyes filled with tears. A sick feeling came over him like rushing water.

"It's all going to work out," she said.

Why did she keep saying that?

"Mom—"

"How about this? I will stop working soon, okay?"

He shook his head, his face puffy with unspoken rage.

"All you need to know is that I put some rubber shoes in the stove with them—I was crafty. They won't be able to tell. I may have had only a few years of education, but I know that melted rubber is a stronger material—it will wipe everything out."

She didn't seem to be that concerned. In the life that he'd left somewhere behind, his mother would be crying now with tears for him and Piet, and for the riches she had destroyed, running through her fingers.

"We sold one and got a pretty penny. Enough money for good lawyers and then some. They have nothing if you don't talk. I told Piet the same thing."

He shrugged very slowly.

"Don't feel bad—don't. I can't explain it now. It will just drive you insane. Take it from one who knows. I have been crazy . . . yes. We never should have done it, but we did, and now—sometimes you just have to let other people handle things and have confidence. I told Piet the same thing."

"What—like these lawyers? What about Gus Maijer? Look at the job he did."

"We have to just move on."

He groaned and put his face in his hands. "It's just such a fucking waste."

"It's over, as far as the evidence goes. Well, almost. You don't get more than four, and Piet less."

"What are you *talking about?*"

"The main thing is, don't talk. It will work out all right, I promise."

"But we're stuck in here, Mom. I'll be twenty-nine when it's over. That is if it all goes according to the lawyer's predictions and you don't end up in jail too. Which is nothing, *nothing* you can count on."

She scoped out the room again, her eyes raking the walls and the corners. "I don't believe that this isn't bugged in here, no matter what they may have told you."

He shook the tears from his eyes, not wanting the guards to see. Something did not fit. She had a strange light in her eye while he was telling her that he would see her only in this one room for the next four years. She was taking it too well. Had she slipped into an alternate reality while he was away? Babbling on about rubber shoes and the stove. Didn't she understand the full horror and the pathetic outcome? They had taken a long shot, trusting a stupid girl who seemed smart. All the details, all the prep—just so they could find themselves here.

"Of course, they are pressuring you." She lowered her voice to a whisper. "Of course, it's been hard. Just deny, deny, deny. If you give them even a small bit . . . they'll grind it out of you. You've got to stay strong."

Luuk tried to rally. But all he could think of was that the visit would soon be over, and he'd be sitting in here, or in the cell, or in the cafeteria, or in the exercise yard, for the next four years of his life. If he was lucky.

He hated this lawyer, Benny Bakker. His mother, still working in that sleazy place after all that had happened. Ineke was clearly at work in her head. If he and Piet confessed, then the charges against her would be accessory to a crime, and she was letting him know it. If he talked, they'd have to give up Ineke. She was acting as if she thought of herself and Ineke only, but that was impossible. Leonie would be miserable if they got stuck for it, but it now looked as though that was happening. Suppose her scheme with the rubber shoes didn't work, and the analysis came back positive for what would have to have been three of the works. Nothing could explain her weird confidence, her fearful excitement.

"You've got to promise me you'll quit your job soon," he said, trying to exert some sort of control. She wasn't listening to him. She was immovable. He thought of Piet, sitting in the other tower after his visit, and the light balsam wood planes they used to fly in the park. The motors were always too strong. If a wing went the slightest bit askew, they would twirl to the ground like maple seeds, smashing on the road.

She looked off, her pointy chin trembling. "I love you so much. You've got to stay on course. Do what I say. Piet, I can convince, but you . . . I can't tell what you are thinking. You are angry with me—"

"Mom, you are talking drivel. How much power do I have one way or another, sitting here?"

Her fingers wound tight around the handle of her bag. "I think only of you. You are my life. You know that, don't you?"

He didn't want to ask straight out but had to know. "Why did you do this?"

She looked him straight in the eye. "They were chasing you, and I had to. You must understand . . . I had no choice. I had to do something to make them stop."

"Mom!"

"I have to get the good shampoo for Piet before the pharmacy closes," she said, rising to go. "I have something for you," putting a smudged, slightly crumpled letter in his hand. "I have no idea what she wrote," she added, pushing the letter under the cubicle.

Luuk's heart lurched a little at *she.* What, he wondered, could she possibly have to say?

Once he got back to his cell, he put the sandwich aside and flopped onto his bottom bunk, his heart pounding a little. His roommate was out, so he had the privacy he wanted.

He tore the end off the envelope. The letter was neatly typewritten on one of the old machines they had at the library, on a lined page torn out of a notebook. He remembered how she had warned them all to never use email or search online for anything related to the job.

She had put a lipstick kiss at the top of the letter, a shade as red as summer cherries. Cute. He wondered what that was supposed to mean since he and she had never kissed. Almost never. There was that one time in the park before she was with Piet. And that time had lasted quite a while. For the sake of convenience, he had put the incident aside in his mind. He had decided not to take it any further because—he had thought at the time—she was too young for him. Maybe, too, she had scared him. It was one of those strange, passing events that looked like one thing and then later turned out to be something altogether different.

Dear Luuk:

The only excuse I have for bad planning is that I'm only eighteen, barely a legal adult. I say it with full awareness that one never gets second chances at certain things. I think about that every day. I'm sorry you are there and things have worked out this way. I truly know that I have you to thank. I have been meeting with Leonie very very occasionally. We leave notes for each other in the frog pot at the bottom of the stairs. I have to sneak in, in the small morning hours. They are cagey though. Very tricky. I try for a meeting spot, go and wait. Sometimes she gets there, sometimes not. Things are slowing down just a bit now.

There isn't too much that Leonie and I need to say to each other at this point. I'm looking after her as much as I can. It's too bad about that lawyer when you were 15. He's dead, did you hear? Don't bring it up to her, she is upset since she paid a lot and she can't do anything about it. Maybe I should have paid more attention. I was so focused on the mission that I never thought to. I knew about your arrest of course, but I believed you when you said there wouldn't be a record. It's amazing that this whole thing turned on one hair. You couldn't have helped it. We knew that something was going on, remember? Leonie couldn't make a move, not one. They did have a constant watch on the house. I'm not sure how much you know. Leonie was under a lot of pressure, the tape running on TV over and over everywhere. They were very aggressive and she went a bit mad.

Once a trial date is set, things will be easier. I write this to you because Leonie has said they've been tantalizing you and Piet with all kinds of breaks and reduced sentences to plead guilty and give me up, but no matter what anyone says you will get the maximum. I've read lots of books on art history, art theft, art forgery and art law. Leonie told me that even her lawyer has chimed in, trying to get your lawyer to make you talk for her protection. I don't even know if that's legal. Anyway, it's STUPID to bargain. Because of the attention to the case they are going to go hard. It would just help them and not you, takes me away from Leonie and worst of all, implicates her no matter what they say about deals. If that DNA analysis of the ashes comes through against her, then it's over, she goes to jail. If you or Piet spill anything at all, that expands the powers of the police and they'll go after her again. Always, ALWAYS DENY. They've torn the house apart stick by stick at least three times. My father and I have watched them do it. (Of course he knows nothing.) Leonie is tough but not that tough. If you hold firm, they'll let up on the pressure.

She is still working at the Yab Yum, no changes right? When she gets home in the morning, I ride my bike down the street I need to see her. If the bastard isn't there we have a signal system. I do a bunch of figure eights if I want to meet. And she'll leave that framed photo of you and Piet and your dad in the window, but turned sideways, if she agrees. We are very crafty, and Leonie has learned how to spot a tail. They're so obvious it's laughable. Though as I said, slowing down now.

I can only say that though you might feel frustrated, you might be able to get out early with doing charitable works and taking classes. Who would want to hear that? No one, but it's the truth. Stay away from the worst of the lot, gravitate more towards your own, relatively mild kind. Things are going to work out very well, I promise. You are only twenty-five. I think of you often and I hope that you will think of me. I'll be waiting for you.

You must burn this letter as soon as you read it. Or tear it up and flush it. If you want to reply send it through Leonie. It will probably take a long while. Let me know if you'd like a care package. Smokes? Candy? Magazines? I'll post it from the other side of the city with no return address or note. But you will know that it was from me.

Ineke (a few more kisses)

P.S. Leonie told me to write that she is tending the garden tomato plants, and is taking good care of those. I don't know what that means but you will. With what I've done, she has relaxed a bit. Be happy for that and please keep our faith. Hope will return, and good things are in the future! I'll make it all up to you, I promise. Don't forget, no internet, no phone. Burn this. Never call me. All of my phones are in the bottom of the Amstel anyway.

"No changes," he said to himself as he studied the creamy quality of those kisses, remembering what she was like. *No changes.* She had a lot of nerve. His thighs began to ache.

Luuk folded the letter in half and then in half again until it was wadded into a small pillow. He chucked it clean across the cell where it landed in his silver latrine.

He had always found a manipulative woman attractive to a degree. Painted nails, makeup, feminine clothes—they showed a desire to please, a willingness. Ineke rarely did any of that stuff, no matter that he had fantasized she should. He wondered where she was at that exact moment, and what she looked like doing whatever it was she was doing. Women could change in their looks like falling off a cliff, especially when as young as that. Early on they'd fluctuate, get fat or pimply, or avoid that and just stay pretty all the way through their teens, then hit a good cruising speed in their thirties if it was meant to be. Then they'd fall off the cliff after about forty-two. If they were wealthy, that could stretch another ten years. Ineke? Anybody's guess.

He stared at the underside of the top bunk, tracing the metal weave of the springs with his fingers. He wondered how long his roommate would be gone. She was driving circles around them all. For example, what had happened to the rest of the money? They had had their foot on the gas for so long, he'd been trained not to ask this question or any other. He was supposed to just take it. Anyway, there was no longer a way of asking, since Leonie was not going to talk about it and he couldn't reach Ineke. The fences were up all around him now. He was trapped, his nerves tingling and fighting underneath his skin. The bars of his cell, the bars on the window, the guard strolling down the hall every fifteen minutes, the lawyers, the trial looming, and worst of all, his mother and Ineke in lockstep. Right now, he hated her. That, and his own helplessness, was turning him on.

CHAPTER 11
OUTSIDE THE LINES

Sagaponack
August 27th, 2012
55 days after the heist

Cracking five eggs into a bowl, Perrin watched as a girl got up for five seconds at most before the wave fell apart. The sea was smooth and curly, and the epic waves of late August were beginning to build. At the shoreline, two young women with big hats traipsed along. Probably Glasgow's friends, probably models. Glasgow's very existence nagged at her viscously—on the rare occasion he went down to the water and stared at it, when the models jogged and pranced by, when the fashionistas who stayed at his house did loud champagne toasts at sunset. She and Chris had seen a few of those from the dunes. Of course, it wouldn't be useful to make an approach when he had guests. Unfortunately, he had guests a lot. Chris said it was up to her, but up till now the opportunity just had not been there.

She poured in a little milk and whipped the eggs into a high froth. Then added a liberal dose of Worcestershire sauce and onion powder like Iris used to do, which George said was revolting. Jack seemed to like it. George always liked his eggs a little soft, and Iris liked them dry; when Perrin was old enough to make Sunday breakfast, she'd make two batches to keep them both happy. George liked Swiss and fresh parsley, which was only possible if someone had been to the store.

As she moved the eggs around, she wondered what George would say about all of this if he knew. He was happy she was painting again and had been up to her studio just yesterday. Though he had an inkling that something was different, he wouldn't interfere, and she wouldn't ask him to. But she knew as surely as the sea beat against the shore how, in a similar situation, things would have to go as far as *he* was concerned. He'd say, you don't owe anybody anything, and you certainly don't owe your life to them.

She sighed with pleasure. Like a persistent child, Chris had gotten into all the crevices between times, when she was in the shower, or putting away groceries, or tending to Agatha. He quelled the sandpaper feeling she had with Jack—he almost blotted Jack out. Opportune, given what was going on. She wondered about what people could realistically expect from a marriage. What would *they* do if a person so absolutely right for them appeared out of nowhere?

And every morning she'd feel fresh and sunny, grab a banana and coffee and charge up to the studio. In the last week, she had added three fast charcoals to the Agatha series, in a sort of Sumi style. She had started another still life. This time, two old apothecary bottles and ripe peaches. She was hurrying that one because peaches would soon be out of season and the hard greenish ones were not the same. She wouldn't work from photographs, especially for something like a still life, having been warned off that long ago by her teacher at SVA. She knew that some people could do it, but there was a flip side to the new life coursing through her—she'd woken up to her own limitations. There was nothing ambitious about a still life. Been done to death. But never exactly the way she would do it, and maybe something more than "just another still life" would come through. She was surprised at how liberating it was to no longer expect, or even want, big outcomes. It was enough to just exist in her own sensory sea.

She heard the screen door slam and vowed again to get it fixed.

Hearing Jack pull a chair out from the table, she poured out two mugs of coffee, set them there, and went back to get the plates. Dividing the eggs in two, she called out, "Did I tell you what Dad said? I was just thinking of it this morning."

"No, what?" said Jack, peering into the kitchen.

"A riddle, something that was a big deal to me as a kid. 'Catch the sun,' I used to say. Or he used to say—something like that."

"Catching the sun?" he asked absently, noticing the two women in hats.

"I wish he weren't so cryptic," said Perrin, setting the plates on the table. Smiling to herself, she thought of how George would approve of something like an art rescue mission.

"It's always about him," said Jack. "It will never be about you. He can't subtract himself from any equation," said Jack, putting his vitamin carousel next to his plate.

Perrin nodded, thinking how true that was, but perhaps less so now.

"And, of course, he's one of the last great romantics—who are those chicks out there?"

"I have no idea," she lied, while Jack reached up to grab the binoculars from the shelf.

"George? Romantic? Really, you think so?" she asked, sitting down.

"That group was working outside the lines, literally," said Jack, scanning the beach and stopping.

"What does that mean, outside the lines?" she asked, though she knew.

He squinted. "They look familiar. Weren't they at Glasgow's party?"

"I don't remember them," she said, hoping to get off the subject.

"Obscure," continued Jack. "Leaving the viewer to make up most of it. You know, everything we were talking about the other night. That overworked *subject.*"

"You yourself said that George was one of the great draftsmen, which was why his work held up."

"I thought differently then. They were all great draftsmen, his group. And so what? We're past realism now, or any derivative of it," he said, putting the binoculars back. "Anyway, I don't call selling two paintings a year 'holding up.'"

The table, strewn with coffee cups and plates, stared at her silently. She thought about that time when she first knew Jack, when everything didn't boil down to sales.

An *uh-oh* issued from the deck. Jack looked in its direction and dabbed at his shiny lips. "How's the bird doing?"

"You mean Agatha?"

"Yes."

"I took her to the wildlife center last week."

"Amazing, I was sure it was finished like the others." He threw a handful of vitamins to the back of his throat and gulped them down with a single slug of orange juice. She could never get over how many he could swallow at one time, like a basking shark.

"No. Not finished—"

"Just don't want you to be sad. If it happens."

Perrin tossed her head, shaking off this idea. "They also told me why she's lopsided when she walks."

"Why?" he asked, delicately setting his plate aside.

"They said that she probably broke her leg when she crashed, and we'll have to see later if she can fly. And survive."

"I hope she makes it."

"Well, I've gotten her this far, and with her leg—they haven't exactly *said* I should keep her, because that isn't their policy. But they've hinted. They seem to think I've done very well with her."

"When are you going to release her?"

"Haven't got a plan—"

"But that's a wild creature, you said so yourself. What about germs?"

"Germs?"

"Like avian flu. And what about the winter?"

"She isn't sick, Jack. She can be on a perch. I'm having one made, in fact. I did some research at the library on how to make it."

"You should take it to the wildlife center if that's their policy. You were up all night for weeks."

"I feel absolutely fine," said Perrin while another loud *uh-oh* came from the deck.

Agatha hopped around lopsidedly, fixing her with that questioning eye that was no longer fearful but had become part of her every day.

Jack pushed his glasses up on his nose. "I changed accountants," he said.

A bolt of alarm. Why was he telling her that?

"This guy had such a great idea, I thought he might be more creative, so I mentioned the thing about George's house."

"Oh, yes?" Jack rarely discussed money.

"We talked about a house for George—me and this new guy. There's a way to do it that would be advantageous, and I think . . . I hope you would be happy with it."

"Okay—try me."

"It's a good solution. George sells his house, then he finds a place . . . We kick in the difference between what he can get and the new place. And he'd have a life tenancy."

"How do you mean, kick in the difference?"

"The part we pay for is ours. It's in a trust. Because of the condition of his house, and what we'd have to cover, could be quite a lot. The house would revert to us when he dies."

"Can't we just buy it for him?"

"It's better this way, tax-wise."

"Tax-wise? We don't have to scrimp, do we?"

"Watching the pennies, or the dollars—and the millions will take care of themselves," said Jack.

She looked into his awed blue eyes and felt she didn't know him anymore. "It would revert to us anyway. He'd leave it to us. Why not just give him the choice?"

"It's generous. The accountant said it looks *less* like charity this way. George can keep his pride. You can call it an investment. The IRS sees it as an investment, that's the important thing. Everybody's problem is solved."

"Jack, it's condescending, like what you would do with a child. He doesn't care about our tax situation. Why should he, after all that he's done for us."

"Have I told you recently how beautiful you are looking these days?"

"Stop it, Jack." His admiration struck fear into her heart. Did he have some way of knowing?

"Truly. Something is going on with you—you are absolutely radiant."

"Nothing . . . nothing is going on. I am painting again."

"Yes, I know. I think it's great!"

"Yes!" she exclaimed.

"What do you think people would say about that house arrangement for George?" she continued.

"One of the things I always appreciated about you is you're *not* a spoiled rich girl."

"You mean powerless." For *once*, she thought, let's just call it what it is. Her phone buzzed in the back pocket of her jeans.

"You are not powerless."

"I am in a way. You keep everything in locked files in your studio." She gestured to the surroundings. "We built this together! But I have no idea how it's set up. I signed everything you gave me and never knew what it was."

"Don't you trust me?"

"Of course."

"What's got into you? I've taken very, very good care of you. If anything should ever happen to me, you'd be set—in the manner in which you are accustomed. And George too. We can sit down with this new accountant, and I'll explain everything."

Jack went to the bookcase and took out a dumbbell. "I take it back. You were land rich—"

"Not at the time. That just happened. And then Dad gave it all away—to *us*."

He curled the weight up to his chin. "This is better in the long run. Your parents didn't plan, they never gave a thought for this kind of thing—the kinds of things *I* am thinking of. Taxes, planning for the future. Too dull for *them.* And look how things ended up. The boozing, the parties, the state of that shack you lived in. Remember how Iris would never go to the doctor, even when she was sick? Then never leaving the house? She really lost it, remember? You had to take care of her. And I had to take care of you. When we first met, you couldn't talk about anything else. It consumed your life."

"At least they had a good time along the way," Perrin threw out, catching herself mirroring George and Iris, understanding them a little more now given what was going on with Chris. Though living for the moment had hardly been Perrin's philosophy, she felt it necessary to defend them.

Jack switched to the other arm. "It wasn't all a good time, especially . . . for . . . you . . . *unnhhh!*"

He was right about this. Perrin remembered when the pipes in the shack froze, and the fields had snow drifts high enough to obliterate the dunes. George was staying with Mia, an art student thirty years his junior, at his studio. They were getting by somehow; he had snowshoes. He used them to get to the general store, claiming the exercise was good for him. *Perry, Iris wants it this way—we can't stop her.* Iris stayed in the shack and had forgotten to pay the oil bill. She hated George with the passion of old impermeable love.

"And now look at him! He lives on the name he made forty years ago."

"He works every day," said Perrin.

"So what? No one cares."

"Jack! There are a lot of people who care! He's got the show coming up—"

"A legacy show. That's the kind of show no one really wants. Like a lifetime achievement award at the Oscars."

"God! You should hear yourself!" She was thinking of Jack's intensity, the way he was looking at her at the end of each curl. "I think I know my own father better than you."

"George will be *fine*," he breathed in short bursts. "Give him the keys to a new . . . dry house . . . with a decent work area . . . and he won't ask one question. It's you that has . . . the . . . problem . . . *unnhhh!*"

The veins bulged in his arm. Something was ticking in his brain, and it was the engine of the way he saw her. It rattled and it revved; a clunky, garish go-cart.

"There wasn't a man at that party that didn't want you," he said with a sort of relish.

"That's not true," she said. "No one bothered me."

"Perrin. I saw it all."

Not wanting him to go into details, she went out to check on Agatha again. Every time she approached the cage, she was afraid she'd find she had suddenly died.

* * *

Usually, Jack did the dishes, but she wanted to take over and do them by hand. While he lingered in the kitchen door, she ran a sink full of hot, almost scalding sudsy water. She scrubbed the pots and dishes until they squeaked, then rinsed them clean and put them in the rack. Drying her hands, she watched the pleasing flow of the water as it disappeared down the drain, taking the grease and flotsam of the meal with it.

"Did you remember that Gia's coming this morning?" asked Jack, absently looking out at the beach again.

"Yes," said Perrin, happy that it would be soon. That scrappy, red-haired Italian was the gadfly that this house needed.

"What about that Pucci?"

"What about it?"

"For the photos. I'll get it."

"I never said I'd do the photographs. I might have said I wouldn't, actually."

Her phone buzzed again and rang on the counter. A phone call this time. What was Chris doing?

"Why not?" asked Jack, slurping his coffee.

"I'm not sure," Perrin said, while the nickname *Cinnamon* flashed in Neon Red in her mind. She felt heat come to her face and was glad she was turned away from him. She was not a person called *Cinnamon.* An inanimate powder. Spice in a jar. She was not something you put on toast.

Her phone buzzed again, another text. She ignored it, grateful that she now had a lock on the phone.

"Who *is* that?"

"It's just the yoga people," she said, sure it was Chris. Something was up.

"She's here," he said and turned to get the door.

Gia set down her gear, her hair in curly corkscrews from the humidity, her skinny curves evident in boy's Levis and a T-shirt. William trailed behind her, carrying power boxes and a few light stands under his arm.

"Holy Crap," mouthed Gia, meaning William, of course. But Perrin no longer noticed William that way.

"Here, look at this," said Gia, putting the paper, still in its blue sleeve, on the coffee table. "I read about it this morning."

Jack slid it from the sleeve and opened it. "Wow! Look at that!"

Woman with Eyes Closed was floating upon the cover of the Arts and Leisure section. Unlike the glossy *Art News* rendition, this was in black and white, yet she came through with all her power.

"What?" said Perrin, trying to read over his shoulder.

He opened the paper, and the headline blazed: ***Dutch Woman's Story Has Art World Fearing the Worst***.

Perrin's heart banged in her chest. "What does it say?"

Jack laid out the paper and took up most of the room in front of it. He gave her a playful shove with his hip. "Why do you care so much?"

Perrin was silenced by this question.

"Funny how this one has become the poster child," he said. "I'd much rather have either of the Monets, wouldn't you?" He peered at it. "Shall I read it to you guys while Gia sets up?"

This was their ritual from their New York days. Though she desperately wanted to devour the article herself, alone, she nodded.

Jack slowly made for an armchair and settled back.

Art world intrigue in the Netherlands—On August 23rd, in a nation with one of the lowest crime rates in the world, the story of the Kunsthal heist took another bizarre turn. On August 2nd, Dutch law enforcement arrested two brothers, Luuk Berkhof, 25, and Piet Berkhof, 19, in connection with the theft of four masterworks from the Kunsthal museum, valued at approximately one hundred and twenty million dollars. Further investigations of the Berkhof home in Amsterdam have revealed the presence of wood, nail, and canvas fragments in a furnace that were consistent with the age of the stolen works. Forensic tests of the remains are being carried out. Leonie Berkhof, 51, mother of the men, and a manager at a house of prostitution in Amsterdam, is the main suspect. Upon discovery of the remnants, she denied any knowledge, but, as of this writing, has claimed responsibility.

The director of the Kunsthal, Kaarle DeVries, had originally said after the theft that all indicators pointed to a sophisticated criminal ring, perhaps in connection with the Abbiate Foundation who had loaned the works to the Kunsthal. That conjecture was vehemently denied by the foundation, and the director later made a public apology. The Berkhof brothers have consistently denied any involvement with the theft. A third female suspect remains at large.

Jack shook his head and put the paper down. "Well, what do you think of *that?* Hard to believe the mother—first she claims innocence, then says she did it."

Perrin attempted a light note. "We can all place bets." Chris had to have known at least something about this.

"The foundation will make a killing with the insurance—correction—Abbiate's heirs will," continued Jack. "Abbiate died a few years ago. It does make for at least a few questions about the targeting. Why those?"

Perrin was speechless as she tried to think of a relevant comment that would not give her away.

"Do you think they're burned?" she asked.

"Doesn't look good right now," said Jack, pushing his glasses up.

"Analysis can be flawed. It's all a matter of percentages, isn't it?"

"For the life of me, I would not want to be Kaarle DeVries right now. He's got a lot to answer for," Jack said, not really answering her question.

Perrin was plunged back into her ruminations. Did Chris withhold this from her intentionally?

"You look perplexed," said Jack.

"Oh me? I'm just wondering whether to go to yoga this morning. Can't get up the steam . . ." Perrin said, as vaguely as she could, while her phone buzzed again in her pocket.

She went to the window. Chris had sworn her to secrecy about the mission, regarding details and absolutely everything else, because it would draw the wrong sort of attention to have this information floating around. God, what nerve! Who would she tell?

And Jack had it all wrong. Two nights ago, Chris told her that all four paintings were on loan from the Abbiate Foundation, along with three others at the museum that had not been touched. So, no targeting. As for that portrait, its subject had since died, leaving her husband and two children, a boy and a girl (which she already knew). She had not known that the family wanted to stay out of the papers, in part because it was they, not the foundation, that actually owned it. She also hadn't known that before his death, Hochberg had created a kind of lease. Abbiate would have the painting for a period of years, lending it and showing it where they chose. Rights of ownership would then revert to the subject's children when both were over twenty-one. The children were now six and eight.

The family wanted no publicity, and of course they desperately wanted the painting back. The husband had re-married and was a playwright—*poor as a church mouse*, said Chris. Puffed up with his insider status, he had described all of this, pushing to find an opening. He had Perrin pegged for soft-hearted, which she wasn't always. And now this galling development!

She couldn't grab the paper; Jack was still reading, the image of the portrait trapped in his hands. Was the woman sleeping? If so, she sat straight up. The light in the room suggested a cloudy day, though her chin cast a shadow. Her small smile was unselfconscious, as if she were completely alone. The painter seemed to have no presence in the room. Because of that—possibly—her face held a touch of hopelessness. She was alone. She was someplace that he could not go, but she was comfortable in her solitude. Perrin did not remember these first thoughts, she only remembered that night on the beach when Chris talked about it, that she had felt envious of the woman, the simplicity and self-containment that seemed to have inspired him so much.

After her last meeting with Chris, she had looked it up so she could see it full-scale, or at least as accurately as a computer screen could display it. Yes, she had thought, one could see that the woman was dying, blue-black shadows across her eyelids, a tired flush across her cheeks, a note of sadness in the upper lip more pronounced. There was a sense of being young and sick and accepting of that, but of being beaten down still further. A sense of pressure and punishment with no reason. A will to let go and a holding on all at once. What made the painting great was the permanence of the moment—one woman, one room, one painter across the room, one afternoon or even one hour. It was one of those works that delivered in such a dose it made one mad to know all the surrounding details. To think of its complicated history and that any mortal eye, especially her own children's, might never rest upon it again was indeed tragic.

But Perrin was the daughter of a painter. She was wise enough to know that she had had her fill just looking and that she would never know more. Art was like that; it could not be analyzed past a certain point. You had to take your scrap of illumination and be happy with it. In a sense, art existed apart from the artist—if it was good, a piece had a life of its own and brought you into its life. Many of the public didn't know that, and for that reason had hungered for every detail about George back in his heyday. They made him into a kind of saint while at the same time trolling for a tidbit about his personal life that would render him human. They wanted him to be a God, and they wanted to tear him down at the same time. It was exhausting to live with. As a child, she became overly attuned to what people wanted, and though it had served her well, it had made her weary. It had gotten to the point where she could tell within three sentences of meeting someone whether they knew whose daughter she was and assembled her defenses accordingly.

"Hey, guys, we're running out of the best light," said Gia.

"No, no—we're ready," said Jack, tossing the paper to the side, while Perrin didn't move a muscle.

Gia cut a glance over to Perrin. "Wrong time?"

"I'm going out, so plan foiled for now," Perrin said to Gia.

"What plan? No plan," said Gia, while Jack reached for his weights again.

"Well, I'm not going to be in these pictures," said Perrin.

"Can I borrow William?" asked Gia. "I'll pay him."

"Sure!" said Jack.

Gia in full work mode, prowled about the living room, looking for the right spot to set up. "Saw your pal at Gandolph's last night."

"What pal?"

She fiddled with her light meter. "Christopher Pinsmail."

Perrin's nerves jumped at the sound of his name. "He's not my pal. We just talked a little. That's all." Too defensive.

"He was asking me about the piping plover," Gia said with a tease in her voice.

"Oh yes . . . ?" asked Perrin absently.

"I told him I have gone by Glasgow's every morning since that party," said Gia. "That *stronzo* hasn't done anything to the fences.

Yet. I've got pictures so I can compare. Maybe I scared him. Anyway, Christopher seemed relieved."

"Why would that guy care about the birds?" Jack asked, putting the weights back, *clunk, thunk*. "He doesn't live here."

"I don't know. He seems to have a supernatural interest in all that goes on at Glasgow's. He wanted to know how long Glasgow usually stayed. How would I know?" said Gia. "I don't hang out with the guy."

Some spy, thought Perrin. Though she was one now too, sort of, because Chris had had her sign that waiver which she understood was a loosely defined contract with his organization—MI6—MI5? She couldn't remember.

"Who is Christopher anyway?" asked Jack, straightening up. "He seemed to just appear."

"He's a buyer for some industrialist," said Gia. "Handsome though . . ."

"Industrialist?" asked Perrin.

"Something off about him . . ." said Jack. "He's playing the fuddy duddy but is too young for the role. I don't trust him."

"He sure doesn't seem to want to talk about his buyer, so I'm thinking it might be dirty money," said Gia.

Perrin reflected that in Gia's eyes everyone's money was dirty. If she only knew how much.

"Maybe he'll want to come over to the studio," said Jack, fake cheerful.

Gia expanded a light stand. "Don't think so. He's not into contemporary. Realism, Impressionists, he told me. And mid-century. I heard that Glasgow collects the same kind of thing. Word is he's got some real treasures hidden away."

Perrin couldn't hold herself back. "Hidden away where?"

"Who knows! How many houses does he have?" Gia said.

"Probably no way to tell," Jack said authoritatively, "guy like that—"

"He's a real *sfigato,*" said Gia. "When people like that start moving in, the place is ruined."

"What should I wear, Gia?" asked Jack.

They left to see what he had in his closet, and Perrin snatched up the paper. Below the portrait, there were three separate shots. Luuk Berkhof and Piet Berkhof were pictured, the one called Luuk definitely older. Both brainless looking. Then their mother, Leonie. A boxy-looking person with a smear of lipstick and smudgy eye makeup. The article said she was 51, but she looked at least 65. A drinker, thought Perrin, and not a methodical one. Perrin studied the photograph carefully. Shoulder-length brown hair above a fake fur fringe on her coat. A bitter, determined face. Had this woman taken four masterworks and thrown them in her stove? She looked entirely capable of such a thing.

Jack poked his head through the sliding glass door. "C'mon. You're perfect. Get some outfits?"

"No," said Perrin firmly and went out to the deck.

Agatha looked up at her, her beady eye a little more dull. Or maybe that was the light; it was cloudier now. Was Agatha depressed? She was no longer fearful, it seemed, and if anything, she was bolder. Perrin tried to take that to heart. She got water from the kitchen and delicately refilled the jar lid. Back to all of these lies, and no way to put them straight. Lies, lies, *lies.* Damn Chris, or whoever he was, *damn him.* And damn Jack too. Her entire life was a pack of lies.

She looked down at her buzzing phone and dialed in the security code. There were five messages, all from Chris. The last one read, *There's still a chance. I'll explain when I see you.*

CHAPTER 12
A LOTTIE

Sagaponack
August 28th, 2012
56 days after the heist

Clink . . . clink . . . clink . . .

To Perrin, it sounded like hailstones on the glass block—that, in August, would be impossible. She looked over the deck railing to see Chris on the patio, lobbing up pieces of coal from the BBQ. She leaned down and delicately removed a few pieces from Agatha's cage. "What are you doing here?"

"You haven't answered my texts or calls," he whispered.

"There is nothing you can say," she said, sadness lodged in her throat.

"How could you know? You haven't given me a chance!"

Jack was in his studio; the coast was semi-clear. This had gone on so long that Chris knew Jack's rhythms. He must have been out in the dunes for some time, waiting. Not so charming now, she thought. And dangerous. She was sure he had plenty of explanations—he was a masterfully articulate person, as he had been from the start. He certainly knew how to talk to *her.* Which, somehow, her own husband did not. And maybe it wasn't a lost cause. But that did not mean that she had not completely lost her mind. She went inside to get a sweatshirt to ward off the damp, intending a conversation of no more than five minutes.

* * *

While staring up at that weird, glowing house, Kit felt like a Shakespearean suitor courting a reluctant maid. Unfortunately, that wasn't at all what this was. He scoped out Jack's windows again—they were still lit. He took off over the dune, holding his phone pointed backwards so she'd see the light. He hoped she'd remember to pocket her phone on the beach, the way he had taught her.

He was very tired, having spent the past week under the eaves in Chaz's tiny spare bedroom at his computer. The briefcase had been set to record from 8 a.m. through to 2 a.m., except on weekends when it was on all the time. He worried constantly about the battery. He also worried that he'd miss something that would turn out to be a disaster like London had been. So he downloaded the files and watched them twice every day. He had another layer of supervision from control, but after the Taj op, he didn't trust them.

One big plus: Glasgow's interior alarm was on the kitchen wall within sight of the camera. He'd gotten the security code when the housekeeper punched it in with her left hand while holding a big bag of groceries with her right that she must have been stealing. Otherwise, why take groceries *out* of a house, thought Kit. She might've not liked the code either: 36-24-36, the supposedly perfect measurements for a woman, which Kit thought rather obvious. Glasgow didn't inspire much loyalty among his people. The security guys sat around with him, but they were paid. The fashion people came and went, mainly with the weather. On cloudy days, they raced back to the city, suitcases skittering across the floor like marbles. Kit had been treated to many hours of Glasgow watching dumb movies with his bodyguards, Glasgow eating nachos and drinking beer, a white napkin placed fastidiously over his front. Glasgow opening the door, 36-24-36, for a young woman in a mini skirt and heels, waving off his bodyguards, and having it off on the sofa with her. A sad spectacle. So far, the only person that was almost always there was a bodyguard named Dave who never smiled and had a Ruger that he was constantly cleaning.

It was a soggy night on the beach. It was surprising how wet it could be here, even when it wasn't raining. Sort of like Ireland but saltier. Looking back, he saw Perrin's shadow trace a line down the left side of the house, her phone pocketed, or just not with her. A Lottie—Perrin was a Lottie now. She'd been signed, she'd been trained up a bit, she'd been briefed, and up until recently, she'd been getting ready. Kit felt he hardly deserved how well things had gone.

Beginning with the luck to land out here with Chaz in Bridgehampton. Chaz didn't seem to mind how long he stayed and didn't question the absurd amount of time Kit stayed in his room during the day. This morning over coffee, Chaz had pointed out the pasty color of Kit's skin in one of the "most beautiful resorts in America," as he had called it. Kit had laughed and said that if this were supposed to be one of the most beautiful resorts, it wasn't very relaxing, and nobody seemed particularly happy. Except for Chaz, unfettered hedonist, who'd been having Gia over a few nights a week. Kit had been surprised, but there was no telling who a woman would go for. Often, they seemed to go for the person who embodied what they most disdained. The dynamic was confusing but useful to know.

Yesterday, he had called Martin. Why had Martin not warned him about the announcement from Holland? Martin had rejoined that they were not briefed by Holland and that it was a surprise to him too. Unfortunately, news came out all at once these days, and there was no stopping it, he said. There was a weird, false note with Martin. He was still gung-ho on this op. No hesitation at all. He'd seen some of the tapes, and he had complimented Kit on his thoroughness. He spoke as if everything was going magnificently well, though that was not the case. He had nothing to add about the Berkhofs that Kit didn't already know from the news.

Kit's leg began to throb, the pain minions gathering forces. He whipped around and saw her ghostly shape in the dark, only a few steps away now. It might not matter what sort of spin Martin was trying to put on this. Here, it might be a different story.

"Okay," she said, out of breath, "I'm here."

"I gather you've heard," he said, cupping her elbow in his hand.

"I don't have much time. Let's walk," she said, shaking his hand from her arm.

"Whatever you want," he said, glad that he'd only taken half an Oxy because he was going to need his wits. Cryptic Pinsmail was not going to work here.

They plodded along in the mottled, heavy air.

"So . . ." she said quietly.

"So."

"It's the whole thing taken together, you must know—"

"No, I don't know."

"I haven't been thinking straight. And this morning, the newspaper—well, it is sad news. When I saw the picture of that woman and her smug, stupid sons and thought about what they did, what *she* did . . ."

He feigned perplexity. "Yeah?"

"It's sordid. It disgusts me."

"A real thing that happened, in the real world, Perrin. Correction—possibly happened."

"I really hate that argument, Chris. Anyway, we know it happened, don't we?"

"There is a possibility that the Monets were fenced soon after the theft, and they are here in his house. Lopez was credible, so we have to go with that, as we have from the beginning. The people running this haven't changed anything." These words felt disingenuous because he didn't understand why nothing had changed. Yet it was true Martin really did like Monet.

"And then there's Jack—what would he say about this?" Perrin asked.

Unless his eyes were deceiving him the other night, this Jack was a complete madman who had no respect for his wife. "Probably not much."

"That's awful to say, *awful,*" said Perrin. She came at him, fists flying at his chest.

Grabbing her tightly around her waist, he said, "I'm sorry, I really am. He would want to care, but he couldn't! He's not capable!" She thrashed in his arms, while Kit held on, grateful that he couldn't see her face.

When she had quietened, he said softly, "Look, this place is absurd. I thought London was bad . . . but here . . . it's lovely, and you have every material want, and *you* are lovely—"

"Shut up," she said, burying her face in his cotton sweater.

"Okay . . . okay . . ." he soothed.

Her voice got tougher as she pulled away. "You're doing it again! Getting into my life and into my head!"

"I'm sorry," he said. "I've nothing but goodwill towards you."

"And I wanted to help you because I felt sorry for you."

"Sorry for me?"

"Yes. You seemed lost—new here, etc. And you were fun, but I see it now. You always had an agenda. If you didn't, we wouldn't be here."

Did any of these people do anything really useful? Did they ever do anything more than generate piles of stuff that were testaments to how wonderful, how sensitive, how visionary they were? This place had its head so far up its own ass, it didn't know the difference between real heroism and bullshit.

"Perrin! So *what* if I have an agenda? What's wrong with that? I'm trying to do *something* for fuck's sake!

"Oh . . . *principles.* I get it, fine! Have your principles! I guess I have none. But the whole thing has gotten all wound up with *us,* and it's dangerous. For *me*. Not for you. For *me.*"

He shook his head, feeling pummeled by her words. "I thought you had some mettle. Obviously, I was mistaken."

"But it's a fantasy trip! I'm not going to take a risk like that. Think of how long we've been talking about it! Because it is *completely insane*."

"Not really. Things go on behind the scenes that you would never know about. All kinds of things. For example, no one would ever know about this if you did it. Because you have been sworn to secrecy."

He looked around. The sea was calm, a muted silver moon pouring onto the water. She was so much more far gone than he would have expected. Maybe it was just the shock of the news. He wondered if she was just taking an opportunity to get out of it. His leg throbbed, and he was too tired to pull the right levers.

"We have that lead. I can only say that the family in Holland, the two brothers, were connected in criminal circles. If my bosses really thought it was a lost cause, they would have sent me home." He could sense his words hanging uselessly mid-air.

"I don't believe you. I think you've known all along. Or you don't know, and your boss is playing you for a fool, or somewhere in the middle. I'm not an idiot."

"I'm sure you're not." Perrin of the sea, Perrin of the sea. It was like this girl had just walked out of the ocean and turned human. He wondered if she wasn't right. There was something off. All around him, soft stars turned slowly. He reached for her, touching the curve of her waist. She batted his hand away.

"Don't count on me," she said. "I have to go."

"Back there? You should never go back."

"I'm not going to blow up my life—"

"Let's just talk about it, get it out in the open . . ."

"That? I honestly don't know what to say about that. It's my fault, too. A kink that just got carried away."

"You don't like it."

"I do not."

"Why do you do it?"

"Guilt, maybe. Because I don't know why I've stayed, and the longer we go on . . ."

"Well, I'll just say it—you are not well-suited. I could see it from the first day I met you. He's this famous, successful artist, but he's soft. And he's crude. And he has no subtlety whatsoever."

She turned away. "Christopher . . ."

You and Jack are a bit of a joke around here—yes, I've heard. People understand more than you give them credit for. Maybe he thinks he's justified because he's so successful. Can you imagine? How does that fit with you?"

"I don't know, I don't *know!* I'm just frightened of worse *things*. And he has taken care of me."

"But what do you owe him now? Don't waste your life! It's all gotten too big in your mind! No one is really judging you. It's a blip on their screen, a hesitation in their conversation, a weird social curio. It's nothing! People are always much more interested in themselves. You should break out, *break out* for God's sake. Do something bigger! That way when you're old—"

"I *have* no regrets. None! Except not knowing much about you. You tell me all this stuff to get me wound up in your scheme, and then try and make it into something I owe the world because I married a rich man. There is nothing about a collaboration between Holland, MI-6, and the FBI anywhere. I could find nothing, *nothing*, on Glasgow. Maybe he's just gross and rich and hates piping plovers. There's no law against it."

"Of course, you wouldn't find that! You can't find anything on Glasgow because he hasn't been arrested yet. That is precisely the point. We're trying to take him down. And that isn't even his real name."

"What is his real name? At least you can tell me that!"

"Grigory Kusnetsov. But you won't find very much there either. He's new to this country. Russia is blacked out for us."

His leg pulsed, then the familiar, pounding ache. He needed her—yes, he did—and so did goddamn Pinsmail.

"How do I know that *you* aren't a thief? How do I know that this isn't all a scheme you've dreamed up just to enrich yourself?"

"Of course, I'm not! Why would I go to all this trouble on a hunch?" *Shit.*

"Exactly. This is all speculation, and you can't seem to show me a thing except a document on your phone where I checked a box."

"You signed a waiver, nothing more. That is because I can't officially bring you in. In the U.S., it's complicated for us. There's no guarantee, there's no pay. It is entirely up to you. The only reward would be getting the paintings back and putting away a real snake for the rest of his life." A little voice in the back of his brain was playing havoc with these words. What was he pulling her into? He wasn't even sure anymore.

"How is this my responsibility?"

"It isn't. It's your duty. For example, what did you do today? Have breakfast with that husband of yours? Read the paper? Get all mad? Regret what happened last time? *What have I done?*"

"You have no idea what I'm thinking, none at all!"

"You *should* be kissing me, and often. Nobody cares about your little infractions. Least of all your husband."

She was silent, which was worse than the argument.

Behind her, three long waves came and went, seeming to take a very long time. He couldn't hear them perfectly, but it hardly mattered. He watched the liquid light break along behind her and settle.

"Look, I wish I could tell you," he continued. "I wish I could lay it all out for you. Glasgow has pretensions here; he wants to keep a low profile. But he doesn't perceive you as a threat. This is what I deal in all the time. Intangibles."

He shrugged, keeping his face in shadow. What, in fact, *would* be the pretense she'd need to visit a neighbor who she would naturally dislike? Under what preposterous circumstances would this event take place?

"I don't even know you, Chris," she said with that awful shrug.

"Okay, well, a bit about me. I can't give you all the details. I can only say that a terrible thing happened. A pressure cooker bomb . . . It's something I will have to live with for the rest of my life. I lost a colleague."

"Oh . . ." she murmured. But still she didn't touch him.

"There was a bomb . . ." he repeated before he could stop himself, feeling the impact reverberate through his bones again. "Yes," he continued. "You must have read about it—in London, at the Taj Hotel. You wouldn't have heard any details. I was there—I can tell you that much. And it was partly my fault."

"How was it your fault? At least you've got to tell me that."

"I got distracted and I missed the person who planted it. I was supposed to have backup looking at the monitor, but they missed it as well. I got this limp. My hearing . . . you know," he laughed. "How many times have you called me out here, and I didn't hear you?"

She chuckled noncommittally.

"My colleague, Meredith, died, and a chauffeur whose name I don't know, and someone on the street—a Mayla Khalife," he said, enunciating her name. Thinking about her dark, solemn eyes, his own eyes filled with tears. It was stupid to talk about this. Just what did he think he was trying to accomplish?

"All of this . . ." she said. "I don't know what to think of it. Who did this bombing?"

"They don't yet have an answer. They wouldn't tell me right now if they did. And that's more than I should be telling you."

She held his hand for a moment.

"I'm sorry," she said, turning and walking away.

Kit stayed out on the beach, his sweater soaking through in places. It was like walking around inside a cloud. He didn't want to go back to that tiny room and watch more tapes. Without thinking about it, he followed until he was in front of her house. The dune grasses etched along the base of it, and the rest of the structure soared high above the beach like a stack of enormous televisions. What a strange place. What a strange life. This might be the future in England too, for everyone. Though it wouldn't be his.

He thought about the type of house he wanted to have one day. It wasn't back in London, it wasn't with Fiona. It was a stone cottage in the deep country with a rose garden and deep window sills, on the corner of a lovely meadow. He wouldn't even mind having to duck through the doorways. It would be perfect. For a moment, he let himself think that Perrin might like it and then shook his head in an effort to get her out of it. This was exactly why he wasn't supposed to get involved.

He watched the cube light up, floor by floor, and then as Jack's windows flickered—he always kept a fluorescent light on at night for security reasons. He could see past the deck into the living room as Perrin came to the top of the stairs. The soaring space was like a museum, bedecked with Jack's works. They looked good; it was right for them. She went into the kitchen, probably to get the cat food and grapes for Agatha, or maybe to get a glass of wine. It was so misty he couldn't make out her expression. Agatha's cage was inside part-time now; she had finally gotten Jack to agree to it. Jack himself popped from the top of the stairs and got what looked to be weights from the bookcase. They went about their separate business, not talking. Watching people was a most intimate thing, and most people wouldn't want to be watched just making dinner. But not these two. Or at least not him.

Kit ruffled his hand through his damp hair; fat droplets were beginning to fall from the sky and wet his face. Fantasy trip, she had said. He'd been on one, that was certain. He loved seeing her studio and her work, and meeting George, Chaz, and Gia, and even Jack, who was probably solid in a depraved sort of way. Jack had gotten onto a good thing, and he was going to hold on to it if he could. *If* he could.

It wasn't any good lurking out here. It would take at least a half hour to walk back to Chaz's. So he got started, wet sweatpants flapping on his feet and pulling ridiculously on his waistband. He chuckled over the collapse of standards—so much for being the chic highflyer that the service somehow thought he was.

Back in New York, he'd been thrown out of his lane, and it had been fun, and he'd fallen into a sort of magic. A germ of a need had been planted in him, a need that was fully contrived, a fool's errand. Then he got out here, to what upper-crust New Yorkers called "the beach," and the need carried over. The wind, the water, her. The play of light on her hair, her brown eyes and coltish walk, the way she felt in his arms. The sound of her voice, her courage and her forlornness. She filled the need and expanded his view of himself in the world. But these people, these rich people. This *place.* They thought they were normal. How often in the past month had he wanted to tell them how useless they were. What good did they do anyone? Often the word *artifice* had come to him when thinking about them and thinking about art—the coin of the realm here.

He shook his head as if to shake it clear. It was all of a piece, and it had gotten to him. It had swept him away. Jamming his sandy feet into his trainers, he knew that he didn't hold it in such high esteem, the way that so many did. He told himself he was only partly invested. It was beautiful, and beauty didn't mean that much. He thought of her as sort of trapped in it too, no matter how, in a way, he loved her. Like a hothouse flower, her values all skewed.

CHAPTER 13
LOST IN IT

Amsterdam
September 10th, 2012
69 days after the heist

The visiting area was full this time. Luuk, waiting in a cubicle, looked up at the door. She was late again, probably over with Piet, bringing him food. Since the verdict, Piet had lost more weight. His eyes were huge. Not at all the burly boy he once had been. It wasn't just the theft, the prison, the trial and the verdict. Very clearly his heart was broken. Ineke was his first love, and Luuk believed that though everyone had to have one, usually they did not go well. Except in the rare cases where they just married and lived happily ever after. Luuk had seen him in the gym, and Piet wasn't there for his health. He wanted to find out what Luuk knew, and usually there wasn't much to tell. He had gotten a letter from her also, but when Luuk asked him about it, he declared it "private." Beyond what Leonie had told him, Luuk couldn't say anything more, though he did tell Piet that the best thing to do was nothing. And to forget about Ineke. He hoped his little brother would listen to him.

He looked up, noticing that the ceiling was the same vomit color as his cell, the effect less pockmarked and dirty since, he reasoned, nobody walked on ceilings or nicked them with shivs or forks or wrote profanities or stuck wads of gum on them.

So far, he had had no notice of when they'd be moved. He was still here, and Piet was in the other tower, though the lawyers had said they'd be transferred out to a different place by the end of the month to serve the rest of each of their sentences. He sighed and rubbed his neck. The same guard scrutinized him, though from the other corner. This morning he'd been to the prison library for the account of the trial, again nicking the paper. Most of the time, the librarian was asleep anyway. He always returned them now, wanting more these days to be a good person, finding himself strangely desirous of that. Though it wouldn't help him, he told himself, as he inched the paper forward on his knee. He had contemplated skipping the story—after all, he *knew* what happened—but his attention had been drawn in by the photo of himself and Piet being led out of the courtroom.

KUNSTHAL THEFT TRIAL

After 7 days of hearings, Luuk Berkhof, 25, unemployed, and Piet Berkhof, 19, student, were sentenced yesterday at the Gerechtshof in Amsterdam for their role in the July 3rd break-in and theft at the Kunsthal museum. Four masterworks, valued at approximately one hundred and twenty million dollars were stolen. Luuk Berkhof, flexing his biceps, showed no emotion as sentences were read. Piet Berkhof cried. When ashes consistent with old paintings were found in the stove on August 23rd, their mother, Leonie Berkhof, had claimed to burn the works. However, during last week's trial, Mrs. Berkhof took the stand in her sons' defense, reversing her previous claim.

On September 1st, the National History Museum in Bucharest announced that forensic scientists had found the ash material from the stove consistent with burned paintings, including copper tacks and pigments of the relevant periods. However, in specific regard to the four missing works, results were "inconclusive." Benny Bakker, Mrs. Berkhof's lawyer, had argued successfully for Mrs. Berkhof's charges to be dropped. Of his client's earlier story, he said bluntly, "She was lying. What she said was 100% untrue. We might never find out what happened to the paintings. In any case, she had nothing to do with it."

Clutching her purse, Mrs. Berkhof recanted the earlier story, saying, "I believed what I said was the best thing at the moment. I did not burn the paintings." Mrs. Berkhof was facing charges of "destruction of private property," as all four of the paintings were on loan from the Abbiate Foundation. The charge carried a sentence of three to ten years, far longer than for her other alleged crime, "supporting a criminal group." She is now free of the property charge, and the criminal group charge, and will not be charged for misleading the investigation.

Court watchers say that the Bucharest Museum's inconclusive DNA findings have lessened the sentences of her sons. The elder brother will serve four years, the younger brother two years. Throughout the trial, the brothers have maintained their innocence. A third suspect, believed to be a woman, remains at large.

Yesterday, after the Berkhof brothers were charged, Kaarle DeVries was asked if he still believed the heist to be the work of a mastermind. He said only, "The whole thing is unfathomable." He added that Mrs. Berkhof's confession and retraction could be "pure invention," and the works could be discovered hidden away somewhere.

Luuk slipped the paper back into his bag. Yes, he had been tense, and flexing was a nervous tic he had when tense. Sort of like going to the gym always improved his mood. Fuck that journalist; he wrote those words to inspire contempt. What a stupid job, writing about people as if you knew them when you knew nothing.

It had taken weeks for his lawyer to decide that he shouldn't take the stand. She talked with Piet's lawyer, and it was decided that he wouldn't either. In the questioning period, the police had done what they could to drive a wedge between them. They had hammered away for a long time. They had their point, but he had his. They were his enemy. He could be just as determined. In fact, he relished his stubbornness as one of his few good qualities. He had enjoyed sitting in those gray rooms, looking at their perplexed and frustrated faces while doing what he could to communicate his technique to Piet. Telepathically, maybe. They had them in the same area, rotating them past each other in the hall to increase suspicions about what the other was saying. But they'd see each other in the gym too and exchange a few words. It was amazing what could be conveyed with so little. Piet, sick with love and fantasies of some kind of reunion, had his own motivations for staying silent. Luuk would have been happy to send Ineke off to prison at the first opportunity, but that would damage Leonie's still uncertain position. He had new admiration for Piet, how he had held on.

But damn that girl. Damn her to hell. Leonie had recently informed him that Ineke had her degree now, and gotten an internship with the art ministry of all places. Walking around free, new clothes, new life. With their money.

* * *

Leonie pushed a sandwich under the partition. Digging around in her white bag, she produced a tin and pushed it towards him.

"*Appeltaart*," she said. "I don't want you getting too thin either."

"No problem there," he said, stretching his torso. "It's the fat I've got to watch. How's Piet?" he asked, pulling the tin toward himself.

She shook her head. "He looks like a scarecrow."

"I know . . . I saw him yesterday at the gym."

"Does he work out?"

"Sometimes, but mainly he wants to talk to me."

"I wish none of this ever happened," she said.

"Well, we know who is to blame, Mom."

"No—no. We knew the risks. I only wish that you were with her instead of him. She's too strong for him."

Luuk rested his fingers on the tin, silently agreeing with her. If it *had* been him all through, things would have gone differently. Very differently. Which inspired his next thought, but she cut him off.

"Ineke said she would tell you about this. Did she? Look at this."

She fished in the bag, withdrew a few packs of Marlboro, and slid them under the partition. She rummaged around again and produced a stack of letters that were tied with kitchen twine. And a folder stuffed with clippings of newspapers about the theft. She untied the twine and arrayed the letters, first separating the envelopes from their content. Lined paper, plain paper, different colored paper, scrawled with angry words. *What's WRONG WITH YOU??* Magic marker, pen, and a few typewritten manifestos. *You must be one crazy bitch!!* One had cut-out magazine letters that spelled *DUMB CUNT*. She lined them up in rows, as many as the table between them would hold. English, French, and other European languages that he didn't understand, but the meaning was clear. Pages and pages with curse words ground into the paper with dull pencils and wrathful biros. Printed-out emails and crudely drawn cartoons.

"Look, *look at these!*" she exclaimed.

Crazy Trut.

Dikzak.

I would say ***GO TO HELL****, but you are already going there.*

I'm coming to your house to burn it down. Hopefully you will be in it.

Leonie hadn't mentioned any of this on the phone. In the Bijlmerbajes, there were no computers, so he wouldn't have had a way to know. Luuk leafed through the stack, reading through some. France, Italy, the UK, America, even Russia—and that was just at first glance. She untied another packet and laid them in stacks on the edge of the orange cubicle, her hands moving hypnotically slow as if to tame the contents. The old toughness, yes, Leonie was tough. Thank God for that.

"And that's just the letters! People were calling me until I got our number changed. Saying awful, dreadful things! From all over the world! Our lives, all that we have been through. Losing Dad, the farm. You would have thought I killed a person!"

A clipping with the portrait of the woman having a daydream poked out of the folder. He fished it out and studied it, thinking of how it had reminded him of Leonie having tea in the orchard when Piet was just a baby. Leonie had had aspirations; she had struggled, just like that woman sitting, her face telling all. He had even felt tenderly toward it as he cut it out of the frame, taking extra care with it. What had happened was a terrible shame, but not for the reasons that these art fanatics thought—no matter their affiliations, their snobbery, their wealth and stores of learning. They had no more claim to it than the Berkhofs. It was a talisman of the past because it had a feeling of the younger Leonie. That it was gone was an equal tragedy for that, as much as for money or the family or whatever the books said. That's what those big shots did not know. He had thought of claiming it from the others and keeping it, at least for a while, because it had to be one of the more expensive ones. His friends might not have liked it, but did everyone have to understand why a person liked something? And there was another side to it, one he had not realized before the possibility was snatched away. While looking at his mother, her eyes hollow, stacking and riffling through these letters, he reflected that with the money they could have gotten for it, they could have reclaimed something in their lives of the painting's yielding and peaceful atmosphere. Wasn't that worth something? To hear her whistle in the kitchen like she used to—that would be worth a lot. Maybe one hundred thousand times the value of the actual fucking painting. Saving someone, even just one person—*that* was immortal. Poetry and payback all at once, and all gone now.

He spoke through clenched teeth. "Mom—these people are cranks. How could you let them get to you?!"

"They are practically crawling in the window of our house!"

"But they have no lives! They sit in rooms with books and never go out!" he said, balling up one of the letters in his fist.

"Give that back," said Leonie.

"Why do you need it? To make yourself unhappy?"

"I might need it one day."

"You shouldn't look at them. If you've got to keep them, put them away. Bury them."

She dug around in the bag and produced another few packs of Marlboro, which she slid under the partition with some matches.

"Mom, this is really bad. But it's time to talk."

"About what?"

"The money."

She began slotting letters back into their envelopes.

"So far," he counted on his fingers, "there was the 55k, times three—that's 165k. Then there was the 150k you told me about last time. Has there been more?"

"No. Haven't needed it, and it's dangerous to move money around."

"Oh—she told you that?"

"Yes, it makes sense."

"Mom, 315k is one drop in a vast, vast sea. I want to know how much she has, where it is, and when we're going to get our cut."

"Ineke would say that it's better for me not to know."

"Why is that?"

"To be careful."

"That's a good one." The image of the portrait going up in flames in the basement stove came to him again and unsettled him. It wasn't a big picture, really just a scrap, and yes, as she had said, just a thing.

"You should see her now, leaving the house these days. I can't be seen talking to her, but it's really a change. On her days off she still wears the kid clothes and rides a bike, but to work she wears a suit and heels. I see her when I'm coming in from the Yab. Her hair is black, regular makeup. Very smart-looking. 'Dress for the job you want,' she says."

"Sounds like she's already got the job she wants."

"We can't begin that kind of blame, Luuk. We can't . . . We have to stay steady and strong—otherwise the whole thing crumbles."

Out of regard for her, he decided not to comment.

She finished tying up the letters with twine and pressed the file back into the white dungeon of her purse, her mouth a thin, resolute line.

Drumming his fingers on the tin, he searched her face for a sign that she was disturbed in any way by the knowledge that they shared. But again he found only that strange excitement glittering back at him, as if the flames of that fire were in her eyes, illuminating her from within.

"No blame," she said. "Just look ahead now."

CHAPTER 14
DECENT RELATIVES

Sagaponack
September 11th, 2012
70 days after the heist

Agatha gave a loud caw for her breakfast. Perrin bestirred herself from her deck chair where she'd been drinking her post-run coffee and looking out over the water. Also training herself to keep her eyes straight ahead and stop scanning the beach for Chris. She made a point of running earlier now so she wouldn't see him if he was out there. She knew from Gia that he was still around, and she wondered why. As far as she was concerned, it was over, and she wanted it to stay that way. He'd have to figure it out for himself.

Agatha's *morning, I'm hungry* call was always a happy sound. She'd had a seamstress from the village make a cover for Agatha's crate from canvas scraps from the studio. Agatha was stronger and fatter than before, with glossy feathers and a brazen eye. She was also having a perch made by Jed Aldrich of all people and looked forward to training her on it. At this point, Jack knew that he'd lost the battle about Agatha and had just accustomed himself to it. There'd been one more casualty. A least tern that she found dead on the patio, its gray feathers tight to its sides, its black eyes cloudy.

She had buried it along with the others under the pilings in that row of small, stalwart graves. Perrin remembered almost every one of these creatures that couldn't make sense of a transparent wall. She was learning about bird species for the first time, George had said. But for the saddest reasons, he had added.

Shifting the boxy fabric up, on second thought she just opened the zip flap to get Agatha's dish and water bottle to refresh them. Every morning, she'd wake up, run, tend to Agatha, and go up to the studio. She'd been trying to concentrate on things that pleased her, that had some kind of a real future. Like this crow she had found, that she loved more every day.

She often felt hollow in the studio, but she persevered. She'd been through breakups before, though Christopher was not what she would have called a real relationship. Nor would he ever be. Her own marriage felt like it had broken up long ago, the days passing in a mostly functional way inside a fabricated cloud that birds did not understand. So there was that. The only way she could stay tough about Chris was to put in the hours, three a day at least, and try to be patient with herself. What did she have to say in paint? Not a lot at the moment. The only thing she really had going was the Agatha series. Agatha, very much alive, pecking at her seed cake. Quizzical Agatha, disinterested Agatha, listening Agatha, conniving Agatha campaigning for more fresh berries. Watching her brought a smile to her lips; the bird preening and cocking her head. She'd do quick sketches on the deck, then take them upstairs and flesh them out. Recently, she was experimenting with watercolors—a brown/cream/black palette with a hint of dark blue, *if* she were feeling courageous. Watercolors were so unforgiving.

She slotted the water bottle into the holder and laid the fresh newspaper in, Agatha gently pecking at her arm. Straightening up, her eyes strayed over to Glasgow's. As always, she could just see the tops of the chimneys. Amazingly, Glasgow was still in residence, emerging occasionally as if to taunt her. One of his toadies would drag a few Adirondack chairs to just above the waterline, and he and whatever friend he could scrape up would sit in front of the ocean with an ice bucket, wine, and a few glasses. Mostly playing games on their phones. Did he ever consider the wonders that were under the sea in front of him? The clouds of silver bunker, massive bluefish and seabass of all sizes, sharks and whales, horseshoe crabs and tuna, flounder surfacing occasionally. They barely looked. Her only comfort was that the summer would soon be officially over, and Glasgow and his pals would be gone.

Her phone buzzed in her back pocket. Lately, Gia had felt compelled to give her updates on Chris. When Gia showed up with Chaz for dinner the other night, she teased her again (out of Jack's earshot) about Chris. She'd seen him at Gandolph's the night before. Which had inspired Perrin to needle Gia about her very surprising choice of a date. What was *she* doing, anyhow?

She looked down. No, it wasn't Gia messaging her; it was Chris. Her heart gave an unwilling lurch.

New developments. Give me five minutes. Tonight at 8:00 same place. Please.

Perrin pocketed the phone quietly and finished her coffee.

* * *

The next day, she held steady, not varying her routine. With a kind of fury, she did ten sketches on the deck and went up to the studio, pushing Chris from her mind. Her hours there felt pointless, wandering across the floor, a loaded brush in her hand. She remembered what one of her teachers at SVA had said: "It doesn't matter if you have a crap day. The crap day can be a bridge to somewhere worthwhile." While cleaning her brushes and putting everything away, she hoped there was some truth to it. She wished that Chris would leave, just leave the area and stop looming out there like some sort of colossal spider. If indeed he was looming.

The following day, she turned off her phone and put it in the studio drawer, sick of its silence. Sick of the way her heart thumped when it emitted any sort of dispatch. Gia with the enlargements. Jed with the perch. Max with a dinner invite. George saying hello. In the afternoon, Jed came, and she helped him put Agatha's perch together in the living room. Once he had gone, she decided to take a walk. The dusk was coming earlier now, and she didn't want to miss it. She wasn't going to stop living her life, was she?

Along the shore up ahead, there was a man walking, the rhythm of his strides broken by a limp. Of course, it was him.

He spun on her, the dark blue of his eyes the same color as the darkening sea.

"Okay—spill it," she said.

"Spill it?" he asked, completely amused. Which was charming. Dangerously so.

"Some kind of news?" she asked.

"Hold out your hand," he said with a chuckle.

She did, and he dropped a dried seahorse into it. There was just enough light to make it out.

"Never seen one of these . . ." she said, peering closer.

"Well, now you can add it to your collection," he said. "I assume you have one."

"I don't have very long, Chris. I think I made it clear last time."

"I'm wondering if you've heard the news from Holland," he asked.

"No."

"The trial, the two brothers—they got relatively light sentences."

"Does it matter?"

"The reasons matter. The DNA from the ashes was inconclusive."

His phone pulsed in his hand, and he disappeared it into his pocket as he had trained her to do. She considered him, thinking that he was both gone for her and somehow still here. He had a new, edgy focus about him.

"Perrin, you are looking right through me—"

"I'm listening to you."

"Everything is different now."

"How?"

"Well, to start with, the brothers pled innocent all the way through. Then the mother, back and forth, and finally, *back.* She said she didn't do it. And she walks free."

"Okay."

"Then the third thief. Very clearly on the tape, a young woman, *never found.*"

"I knew that."

He shook his head. "You are dead set on arguing with me."

"I'm merely interested in my own survival."

"As am I, Perrin," he said. "Let's walk a bit."

He pitched in. The DNA from the stove had been reported inconclusive. However, in terms of DNA, "inconclusive" generally meant negative. But not enough to confirm negative. There wasn't much room between the negative of not confirming or "inconclusive" and the negative that was just negative. Authorities waffled; that was what they were paid for.

"They are covering their ass, as you Americans like to say. There's the third thief, the crazy mother, and the sons that never said a word. That leaves a lot of questions."

He continued to speculate, specifically about the portrait and its fate. Unfortunately, most civilians did not understand the subtleties involved in the case. For example, very likely the children of the woman who had posed for the painting had been told by relatives that the likeness of their deceased mother that was all over the news was a carefully cataloged bag of ashes in the basement of the National Museum in Bucharest.

"Yes," she said, becoming intrigued in spite of herself.

His voice became quieter. "And if those relatives are *decent* people, they very likely would not tell the children that this had happened because the portrait was worth twenty million dollars. Or at least turned off the television."

"No . . ." she murmured, struck by the sensitivity of this statement. She hated the thought of those kids having to contend with their loss and the rapaciousness of a market.

"*Supposedly* happened," he added. "Too much that is unresolved . . . you see . . ."

"I hope they are decent—the relatives," she added.

"There's more," he said, shaking his head.

"You like that painting, don't you?" she cut in, thinking of the dreaming woman with closed eyes.

"I do," he said.

"Why?"

"I don't know," he said. "I just do. C'mon, let's keep walking. I've got more, and you are not going to like it."

"What?"

"You notice that he hasn't left?"

"I've noticed."

"There's been a break in the London bombing case, the one I told you about."

"The one you were involved in?"

"It was him. Glasgow, aka Grigory Kusnetsov. It was him."

She was horrorstruck.

"He was targeting another crook, Demyan Egorov. He's responsible for those deaths. How's *that* for a neighbor?"

"It's sickening," she said, her body tingling with revulsion.

"In London, an agent was blown—fortunately, they got out. But through that and other inquiries that have been made, Glasgow is now well-aware. He has many layers of protection, but he'll probably stay here where it's better for him, under a sort of cover he's created. Very low-key, making donations here and there. Hate to highlight the bad news, but he probably won't leave unless he's busted. Unless we have something on him, and the cops can search his house. I've talked to people around in the town. *Nobody has a clue.* People think he's great and are willing to overlook—"

"Uggh," she said. "I'm not sure I can take anymore."

Suddenly, he froze up. The abstract work that Chris once was organized quickly into a sort of wall, a stage. This was the part of him that was doing a job, and it had informed him that he had gone too hard. There was the business side, and this was it. All the rest was on a shelf. And in a way, this let her off the hook. She needed to be dispassionate. It was best that all this information remained separate from them, whatever constituted *them.* There was no other way to keep her head.

"The only reason I can tell you this is because you are no longer a civilian, Perrin. You are not. It's all there in the official secrets act you signed and I sent to you. One thing is certain: If you decide you want to stay out of it, you can't ever say anything that I've told you to anyone. Not a soul—alright?"

"Al*right,*" she exhaled, feeling swamped with unwanted news. That mandatory secrecy would be welcome in the future. It would make it easier to forget. "My head is spinning, Chris. I've got to go home."

"Wait. Just a minute," he said softly into her ear. That voice, again. Brushing his lips along her forehead, slipping his arms around her waist. Gathering all of her in close, so close.

CHAPTER 15
A GIANT HAND

Sagaponack
September 16th, 2012
75 days after the heist

"All those paintings are toast," Jack said at breakfast, a hand arcing disdainfully as he closed the paper. "Who would do that?"

"She did that, it seems," said Perrin, preferring to keep Christopher's opinion to herself. The paper was an old one that Jack had picked from the stack next to the fireplace. The front page carried a picture of Leonie Berkhof. It was hard to believe she was only fifty-one. Her head was driven down into her neck, as if she'd been flattened by events.

"It's a real shame," Jack said, "especially those Monets. The Picasso was ugly; the Hochberg too."

"I *liked* the Hochberg," she said.

"Well, you would. Most women would. Women like to dream."

"Hmmmph . . ." she uttered, resenting being lumped in with most women and being classified as dreamy. And even if she were dreamy, that was not a point against her.

"Don't you dream, Jack?" she asked.

"Not unless I'm asleep," he said, pushing up his glasses on his nose. "Well anyway, rarely."

While watering the big pots on the patio, she could almost smell the mixture of dust, clay, and oil paint of the *Mbweebwee* collective on Houston Street, where she had first met Jack. There was a Christmas bash there; she came along with a friend from SVA. He had one of the drafty studios that had been hacked out of an old fabric warehouse. A vaulted skylight ran the length of the building. The place was freezing cold but had terrific light. Jack himself was from Indiana, tall and slightly goofy, with longer hair. He brought her a dubiously washed mug of *glögg* from a big steaming pot in the hallway.

While pruning a dead rose, she remembered his fingerless gloves as he handed her the *glögg*, and that she did notice his casual air was somewhat studied. He wanted to appear a certain way, and being good at appropriation, he did. His cubicle was filled with paintings of flowers and sea creatures, glossy and ultra-cool. They were a complete departure from the jagged lines and frenzied color of George's work at the time. She thought of Jack as more of a craftsman. Jack's paintings were organized, as if done by a precocious, cheerful child—she later discovered that Jack himself was like his paintings. That was usually the way. Maybe someday it would be said of her work. It was the reason why any of them did this work at all. To take the hazy atmosphere within themselves and try to pin it down.

After watering the allium bed, she leaned to turn off the spigot. The rest had been on repeat, more so than before—the distracted attention, the screen door slamming, the obsessive weightlifting. The campaign about the life tenancy for George. She'd whipsaw back to Chris, the way he loved her. Chris, in that strange, bowstrung garden at the beginning of things. Chris, waiting for her.

Later on, Chris texted her from Chaz's to say that Chaz was at Gia's for the night. Because she didn't want to start up the car, she snuck to the storeroom for her bicycle and pedaled into the village.

He'd led her up to the spare bedroom under the eaves, where he was barely able to stand up. He gave her tequila in a teacup, he swigging from the bottle. "Nice to have a bed, such as it is," he joked while flopping onto it, his feet hanging off the bottom. Smiling, he seemed perfectly at home. She noticed the bottle of pills on the tiny table. A knee brace was flung into the corner on the floor. "They don't work," he said, "just make you sweat." He hitched himself up to make a sort of place for her to land. Bending at the waist, she crawled into his arms, and feeling like a contented cat, stretched along his side. Absently crunching her hair with his hand, he propped up his laptop to show her the view of Glasgow's he'd had all these weeks: half the dinner table that stretched along the windows, and the sofa, chairs and coffee table where Glasgow spent most of his time. Glasgow's code—36-24-36 on the outer kitchen wall—was needed to get *out* of the house as well as into it, which Perrin thought a chilling fact. "He's mostly a night owl," Chris said, adding that he'd never seen any violence or anybody who was trapped.

At four the next morning, she hopped on her bike and pedaled back against a furious, metallic-smelling gale. Instead of creeping down to the basement room as usual, she sat in her chair on the deck, just to feel it. Pushing at her from all sides, this was not a playful wind. It had a mind of its own and a cavalry following right behind. She was tired, and it was still warm, enough to sleep a bit. So she curled up tight and closed her eyes, wind buffeting her ears, Agatha piercing the scene here and there with a cry. Her dreams were spokes on a wheel—intensely important and completely nonsensical—the sea kicking up, George in his basement in a rising flood, unable to scale the stairs, Agatha flying under the house on broken wings, Chris fiddling with his phone, imploring her wordlessly.

A few hours later, she rose and stretched and thrust her nose into the air which had not calmed down. The sea was agitated, seagulls flying erratically over it, whirling and dropping like stones. Jack would be up soon. The metallic tang in the air persisted, and the sky held a crepuscular glow.

She went to the market for staples—coffee, canned tuna, hard candy, peanut butter, Sterno, batteries for the radio—all the things that George liked to keep on hand under the shack. Wheeling her cart down the aisle, she ran into Jed Aldrich. The Claytons and the Tripletts and their ilk had inspired a grudge among the locals because of the cost to taxpayers to shore up the beach after one of these storms. He was predictably curt with her, his eyes slicing to the contents of her cart.

"Those candles won't last, burn down in a half hour," he said, redirecting her to his cousin's hardware store for the right ones.

She laughed and said, "I'll just buy twice as many." Forgetting that she'd lived here as long as he had, she looked into his hooded gaze for some sort of evidence of how bad it was going to be.

"But that would only get you an hour," he said. As if reading her mind, he added, "This is going to last longer than that."

"Why do you say that?"

"The weathervane on the barn is schizoid."

She went to the hardware store and got candles. Without knowing exactly why, she also bought two kerosene lamps, red ones, and extra kerosene.

She sped home, cursing the storm, and cursing Jed and his smug attitude. Humming nervously in her kitchen, she loaded fresh batteries into the radio, tested it, and cut up apples for Agatha. Worried that the cage would blow over, she hauled Agatha inside next to the fireplace. *Uh-oh, uh-oh,* said restless Agatha, hopping on her bent leg, nipping at the fruit. Perrin refreshed her water while noticing the red windsock on the deck drooping, then extending straight out as if electrified.

Jack surprised her, making her jump. He looked at the empty grocery bags on the counter and said, "Let the panic buying begin!"

Perrin said nothing. A Midwestern boy to the last, Jack had more respect for tornadoes. He didn't take hurricanes seriously because he'd never been through a real one.

He put his hand on her shoulder. "Are you alright? You seem kind of distant," he said.

"Are you kidding?" she asked, her heart lurching in her chest, longing for him to go away and stop pretending. At the moment, he was playing at concern, cool concern. Everything-is-under-control concern. *You-might-be-nuts* concern. He squeezed her shoulder and smiled, sending a shudder through her body. She saw everything through Chris's eyes now, as if she *were* Chris—meeting her that first night when she wore the Pucci, fumbling the champagne, making love to her on the beach and in the spare room, and, with deep incredulity, looking up at their house a few weeks ago.

She pulled away and stood separately from him. "Jack. It's a storm, a big one."

"You're overreacting," said Jack.

"Am I?"

"A little, I think. And I do remember the last time. And the time before that. But all you really need is a full tank of gas. That's how it turns out. Right?"

"Generally . . ." murmured Perrin. There was no point in engaging with him. This one did seem worse than the last. From the kitchen, the radio squawked and coughed, and the mechanical weather lady droned an alert. Perrin turned to the window, transfixed by nature's disarray. The Napoleon was losing its form as it blended into the sea and the gloomy sky. Bands of luminous gray advanced; the wind keened; the sun was a piece of mottled marble.

She remembered reading about the surfers who were swept out in '79 when she was only two, and the kid who was electrocuted in '95. When she was nine, a blizzard knocked out the power in the shack. George was stuck in the city. She remembered being very cold and crawling into bed with Iris in the morning. Iris's electric blanket was cold, and she smelled like a stale glass of wine. Her skin was clammy and pale. Perrin thought she had died. She spent a few frantic minutes dripping ice water onto her forehead until she began to stir. It was Perrin's idea to go away across the field to the Aldrichs', where the lights were on and beckoning. Otherwise, they might have frozen in their beds. She opened the door to a powdery drift that was taller than herself, and beyond that, a stark, glittering world of endless white. Trudging across the field, Perrin was up to her waist in snow, and Iris had on tennis shoes. They were given dry clothes and tea and the most delicious scones Perrin had ever tasted.

The screen door, caught in a wind gust, slammed and rattled on its hinges. Jack was back, hovering again, looking out over the deck with her. "Well, now we're all set, thanks to you," he said with finality, as if trying to put a lid on the agitated sea, white caps beginning to pull and race toward Montauk. Then he was gone again, presumably to his studio.

Agatha flapped her wings, as if feeling the agitated air with them. Jed didn't remember that blizzard, probably. Perrin hated it when people didn't remember things. It was as if a piece of herself was lost all over again. Together, she and the bird watched the clouds and rain swallow up the day.

The door sounded. William.

"Hey, Mrs. T—blowing hard out there. Just getting something for Jack."

"You should duct tape Jack's windows," she cautioned, pointing to the sliding door she had already done, hatched now with big gray X's. Or get *him* to do it. You should probably go home."

"Yeah, I should."

"William, I have a special favor to ask. I'll pay you . . . can you take the crow?"

Jack was suddenly there again. "Hi, William. What are you doing?" His voice was tight.

"Just watching . . ."

Jack moved to turn on the lights.

"Don't. You can see better with the lights off," she said. "You should probably bring the radio in here."

"Sure," he said. "We also need a game plan, don't you think?"

Both William and Perrin looked at him quizzically.

"Sure, Mrs. T, I can take the bird," said William into the silence.

"Take her where? Where are you going?" Jack asked William.

"Got to be getting home to my mom."

"Oh, right—of course. What's to be done here, do you think?"

"Category four?" said William with a small degree of relish. "All you can do is watch."

Jack came up and stood by them, "Look at that windsock. Never saw it like that before."

Illuminated by the deck light, it was now straight out sideways, rippling finely in the wet wind. She didn't feel an urge to tell him it was all going to be okay. In part because she wasn't sure.

"If it's supposed to peak in the early morning hours . . ." Jack meandered, "wouldn't they call an evacuation if they thought it was going to be really bad?"

"They might, but you'd have to get out in front of it. Only one road," said William. "But you already know that."

They were transfixed. The usually clean horizon line was blurred as if by pencil, which Perrin had never seen before.

"Look at that . . ." said Jack. "My God."

"Pretty amazing," said Perrin, a chill crawling up her back as she remembered where she had stashed the extra lamps and kerosene. "Jack, William has to go."

The radio belched and screeched an alert tone, followed by the computerized voice: *Direct strike of potential catastrophic and life-threatening hurricane expected late tonight and early tomorrow morning. Rush protective measures to completion. A hurricane warning for the Suffolk County area . . . Squalls spreading over North Atlantic with inland conditions deteriorating . . .*

"Right. And we should too. Get the jump on it," Jack exclaimed.

"Where?"

"The city—"

"The city?"

"Yes," he said, his voice tight.

"Jack, I'm not leaving," said Perrin, leaning over the table to write out instructions for Agatha.

"What?"

"William! That's five hours. I'll mark you down," said Perrin, handing him the paper and fitting the cover over the cage.

"Okay, I spoke too soon," said Jack.

William lifted Agatha and her house smoothly from her corner spot.

"Don't forget the cat food! There's a bag in the basement," she called after William.

"I admit that this is looking a little scary," he added. "Not like before."

"I'm glad you see that. Did you duct tape the windows in the studio?"

"Perrin!" said Jack. Didn't you hear *rush protective measures to completion?* For us, that's *leaving.*"

"I can't leave my father."

"But what if the sea comes in?"

Feeling guilty about his real concern, she wangled, "Max's design—wasn't it supposed to be so great?"

"How would he know? They don't have hurricanes in Italy," said Jack, his teeth chattering though it was not cold.

"There are standards here; otherwise, we'd never have gotten insurance. I'm not going to leave my father. If it comes up on the beach, then I'll go to his house. If the field and road aren't flooded, I can just put on waders," she added.

"Oh Jesus!" wailed Jack. "We can *bring George.*"

"I already talked to him this morning; he's not budging. You know how he is," she added, enjoying that part a little.

"But how will we *know* what's happening?" said Jack. "We won't be able to see it—it's getting black out there!"

"You could just wade out and tell me what you find," she said, suppressing a smile.

"Perrin, this is serious! I could lose all my work!"

"Do you think he's going to leave his work to a flood?" Perrin asked, thinking of the sawhorses George had already made. He was probably setting them up now.

Jack worked visibly at calming himself, his eyes scanning the fast-coming night. "I don't really want to go to George's. Let's head for the city right now. We can bring him. I'll get a hotel for him if he wants to be alone."

Perrin bristled at the idea of her father being managed by Jack. "Of course, you don't want to go to George's. It's a dump! How do you think he feels about living there!?"

"This is hardly the moment—"

"It is to me."

He flicked the lights on and stared at her. "Are you *nuts?* Suppose the pilings collapse. Jed said that in '38 the water was all the way across the field."

"Nothing you can *do* about that," said Perrin, finding her inner fatalist in regard to the house, and especially to the mouse burrow underneath the pilings. How many lonely nights had she spent there, hiding? She wouldn't be at all sorry to see it go. The percale sheets, the thin carpet, the high little window that let in the noise of the surf. What a life.

Yet the last time she had seen Chris was in that very basement room. Her place of refuge and miserable self-solace, where, in Jack's absence, a sort of fantasy was free to come to her—that she had never met him, that she was with someone different, who desired her in an ordinary way, who appreciated her. A private man who found just her presence in bed with him to be as much as he needed or wanted. Who touched her lovingly and passionately. She had imagined that person through so many nights, the sea tumbling a few hundred yards away, that when Chris came in, his sweatshirt damp with salt spray and his dark blue eyes ablaze, she took his hand and led him down the steps without thinking about it, flicking the doorknob lock behind them. And then, perfectly, he said, *Perfect.*

"What is this new passive-aggressive thing you're doing? Complete bullshit," said Jack.

Perrin let that settle before she played her card. "If it hits really hard, we'll be okay for a few nights, maybe a week. Dad's got some sleeping bags in his garage. They should be clean enough."

"God*damn* it!" said Jack, grabbing a bag in the kitchen and dropping bottles of pills, vitamins, and protein powder into it.

Perrin felt a twinge of guilt for how easy it was—it looked as though he was really going—and yet she'd have to follow through now. No more stalling.

"We shouldn't have let William go," Jack said, hurrying away to his studio.

Together they worked, getting everything off the floor and selecting works for transport to the city. He separated out the one-of-a-kinds and models, and Perrin wrapped them in blankets for the back of the BMW. Jack loaded in all the legal papers, and Perrin did not protest. Two boxes went into the passenger seat, lashed together and judiciously secured with the seatbelt. They wrapped the small three rocket models in bubble packing, stashed them in the trunk, and packed the Trick Mirror series in the back. The rain slanting down in the floodlight, Jack rearranged things so he could see to the rear.

His pinkish face flecked with rain, he licked some from his upper lip. "*Waxing Space* has twenty," he said, referring to a gallery in Santa Fe, "and there's more in storage, so that's good . . ." He looked down at her as if that was all she cared about too. He puffed out his chest. "I'll get a truck with all-wheel drive in the event that this happens again."

He kissed her cheek, while a gust of wind behind her felt like a giant hand. She wondered how she would get through the coming night despite the opportunity that had come along with it. In the past, given a similar predicament, she would have found herself hoping that Jack would realize he was actively deserting her. But her feelings were distant now, knocked down in size. Feeling deserted implied that one expected not to be, that there was a bond that had been broken. Here the sensation was almost non-existent, like fingers numbed with cold.

"Well, if the electricity goes out, you'll still have the landline," he said. Perrin cut a glance down the dune to see if Glasgow's lights were still on. They were.

By the time he drove off, the sky was dark gray and the sun was gone. Perrin would never forget the *thwunk* of the BMW's door, the wind pushing at her back, and his taillights receding in the driving rain. In some ways, Jack was cut from the same cloth as George. In her mind's eye, she could see George struggling with the sawhorses in the basement, balancing his paintings on them, schlepping the more delicate sculptures up to his kitchen counters, barely giving a thought to her as the storm rolled in on the old dune they called home.

* * *

Everyone had gone, and the house, but for the blowing outside, was silent. It was only eight o'clock. From the deck, she saw that the glow from the city, a hundred miles down the coast, had been mostly extinguished. Did Glasgow know what it was like to be plunged into darkness in the country? It was a lot blacker than an urban area. Maybe he was from a place with no electricity at all, and it would be no big deal to him. But it was a sure bet that the lights would go out, she thought. That would be her opening line, her reason for neighborly concern. As she had promised, she sent a text to Chris, notifying him that she was going to try to do this thing.

On her way to the storage closet, she looked into the little room with the high window. How odd that this Brit who wasn't even much of a swimmer made her feel newly a part of her own life. In the time they spent together, in the things he had unwittingly recalled for her—namely that she was free and had always been. It was as if a trap door had swung open to a brilliant sea—the same sea that she had woken up to every day of her life and yet had never seen properly. She kept her mind on that—in fact, she could think of nothing else—while pushing down the terror that she felt. With white and shaking fingers, she reached for the closet door where the lamps and kerosene were.

She could almost make out the white edge of the water, boiling vigorously, not yet licking the foot of the dune. Too early, she thought. Still a ways off. Might never, and yet, *might.* It wasn't so much that the shoreline came up as that the waves pushed deeper and deeper in before retracting. A jagged line, a slow advance, and then without warning pools of water behind the dune, in the fields, reaching into the interior of the land. An incredulous but silent earth under the weight of water. In '95, they couldn't get back in for a week. And what would she do if it happened again—wade to her father's? He'd be there with a jug of Gallo and a pack of American Spirits, wiling away the hours, dragging work up to the roof if he had to, endangering himself. She envisioned the two of them huddled together on the shingles, the outer fifth of the entire island underwater as it was then.

Extra matches in her pocket, a plastic bag to protect them from the wet. The lamps and the bottle of kerosene jammed under her arm. Now *she* was the wise local. In the inky dark, she knew the hills and dips of the dunes with her feet. She sang a little, high and faint in the wind, the beach grasses scraping her ankles.

As she came around to the front of Glasgow's, the muffled sound of blaring rock and roll registered right through the wall. After several heart-pounding tries at the doorbell, she decided to knock loudly. Glasgow's big wooden door swung open, the music spilling forth from the living room. His small eyes were narrowly spaced, his mouth ugly and plump, a few days' growth of beard surrounding it. He looked very surprised to see her. Of course, he would be. It occurred to her that though every other characteristic separated them, he was about thirty-five, her age. The band was Night Ranger, popular in her school days.

"Hey, you're married to the guy with the big studio . . ." he said, taking the bottle of fuel from under her arm without thanks, raking her top to toe with his eyes.

She did not affirm it. Next, he would want to know where Jack was. And she certainly couldn't answer that. It would sound bizarre to foreign ears, even his: *I have been deserted in a hurricane by my husband.* In the room, the guitars were loud. What looked to be a security guard sat very still in one of the chairs around a coffee table. Upon it a bag of white powder, a large mirror, and, judging from Glasgow's intensity, lines of what must be cocaine.

"Haven't heard that one in a long time," she said, holding up the two lamps, wondering at her own compulsion to provide reasons and be nice. He was a killer. She was supposed to be playing *him*. It occurred to her that a blasé attitude was called for, like the models she had seen at his party and decorating the beach in front of his house.

Motorin'
What's . . . your . . . price for flight
In finding Mr. Right
You'll be alright tonight . . . blared the vocals.

"Where is he?" Glasgow asked, meaning, of course, Jack.

Perrin ignored him and walked to the center of the room alone. Glasgow remained at a distance, as if he didn't want to spook her. The air was supercharged with the storm and the music. Finally, she plunked the lamps down on the dining table.

Motorin,'
What's . . . your . . . price . . .

So loud. *LOUD.* The ceilings were lower than she remembered, or maybe it was because the windows were so black, filigreed with water running up and sideways in strange star patterns. She could almost see the glass vibrating. Somewhere outside, an object was loose but tethered, making a banging sound. She couldn't see what it was. Hugging her sweatshirt close, she tried to shut it out and look at the scene for what it was—a house on the sea in a storm.

"You look like you need a drink," said Glasgow, still at a distance.

"Do you have any duct tape?" she asked.

* * *

Do you have any duct tape? She's stalling, thought Kit, she's looking for an angle. He shook out his leg and bit off half of an Oxy, which he swallowed without water. Someone, probably the housekeeper, had moved the briefcase to a spot next to the door, perhaps waiting for him to finally pick it up, and naturally he hadn't. His view was now a straight shot through the living room, showing almost all the dining table along the windows. He could now see only half of the cluster of oversized furniture and the coffee table, which was frustrating since that seemed to be the locus of the house. Over the last twenty minutes, Glasgow and Perrin crossed the room like people on a train platform. The sound was terrible and made worse by his inferior hearing. After some minutes, they slipped from the eye of the briefcase, and their voices receded—it was impossible to determine in which direction. All that was left was the blasting stereo coming across his headset. In Chaz's spare bedroom, he cursed and banged the volume button on his computer.

The security guard, who he knew was called Dave, appeared and bent down to the coffee table with a curious duck-like movement, his head thrown back. Okay, cocaine. She was gone, and that damned album was still on. What a stupid, stupid song. Kit hated everything about Glasgow—his bombs, his crappy eighties music, his Fila sweatshirts, his height, his gold jewelry, his view that he didn't deserve, and especially that he was right now out of range, probably trying to get his hairy hands on Perrin. The idea of it was so enraging that he thought the top of his head might blow off. Upon the discovery of Glasgow's role in the Taj op bombing, they should have pulled him from here immediately. On principle.

But who else could have seen it through? Who else would have gone to such lengths to try and bag the bastard? And how was it that they had *just* let him know as the summer was coming to a close? With a shock, it occurred to Kit that they had known about Glasgow when they sent him here. Of course, they did. There was the big mystery solved. They *knew* about it and they had delayed telling him until now. They were as bad as the crooks they were supposed to be chasing.

When Dave stood up, Kit saw the gun he had shoved in his waistband. Martin had said that Dave had no alliances except to Glasgow, and perhaps not even really to him. Dave was strictly a for-hire type. That *was* helpful because if Dave were not a disinterested party, he might step in and try to save Perrin, putting the whole thing in jeopardy. Kit loathed himself for thinking this way. He felt his mouth going dry as the seconds ticked by and the horror of them alone together took root in his mind. Not just a concept anymore, but a reality.

His leg throbbed. She was not a pro. *She was not a pro!* The suspense was awful, yet if he interfered, he'd ruin whatever chance there was. He absently shook another pill from a foil pack and swallowed it whole. He tried to face the moment head on, what he had put into play. Basement. Mermaid girl. Lover. Paintings. And last but not least, Vengeance. An avenging SIS would have deconstructed the housekeeper's story, Leonie Berkhof's story, and the inability of the Dutch police to get anything out of her sons. They would have made a calculation with the resources they had, which, along with the FBI's, were considerable. Yet they were going on with it. And they knew that he now knew about Glasgow, the bastards. It was full steam ahead.

The door opened behind him. Chaz apologized. "Sorry. Didn't know you were here. I was . . . Hey—isn't that Glasgow's place?"

"Can I borrow your car? Want to get a pack of smokes."

"In this weather?"

"Yes. Desperate."

"You better hurry up before the road washes out."

Chaz tilted his head to get a better view of the computer. "What's that you're doing?"

"He sent me some video. Wants me to find a sculpture for the deck, and maybe a few items for the living room. Pretty bare, isn't it?"

"That goon has no taste. Couldn't even get him to buy a Triplett. Keys are on the sideboard. Don't drown my car."

* * *

Kit inched down the dirt road behind the dune, the rain spiking his high beams. Soon, he thought, the road would turn to mud, so he brought the car to a halt. A spotlight from under Perrin's house showed her Land Rover, Jack's space empty, and the corridor to that strange little room she liked. A bit of an odd arrangement, but when Chaz was here, where else could they have gone? At least the room had a lock. The others didn't. He knew because he had been all through the house while she was sleeping, avoiding the bedroom where Jack was, of course. How she ended up with someone like him was a mystery, but a lot of great women were with men that didn't deserve them. Look at Susannah, who had endured his interest and said yes. He knew she regretted it, and what was worse, she would never own up to it.

He could barely make out the top floors of her house, lost as they were to the black raging night. Christ, oh Christ. *Christ.* He wasn't supposed to think of Perrin's motivations about anything, but especially this.

It was slow going, the wind pushing him steadily back, while his feet sunk deep into the soggy dune. He climbed up, the rain pummeling his skin, the wind plastering his shirt to his front. The ocean sounded much closer than before—or was that just the nighttime? Or was it the extra pill he had stupidly taken? It was an auditory illusion, she had said the other night. He experienced it firsthand in that room, the rolling surf sounding close enough to wash the house away. He almost wished it would have, with them in it.

Now poor Perrin was a Lottie, and it was his fault. His heart sank. Yesterday, Martin had gone over it again, adding, *There are all kinds of ways to protect you and her. Just you hold the line. Just don't lose your head. You have us all behind you.*

But in truth, there was no help nearby, and he didn't even have a gun. The trail had fallen off in chunks in places; he had to be vigilant to keep his footing. Lights were still on at Glasgow's, as well as twinkling across the potato fields. A bit of luck that they still had power; Chaz had said it would go out soon. If only these favorable strokes would come together and return her to the sane, living world this very night. Let her not be doomed, and he would give just about anything. Anything. As he got closer, he saw the sea throw a casual tongue of water under the deck, lick the pilings, and withdraw. He stopped, not believing what he had just seen, till yet another sinuous wave bowled in, dispersing against the foundation. Very likely they had no idea. From what he had been able to discern, no one had been outside for hours.

He abruptly gained a wooden walkway, the rain stinging his face. From there, he could see a set of stairs that rose along the east side of the place, while from somewhere came a curious, rhythmic banging. He was able to clamber onto the walkway and make his way to the deck. Four large picture windows looked out onto the night. They had big black X's taped on them—the duct tape? He was relieved to see Glasgow and Perrin on the sofa, and Dave rock solid in the armchair. A pile of chairs lashed together in the middle of the deck would make a good cover. He darted across, first wedging himself behind the enormous stainless-steel barbeque, and then slinking along the railing to the chairs. From this vantage point, he could just see through the latticework to the living room. It was like watching a movie with no sound.

Glasgow sat down, plunking the duct tape on the table with the coke. He was talking fast now, firing words at her in his thick accent that she didn't completely understand. He had shown her the house, and she was relieved to be back in the living room where the other guy was, to whom she had not been introduced. With the flourish of a sommelier, Glasgow fished a marble mortar and pestle from a side table and added it to the paraphernalia on the mirror:

an American Express Gold Card, two razors, a few rolled-up bills, and a sparkling pile of white, rocky powder. Next to the mirror, a gun.

Seeming to read her mind, Glasgow said, “Don’t worry. He just cleans it. It relaxes him.”

With the credit card, he removed the rocks to the smooth interior of the mortar. Its white and gray surface made Perrin think of that mottled sun of a few hours ago, now swallowed up in the night. Looking at the top of Glasgow’s shiny head and the immobile Dave, she thought about what a very long shot she had gotten herself involved in.

Fueled by the coke, they went from cool acquaintances to light chatter. They knew some of the same clubs from the glory days in the city—Area, Danceteria, Studio 54, the Red Parrot, Limelight, Pyramid. Glasgow explained that he had been at NYU, to the film school. He saw the B-52’s when they were nobodies. His family had wanted him to pick up English and go straight, so they indulged the film school idea. He never graduated. He shrugged and handed her a rolled-up bill. With speed, Perrin left her reasoning, rational self somewhere back in time, not very far back, but a clean break nonetheless. A few hours? An hour? A few minutes? *Wasn’t that the point,* Glasgow’s smirk seemed to say. Without breaking eye contact, he pushed the mirror toward her while saying to Dave, “Get the champagne, and make sure it’s cold.” They laughed together, feeling the buzz of the storm. This happened so fast that somewhere in the back of her mind Perrin began to think there was some kind of a chance that she would be able to sway him. After all, he was high too. There seemed to be some sort of joke in the air—a riddle. What was the riddle? She was the riddle.

“Okay, really—what are you doing here, little Miss . . .” Glasgow asked with the sort of bemused cheer that didn’t require an answer, and she did not feel obligated to provide one. He was not very tall, but burly and strong with a hint of gut above the line of his designer sweatpants. When he reached for his flute, a tattoo of small numbers and letters peeked from his shirtsleeve. He was unshaven and sweaty, which was not helped by the expensive cologne he must have splashed on when he went to the bathroom. His narrowly set eyes, black as the sea now, drilled into her.

The scene was not one that she was unfamiliar with—words were rolling off her tongue so fast she wasn't certain what she had said, like her party days in the city when she still had Solo the cat, when people sat around bowls and mirrors of white sparkling powder and consumed each other passionately in wide-eyed conversations that might as well have been conducted silently, unclothed, and in bed so confessional were they—listening deeply and carefully and totally to the string of associations careening through the mind of another—*Remember that fuzzy sun? Doesn't this color look exactly like it? Wow! I loved that!*

She drained half of her champagne flute—the champagne warm because Glasgow hadn't had another bottle chilled, he explained with no apology whatsoever. He had no social niceties, and he wouldn't have had them on the sunniest day of the year. He was a completely uncensored person. Willfully ignoring his pointy stare, she tried to think of him as interesting, like the id that George claimed was lurking in most of his work—that thing that he would never tame or quell for the sake of his art. Yet it was a dangerous thing to be *all* id, or even be near someone who was. Perrin had never before encountered anyone like Glasgow at close range. An hour passed, while in her confused mind it became clear that her usual manipulations and charms were mostly useless. He had no language for them.

The lights went out, and the entire house went black. Expected, yes, but no less terrifying for that. For a minute, they fumbled around, until Glasgow got a candelabra from the breakfront, which she lit, her hands shaking again, with matches from her pocket. With that, she was able to fill the red lamps with kerosene, losing just a few drops and wiping them up with the sleeve of her sweatshirt. A yellow glow jostled the walls, while Glasgow watched with the air of someone accustomed to people doing things for him.

"You are kind of like local royalty, aren't you?" Glasgow asked, jamming another bottle of Dom Perignon into a bucket of ice Dave had fetched.

"No . . . uh . . . no!"

He waved her away. "You are. That big guy Chaz, he was trying to sell me your husband's work. But I don't like it. Don't like it, no."

She noticed the tattoos again, that they were blurry and crudely done. It occurred to her that his tattoos had been done in prison—some kind of gang thing.

"If I thought you were coming, I would have shaved," he said. He rubbed his chin, signaling to Dave that he should leave with an awful flicking motion of his index finger and thumb, as if removing an ant from a table.

Perrin fought her revulsion and thought of Chris, the mission—*their* mission now—pursuing a jumble of paintings, that the connection of any single one to Glasgow would be able to bring down his entire operation. Any single one. And for those English children that lost their mother, and afterwards that terrible sting—the painting that captured her likeness seized by fiends, destroyed. Did they know? A brutal, distant pain that was far away across the sea and suffered by someone else, yet deep inside herself, she felt it. Glasgow wound his hand into her hair. She took it in, every bit of it, including him, felt her body soften under the weight, somehow knowing those kids, knowing how it would all turn out. The loss would be absorbed and assimilated into time and themselves day by day and week by week and on into the future, the mother they might have had and the people they might have been trailing them like ghosts and never leaving. *When life gives you lemons* and all of that, thought Perrin, the same way she had had to willfully re-create herself against the odds, and was doing it still, having had to grow up too fast because her mother was useless and her father was mostly inaccessible. The good part was the drive you had from working that survival muscle all the time, just to keep an ordinary day from falling apart. It could make you resilient. *When life gives you lemons, make lemonade or die,* she reflected with a sinking feeling, coming down from the last line of coke, knowing what was coming.

Glasgow rubbed her neck with surprising sensuality, while she couldn't bear to think of him as him and tried to fantasize that he was some faceless man she had never met but must endure, say an actor with a different face and a different past, she an actress playing a role. And the others that Chris had told her about, the Picasso, the two Monets. Personal, lovingly done work that could never be replicated. Look—any one of these, he had said. *Any one . . . You can do it . . . This is your power . . . Don't shrink away . . .* I won't, I promise, I will do this thing . . . If at all possible, I will . . . you see? I'm still here.

Glasgow pulled her sweatshirt and then her shirt over her head while a winged, coke-propelled vision brought her back to that haunting marble sun again and went back further, to Chris's slumbering back, rising and falling in that pokey little room, so deliciously *there,* while she cracked the door of the corridor to see Jack's BMW parked in its space and realized that he had come in without trying to find her, thank God, remembering her relief at that freedom.

She sank back into the sofa. Well, she was free and clear here too. Glasgow pulled her close, slipping his hand to the small of her back and under her leggings. Over his shoulder, she saw the keypad to the left of the doorway, 36-24-36. Freedoms small and large came along unexpectedly from time to time and certainly odder than one could have foreseen, but still one had to grab them or live with regrets. What should stop her now? This was the role she was born to play. The bunker. The pilfered treasure. And she the Queen, *royalty* if he said so, risking it all for the kingdom.

She pulled herself up. "This used to be an old train depot that was moved here. My father rented it and worked here for years."

"I met your father . . . a real Gregory Peck-type guy."

"Have you seen his work?"

"No."

His eyes traveled down to her bra.

"Maybe that's why there's an "art vibration" here," she continued, deliberately keeping her voice soft, remembering the effect that Chris's voice had on her. "I heard some say that at your party," she lied. Keep him talking.

"Great works," she continued, "my father's works, were done on this very spot. Didn't I tell you? I'm sorry you've never seen them. That sort of thing leaves an impression, an *imprint*," she reached for the word. "It leaves a *sign*."

He gestured to the grand surroundings as if they had all the atmosphere needed.

The role of local sage, even a half-dressed one, was falling flat. Through her sped-up thoughts, she remembered what Chris said. You can get him on the guilt. Some of these thugs, after they make a pile, start to evolve—believe it or not. *Some.* He's had a life of such excess . . . it can ring hollow after a point. They have children and send them to good schools, they want to be respected and taken seriously. They make donations like he's done around here. Glasgow's a pretty crude item, but you'll find his soft spot, what he wants to *be.* What is his *future.* He has a museum in Brasilia—that should tell you something.

"Do you have kids?" Perrin ventured.

"Yes, one," he answered, more prickly now.

She teetered on whether to ask him if he was married. It would be rude to assume he wasn't.

"Are you married?"

"No. The bitch got me on child support. A DNA test."

"Oh! Well . . ." Where could she go from here? Amid the pugnaciousness was a surprisingly attuned character. She tried to take the attitude that their situation was a tantalizing puzzle that could be solved in more ways than the obvious one. "I just thought, we're about the same age—most people have done it at least once by now! Got married, I mean—"

"I was married a long time ago. Didn't work out." A strange contraction of muscles on his pockmarked face, as if he were not used to sorrow. He reached for his drink.

She sat down and asked, "Is it true you have a museum?"

"Yes—true."

"That is such a noble thing. You must have a real feel for art."

"They tell me that. They lie," he said, with a change of aspect.

"Why do you do it?"

"Good way to store cash," said Glasgow, looking away. "I just buy the things I'm told. I don't have a preference."

"I find that hard to believe."

"Well, I don't like . . . what do you call it . . . this concept art."

"What kind is that?"

"The kind that has to have a story. I like when you look at it and you know what it is. Or it does something, reminds you . . . of something."

"Isn't that funny, I agree! We aren't so very different, you and I."

"So, you don't like your own husband's work?"

"No! Not really!"

She saw, through the glass top of the coffee table, *Janson's History of Art*. She pulled it onto her knees. "We used to have this before we moved out of the old place. Hey! Maybe this is the same copy. I don't know what they did with it."

Glasgow looked at her strangely, failing to believe her.

"What are you doing, little Miss? I don't want to talk anymore."

Perrin went full-steam, having nothing to lose. "I think you are more than you say. I think you have fine sensibilities," she announced, hopping up, holding her shirt to her front. "I'm a very visual person, and I . . . I . . . feel that something is still here. And that you . . . you . . . were the right person to have this spot."

Glasgow leaned forward with a look of desperation. "What do you want? Do you want me to *buy* some paintings?"

"I just want you to know how special this is, and *you* are. There's a reason you and I are together here in this place, isn't there? I can feel it."

CHAPTER 16
"MIKE"

Sagaponack
September 17th, 2012
76 days after the heist

Behind George's house, saffron skies had faded, and the color over the fields was faint as if water-washed. The name "Mike" did little to describe the calamity that had just passed. A hurricane was like a woman, a screaming banshee of a woman. Men didn't get angry in the same way. Men lashed out pointedly, forcefully, a means to a specific end. The emotion was contained in the action. But a hurricane was a fury from the heavens, a wrathful, passionate Valkyrie. She moaned and shrieked for days, throttled trees and felled them, carved away beaches and flooded crops. She lifted away roofs, made powerlines dance, killed all manner of life. Her rage was widespread and indiscriminate and persisted until she exhausted herself. Mike was a guy that dropped by, stayed for maybe ten minutes, and said little. Even if he wanted to shoot you, he would get the job done and leave.

Putting his nose to the wind, George noticed a sharpening, as if the air had contracted again after its wild expansion. Most of the summer crowd had left early, and those that had stayed were probably cleaning up the mess the best they could right now. This was usually the time he felt the exhilaration of being new here so many years ago. Beaches empty, or with just a scattering of folks reading and sunning, and no lines at the stores. But this year would be different. To begin with, half the beach had probably been chewed away. And there were too many disturbing questions floating around.

Like a half-drowned cat, Perrin had shown up at his door, alone, in the very early morning when the storm was still going. All she had with her was a small flashlight turned off. His first question—*Where was Jack?*—was met with facts only—*In the city.* He thought this deserved more of an explanation, but she pushed right past him. She hadn't wanted him to light his lamps—no explanation. He had a small candle in his hand, and even in that light he could see that the left side of her face was red and purple and her left eye was swollen. She went directly to the bathroom, then asked him for cleaning things and another flashlight. She had stayed in there for an hour, banging around, before crawling off to the spare room. In the morning, she was so icily silent he didn't dare ask what had happened. She had grabbed her phone and hid out on the side porch for hours, talking quietly, wrapped in an old wool blanket.

Just like Iris, she didn't seem to want to go back inside. So he had gotten Iris's old chaise from the shed and set her up in the garden, with the blanket and her coffee. Under the beech tree, it was relatively dry.

He had spent the time cleaning up and willing the flooded bottom-third of his lawn to drain. The power was out, so he took advantage of the post-hurricane light, beginning with a big block of clay that he had ordered and had been neglecting. It was a bit dry, so he put it in a garbage bag with about a cup of water and rolled it on the grass to wet it evenly. In about an hour, he'd be good to go. Working with a low-tech medium required only tools and daylight—that was the great thing about it. And it would help take his mind off all of this madness.

In the afternoon, still waiting for her, he took his bike out for a look around. The waters had receded, leaving swamps here and there across the fields. The sky had keyed up to an intense blue. Jed came by in his truck, warily asking about Perrin and Jack. George assured him that they were okay. Then Jed told him about the house. The pilings "just went," he said, and that was it. The access road was all mud, but if they wanted, they could go along what was left of the beach to see it. Jack's studio had survived, though it was in sorry shape. Its foundation had been completely flooded and had sunk on one side, causing the entire structure to lean. The Napoleon, that bizarre glass cube on the dune, was no more.

The news had upset him. A little more perhaps because some of his early work was there, and that was the site of his first years here. And the state that she was in—what had *happened? God.* While arranging some sandwich things and fruit for her on the counter, he had the same black thought he'd always had, that everything would be reclaimed by the sea in the end—the shack, Iris, himself, all the work, and eventually, even his daughter. The end of things would come in dribs and drabs, like this. Sections of the entire fading picture seemed more dramatic close up, but in reality they weren't. The ocean had taught him that. They just had to be looked at another way; they had to be endured. It occurred to him that this kind of clarity was depressing, and also the burden of the old.

He remained silent around Perrin, making the extra coffee each morning, setting out the yogurt and fruit that she liked for breakfast. After a few days of this, he thought it was odd that she wasn't curious and hadn't mentioned anything about returning to what had been her home. Instead, she was always on her phone, completely absorbed, as if conducting some sort of important business. If the phone wasn't charging on the kitchen counter, it was plastered to her ear. Maybe Jack had already told her about the house? He hoped very much that he had.

But then Gia called on the home phone, asking about Perrin and Jack.

"They're fine," he said. "All A-OK."

"Good! There's a lot of buzz at the bar. Because of . . . the house, and because no one has seen them."

"Yes, we heard about it. We're going out there soon." As soon as he could rally Perrin, he thought.

"I guess they haven't gotten in touch yet?" asked Gia.

"Who?"

"The police—"

"What?"

"About the Russian. A lot of the people who were at that party are getting visits from the police."

"Why? What happened?"

"He's dead. Found dead in his pool."

A blade of fear fell through him. George immediately located Perrin outside and saw that she was dozing in the chaise with headphones on.

"George?" asked Gia.

He worked to maintain his composure. "What? When did they find him?"

"They did a routine search of all the houses up and down the dune."

"Why'd they do that?"

"Don't know . . ."

A long silence while he cast about for an obvious question. "How do you know all of this?"

"A lot of people know. I got some extra detail from that British guy, Christopher. The other night at the bar . . . He and Chaz were among the first they questioned. It was his idea to call you—"

"She's okay," George said, watching Perrin pull the blanket a little tighter around her shoulders. "They're fine—"

"So sorry to give you the bad news. I'd love to hear from Perrin. Tell her to call me."

How was that possible, George wondered while hanging up the phone. The Russian, drowned in his pool! Dead!

* * *

Once more, Perrin dialed the number she had for Chris. A pause, and that weird, overseas double ring. Then the message again. *We're sorry, but the number you have dialed has been disconnected.*

No no no, said an inner voice, though she hadn't really believed the message would change. Listening to it repeatedly was a way of drilling down into the facts and facing them. *We're sorry . . . the number . . . disconnected . . . disconnected . . . You have dialed . . . sorry . . . We're . . . You have dialed . . . the number . . . but . . . has been disconnected . . . sorry . . .*

She thought of that night, only three nights ago, when Chris showed up at Glasgow's, cut her free, and ordered her to get out. Since then, he'd been unreachable, even though she had heard from Gia that he was around. He didn't answer his phone, and then this recording. She felt utterly deserted, especially after hearing about the death. Everyone knew about it, and Chris was off the map when she needed him most.

Her phone dinged with a text from Jack about the insurance. *Yes,* she answered, to whatever it was he had asked her.

The phone rang; Chaz's number came up. He was sorry about the house. Was she okay? She was fine—just recovering, she said, just trying to absorb all the news. Had she seen it? No, not yet, but she was going soon. George was working up to it. They were going to go together.

Her call waiting came up, a number she didn't recognize.

"Chaz, I've got to go." She clicked over.

"It's me," said the voice she knew so well. "Are you alone?"

"Yes. Where are you?"

"At JFK on a public phone. Only way now."

"God . . . what happened, Chris?"

"I had to leave. No point in me hanging around for the townsfolk to start stitching together theories, right?"

"But he's *dead.* Why didn't you tell me?"

"Hardly had an opportunity. Best to have you surprised anyway, heartless as that might sound."

"It does sound heartless."

"You're at George's—he's taking care of you?"

"Yes, surprisingly well given that I'm lying to him, and he knows it."

"And it has to stay that way, Perrin. It will blow over—just wait a little."

"I've just kind of checked out for a little bit. You are going to have to tell me what happened."

"Can't discuss it." He sounded gruff.

"My prints are all over that house! How are they not going to find out?"

"Because he drowned. Much simpler."

"It *looks* like he drowned—that's what they are saying. How could that possibly have happened?"

"It's better that you don't know."

"So *you* know."

"I don't want you to worry. We've had a fair amount of luck."

She was silent. Just as he had coached her to do, he wasn't telling her anything.

"Not only that. You've done a valuable, brave thing. You can be proud of it for the rest of your life. Perrin?"

"Yeah, yeah. Okay." She did not care for his praise. He was not telling her. *Him.* When so much had happened.

She kept trying for any crumb she could get. For example, the body. Where was it? Would it be transported back to Russia? Yes. They'll do their own autopsy? Probably—but there was nothing to find. Then she asked him if he was used to dealing with fools.

"Let go of all of that. Let go of who you think you are and what you think it is. Keep it very simple in your mind, very black and white. How's your face?"

"Healing."

"What are you saying about it?" Gone were the honeyed cadences of before.

"Haven't had to say anything about it yet."

"You walked into a door at your house, anxious to get everything and get out."

"Okay. Where are you going?" she asked, already knowing the answer.

"England." There was a pause. "I'm sorry for it all, all of it. I truly am."

She wasn't going to change him. No matter what had happened between them, he didn't want to be reminded—not now. This—what he wanted to talk about—was a conversation about facts.

"I did it for you," she said, regretting it as soon as the words were out.

"It's impossible," he replied, a dreadful quiet to his voice.

"Just don't forget what I'm telling you right now. There's no skimming by it, Chris. Whatever happens, that's the truth of it."

His voice softened again. "Those are more intangible things . . . fleeting things."

"Are they?" she asked, tears welling in her eyes, wondering what sort of result she was after. It was surely not this conversation.

"We had perfect timing. The lights went out at one-thirty, about an hour before I got there. That was a very good, lucky break."

He continued politely, laying out all the information. The timing was perfect, said he, because no one would be able to claim to have seen her on her way to her father's, or anywhere else for that matter. On a dark night, one could be anywhere one claimed to be.

"Did any cars go by when you were on that beach road?" he asked.

"No, there were none," she said, digesting the fact that he was going back to London. Probably for the rest of his life.

"I thought there wouldn't have been. That's good, that's very good. I want you to say you left earlier, say, nine o'clock. They've got nothing—remember what I'm telling you. *Nothing*. It's the best we could have hoped for. That hurricane was a gift, and you took the opportunity. *You, Perrin.* You did it."

Then she really knew that he was leaving.

"Listen. They are going to question you. They'll want to seem competent. You have the same story always. Straight and true. You are not obligated to elaborate—"

"Chris, I can't hear you."

"The gate is closing . . ." There was a pause. "My name is Kit, by the way. Kit Hobbs."

Kit, she thought as her phone went silent. *Kit Hobbs.* She wondered if she'd ever see him again.

* * *

The police did call her into the station. She borrowed George's van and was relieved when he handed her the keys with no questions. For now, his hands-off parenting style was welcome. She had nothing from her house, not even a small bag, so she bought concealer and makeup at the drugstore and applied it in the van's rearview mirror.

One of the cops, Bob Wilken, she had been in school with. They had gone out in fifth grade. The other, Nick someone, she didn't know. With Bob, she could see that earlier context written on his face, as well as a small edge of alarm at the marks on her face. Her face that he knew well from make-out sessions under the bleachers at the park. Blood pounded at her temples as she tried to remember what Chris, now Kit, had said. *Keep it simple—black and white* . . . But she didn't really feel simple; she felt soiled and dirty and ready to lie. A person had died there on the dune that night, in the same house where she was, and she was at least partly responsible for it.

A woman came in to take her fingerprints; it seemed to take a very long time. The atmosphere thickened around her as a surprisingly grown-up-looking Bob studied the file. She cast about for her new role with him—suspect? Person of interest? Old friend? Bob, riffling through his papers authoritatively, was clearly trying to be gentle. He asked if she could help with a few items.

"Yes, I'd be happy to," she said, adding that she'd have to get back to George soon because he needed his van.

"Right. I get it. Well, across the fields at the Aldrichs', Jed was filling up the generator that night. This was late. I haven't got a time. Only approximate, but late. Not that long before the lights went down. You see?"

"What night?"

"The night of the hurricane, and the death."

"Of course," she said, admonishing herself visibly with a flutter of her hands.

"He said your house lights were on, and Kusnetsov's were too. No other lights were on."

"Okay."

"He seemed to think there was a kind of connection there."

"Jed? Between whom?" asked Perrin, eyeing the smudge marks on her fingertips from the ink. Had Chris wiped the house down? Suppose he missed a spot?

"Between your two houses."

"I don't know why he thought that," said Perrin.

"Did you know Mr. Kusnetsov?"

"Hardly," Perrin scoffed, with a little local-to-local disdain. In Sagaponack, characters like Kusnetsov were considered to be a scourge on the very ground.

"A lot of people had gone back to the city. But a few didn't, I guess. Jack did!"

Bob gave a bit of a start at that, as she knew he would. The code of the country, his wide-open, patient eyes seemed to say, would never have allowed that kind of thing—and furthermore, he didn't feel sorry for her because she had gone for the guy.

Following a logical thread, his attention then moved to her face.

"Yes—it's the silliest thing. I walked into an open door. The edge." She shrugged and sighed, hoping to dredge up a little sympathy in him. "I was in a hurry."

A shadow of a smile crossed his face. "Totally understand."

They went on for another ten minutes, talking about the destruction of her house, Bob pointedly not asking the question she'd expected and for which she had prepared. Sweating a little in the close room, she wondered if she should offer it up or whether that would look suspicious. She averted her eyes, digging the leftover ink from under one nail into a little ball. Why didn't he ask? After all, she couldn't have spent the night at her house.

"I've got to get the van back. Is there anything else?"

"They've opened the road," he volunteered. "Think you'll be able to salvage anything?"

"I don't know. I haven't seen it."

His mouth hung open perplexedly. "Not even from the beach side?"

"No. It's kind of upsetting, you know."

"Sure, sure it is. So where did you go that night?"

"I went to my father's," said Perrin, with a dash of irritation.

"Right, okay. Though we might want to talk again. Oh—what time did you say that was?"

Finally. "About nine. Can't say for sure. Things were a little dramatic at that point."

* * *

George cleared away the coffee beans and grinder and then set out a pitcher of milk instead of pouring from the carton the way he usually did.

"Good morning," she said, sliding the pot from the burner. "You?"

"Thanks, already had," he said, motioning with his mug.

With a rectangle of sun warming his floor, he was surprised at the rush of hope those two small words, *Good morning,* gave him. Yes, yes, it might be good—or at least better than before. Her face looked better; those red welts had calmed down.

"You can still feel it," she said.

"What?"

"The storm, like a mushroom-y smell."

"Yes, and fresh water mixed with salt."

"A kind of dankness."

"From the fields, and all of these basements," he added.

"How's your basement?" she asked.

"Flooded," he said.

"Oh, Dad . . ."

He surveyed the garden. "Glad I got the work upstairs. Glad I made the sawhorses. Though I didn't end up needing to use them all." He paused, turning to her. "It's all pretty incredible, isn't it?"

"Yes," she said, her voice clipped. Obviously, she didn't want to go into a lot of detail.

"Let's go out to the dune," George said, digging his keys from his pocket.

The road was still a mess, so they parked at the lot, deciding to approach on the beach side. The sand was cut away by half, ending in shallow cliffs that dropped to the water. Together, they walked on the strip the ocean hadn't dispensed with, murmuring oaths to each other. George counted seven houses to his old place, noting that the neighbors had gotten through intact, if a little bare-looking and emptier than before. A slight curve brought the Napoleon into view. Or what had been the Napoleon. It had had the misfortune of being built closer to the water and had also been taller, and so it lacked the center of gravity that the others had. "Mike" had dashed the house to its knees, the pilings collapsed, and the entire front edge sunk deep into the sand. The upper deck had broken off and was twenty feet away, half-buried from the last few tides. The cellar rooms were crushed, as was her Land Rover underneath. Jack's space was, of course, empty. What a bastard. It had been upsetting to see her in such a state—her hair stuck to her neck in vines, her eye bruised and bloody. It must have been three a.m. at least. Of course, he had asked her if Jack had hurt her and was deeply relieved to hear he had not. He was too old to take on Jack. He had never been an *I'll deck anyone that hurts my girl* sort of dad anyway.

Now that they were finally here, George was awestruck. The studio was leaning precariously, sand drifts piled up to its lowermost windows. The house where the shack used to be had come to rest at an extremely odd angle. An 8x10 of Jack's that had been over the fireplace was doubled up against the living room window. Iris's pots in the front had been knocked over by the storm surge, purged of soil and Perrin's flowers. They peered in, George venturing a step closer, recognizing the white sofa, rugs, fire irons, and Iris's pottery piled up in the windows and in the corners of those odd transparent walls. In the very back, he could see a few of his early works flat on the floor and wondered at how the impact of the collapse had popped them off the wall. A few of the Peruvian things he and Iris had collected were still whole; he wished he could get at those too. He pushed past the yellow tape.

Perrin grabbed his sleeve. "Dad, it's dangerous."

She didn't seem all that bothered. *He* was the one shaken up. She seemed more leaden than hurt or even surprised, but of course, she was out here when this happened, or was beginning to happen. Doing what? He didn't know. Together, they dug the remaining earth out of the pots so they could move them to the driveway side to be picked up. A quarter-mile down, the Russian's house was still standing, the front-third of the dune shorn away.

George proceeded gingerly. "You were out here—did ya hear anything? See anything?"

Pulling a camera from her bag, she fiddled with the settings. "No."

"Did the police question you?"

"Yes. You know they did."

"What happened?"

"Nothing."

Okay, she was stonewalling. No point in pushing her.

"Where's Jack?"

"He'll be out soon. He'll stay with Chaz."

He looked at her imploringly. "Perrin—what the hell—"

"It's over now. You don't have to worry about it." She took pictures from various angles, like some sort of reporter. As if the house were not hers.

"I'm not worried . . . you show up like that and, well . . . what do you expect me to think?" They'd always been a peaceful family, hadn't they? Eccentric and countercultural, sure, but there had never been any violence.

"I walked into a door, Dad. I was drinking."

She crouched to get shots of the interior. "Jack's bringing out the insurance people. And William is coming."

"You know, I *was* trying to reach you that night," he said, wanting to make a point of it. "Are you going to be able to get inside?"

She pointed to the yellow tape on stakes that wrapped around the beached structure. "It's condemned, Dad. We're not even supposed to be this close."

"Don't you care? It's your *house*! What about Mom's things?"

"Maybe Jed can help," she said, putting her camera back into her bag, meeting his eyes.

He looked at her for a long moment, now absolutely convinced that something bigger was going on. "What have you heard?" he asked, motioning up the dune.

"Drowned? I don't know. You know as much as I do."

"Drowned in his pool? That doesn't sound right. Who goes swimming in a hurricane?"

Her tone was so flat, he wondered if she was in shock. He looked up and down the bald dunes, feeling as if they'd both been thrown back to Hurricane Celia in '95. He remembered waiting that one out with Perrin and Iris in the school gym, playing Gin Rummy, hearing the wind bang on the roof. A reckoning like that usually wiped away any remnants of self-pity; superficial problems seemed to go right down the drain. But then they'd return. Perrin was holding onto something, tight.

He eyeballed the tattered windsock that was still attached to the deck. It lifted in the exhausted wind. "At least Mom's pots are okay," he said, trying to keep the conversation going. "Jack's going to be pretty pissed about the studio—"

"Dad? Do you remember when you ran up all that credit card debt in the nineties?"

"Well, yes." Reptilian pea brains hounded him and threatened him, alternating with honey-toned, soothing words. Collection agencies were workshops for the sadists of the world.

"Why?"

"I don't know—I was just thinking of it."

She noticed the upstairs bedroom windows were now staring bleakly into the sand. Behind them, a small mountain range of mattress, bureau, and side tables, and an early Jack that had hung over the bed.

Behind her, the sighing, listless sea was slowly receding, taking with it something that was precious and of limited quantity. After Glasgow had shown her the two Monets in his kitchen, his gloating had turned into an ugly taunt. It was as if a light had gone on in his muddied brain.

How do you know about my museum? How? He had poked his finger into her face. *No one here knows about that.* And she hadn't been able to come up with a reason. She could have deflected by flattering him—something about an underground art world gossip network that knew about anyone who was *anyone*—but she had been too frozen in fear to think. A little while before she had been in his king-sized bed, the wet wind hammering the windows. She had to struggle to appear willing, imagining what a prostitute feels. Slick with body heat, sweat, and stale champagne, his tank-like body smothering her, she had been unable to transport herself out of the experience. All the fanciful imaginings of an hour before had deserted her. She hadn't been able to imagine him to be anything other than what he was—a criminal, unfeeling thug she disliked intensely, using her, though he was too soft to enter her.

Afterwards, while she pulled her clothes on, he had appraised her with a proprietary twinkle. "I won't tell if you don't."

Was he kidding?

He was still high, and in sort of a good mood, as much as a deadened person like that could be. He had gotten what he wanted, sort of, hadn't he?

He had asked if she was hungry. A little, she said, thinking that the kitchen was that much closer to the front door.

"Just a bite," she had said, the idea of food making her want to retch.

And then, in the kitchen, he got out some sandwich things and became impish again. His black eyes twinkling, he plucked two cardboard tubes from the top of one of his kitchen cabinets. *If you want to see art. No one would ever guess . . .* His accent had thickened *. . . No, no, no . . . what I have in my kitchen here, little Miss . . . you won't believe . . .*

He had rolled them out on the dining room table and fixed them with lamps and two rock glasses. *Bridge paintings,* he announced, noting the brushwork, praising the colors that Monet had chosen. He had pointed out the signature in the corner of one of the canvases, and there it was, plain as day. *Monet, '99,* inscribed several lifetimes ago, just there, a hairsbreadth away from her fingers. They were exquisite. Especially the lighter, less moody one captured her—it was a portal, a pool, a watery sanctuary far away from the dark incalculable night in which she found herself. She was too high, straining to keep her thoughts straight, aghast that her gamble had worked. She was here, and they were here, the lamps that had been her ploy going on either side, the kitchen and living room lit with candles, the figure of Glasgow an indistinct smudge amid her churning thoughts. Christopher would be so pleased. She had done it! With this thought, she was brought up sharply into the present, her mind clearing, her skin crawling as the numbness of the coke left her, and the physical memory of Glasgow's hands on her body had taken on a first life among many. He reached for her again. Of course, she had to go home—her father. Logic would dictate that she must go home and check on her father. He was older, she hadn't been able to reach him. She told Glasgow about the radio at her house, gambling that he wouldn't try to come with her and use it. Quickly, she added that Jack might've returned, just might have turned around on the main road because it was blocked—or maybe he had thought better of leaving. She had to get home, *now*. Jack did not deserve her, Glasgow said. She should stay with him through the storm. Yes, she agreed, Jack was a brute for leaving. She knew her face was bright red. Her heart was accelerating, pounding in her ears. She was full of terror and joy, and it was overtaking her, and she must *stop*. She had imagined, she had hoped that in the low light he couldn't see her well. She had wanted so desperately to get away, to shower and brush her teeth until her skin and gums bled. She had wanted to scream. He had looked at her, a queer, inquisitive expression on his face. "Wait a minute, little Miss, wait a fucking minute . . . Why do you have to go *now*?"

The memory made her shudder deeply, tears jumping into her eyes.

"Perry," said her father, his old nickname for her. He wrapped her up tight in his arms without thinking twice, as if it was the most natural thing in the world. This was Perrin. She wasn't made out of stone, and she had had a very rough time.

She spoke into his jacket pocket. "I loved your attitude about the credit card people. You weren't going to let it get to you."

"Christ—remember that?"

Collection agencies were calling night and day. Iris would lift the receiver and just slam it down, especially on the regular early Sunday call. George would stand out in front of the shack, opening his arms wide to the sea and say, "Glorious! Fuck it! I am

STILL HERE! A financial midget, yes, but solvent in every other way!"

They laughed together, Perrin through her tears.

He said, "Can you at least promise me that you are out of danger now? That this madness—whatever it is—isn't going to go on?"

"I think I can," she said, without being sure at all.

"What's going on?" he asked, studying her face.

She explained it to him again—she had had too much wine. *The hurricane made me nervous . . .*

Her father looked at her intently, as if weighing the amount of truth in her words. If she had ever wondered what it would take to really get his attention, it was now clear. A collapsed house, a death nearby, and something he had to do without knowing why.

"One day I'll explain," she said.

"I don't have until one day. I have only now."

"I need you to say that I came to you earlier on the night of the storm, around nine o'clock. Can you do that?"

"Of course."

"Just make sure you tell them I was there at nine. And I need to stay with you for a bit more. That's all. Can I?"

He agreed to this as well, thinking there was always a melancholy playing about her face, but today a luster too, a liveliness that he couldn't figure out.

* * *

Spooked by the visit to the police station, the next morning Perrin took the leggings and the sweatshirt to the dump and bought some new clothes. Jack, still in the city making his arrangements, was fired up with plans to re-build everything. He was calling several times a day. He told her he felt terribly guilty about leaving, and his guilt, while noteworthy, had no effect on her. She felt herself in limbo again, while Jack worried that the cost of materials had escalated, and the insurance wouldn't cover it. He insisted that he was ready to settle for a "more simple" house anyway and that at least some of the studio could be salvaged. Most adamantly, he wanted Perrin with him at the apartment. She didn't really need to be in the city, she told him. She found herself continually drawn to the garden at George's, which had gone from a small pond in places to soggy grass. Some of the plastic supports had popped on the chaise, but it was still workable. She lay in it, a scarf tied around her eyes like her mother would have in such a situation. Only the beech tree, the birds, the fresh air, and the distant sound of the sea for company.

She missed Kit fiercely. She missed the soothing balm of his voice, his blue eyes and enfolding arms that had acted as a sort of shield. In the slow ebbing back of the sea, the empty spaces in her life opened up again, more vacant than before. From a very temporary-looking email address, he sent a few paragraphs that were just to tell her to look out for a ceremony of some kind in the future, when the Monets would be restored to the public. It was a love letter of sorts, a tribute to her, and to the recovered Monets. Valuable and historic, yes, but only canvas and paint and wood. They were not living, and she was.

She had no idea of time passing. She could not face Jack, nor her friends, nor George. Her face had to heal. She ignored the texts and asked George to fend off calls to the landline. Finally, she put her phone on silent.

Listening to music helped, bands from her high school days, though not Night Ranger. After a while, it all began to sound like Night Ranger. Bad eighties rock all sounded like Glasgow—his doughy face, the way he was a criminal while also playing at being a criminal, and what had happened. Her skin crawled; she couldn't stop thinking about it. Her impressions were blurred but powerful—sharp stubble, sad eyes, small and stupid, that banging noise that had gone on all night, and no one had checked what it was—probably a garbage can tied to the house. She remembered her relief when she saw the paintings, and her internal plea, *Dear*

God, get me out of here, and then trying to explain about the radio and George. The hardness of his fist. Well, she was alive, and he was dead, and she didn't even know how.

She switched to Mendelssohn on her iPod, which Iris had liked. Through the variety and various colors of the sound, she felt Iris closer to her. It gave her some comfort to know that no matter how disgusting she felt and how frightened she was, Iris would have been impressed. Of herself, Iris hadn't left much in the world. Not a book, or a journal, or paintings—she had destroyed most everything. There were some family pictures, the pottery, boxes of records, jewelry that she never wore, but really not much beyond the two giant clay pots that had survived the storm. The only clear impression of Iris that remained was her particular alertness for something otherworldly, something extreme, something *conclusive.* For Iris, simple living was inadequate and frustrating because the cumulative, final something that she craved never happened. (Until, thought Perrin, perhaps it did happen when she died.) With Mendelssohn as her guide, Perrin felt and saw the events of the past week through her mother's eyes. A strike for our side, Iris would have said. A *secret* mission. She would have loved that especially. It would have put a real smile on her face when few things did. If only Iris were there, Perrin would have told her everything, official secrets act be damned, and she would never have had to worry about Iris telling. Iris wouldn't have bandied it about or bragged because Iris was not in possession of any kind of a scorecard. The great thing that happened for which one had sacrificed and that no one ever knew about, that was not a part of Andy Warhol's fifteen minutes or made the pages of the *Times*, was the deeper and more meaningful act. With that germ of a thought, she turned up the Mendelssohn and pulled the memory of her mother close.

Occasionally, she had to leave the chaise to grab something to eat or go to the bathroom. On one of those trips back, she stopped short and sidled close to the house. The police were talking to George at the front door. It was Bob White again, and his partner Nick. She tiptoed closer to listen.

"Where did you hear that?" George asked.

"Aldrichs'. Mary and Jed. Standard procedure to interview everyone in the vicinity."

"When did you say the lights went down?" asked George.

"1:24," said Nick, with a clipped tone.

"Amazing we had them for that long—"

"Aldrichs said Perrin and Jack's was lit up until the lights went," said Bob.

"Well, that may be true. She probably ran out without turning everything off. I would. Bob, have you ever been out on the beach in that kind of weather?"

"No, I haven't."

"The ocean sounds like it's coming in, and you don't know, it might come in. How can you tell? It's late, it's dark," said George. "Would you like a cup of coffee? Just made some."

"Okay, thanks."

One life-size sculpture ensconced in bubble wrap blocked the view to the kitchen, so Perrin snuck around to the living room window. It was almost covered by a privet George had never clipped. If she wedged between it and the house, she could just see across. She heard chairs scrape back. Someone would definitely have to stand because there wasn't enough room.

"Not to be nosy," intoned Bob. "Well, I'm paid to be nosy—"

"Go ahead, Bob, ask anything you like," said George, putting mugs of coffee down on the table. "Sugar? Milk?"

"Okay . . . yeah . . . milk—sorry to have to ask this, but where was Jack?"

"Ahhh . . . well . . ." said George. "You know how it is. Sometimes . . ."

Bob kept on. "Yes, but was he there? He says he wasn't there, but that's hard to believe."

"He wasn't there. He left earlier that night. Marital discord. Don't say this around, but I think Jack was shit scared," George said with a chuckle.

"Okay. Perrin came here, you say. 'Bout what time did you say?"

"9 . . . 9:30. She had had a few drinks . . ."

She exhaled, hoping that he would know not to keep talking.

"You know, Perrin—you went to school together, right?"

She could hear that Bob was a little intimidated by George. "Sure did."

"She's a lightweight. Had some wine—"

"Yeah, got a pretty good black eye on that door—she said. We saw. But okay . . . Why was she still out there, even then?"

"I don't know. I couldn't reach her—she has that newfangled phone that goes with the internet. Internet wasn't working, so . . ."

The conversation mumbled back and forth while George played dumb, talked about his flooded yard and embellished at the same time, saying that she had come out of concern for him. Perrin held her breath, hoping he wouldn't go on.

"How did you get through?" asked George.

"We came out okay—a tree fell on my neighbor's car, though. Totaled," said Bob.

"What about you, Nick?" asked George, pouring more coffee.

They went on like this for a bit, her father's gravelly voice doing its charming best. "Don't know about you, but I would *never* give up my old-fashioned landline. Can't imagine why anyone would want to have to rely on a computer telephone. What happens when the whole damn thing goes down?"

"Yep, yep, yep . . . What did she bring with her?" asked Bob, manfully steering the conversation.

Perrin's heart dropped a little. She hadn't prepared George for this question.

"What do you mean?"

"Well, in a situation like that, most people bring something important—jewelry, house deeds, family pictures."

"I don't know. She was tipsy, as I said. She could have had those in her jacket."

Perrin was cheered by George's protective words, that he was handling things in the way a father would for a child—but didn't when she had actually been a child.

"Her jacket around?"

Perrin heard the tension in his reply. "I don't know. You'll have to talk to her about it."

"I did. At the station . . ."

For the moment, Perrin hated Bob. She had rebuffed this question at the station, not wanting to make another mistake. As with Glasgow, she couldn't lie fast enough, so she was silent. Since then, she had thought about it often. To not have taken anything implied that she was abnormally distracted. But then again, why wouldn't she be with a hurricane raging outside?

"She wouldn't say," volunteered Nick.

"Well, for Chrissake, Bob, she had just lost her house!" George exclaimed.

"She lost her house *later*. That doesn't explain—"

"I mean when she came in to see you!"

"Okay . . . okay." Bob put his mug down. "But here's what I can't figure out. You are in the house, the hurricane is going crazy, you're drinking a bit. You know how bad it is. You aren't somebody who wouldn't know, like, for example—the Russian who died. What are you doing? Why are you there? Why would you take the risk and wait so long, and still not take anything when you finally leave?"

"What are you getting at?" George asked with a chill in his voice.

"I'm just asking the question. It's unusual, especially considering all that went on out there that night."

George leaned over the table, writing something down. "Here. Here's Jack's cell phone in case you don't have it. I heard that he's coming out soon. Why don't you haul him down to the station too."

"Is Perrin around?"

There was a pause, and George said, "I just came in, Bob. I don't know. You can check around if you want."

Perrin heard his chair scrape back to indicate the meeting was over. She stayed hidden in the privet, while three disgruntled men walked through stacks of paintings. She wondered if she should stay put or try to make it back out to the chaise. To her intense relief, there was the scattershot sound of voices in the front yard followed by the engine of the patrol car turning over. Gingerly, George clicked the front door shut.

* * *

Later, she took the van for hamburgers and macaroni salad, a six of Heineken, and the navel oranges that George liked. It was still warm, so he got the barbeque going. On a card table set up in the garden, they ate on paper plates, with beers chilling in an ice bucket in the grass.

As the embers died out, George asked, "So how'd I do, Perry?"

"Pretty well! Now we just have to see if it will die down."

She saw that he didn't like being in the dark but was living with it.

"I think it will," he said.

"What makes you think so?"

"If Bob were serious, he'd have searched right then and there."

"How did you know he wouldn't?" she asked, grateful that she was now the one with the questions.

"Honestly? I wasn't sure. I thought I would take a chance."

"Whew," she said, sipping cold beer to the back of her throat.

George puffed up a little, pleased that he could soothe her fears. "He was only posturing. He is essentially too timid to come barging into my house. What are you going to say if they ask you again?"

"That I was overwrought. That I didn't want to tempt the fates. Do you think he knows the meaning of that?"

"Probably not," said George, "but you never know."

"If he doesn't know, I can explain it, take up some air," said Perrin.

"It is a good question," said George. "You didn't take anything, did you?"

She thought about the photo books that Iris had put together, that had family pictures in them. “No,” she said, sorrowfully.

“Why didn’t you? Not even a computer or the photo albums? Mom’s jewelry?” he asked gently.

“Jack had taken all the important papers. I just had to get out of there, Dad.” She stood up and collected the plates.

“Maybe we can get some of those things later,” he said, not moving.

“Yes!” she said, taking the tray into the kitchen, feeling autumn’s chill upon them.

* * *

Jack had stayed in his city studio but had now come out to work with William, salvaging what they could of the rocket. He seemed to want to give her as much room as possible. He refused to be a part of the demolition of the house, appearing to walk by it with blinders on. He had begun to work on plans for a new house, “a completely different, straightforward wooden house,” he had written in a text. It became apparent that he was deeply embarrassed by having left her that night and that he thought a new house was the key to a future of some kind. “Let’s just get through the boards quickly,” he’d written. “You have to be happy with it—no one else.” During the week, George went with her to the dune to oversee the demolition of the Napoleon, as they both freely called it now. She was grateful that he didn’t ask about Jack. He’d put in his hours in the morning, and they’d go over together in the old van.

Jed and his father came with their cherry picker to help. Mr. Aldrich ran the machine, while Jed, using a kind of sling into which he strapped himself, retrieved Iris’s photo books and, amazingly, Iris’s jewelry case from the dresser on the top floor. They had brought a tool from the hardware store, used to take items down from hard-to-reach places, which George thought ingenious.

They got George's paintings from the second floor and plucked a painting of Jack's from the top floor. Looking at Jed swinging from the harness, Perrin felt thornily appreciative—it was the least he could do given his theorizing to the police. And despite everything, she was pleased to give Jack his salvaged work. It would placate him, at least while she sorted herself out.

The demolition took two weeks. It went section by section because it was quickly discovered that the glass block broke into sharp pieces that were hazardous in the sand and earth around the plot. It had sliced through the shoe of one worker already and cut him badly. After a few days, a team of termite fumigators was brought in to balloon-tent parts of the structure as it was demolished. For a while, the Napoleon looked like a giant red and blue beach ball or—Perrin joked—one of Jack's creations. Max hadn't considered his building materials, said George. Glass houses, like the Wright houses in Connecticut, were probably built with block that was treated for just such an eventuality. Likely, the Napoleon wasn't to code, or the local board hadn't seen materials like this before and just gave it a pass because the right palms were greased. Hard to believe, George said, shaking his head. He noticed that Perrin seemed to want to be there for every bit of it, every chunk of concrete, every time the big dumpster was carted off and returned empty. Sometimes she cried, which perplexed him. Still, she would stay.

One day towards the end, the deck was dug out of the sand. Too big to go in the dumpster, it had to be cut up into pieces, and so they hired Jed to help again. George wanted to use the wood framing in his fireplace, but Perrin wouldn't let him because, she said, it had been chemically treated. Before Jed fired up the chainsaw, George unscrewed the windsock. What had once been a bright cherry color was now the color of a dead salmon. That was the thing about living near the sea—salt and wind wore away colors, chipped away at things and people, diminished them. But it was better than rotting away inland in an airless garden of boxwoods and hydrangeas or some sort of rest home. The sea was active; it was an *exchange*. The sea held one's fate somehow, which is why people loved to stare at it. From whence it all came, including every living thing on the earth. And where, when he moved on from this world, his ashes would be thrown. Might as well be near that force while he was living, might as well be awed by it and reminded every day. There was no protecting oneself anyway. Time did its work—that was the built-in tragedy.

Jed and a few of the workmen first had to dig the deck out, and George grabbed a shovel. The sand was wet and heavy, so it was slow going. He surprised himself by getting misty-eyed. He was thinking back to when the shack came down. Now, that was sad. But of course, he did not cry. Digging out the deck took no more than forty minutes, and then there was only a rectangle of cinder block in the dunes where it had been. A small imprint—nothing like this. The workmen thought Perrin was upset about the demolition and were sympathetic, averting their eyes politely at the tears that slid down her face. They'd seen all of that before. George took their cue and caught onto what he thought were the feelings of the moment—that she was having a delayed reaction to what was the end of an era for her. Perhaps it was just as well. She had never seemed happy in that place.

He stuck the windsock in his back pocket and went to squeeze her hand, while Jed's chainsaw kicked up and whined its call of destruction. She was really gone now. Was the deck her favorite part of the house? Maybe—because it wasn't *in* the house. He put his arm around her and held her as it got carted off. Less ridiculous structures had gotten through this hurricane intact. Even the Russian's house had made it through, though no one was there now. He wondered if it would be sold.

With a coordinated pull on ropes, a piece of the tent came down, billowing over a pile of glass rubble, shards, and dreck. He had always felt the Napoleon overly insistent. It had no grace, no humility; it refused to cooperate with the surroundings. A confection sitting high up on the dune, it was oblivious. It was too tall and transparent; it tried too hard and asked for too much attention.

It had killed too many birds. Inner lines of tension and support that might have held it together under attack had failed because they were weak. This was the Eastern Seaboard—an unprotected outcropping of it besides—a point Max and Jack seemed to have completely missed.

Large pieces of wood clunked and rumbled as they went into the dumpster, while Jed's chainsaw howled gleefully on. George could never say how satisfying it was that the Napoleon was going into the ground and would live on only in the lore of Hurricane Mike. It especially pleased him that one of his most closely held theories was proved out—that arrogance could not endure. That there was such a thing as too far and too fast and too much, and that if entities, people, and even buildings did not in some way fit around each other and allow each other to exist, they would not survive.

Perrin leaned in to his side, and he pulled her close, content that he could help her, if that was in fact what was happening. So often he had been unable to, or didn't have the time, or—if truth be told—didn't notice her. He had been too busy. He wasn't sure what her reaction was about. Maybe she herself was not sure but would sort herself out eventually. Perhaps one day she'd tell him the story, although it was also true that he might be better off not knowing. Her weight was heavy against him. He let himself feel her animal self, that she was a part of him. It didn't have to be dangerous. She was his girl, his daughter.

While the demo went on, he found a fishing rod in the carport and baited it with a bucktail lure he had in his jacket. He took her hand, and—retreating from the noise and machines—they went down to the shore. But it wasn't the right spot, somehow. So they walked down a half-mile towards Bridgehampton until he found a patch of ocean that looked promising. They took turns casting out. Eventually, she got a nice fat blue, and that seemed to cheer her up. They roasted the fish on the barbeque and ate well, Perrin still not talking.

Along with the now tepid beers on the card table, an air of finality hung about. Perrin had cleared the plates, leaving the dishes to George, who had gone inside to watch TV. She was tired and she knew he wouldn't mind. He seemed happy to have her around and quiet about everything, thank God. As her mind cleared, she reflected that her house was now in ten large dumpsters that had been carted away. And that soon she'd have to decide what the future was going to be. Jack had left messages for her today. She hadn't listened because she knew that he wanted to finalize the plans. She was not ready to.

She decided to hunt for more blankets inside the house. After finding a dusty one, she went out to the chaise again. It was early, but all she wanted to do was sleep. Snuggling deep, she concentrated on the wind in the trees, just as Iris would have done. A car passed by occasionally, and the ocean's distant roar lulled her. The fresh night air filled her nostrils as she slid again into the chaotic half-world that had so recently plagued her. Kit was there and also not there. He was a ghostly presence, stretched here, compressed there. He didn't look or sound the same, though it was him and could be no other. He either could not or would not help her. Glasgow was the last person to have touched her, not Kit—the illusion seemed to insist this. She was pulled down into the dream, trembling with revulsion, replaying his soft, pushy hands on her body, his stale cologne, his small metallic eyes, his hanging red mouth. In between, there was the steady banging of the can on the pilings and the swirling dark above the house. Stretchy skull faces like Munch's "The Scream" brimmed up out of the night, encircled with their own bony hands, disappearing below or to the side, blinking in and out. Peculiarly, these faces that tormented her also felt sorry for her, and that made it infinitely worse. She tossed around in the black ether of sleep, wanting to retch, her skin sweaty with fear.

Then suddenly, she found herself awake in the dream, in a new chapter of it, a lovely one. She was as awake as she had been earlier, eating bluefish and drinking beers with George. She was flying somewhere above George's hollies and higher, even higher, between the branches of the big beech tree—free in the autumn night and completely untethered to anything. It was delicious. She wanted to stay there forever, among the branches of that sheltering tree. But the dream impelled her to move in order to stay aloft, so she did, flying away over the fields in the morning sun and down to the water, saying to herself, up! up! up! and actually staying up through force of will. Darkest night had turned to midday. She flew over the town, watching the waves break far below, the fields, the dunes, the beach, up and down the coast for miles, always remembering the sheltering tree, and that she could return there anytime. The dream seemed to go on for hours, and her heart ached with joy, wanting to stay in it forever, while at the same time she knew that she'd have to return to the life she had left.

In the morning, the blanket was wet with dew, and the chaise felt like the floor of a lifeboat. The sky hunkered low, gray and strange. Turning away from the colorless light, she wept for all that was lost. There was nowhere to hide. Like an army, the whole world was coming across the fields, through the hollies and into the garden.

CHAPTER 17
OLD CANVAS, OLD NAILS

London
October 8th, 2012
97 days after the heist

A cool October moon stared down upon the tarmac that flew underneath Susannah's wheels. They had a new black BMW, the model she had wanted for a long time. Black rims and privacy windows extra.

In the glow from the car radio, he saw that she was wearing a new blue frock, bought specially for this occasion. She was looking forward to getting to know Martin and his wife Fiona better, as Fiona was on the board at the Art Institute and might help her along at her job at the Tate. She sang along with the radio, happy they would have a night out with people she found interesting.

He wished he was as happy and felt guilty that he wasn't, which added to the throbbing in his leg. The pills had maxed out; he had begun suffering withdrawal when he didn't take them. A month ago, he had started to wean himself off them, only using them occasionally when the pain was too much. He was due for another surgery too, to remove a relatively large piece that had migrated halfway up his thigh. Another thing he didn't like to think about, yet, in another way, it felt like something he deserved.

He patted his pockets to make sure he had cigarettes while looking forward to his first drink at Martin's and the smoke he'd have with it. Fortunately, neither Martin nor Fiona were fussy, and they had a sunroom where smoking was okay. Small simple pleasures were more important in the life that he had returned to—they were touchstones along the way—a smoke, a good book, a flirtation with any attractive woman in the vicinity, and enough alcohol. These were the things he lived for, self-hating faker that he was. He smoothed the black vinyl of the car seat, the "leather" slightly nubbly under his fingers, the green numerals of the dashboard soothing to his weary eye. The car was that of an important person, or someone who wanted to be important. While Susannah prattled away, he tried on a few personas—a dignitary on their way to Whitehall, the wayward offspring of a Chinese shipping magnate, a housewife on a tear with friends (chauffeured). Or the worst—one of Kusnetsov's gang outside the Taj hotel. He'd probably never drive this car for that reason. Which was fine—it was really meant for Susannah.

Once the first child comes you will never be the same, said every parent he knew. And it might happen soon because a recent test had shown Kit's sperm were absolute stallions. It might happen, and maybe it would be enough. He had seen it before—a first child and its needs grabbed marital unhappiness and stuffed it into its great, greedy maw. From which it might emerge later. Only to be hidden away again. Or never emerge, due to a reshuffling of priorities. One could never tell—it wasn't the sort of question one could ask of friends. Was it a slow settling, like silt to the bottom of a lake? Was it a real unity? Was there a difference? He often wondered about it. One didn't try to nose into a marriage, though he always found himself looking for clues that told the real story. He had never gotten a clear answer as to why Perrin had stayed with Jack, trying to dodge him and placate him at the same time. They were imprisoned in that glass citadel as much as he could tell. But now the citadel had been destroyed.

Susannah leaned in to turn up the radio. . . . *London will rejoice tomorrow as two stolen Monets believed to have been burned will be unveiled in a ceremony at the Tate . . .*

"Not just the Arts segment of the news, but the *Headline News,*" said Susannah, her voice upbeat. After all, she worked in a museum. "That is unusual . . . Do you think the average man on the street knows the story?"

"Perhaps they will know now," said Kit, enjoying her ignorance for the first time.

. . . paintings were stolen from the Kunsthal Museum in Rotterdam . . . was brought about by a collaboration between American and British authorities . . .

"Not you, of course," she said teasingly.

"Of course not. They'd never give me something like that," he said, playing the game.

"But you couldn't say anyway, so how can I trust you?" she said, which was her way of beginning to pry.

"Susannah, you know—"

"I'm kidding," she said. "I won't ask."

. . . Kaarle DeVries, director of the Kunsthal Museum, called it an occasion to celebrate, adding that the recovery of works from museum thefts is rare in most cases . . .

Yes, thought Kit. They'd pulled off the impossible.

. . . Queen Elizabeth and Prince Phillip will be in attendance, along with various prominent figures of the art world. One hundred of the Tate Britain's members, selected by lottery, will also attend . . .

"The Monets will do something for relations with France, don't you think?" she added, while Kit flinched, not caring about relations with France, an item that seemed irretrievably small, though of course, it wasn't small at all.

They left the M40 and soared onto a dark country road. The BMW was smooth as honey, he could say that. Money did soften the hard edges of things. Death and destruction—he felt as though he was dripping with it. Kit found it hard to believe that in the training he'd received there was nothing about how to contend with having killed someone. Could that kind of thing be taught? They especially never talked about revenge. The objective was to turn out professionals who were guided by duty rather than emotion, and so revenge wasn't supposed to play a part. Perhaps because of this, in the three weeks since *Viridian* had ended—excepting a goatish interest in Perrin—Martin had not once touched upon the events of the operation. No interrogation whatsoever. Though it was unsurprising, Kit felt the lack keenly. Between the two of them, Kit felt there should have been some sort of formal acknowledgement. All around him Kit felt the pink buzz of progress, which was really things being wrenched back into the shape they had before, or at least what that shape had appeared to be. The Monets had been restored. Glasgow was dead, and Glasgow's operation was busted wide open. Meredith and the service had been avenged. Everyone at the office knew that he was responsible in some way. The details of his epic screw-up at the Taj had faded, and people were buoyed by his success—much more than he was. It had nothing to do with them, and in fact, they had no idea what it was like.

Revenge was satisfying in *concept,* as one might hear about at work or read in a book. Carrying it out was grisly and sad. No matter how bad Glasgow was, what remained was that he had been alive as Kit was alive, going through the same days, the same life, in the same pocket of time. Kit had had to play God, and in effect, had to be God for some moments. It had affected him. Though he had cut out the pills, he was drinking again, a lot. He startled easily, and every now and then a chill of undisclosed origin crept through his limbs. Revenge—his own—theirs? The lines were all blurred. At the moment of action, it was only between himself and Glasgow, and it couldn't have been more simple. Now, he second-guessed himself constantly, and did once again as he looked out at the trees in the moonlight, a silver blur along the road.

While trying to work through the labyrinthian tangle that had had to serve as justification for *Viridian,* he kept coming back to Perrin. He couldn't get out of it then and he couldn't now. He thought of her constantly, wondered how she was, and if it had been worth it. He tried not to think of her as the reason for what had happened because that was an unnecessary burden on her, even in his mind. He restricted himself to the comforting but probably false idea that she would understand his anguish because she knew the whole story, or at least most of it. She had been there, gathering impressions that would stay with her always—the gloomy, wind-battered dune, the black night, the shuddering windows, and belligerent, forlorn Glasgow. There was not anybody else he could tell about it except Martin, and somehow that had been declared off-limits.

He was sure she didn't care about the house. For a while, the news showed a white box toppled onto its front edge, that one windsock fluttering on the dispatched deck. The camera would then travel down the beach to Glasgow's, the BBC reporting that Russian businessman Grigory Kusnetsov had been found dead in his pool. Perrin had guessed right—the body was sent to Moscow, and an autopsy was performed. Between GCHQ and the FBI, the cause of death was official: Kusnetsov had drowned. Moscow, through a mechanism that he wasn't privy to, had been shut down.

Those were long moments hiding in the stack of chairs, peering into Glasgow's living room still ablaze with light. Dave the security guard came out on the deck and wandered about, his expression strangely invigorated, as if he enjoyed being buffeted by the wind. Kit remembered thinking that Perrin's beloved sea was turning into a monster. At the time, he wondered if she knew how bad it was. She'd glance furtively toward the window now and then, as if trying not to think about it. Glasgow refilled their glasses again and again, while the two of them took turns with the mirror and the straw, though he could see only half of them. Periodically, they'd fall back into the sofa, disappearing from view. That had been unbearable, but he'd had to endure it. It was nothing compared to her ordeal.

Sometime after one o'clock, the lights went out everywhere, and the living room window went completely black. The water beneath the deck roared a white fury, sending spray shooting up through the boards. For some long moments, Kit couldn't see anything, the chairs rattling around him like a deranged cage. The banging on the side of the house ratcheted up. It was incredible that no one inside tried to do anything about it. They were all too high. Up from the sofa again, Perrin lit a lamp, her soft brown eyes shifting in its warm glow. He clung to the sight of her, believing that as long as he could see her, it would be all right. With the exaggerated concentration of the intoxicated, she fitted the glass globe back on, while in the diminished light, her eyes became hollows. She was lost to a terrible void not thirty feet away from where he crouched. Glasgow came up and looked over her shoulder into the wet night, as if daring anyone to challenge him. When she was done, he put his arms around her from behind, his thick shiny face illuminated by the flame.

It took all the resolve Kit had to stay still.

"It was in the cards, Chris," she had said a few days later on the phone. Her voice was sing-songy, like a person in shock. "He couldn't do it. But it was disgusting anyway. I will live."

Outwardly, he had been full of praise, steering her towards what was supposed to be the main point. He had asked about her face. It would heal, she replied briskly. Yes, she had done the job, and that was all that he had wanted. Officially. It was unnerving how detached she sounded.

And then she said that last thing—principles, *Viridian*, England, the service, and the art world chucked neatly into his face. *I did it for you. No matter what else happens, that's the truth of it.*

For him. Why? Was she a bit of a masochist? Or was she simply undefined, a muted presence that once given a shape could inhabit it with unexpected strength? A case of pent-up energy looking for a port? Maybe that was what was attractive about her, besides the obvious things. That morning on the phone, she also explained how the intelligence about Glasgow's museum had worked. Yes, it had, at a great cost to her. He was a piece of shit; he was worse than a piece of shit. He had wanted to tell her that right there, but it would have been too dramatic for the out that he was trying to create for himself.

That night he had waited, watching the candles on the table fatten and straighten as massive winds sucked at the house, and the two of them getting up periodically and going back to the sofa. When Dave came out on the deck again, Kit strong-armed him and took his gun, warning him off with a list of threats and oaths he knew that Dave, who had a long record, would find meaningful. He had then slipped into the house, the gun tucked in his jeans.

He had maintained a long vigil, back tucked against the wall, his ears pricked for signs of trouble, knowing that there would be. From his new standpoint, he could see the coffee table, the candles with waxen scree, the mortar and pestle, scattered granules and credit cards. A puddle of water had formed where the ice bucket had sweated onto the glass. He heard voices drift from the kitchen. The wind was hard on the windows; he could feel them bend and the pressure change in the house. Now that Dave was gone, all he had to do was wait. He held still. Even with his bad hearing, he was picking up that Glasgow's voice was louder than hers. Then he heard the crash and Perrin's muted scream.

He followed the direction of the noise into the living room. Her mouth was taped, and she was taped to a chair. Glasgow had hit her so hard the chair had fallen over. On the table behind them, the two Monets were spread and held down by glasses. Kit crept up behind Glasgow, put him in a chokehold, and put the gun to his temple. He saw ahead, down the barrel of years. They could find her, while he, himself, was protected. Still holding Dave's gun on Glasgow, he got a knife from the kitchen and cut Perrin free with one hand. It had to be fixed. Otherwise, she would never get out of it. He saw through to what the best thing was for her and for him, and indeed the world. "Bring that briefcase to me!" he barked, doing a double take on the welt on her face. "Hide that mark, fix yourself up. You were at your house. Get out—get *out*!"

Martin swung open his heavy blue door. Classically English-looking, with a long red nose and thinning blond hair, he led them straight to the bar. "Glenmorangie and water, right?"

Martin knew very well what it was. He poured him three shots at least, with a few ounces of water. Kit sipped and followed Martin back into the stony splendor of the Greens' sitting room. Small leaded windows with deep sills looked out on a garden that was gray-green and going to sleep. Walls lacquered a red somewhere between dark red wine and cherries were studded with late-nineteenth and twentieth-century art. Lights from under the moldings illuminated works that went up to about 1955, with a concentration on realism. A John Singer Sargent had a place of honor over the piano. A very serious burglar alarm was on standby.

Plump Fiona Green greeted them, her hair tamed into a bun, wearing a caftan of orange silk. Kit exclaimed his admiration for the artwork. Since their tastes were broad, he asked, loud enough for Martin to hear, if they had a Hochberg, whereupon Martin's shoulder flinched just a bit.

"Funny you should ask—a sketch right here . . ." Fiona said, pulling the door back to a small gallery of ink, pencil, and charcoal portraits.

"Can you tell which one?"

Kit pointed and knew he was right. It was that line, tender and ruthless at the same time. A representation of another friend; he guessed it someone the artist was fond of but who seemed content by comparison to the portrait of the woman. Nothing too much swirling around him.

As if reading his mind, Fiona exhaled, "Too bad about the Boseman portrait."

"Yes. Do you mean the *Woman with Eyes Closed?*"

"Right," said Fiona.

"Did you know her by any chance?"

"Only through Sara," said Fiona. "She's here tonight! I do know that the Boseman family is warring over it—that is, if it survives. The father wants to call it a loss and collect the insurance. Julia Boseman's sister, Lily, wants to hold out for the sake of the children."

"Because of the Monets—"

"Exactly. If they call it a loss and take the money, it can become very complicated with the insurance company."

"How so?" said Kit, his blood quickening just a bit.

"The appraisal—the payout. The high numbers can create a legal quagmire. The sister wants to hold out, though there might not be much to hold out for . . ." She fluttered two fingers to her chin in perplexity. "What do you think, Kit?"

"I have no idea . . . wish I did," he replied truthfully.

There were two other couples in the dining room: Barbara Asher, head of a girl's school, and her husband Frederick, a retired banker. Hugh Rhoades was a curator from the British Museum, and his wife Sara was on the board of the Tate. Normally, Kit and Fiona would have been junior to this group, and that might have been at a big Christmas do. But they all seemed delighted to meet them. He wondered if the events of the summer had somehow steeped him in a new cultural seriousness which they responded to and immediately dismissed the thought. No, this was an unofficial thank you. Fiona had invited her high-powered friends that would be useful connections for Susannah, and Martin had quite a lot to thank him for.

A waiter with beads of sweat on his nose brought a first course of leek soup in a silver terrine. At first, there was much talk of the unveiling of the Monets. Sara and Hugh were attending, and so were Martin and Fiona. The Ashers said nothing on the subject; Kit guessed that they hadn't been invited and were not happy about it. Kit felt so far away, it was almost no use trying, and with this distance came an eerie clarity. Instead of people merging into one as they usually did, each guest was separate. Susannah, in cobalt blue, hoping. Martin, a fried lock of blond hair on his forehead, dodging. Fiona, his favorite, mothering. Frederick Asher, put out. Hugh, assessing. Sara, her small, fine features actively composing themselves. The service, not a guest—but there anyway, admonishing. Perrin still in his head, lost to him.

"The Queen—I don't think that's happened before," said Frederick disapprovingly.

"It has, actually," said Fiona. "I think they mean to . . . to . . . at least state, in a clear way, that our SIS had everything to do with it. Well, along with the American . . ." Fiona stopped herself.

Martin, mostly preoccupied with the *Chateau Musar* he had crowed about earlier, shot her a glance.

"I met Julia Boseman before Hochberg made his bequest to Abbiate," said Sara coolly but possessively. "I had lunch with her because she wanted my advice. Hochberg would have done anything to make her happy. He had come to her house for several months before she died to paint the portrait, instead of her having to go to him. At the point I saw her, she was very sick."

"Did you get to know her?" asked Kit.

"Yes, a little. I think she wanted the world to see her portrait because, perhaps, the world would no longer see her."

"Toadies," interjected Frederick, still grumbling about the Queen. "A desperate search for meaning. A complete farce."

"Oh please, Frederick. You're as big a royalist as they come," said Martin.

Sara went on. "Her kids were in the same school as the boys. I helped her structure the lease that they had with Abbiate. She was an absolutely lovely woman. That painting hardly did her justice."

"No," agreed Fiona, while Kit thought how little it mattered.

"Though it isn't really a painting about beauty, is it?" he said, feeling completely out of depth with this crowd.

Martin, swirling a plug of wine around his goblet, paused for just for a moment.

"Past tense, I think," said Frederick with a quick glance Martin's way, which Martin did not return.

"I agree," said Hugh. "Absolutely not about her looks. Anyway, I met her once. She was what we used to call a *jolie laide*. Bit too much fuss if you ask me. Though I always like a *jolie laide*."

"You are still reducing it to a question of attractiveness," said Fiona. "Kit is saying that attractiveness has no part in the worth of the painting."

Hugh looked weary, as if he might never get out of the minefield of this conversation.

"Never did with Hochberg anyway," said Sara. "His portraits are universally unattractive—"

"What's the opinion of the service?" Frederick asked Martin directly.

"On what?"

"Its recovery."

"We don't talk about that, as you know," said Martin, poising the bottle over his glass.

The heavy soup terrine gone, the nervous waiter leaned between each person with the main dish of poached salmon and asparagus. Kit laughed silently. It was that the sweat had accumulated at the end of the waiter's nose and was just . . . *just* . . . about to fall onto someone's salmon. And then did, onto Martin's salmon, which was delightful. Susannah frowned at him, the first of many he would receive this evening.

Jesus Christ, what a worm he was—under the heel of the boot of these people. He skimmed over Martin's face as he jawed the salmon in and took another showy sip of wine. *Jesus H. Christ.* Had he been so predictable? A design on behalf of the service was unsurprising. These were people who sat at headquarters all day pondering just these sorts of questions. He had done it too. He had assessed Chaz, what he would have to do or say to get him to take him where he needed to go. He had assessed Perrin, what she would do for him. There had been no limits to that, and it would now prove to haunt him. He tried hard to keep his face from falling, tossing back the wine as soon as Martin topped him up, smiling at jokes and punchlines he didn't hear through the ringing in his ears and the flurry of his thoughts. What, if anything, had they worked out about Perrin? She would be as good as gone if he hadn't forced Glasgow at gunpoint to drink half a bottle of vodka and then waited twenty minutes in stony silence while Glasgow wept and pleaded. Kit had worn gloves to make sure that he didn't bruise or scratch him and held him under the water in the pool while standing in the shallow end up to his waist. Glasgow fought listlessly for a few minutes, pawing the water until his bullish arms relaxed into an embrace of his own fate. Kit stayed holding his arm for what seemed a very long time, just to make sure he was really gone. His mind recorded every detail: the silent, pushing gale, the guttering lamp, the Russian's T-shirt ballooning on his back, rippling in the water and wind. Or maybe this was what they did work out about Perrin.

"Would you mind if I guessed?" said Frederick. "Based only on what I have read, of course."

Martin smiled with a tight sort of patience. It was clear he didn't like Frederick and only had him to dinner because Fiona was friends with Barbara.

Frederick continued portentously. "They surmise that the Monets were sold by the gang, if that duo could be called a gang, and the rest went up in the stove. They aren't going to spend any more on it. Coffers shut, eh Martin?"

"I cannot comment," Martin said lightly, annoyance flickering across his brow.

Frederick sat back contentedly. "That is why they are absolutely mum on the subject. And many have speculated about it. Did you see the editorial in the *Times* last Sunday? They can't say they've given it up, and so have just left it hanging."

"Don't tell Lily Boseman that," said Sara.

"I'm sure she knows," said Fiona.

"One priceless work, more or less, isn't going to hurt too terribly much," said Frederick, winking at Martin.

Barbara was scolding. "Don't be so cold, Frederick."

Frederick was casual. "Have another portrait painted, a more flattering one—"

"She's dead!" said Barbara.

"Right. Never mind then. But think of all the problems they'd have down the line. Inheritances. Legacies. Sentiment. Who wants to keep it, who wants to sell. Might be better that it is just gone."

"What a callous thing to say," said Barbara, not without admiration for her red-cheeked banker.

"They can't know for certain," said Kit, but not loud enough. Only Susannah heard and, reading Martin's expression, nudged his leg to stop.

"Why the Tate, Sara?" asked Barbara. "The Monets were owned by Abbiate, were they not?"

"There was a planned Monet exhibition that is now going forward—whole—which no one expected. No one in their wildest dreams believed they'd be found. They'll go back to Abbiate afterwards," said Sara.

"Can't get better publicity than that," said Frederick.

Sara leaned forward. "What has happened with this recovery is that the outcome for the others is further defined as an open question. The claim for the Picasso is proceeding, I know that."

Everyone, excepting Martin, continued to look at Sara expectantly.

"Just the lunch, as I said, and in passing. She was a librarian, and he is a sculptor of no reputation. But I do know through a friend that there is no money to speak of. The father has re-married, so there is a baby and a new wife. If I said any more, I'd be speculating. Really, all you have to do is use your imagination."

"What a mess," said Fiona. "I feel sorry for them."

"I say better off," said Frederick.

"Oh Frederick," said Barbara.

"But it isn't necessarily gone," said Kit, more loudly this time. He was surprised at the sound of his own uneven voice. There was dead silence, which meant that, to varying degrees, everyone knew of his involvement.

"Page four of the arts section," he continued, "first week of September. A column. Not very dramatic, not the kind that sells a lot of papers."

"That's right," said Sara. "That's exactly right—the DNA results from the stove. Old canvas and old nails, but not definitive."

"And really, how could that old Dutch woman have done something like that, really done it?" asked Barbara with restraint. "It never made any sense."

Sara said, "There were many loose ends."

Kit drummed his fingers on his empty glass. "And the brothers never admitted the initial crime. The mother, who was supposed to have done this, has shut up completely."

Susannah looked as if she might cry, and he wished she'd pull herself together.

The atmosphere in the room thickened. Kit stood up, grabbed another bottle of *Chateau Musar* from the center of the table, and poured himself another glass. He was not being reckless, he told himself, because he hadn't said anything that wasn't in the papers.

He toasted the silent group. "To your dying brain cells. And to mine . . ."

Susannah said, "Kit—"

"Kit! *Kit!!!* What are you *doing,* Kit?" he shouted, mocking her, knowing how ugly he sounded and how ugly he was.

Martin plucked the bottle back from him, reaching behind himself to put it on the breakfront.

Kit barely noticed. "Because that, *that,* is a shame. Everything that happened, everything that went on, all for some stolen art. And then that little painting. Fuck the Picasso—no one cares. The portrait, Martin, is the one. How big is it, or was it? Do you know? Martin?"

Kit was at a loss to express the cauldron within himself. Martin now seemed to be getting up and going somewhere—that much he could tell, though the room was beginning to spin.

"And you don't know the half of it," he said, flopping back in his seat, taking the deep breath of not caring. The amber sconces on either side of the fireplace, the deep leaded windows, more pictures in tasteful gilt, brown and black frames, Barbara and Sara, kicking up a bit of nervous conversation. Bowls of fruit, landscapes, the very old portraits. He searched them, looking for a presence within all the black lacquer and aged gold leaf. A few . . . yes, there were a few *there*, speaking, living somehow on the walls, though the subjects were long gone. A young, affronted vicar. A girl with a basket of flowers. A severe woman in a stiff bonnet. There were three in the group he liked, but they didn't quell his longing—they weren't specific enough. They weren't anyone he particularly wanted to *know*. Like magic they spoke from the past but were not her. Not *her*. His eyes lowered to the people, the actual, living, dismayed and shocked people. Susannah, twisting her napkin as if pleading with it; Fiona, frowning slightly but also watching him with interest. The banker, his shirt straining at the buttons as he leaned back and sighed and stifled a contemptuous belch.

A fresh pitcher of water was there at Kit's elbow, and a tall glass.

"Have some water, Kit," said Martin, putting a hand on his shoulder.

CHAPTER 18
FOR THE RECORD

Amsterdam
October 20th, 2012
109 days after the heist

Generally, if she were feeling hopeful when she awoke, she would circle a TV program in the paper with the intention of watching it later, before heading out to the Yab Yum. This was an old habit because more often than not she left the TV off. Prior to the boys getting caught, they'd all watch together, speculate about plots, and make fun of the actors. Contrary to any kind of logic, that dispelled the artificial quality of little people in a box with their tiny houses and tinny words. Alone, her bulbous RCA television with rabbit ears looked so old. Alone, Leonie could see the actors strain and all the glaring plot holes.

So she read instead—there was something cozy about it. She'd once been a very good reader. Mysteries, Harry Potter, True Crime. Occasionally, her mind would drift, and she'd just look out of the window into the inky darkness. She got everything from the library, though they were snooty there, those people she had known for years. Everybody had an opinion.

Now, the wind was getting colder, lifting through the small forest behind the house. She had spent the day before in the root cellar, cleaning out her antique furnace, which was the old way people used to heat their homes around here. Now, she used it mostly for garbage. She also made room for a new crop of baubles and paintings she had bought last week at the flea market. She had always liked to have a collection on hand for gifts—things that appealed to her, bought for a few euros here and there at street sales. Even with all that had happened, she still kept on with it. It wasn't illegal.

She visited the boys a few times a week. Luuk liked new clothes (though he couldn't wear them, he could look forward to wearing them) and gaming magazines. She brought them both cooked dishes like *jachtschotel* and *snert,* which she believed would help them feel okay. For herself, when she had time, she'd taken to visiting cousins and second cousins and people she had known in school who lived far away, who didn't care so much about her supposed crimes. In fact, they were sort of fascinated by all that had happened. She'd bring them a little something from a sale—a clock, a pillow, a painting. They seemed to understand more what she had been through—that her only real fault was being gullible, falling for an idea. The gifts she brought helped to soften them.

In a light rain, the trees sighed, and the birds sang their weak, end-of-summer songs. On her way to the shed, leaves crunched under her step, reminding her she'd need to rake out the garden one of these days. She had been coasting along with tips and wages from the Yab Yum, determined to leave what she called "the capital" in the coffee cans alone. However, after all the lawyer's fees ,she was running low, and Ineke hadn't been to see her for a while.

She nosed the shovel in, heaving up a brown pancake from the damp ground. She sighed—another piffling, back-breaking job. The ground, laced with the stalks of dead tomato plants, would have to be tilled in later. She plucked the remaining vines from the stakes, dropped them in the dirt, and tossed the stakes to the side.

The earth was heavy and mounted slowly into a pile on the side of the hole—at this rate, she'd be digging all morning. She felt the shovel edge through her boot and sunk it, deeper this time. Most people her age had grandchildren, or at least the possibility of them. It would do no good wishing. She remembered the thrill leading up to the job, how she'd enjoyed plotting with markers and pictures on the kitchen table, believing she was in control of this great scheme. Being a rebellious old woman never worked out. That was for kids to get out of their system; adults were supposed to stop them. What a job she had done of it. She searched for a strand of hope to match the change in the air. Luuk would be almost thirty when he got out. If Piet couldn't get his credits at the prison school, he'd have to go to class with those he knew as small children. The four of them were tripwired together, the wire made taut while she was too desperate to think.

Early on, Ineke had continued checking in after her normal work hours—leaving DVDs from the library, sometimes paperback thrillers, never staying for long. Of course, they could not be seen together. Leonie, newly alone, had found her mental toughness waning. She would wait for the weekends when Ineke would dress in her old punky style, ride her red bike up and down the street in figure eights, and bring her a little something after night had fallen. It had been nice to be cared for, even if she was beginning to be suspicious. She had had no one else. Her old friend Marit looked right through her at the market. Her lawyer Benny Bakker took weeks to get back and had cut his visits to less than once a month. She didn't go out, except to work, and that was all hookers and night owls, people she no longer wanted to be associated with. Mistakenly, she had believed she wouldn't need to associate with them anymore—but ended up talking with them just the same.

Ineke's air of certainty had been a panacea at a time when Leonie had agonized over simple questions like whether to walk or ride the bus, or what clothes to wear. With her silk shirts, dresses, and heels, what had started as an internship at the Art Ministry had turned into a real job. She said that she, too, was alone, and troubles borne alone were burdensome. So just accept it and leave it all to her, and they would bear it together. She was especially helpful right after the boys had been taken away and Leonie felt as though she was losing her mind.

The shovel hit something, sending a jarring sensation up to her shoulder. She knelt down and brushed the dirt aside. She reached down into the hole but couldn't get any purchase on the can. She popped the lid off and grabbed the tin by the edge. A few small bugs crawled out from between the damp notes. She sifted through the euros in her hand, which smelled of earth after all this time underground. She began to count it out—hundreds in one pile, fifties and twenties in another. It would make up for the lost income from Luuk for another six months. She stashed it on her windowsill inside and came back out, intending to fill in the hole.

Behind her, the sound of footsteps came up the walkway. Though she had not had a daytime visitor except the garbage man for months, there was someone at the gate. Wedging her shovel in the dirt, she turned around. Not a friend, not a Dutchman, not a cop. He was tall, wearing a dark straight-cut raincoat, moist with rain on his shoulders. He had damp dark hair and striking blue eyes that radiated toward her. He was intent. A shorter academic-looking type stood a little behind. The tall man was bold, resting his hand lightly upon the latch. He seemed certain she'd invite him in.

"Mrs. Berkhof?" he said.

Though she didn't speak English, she thought she detected a British accent in the way he said her name. She had never met a Brit, but she had watched all those shows on Sky TV.

"Ja," she said, telling him with her eyes to take his hand off the latch.

He lifted his hand quickly. The younger man stood back; he was either an apprentice or being paid.

"I'm wondering if you might want to clear things up a bit," the tall man said, which the younger man translated into Dutch.

"For whom?"

"For the record," he said, with a firmness and resolve that

made her consider for a moment how *the record* might in any way be important to her.

"All of that has already happened—you're too late," she said, turning back to her work.

"It's a delicate subject, I know. You've been through a lot. I won't stay any longer than you wish." He handed his credentials to her over the gate, the other man translating again.

"Paul Alder, Private Consulting and Investigating," the younger man translated. It was followed by a London address.

Investigating! Investigators had plagued her for months. If he wanted to be accepted into her home, how did he settle on that? She threw her head back and laughed.

The younger man then piped up nervously, asking if it wouldn't be better if she agreed to continue this conversation inside the gate where they couldn't be heard. He was not much older than Luuk. Inwardly, she sneered at them, pretending their intentions were somehow honorable, sniffing around her house. When she, herself, was innocent! Mostly.

This Paul Alder put his hand on the gate as if it were a thin-shelled egg. "This is Jacob, from Amsterdam, whom I've hired to help me today . . . He is a language student, and a very good translator."

Leonie nodded. "You can come in on the condition this conversation is confidential between us three only. There will be no records, no recording. In fact, you'll have to empty your pockets before we speak."

And that response was communicated to him.

"Phones and anything else in the middle," she directed them as they sat down around her kitchen table.

It had been a long time since she'd had company and prepared something for another person to eat or drink. Standing at the refrigerator, she almost froze. A sense memory began to direct her: pluck a tray from behind the toaster, measure out grounds into the percolator, and flick on the burner. She remembered that she had an extra breakfast pastry to cut up for them and was relieved.

"Who are you working with?" she asked as she puttered around.

"I am not affiliated with any police or organization," said Paul. "But first I'd like to give you a house present, just a little thank you for talking with us."

"I haven't said anything yet," she retorted, opening the bag and taking out a bottle of Fishers Gin. She set it in the middle of the table amongst the phones. Luuk might like it later on. Come to think of it, she might like it.

"Best of Britain . . ." he continued, motioning to the gin. "I do investigations in the UK. But my business here is personal."

"Personal?" she asked, filling the coffee pot with water.

"My own satisfaction. Strictly confidential," he said, noticing the stacks of cash on the windowsill. "There's quite a lot about the story that doesn't hang together."

Her chest felt tight. Why did *he* care? There was a gentle, non-judgmental tone in the man's voice, a sweetness there. He seemed unattached to any particular outcome, though that might be how his charm worked. Still, she didn't like him.

Kit leaned forward. "There was a lot of press, I heard."

"You could say that," she replied. She retrieved the hate mail, press clippings, cartoons, and slurs she had jammed into a basket on the floor. "There you go," she said, dumping it all out on the table next to the phones.

While she unloaded the things from her tray, the two read through most of it, Jacob translating. She was able to pick out a few words of the English: *priceless, crazy, burned, works, bitch.* She had put the worst on the bottom, so she wouldn't see them easily. But in another way, it was useful to be reminded of her ordeal, which was why she hadn't put the whole thing in a closet. It was right to suffer for being so stupid. She still had at least a third of her life to go—could she ever learn to be a better person? She poured the coffee and gave them each half of the pastry on a napkin and a few wedges of cheese.

"How absolutely awful," said Kit, his eyes downcast, reading the letters rapidly. "I never understand how people are able to find addresses, like *your* address, and then take the time to write something like this."

But Leonie resisted the urge to commiserate with him. These two *dwazen*, so pleased with themselves and their virtuous love of art—that was why they were here, of course. Well—the Dutchman was getting paid. What did this Paul Alder think was so awful? She mused bitterly upon the question. Was it that pile of papers? Was it that her sons were in jail and she had no one? Was it that her friends had deserted her? Was it his florid imaginings about cultural crimes? Was it a pile of burned paintings? She decided to make a game of it, to see how much she could say without telling them anything.

"What else could you do?" asked Jacob.

She ignored him. Her eyes slowly shifted over them, taking in each detail: the younger one's earnestness, the older one's weary, deflated pride. He might have been trying to play to her womanly sympathy, not knowing how little she had.

"You are welcome to the coffee, but what do you hope to get from me?" she asked.

Couscous padded into the kitchen and curled around Paul's leg. "Girl or boy?" he asked, smiling and stroking its back.

"Girl," said Leonie, thinking of how Couscous loved Luuk. It was just the same. She had a thing for tall, handsome men who had thoughts brewing in their eyes. Maybe she sensed the tension and wanted to relieve it. Leonie steeled herself. She had no intention of solving this man's problems.

"I'm sure you have been through a lot," said Kit, holding up his cup of delicate porcelain, noticing its worn gilt rim, the last of a beautiful set she had brought from the farm. "I have no interest in seeing you in jail. I'm not affiliated with the art world, or any of the people who wrote these letters, or the press. I just want to tie up some loose ends."

She nodded, still silent.

"I notice you have a lot of artwork on the walls. Do you like art?"

"It's okay. I like pretty pictures," she said, getting out her tobacco and rolling papers.

"You must have been to the wonderful museums in Amsterdam?" he asked, purposely avoiding questions about Rotterdam.

"No. I am not that type," Leonie said firmly, depositing a log of tobacco into a paper.

"What type are you?" he asked.

"I don't have the luxury to be a type," she said, narrowing her eyes at him. "I work in a brothel. I go to work at 18:30 and come home at 4:00." She began to enjoy herself a little, throwing up stone walls all around herself. She could see him thinking, trying to angle his next question. "Would you like me to roll you one?" she asked him.

"Yes," said Kit. "Absolutely."

"Yes," said Jacob, who hadn't been asked.

"And let's crack this open," she said, reaching for the gin. "It's my day off." A complete lie, executed just for the practice. "What do I put with it?" she asked, never having had English gin in her life.

Kit smiled. "Do you have lemons and sugar? Ice?"

"Yes," she said. "Yes, I do."

"I'll do it," said Kit.

Kit became a man making short work of something in the kitchen, a role that he was fond of. She handed him the sugar and lemons.

"I need a pot, a small pot and a flame," he said to Jacob, who translated.

"A half cup of water—no need to be exact," he said, pouring sugar into the pot, along with the water. He handed Leonie a spoon and told her to stir.

"*Roeren,*" said Jacob.

The simple syrup beginning to bubble, he found a bag. And with the underside of another, bigger pot, he crushed the ice in it. Mr. Paul Alder seemed so at home in her house, she found herself relaxing just a bit. The afternoon sun came slanting in, showing the worn linoleum floor with dust bunnies and the empty basket on the floor.

"You don't hate art though, do you?" Kit asked, squeezing the lemons over a strainer she had provided.

"Why do you ask that?" said Leonie.

"Because that's what people say about you. In those letters and clippings . . . and other things I read in the UK papers."

"No," she scoffed. "That—they created."

"Who are they?"

"The press, the police, the art world . . . all the people who wanted to send us to hell." She felt it all over again, how she and Luuk and Piet had been pulled into a web rife with bad advice and sniping hoards who had nothing better to do. Who didn't understand the difference between valuable things and living beings. It felt good to talk about it, to tease out the difference between what she felt responsible for and didn't. Somewhat like a cheap therapist.

"So you had nothing to do with it?"

"Yes and no."

She emptied the ashtray without another word. Kit told Jacob that he hoped his translating skills would stay intact while gin-sodden. Jacob replied that he was in fact a better translator after a drink.

"What?" she asked Jacob, who repeated his theory.

"I can almost understand English after a few of these," she said, setting drinks on the table next to the papers and the phones. Though these men had not presented any solutions, she suddenly felt hopeful, almost girlishly so. Though, not because of them, she insisted to herself.

"Is there anything I might do to make it worth it to you?" he asked. "Again, you do not have to be involved with outcomes."

"Hasn't everything already come out?" asked Leonie.

"No, it has not. Did you hear about the DNA? Have you been following the story? You might not have heard over here."

"Of course, I heard. I have a good lawyer now—unlike the people I've had in the past."

"That's good, that's good," said Kit, filing that away for later.

Behind him, the Soviet-era refrigerator hummed to life. She was not heartless, but she was extremely canny. Kit thought he rather liked her, and that she would make a good spy. He was glad he'd brought the gin. *Yes and no.* What did that mean? He was certain that she wasn't the driver because she was too big. The woman in the museum was much smaller.

She continued. "The DNA said nothing—they could not be sure. No results. Hah! What they accused me of was only speculation! But nobody cared about that part."

"Didn't they publicize the outcome here?"

"Yes, but not on TV. The lie was the big news," she continued. "The truth is the small news. It was in the paper, in the back pages. Like I said, nobody cared about it."

"I'm sorry about that. It often isn't fair, the way the press works. You have been through so much. Tell me about your lawyer. You said he was not like what you had in the past . . ."

"I'm not going to go into that," she said, pulling the basket from the floor and sweeping the clippings into it.

"Good thing you kept those," he said.

"Why is it good?" she asked, with an edge.

"Because then you can say, to a judge if it comes to that—which it will not—that you have already paid in misery. That's a lot, a *lot* of vitriol."

"Then there was the dog shit," she added, nailing him in the eye with it.

"Where?"

"On my top step. A few weeks ago, someone left a pile wrapped in newspaper articles about the Kunsthal. Then another last week, another one, on fire. Right on the front step. And no—if you were going to ask, I did not call the cops. I do not want them around my house again. And I don't for any reason having to do with you. Do you understand?"

"Of course! You have my word. I hope you got pictures."

"No. It won't be necessary because as we have discussed, the DNA results turned up nothing,"

"Yes, the test turned up nothing," said Kit, treading as delicately as possible. "And that puts you in the clear . . . however . . . I understand . . . there was a lot of pressure."

"Do you have kids?" asked Leonie.

"No, I don't," said Kit.

"You?" she motioned with her chin at Jacob.

He shook his head.

"Then neither of you understand at all."

"Ok. Probably not. I can try to imagine though . . ." he said, his hopes deflating fast.

"It isn't the kind of thing you can imagine," she said, her mouth settling into a hard line.

"Your sons were in danger . . . Is that when something happened with a lawyer?"

"None of this would have happened without a bad lawyer, I can tell you that. None of it. The whole mess."

Kit quickly ran through options as to what this statement meant. A bad lawyer . . . a lawyer for whom her resentment was deep. As the afternoon wore on, two things began to emerge: First, she was enjoying their company. Second, though trying to sound resolved and sure, there were vast areas of ambiguity for her as well. Despite having an eccentric, combative nature that wanted to see the world in black and white, for this woman, there was lots of gray.

He looked at Jacob with dramatic incredulity. "Jacob, have your translating skills deserted you? Did I just hear that this was all the fault of a *lawyer?*"

Jacob looked quickly at both of them. Kit nodded that he should translate that.

Leonie listened and laughed again, a wide, encompassing fuck you of a cackle. Kit and Jacob laughed too. She was completely infectious.

She took that as her cue to boot them out. "Come back tomorrow—we'll finish the bottle."

In the car, Kit asked, "Do you think she's telling the truth about the dog shit?"

Jacob nodded wisely. "Oh yes. You have to understand what the Dutch people feel about the art. It's very personal to them."

"Yes, but none of those works were done by a Dutch artist—"

"It doesn't matter. The Kunsthal, along with the Rijksmuseum and the Kunst, it is a point of national pride. You have to understand, the Netherlands is small, yet we have such an art history here. That's why people were so furious at the Berkhof's beginning with the theft . . . and then. She made the Netherlands into a joke. We don't like that."

"What if she didn't do it?" asked Kit.

"She's good at making you think that," said Jacob.

"Let's see what happens tomorrow," replied Kit.

Kit treated Jacob to dinner at the hotel and then went to his room to get on the phone with Martin. Martin was surprised to hear that he was in Holland on his own dime. And as he had suspected, Martin tried to stonewall him about the *Viridian* file. Because, he said, he'd have to contact the Dutch police. Kit didn't doubt it, and he also knew that Martin would come up with any excuse he could muster. It was almost fun to hear him bluster, until Martin told him to "do whatever you like" and that the case was closed. Which meant that all the Dutch records in the file were off-limits.

"I don't believe it. Who told you that?" asked Kit.

"Don't need to be told—that's policy. It's over and done. We were lucky the Monets had been fenced."

"As you said," Kit replied, "Berkhof is crazy. Does she know the difference between the truth and her own lies at this point? And there are other players in this scenario. She herself might have been kept in the dark after all of this publicity. I don't see how we can ignore the *fact* that the driver is still out there."

"That's for Holland to deal with. Not our purview."

"But they're incompetent!!"

"Not true. Kit, don't forget, we aren't officially involved now. No matter the fit you threw at my house."

Boiling with frustration, Kit watched the *Westertoegang* flowing by five stories below his room. "Martin, I'm so close! There's something going on here, a deeper story, I promise you. Why wouldn't you want to finish it?"

"This is about that girl," ventured Martin.

"For God's sake, Martin, she isn't even in Holland. And anyway, how would that equate for her?" Kit seethed at having the tangle that surrounded the portrait reduced to a sordid obsession.

"Listen, this happens. It's happened to me. You get overinvested in people, you want to make it right for them. A few years down the line you'll look back on *Viridian* with pride. It will become clear to you what part of this really mattered."

"Never going to happen. By the way, Perrin—yes, that is her name—wasn't just a Lottie. She was a person, and we put her at great risk."

"Well, I'm sorry about that, and for all that you went through, and *she* went through. Unfortunately, we cannot predict—"

"Exactly. You can't. Suppose the other two turn up somewhere . . . say in a rubbish bin. How will that look? As if we didn't care. Nothing the Berkhofs say is reliable—you can't argue with that. If the two paintings are found in any condition at all and we aren't involved . . . well, it really couldn't look any worse."

Martin was silent and then said, "Kit, what happened that night?"

Though this was the question Kit had hoped for, it felt like an intrusion. "I'm not going to go into it. I can only say she was reaching across a very deep chasm before things fell into place—finally. The service really didn't give a damn about the outcome, Martin. Don't try and gloss it over."

"I'm sorry, I really am. It's just the way it goes in our line of work."

A glimmer of sympathy is sometimes more powerful than a surplus. Kit collapsed in a chair, half-watching as a tourist barge went under the *Aluminiumbrug* bridge.

"Why did she do it? Why did she help us?" he asked, only because Martin was the only person to whom he could safely confide. "I wish she had complained at least once, and that she hadn't been so reliably brave."

"Kit, people do all kinds of things . . . sometimes it's the glamour, the subterfuge, the fight for the good. But don't forget that she signed on."

"She liked the Hochberg the best . . ." Kit said, feeling as if he were talking to himself. "She didn't even really like the Monets. She said they were artifacts."

"Hah! Opinionated!"

"Yes."

"But I think if we're honest here about her reasons, Kit, she was—don't fly into a rage—doing it for you. You did your English lad thing. It worked, and you feel guilty."

"She was *not.* In fact, she didn't even tell me she was going to try until the last minute. In the middle of the night, in a *hurricane,* Martin. Have you ever experienced one? All I had was a text. She was going it alone, and I must say, her instincts were very good. And we were *very* lucky that the briefcase was there and I could monitor. It might have been her in the pool instead of . . . of that bastard—and no Monets for you. You can't speak about it in jest, Martin. I'll hang up, and you'll never hear from me again."

Martin was silent.

"She was inspired, she really was, by something more elevated than you might be thinking," Kit continued, sadness in his voice. "And I did the dirty work for you. And *she* did. Right, Martin?"

"That's the risk. And you knew it too when you got into this work. You were attracted to it for some reason—it suited you."

"You set me up to finish the business with Glasgow. I was your only choice for that, and I delivered. Beginning with the gimcrack operation at the Taj and then siccing me on him like a rabid dog. You can't deny it. We will never again be on the same footing because I know the depths to which you have sunk. But now I'm your star player. If you want me to play along, you are going to have to work something out."

"Okay."

"To begin with, I want that file. *And* I want back up if I get onto something—"

"*What* something. You aren't being realistic. I'm saying this to protect you from false hopes. The woman burned the Picasso and the Hochberg. The Monets were fenced early. I think you'd better accept it—"

"You have never talked to her. I have. Logically, it comes down to the driver. She and her two sons are shielding that person—why? For what possible reason? I think that they play a big part in all of this. Things are murky—"

"Kit! She's *kept* things murky, the reason being she doesn't want to get charged for what she did!"

"You're just going to have to cough up the money and the file. I think I'll need at least seven thousand. I'm staying at the Ibis Amsterdam Center."

* * *

Tired from the club, Leonie got up around noon the next day. Her first thought was that she had left the shovel outside on top of a half-finished job, in the rain no less. And the second was that they were going to be back soon. She powered down a cup of strong coffee and went outside.

Before all of this, she hadn't been exposed to the legal system. Now, instead of finding it an instrument of oppression as she had believed, she had discovered in it a meandering but relentless logic. Did Luuk and Piet deserve four years for the crimes that Ineke had led them to? Yes, but Luuk much more than Piet. Because Piet was more innocent and truly in love, whereas Luuk was just hormone and cash-addled, wanting what he couldn't have. And that was reflected in the sentencing, Piet getting half the time Luuk did.

As she heaved a shovelful of dirt into the hole, she thought about her art collection in the cellar, how she was always hoping that one would be a big winner at Hessink's, or the artist would suddenly come into favor. Though she prided herself on picking "good" pieces, she didn't take it very seriously, and now it seemed more a fairy tale than ever. What was a painting really, but a scheme? A bid to play upon the imagination of the viewer, to exploit their feelings or appeal to their vanity. Most successful portraitists were paid to make people prettier than they actually were or, in the case of the artist that did the portrait of the woman, say something about who she was. That was the game. But it was up to an individual to know themselves, what they would and would not do, and up to the people closest to them to know them without the aid of a stranger's perception. Therefore, she was not sorry.

* * *

The *Viridian* file and the cash were delivered to Kit by courier, landing at his hotel at 9:00 a.m. That gave him enough time to prepare before they went back. Fortunately, Jacob was available and almost eager for another drinking and delving session. They sat in a corner of one of the conference rooms of the Ibis and laid the file's contents out. First, the Dutch dispatches from the *Viridian* documents. He wrote out a timeline of *Viridian* dates, starting with the theft, the commencement of the liaison with the FBI's art crime unit, removing sensitive information like the housekeeper's name and Glasgow's name and addresses, leaving only what was safe to tell. Then, from the Dutch police dispatches, he extrapolated a timeline to run concurrently with developments in the U.S. As he passed each of the Dutch documents to Jacob, he noticed their quality of being undisturbed—he was almost sure that in London's haste to cut losses and move on, they'd never been translated or read. Jacob took it piece by piece, translating for Kit, notating in Dutch and English. These items were then inserted into the *Viridian* timeline which was translated to Dutch for Mrs. Berkhof. Kit made sure to leave in juicy bits from *Viridian* that had made it into the news—like just how far the Monets had wandered, and the glamorous village in the U.S. where they were found—in the hopes of tweaking Mrs. Berkhof's curiosity.

When they were done, they had lunch near the hotel, their table wobbling persistently, no matter how many packs of matches were jammed under it. Beyond the state of the table, Kit did not provide much conversation and hoped he didn't seem grumpy. This day of all days, there must be no fissures in the personality he would portray, though he felt strafed with them.

A slow drizzle pecked at the puddles on the road outside their window. There were revelations in the *Viridian* file that Kit hadn't been prepared for. Some were very helpful, and some were not. The potentially volatile connection between himself and Glasgow was never mentioned. The choice had probably been so obvious that it did not warrant even a few words jotted down. Once they'd identified that Glasgow was behind the Taj bombing—the choice of Kit for Sagaponack, NY had likely existed as a suggestion only between Martin and the others. Was it a raised eyebrow? A nod? Were both a raised eyebrow and a nod expended on the decision to put him on *Viridian*? It sickened him to think of it.

Susannah came to his mind, his leg beginning to throb in the dampness. He knew that his marriage was over, that the way they had loved and known each other—if indeed they had ever really known each other—was too far in the past and could not be resuscitated. She had barely spoken to him since that night at Martin's. He had felt so sheepish about it that he had hardly been home in the few weeks since then. She might have intuited that something had happened while he was overseas. But typical Susannah, she wouldn't pry. If he knew much about her at all, he knew that. They could go on, his vile attitude and his drinking unchanged, and she would bear it. Which was insufferable. He remembered driving back from London that night, she at the wheel because he was so drunk, each of them cocooned in hard and unforgiving silence.

Kit thought of Perrin last, and not until then did his mind release the past and old treacheries as if they didn't matter. It is better to be free, he mused, watching a small houseboat appear on the canal and chug away sweetly and waywardly, a girl of about eleven at the wheel. If one's life feels like a bench vise, it is only freedom that matters. Though freedom hinged on intangible things, it was possible—all that was needed was faith. This was the revelation. Perrin was last in his thoughts because it all led to her. He missed her terribly. She, *she* was the place, so many miles away over the wide and wild sea, where his thoughts and entire being converged, where the fragments of himself flowed into one. That stretch of time afterwards, consumed with tying up loose ends in New York and trying to resume his farcical life in London while thinking so often of her face, her eyes, her yielding body, the way she took him into herself without hesitation, as if knowing the same thing as he—that they fit together perfectly, that there were worlds to discover in the other one. After such grace, he had reverted to the bloody book—wind up job, sever ties, and skulk back to the UK. He wouldn't blame her if she hated him now.

Then they were there again, at the woman's house, so fast. Too fast. He wished he'd had a little more time to prepare what he was going to say, though he felt certain that he had uncovered some interesting things that she would want to know about. He thought back to his school days. Even if you flubbed an oral presentation, the text and the ideas were mostly what mattered, even if you were rattled. You had to believe that people were capable of discerning what you meant.

Leonie was near that same spot, her face averted. The little wood at the back of the property dripped and creaked, alive with the hard twitter of birds. Leonie—*Leonie?* Or was it best to err on the side of caution and stick with Mrs. Berkhof?

He watched her, and for a moment, Kit thought the two paintings might be deep in that damp ground, or the ashes of them. Martin's words—*I think you better get used to it*—nagged at him. Why did she hover there? It was true that she knew they were coming and that she liked a game. It might be a tease. A number of interrogations in basement rooms told him to follow his instincts, and his instincts told him that she had a playful side. She walked back and forth meditatively, tamping down the earth with her weight. A lit, home-rolled cigarette dangled from her lips, and she plucked it from her mouth upon seeing them.

Jacob, who was a cautious fellow, waited for her to open the gate. She deposited the shovel against the side of the house and went inside, beckoning them to follow.

"Looks intimidating," she said, regarding the file that Kit held. Rummaging around in her bag, she plucked out her tobacco. "Are we having coffee again?"

They both shook their heads. Jacob retrieved the bag of lemons, cheeses, and crackers they had bought from his backpack. He set them on the table, making some sort of Dutch joke about drinking in the middle of the day. Kit noticed that the basket of notes and clippings was nowhere to be seen.

"Okay, here we go again . . ." she said, sitting down with a sigh.

"We'll make this as quick as we can," said Kit, and Jacob translated that. By giving Jacob a few sentences at a time, Kit hoped to follow along with her reactions.

"So there's the act," said Jacob. "The museum, it's tantalizing—the pickings look so easy. So you plan this, you all decide. Easy money, right? But it isn't . . ."

In Dutch, it sounded like gibberish to Kit.

". . . the cops are circling, your sons are caught, one after the other. Your relationship with the third person—a woman?—it begins to deteriorate. Your only desire is to protect your boys . . ."

Leonie, in command of herself again in the daylight, was giving away very little. While she listened, she felt as though she were being attacked. After all, it was *her* life, not Paul Alder's. She was surprised to hear that the two Monets that were found in the U.S. were now back in a British museum. But she found herself more interested in the way Paul was speaking about it. He was in very deep somehow. Some way that went beyond just paintings, no matter how valuable they were.

After quite a speech, Jacob kept translating bits from Paul. "And from this I concluded that you, or someone, sold two, maybe on the cheap side. Early on. You didn't think or contemplate much . . . you just needed the money."

At this, she shut down completely, though he kept blathering on, talking about the fallout from the heist. Here was the *big picture,* he said. With mounting excitement, he veered into broader territory, becoming philosophical about how people, Holland, the art world, and the family of that woman in the painting who died were connected by the crime. Oh, that woman, that *woman.* People just went on about it. Didn't he know her by now, even a little bit? Like a salesperson trying to paint a picture for a hapless listener, it was baby talk. It was nothing talk. One big fat zero.

As he expounded on, she dumped peanuts in a bowl, poured Couscous some food, and plunked down ice for the drinks. Was he playing on some idea of karma? She didn't believe in karma. That was just a basic fear that everyone had. Buddha, karma, Allah, and good old God, the one she had grown up with, foisted upon her and in whom she never believed. People attempted to do everything the right way, so they would be spared on judgment day. As if anyone really knew what happened on judgment day, or if there was anything to be done about it. She only knew that there was no way to avoid leaving a footprint in this world. Actions led to other actions rippling away from the center, and many centers in a day, in an hour, in a life overlapping. It was confusion—complete chaos. The only certainty was the repercussive effect, the rippling out—that he was right about. As for what had happened to whom, she would not take responsibility, except for what had happened to Luuk and Piet.

He soon ran out of steam, arms falling to his sides. He had not gotten his foot in the door the way he had planned. With that velvety voice and style of delivery, almost like an actor, it must have worked on lots of people.

Jacob scratched his head, and they both shifted around, sipping their drinks, looking here and there as if fascinated by her shabby kitchen. Jacob tossed back a handful of peanuts and chewed wolfishly. Leonie wondered if anyone fed him in the mornings, he was so thin. Not so the well-fed tall one who called himself Paul. He looked like a Paul, but that wasn't his name. He sighed and riffled through his papers, Couscous winding around his leg.

Finally, he seemed to pick up that the passionate approach wasn't working. Out of weariness or strategy, he shifted to a flat, almost bored tone, and Jacob copied him. And yes, she was more comfortable with that. Together, they began to itemize the timeline, Jacob translating each item.

"Okay. *July 3rd, 13:45. Officer de Haan responds to alarm at the Kunsthal.*"

She felt herself nod infinitesimally.

"Call from Kunsthal director Kaarle DeVries, July 1st, 14:03."

"July 6th. Press is formally briefed by inspectors Dijkman and Groot, and Kaarle DeVries."

"July 7th. Tip line opened and publicized. 17 calls received."

"July 8th to July 13th. Follow up calls and canvass."

Paul stopped for a moment and said something to Jacob, who explained the tip line follow-ups and canvass procedure for her. If the tips didn't go anywhere, there wasn't a report on that grouping. Leonie had a sinking feeling as to why that was important and braced herself.

Paul drummed his fingers on his knee. "*July 13th. CCTV of Kunsthal robbery released to public.*"

"July 10th. Re: 1 Hochberg, 2 Monets, 1 Picasso. Liaise with Art Crimes Division UK."

"July 14th. Press conference, Inspectors Dijkman and Groot with Kaarle DeVries. Call for tips."

"July 15th to July 17th. Follow up calls and canvass."

"July 19th. Tip line screeners report. 15 calls. 1 flagged. Female. Anon. Burner."

He stopped for a moment, as if looking for a reaction. When she gave him none, he began again.

"August 1st. Canvass visits to residences: Kulper, Lange, Jaager, Berkhof, Visscher."

She licked her lips. "I remember. They came. They came to my house. And those are all people that live on my street."

He stopped. "Yes. They had narrowed down to your area. Because . . . let's read on. I'm sorry if it's painful, I truly am."

"What is a burner?" she asked.

"That's a cheap phone that can't be traced."

She felt herself nodding again and stopped.

"August 2nd. Dispatch to Piet Berkhof's school and Luuk Berkhof's place of work, The Blue Parrot. Piet and Luuk Berkhof arrested."

Leonie lowered her head into her hands and groaned.

"Do we need to take a break?" asked Kit.

"Just get through it!" she barked.

"August 23rd. After repeated visits to the Berkhof residence, ashes were discovered in the basement stove. Mrs. Berkhof stated, 'I burned them all.' Berkhof unsteady, had possibly been drinking. Ashes bagged and labeled for testing." There was a pause, and then Jacob translated, "Did you say this, Leonie?"

"Yes, yes, I did," she said, looking up, her eyes wet.

Jacob put a hand on her shoulder to steady her. She did not welcome it.

Kit dropped the file to his lap and looked hard at Leonie. "Did you say then that you lied?"

"My lawyer told me to say that!"

"It's true though. It *was* a lie!"

"Yes, *yes*, it was a lie. He said I could go to jail, and I hadn't helped the boys at all! So I took it back! I don't know what got into me that day. It was all too much, and I was so angry . . ."

"Is that the lawyer you were so unhappy with?"

"No, *no*, it was the first one."

"What first one?"

"Guus Maijer. The one we had for Luuk when he was fifteen."

"For what?"

"Shoplifting. Don't you know about it? The police do."

Jacob opened up the file. "Not in here," he said.

Leonie's lips pursed in frustration. "He did fifteen hours of community service. The record was supposed to be sealed or thrown out or I don't know what. Then the DNA, the goddamn hair in the van!"

Jacob pulled from the file anything he thought might be relevant, while Kit found the sheet for Luuk. Fortunately, Jacob had taken the time to translate it at the hotel.

Kit read up and down and said, "I see nothing here about when your son was fifteen."

Jacob piped up. "That wouldn't have been in there anyway. That was trial evidence and so forth. These are police files."

"Yes, right—of course!" said Kit.

"Okay, right. That was a part of the trial," said Leonie.

"Yes, I read the transcript. Of course, it was," said Kit. "Which leads me to—"

"Benny said they couldn't do anything until the analysis of the ashes. Then, in the end of August, I guess, someone from the police leaked to the press what I first said."

"Which wasn't true," said Kit.

"No! Okay, no!"

"Or—it could have gotten out another way . . ." said Kit.

Leonie felt pins and needles under her skin, along with a kind of heat that was clouding her vision. She tried to breathe and open her eyes.

"To begin with," Kit continued, "I am surprised that no one

bothered to mention to *you* about this call to the tip line, seeing as the third thief was female and never found."

Leonie snatched the paper out of Kit's hands, though she couldn't read it. Jacob handed her the translation.

"Who do you think this woman is, on a burner phone, tipping the police to concentrate on your street?"

"That was what she said?"

"Yes. I would say absolutely, yes, because of the action that was taken. They hadn't unsealed your son's record yet. That took a while."

"What about the trial? Why didn't they mention it?" she asked.

"Because an anonymous tip is hearsay and not admissible as evidence. Your friend probably knew that."

Leonie sat back in her chair with a ragged sigh. "She's not my friend," she said, bracing herself. This guy, *Paul*, was all set with the news. He was dying to tell her all that she didn't want to know.

Jacob translated every two or three lines as Paul went through his theory.

"So, here's what I think happened, Leonie. Because of this tip, they did an analysis of all the households on your street. Because of the tip—this *credible* tip—they went further. They found everyone in the neighborhood who would have fit the description, and then they did a deep, deep dive. It took them a few weeks, but finally, as you know, Luuk's juvenile record and DNA records were unsealed, and they made the match with the hair in the van. But that connection would never have been made without them concentrating on this neighborhood."

"What made this tip so credible?"

"She probably had details that no one else would have known. Which makes it even more of an outrage that they didn't share this with you."

"Is there anyone you think could have made this call?" he asked, as gently as he could.

But she had stopped listening. Benny Bakker, who she liked and even trusted, might have said something about the caller. A woman caller to the tip line, especially when there were so many stories in the press about the third thief, the driver—how could he have missed it? Wasn't it his job to keep her out of jail?

"Is the woman still around?" asked Kit.

Leonie expelled a puff of air that told him yes, she was.

"I'm really sorry about all of it," Kit said as Couscous hopped onto his lap, purring mightily.

"I think I can guess how this is all adding up for you, and I want to help." Balancing the cat on his knees, he reached for his backpack.

Leonie, as she waited for Jacob's translations, remained silent. She felt she needed another gin drink to temper the shock. There had always been too much mystery about Ineke. The boys loved it, but men always love a mysterious, dangerous girl. She herself might have been drawn to the long shot, the chance hit, the odds of a million to one. She might have thought a turn for the better was overdue, and that Ineke was the agent that would deliver it. Wanting things, or believing you deserved them, did not make them real.

Having retrieved what he wanted, Paul tossed it into the air and caught it. "See how little this is?" The device was dwarfed by his hand. About a quarter of the size of a pack of cigarettes, he placed it on the table next to the phones. "Jacob downloaded the manual in Dutch. I wasn't sure that we were going to get to this point, but I think, I hope that in the long run, you will see that this is the only way to put this right."

She felt herself nodding almost imperceptibly.

He ran a hand down the cat's back. "You know what this is for and what you need to do? We need the location of the remaining paintings. I am guessing that she has them or knows where they are. But the most important thing is to get her on tape talking about the theft, her part in it. Can you pull this woman into your sphere and get her to tell you? Is there a reason to hope?"

She nodded again, very slightly.

"Couldn't be any easier to work it," said Paul.

"Make sure to keep it charged," Jacob said, as if he was rooting for her.

These men, *these men,* they were getting to her. She watched with empty eyes while Jacob plugged it in next to the coffee maker and then placed the manual neatly in line with the counter tiles. "It's easy," Jacob continued, "especially for a big smartie such as you."

So easy, she thought, sitting at the kitchen table the next morning, rolling her first cigarette with shaking hands, trying to ignore the device. It waited in the corner of her eye—black, shiny and slick. It seemed to want her to start something. Right now. Leonie approached, wrenched the plug from the wall, and gingerly re-positioned the whole lot under the table out of sight. She sat back down and drank some of her coffee. She needed to pull herself together before thinking about any of that. She felt that if she touched it again, it would take control of her.

At the beginning, Benny Bakker had suggested that *she* was the driver; at first, he did not believe her when she told him she was not. Even though it was very obvious on the tape that she was not. She was too big. She took a deep drag of the cigarette and coughed. She had trusted Benny, *as much as she trusted anyone.* That was the trademark of the old: getting things stuck in your head the way you wanted them to be or the way they used to be, the way you heard them someplace, that time when you were really listening. She thought that because he was about her age, and because he came from the country, that he was her ally. But he might not really have been. He might have just been getting things done his way.

Before they left, she asked Paul, or whatever his name was, to have Jacob read out that transcript a third time. For a while after that, they just sat together not saying anything—Leonie absorbing the facts, Paul fending off Couscous's advances, the three of them mostly quiet. Eventually, Paul had asked about more drinks. Yes, yes, to that. An old hand in her kitchen now, he found the simple syrup he had made in the refrigerator, crushed the ice for the glasses, and squeezed four lemons, carefully extracting the seeds from the juice.

After that, she spilled it, the thing that they so desperately wanted to know. Finally, finally, *finally*. It felt good—the one good outcome of the day—to just throw it all out there. Paul, in his rough friendly way, did not judge her. Jacob, as he translated, had a look of wonder. He couldn't hide that he thought her cunning impressive, or that she was totally nuts, or some combination of the two.

Two that she didn't like very much, all four on display in the house, all similar in size to those four that were called the Kunsthal masterpieces and considered irreplaceable. Well, they weren't, were they? She had, of course, asked Paul that, unable to resist the question. All made out of the same stuff—canvas, nails, and paint. Yes? *Yes*. Just an illusion, nothing more, tossed into the stove with a pair of rubber shoes. All of those tears, and all of that hatred. Trash, trash, *trash*, she muttered, grinding out her cigarette, thinking of the day the experts came barreling through the door, their arms encased in orange gloves up their elbows, and filled twenty glass jars with ashes from her humble stove. Did she believe they'd stop the prosecution of the boys? No, it was a short-term fix, a blind explosion of frustration. Not knowing what Ineke had done with the real and actual works was a problem she didn't trouble herself with at the time. And stupidly, she kept putting that question aside, over and over again, while letting herself be plied. She sighed and leaned back, avoiding the black wire under the table. If she did this thing, the girl's life would be ruined.

She felt her own eyes becoming sad again, emptying out. She had barely cried over any of this, and she wasn't going to start now. She hated sad-eyed people. Mainly, she hated what they were sad about. It was awful—sadness. It was contemptible. Life dealt its blows, and that was that. You had to keep on.

The next day Leonie knew that Ineke would be off from work. The night before, she had put the framed picture sideways and a note to Ineke in the frog pot, saying that she wanted to meet as soon as possible and that Ineke should set aside some time. After work, in the park? Paul had coached her not to set off alarm bells but be absolutely firm. As instructed, she called Paul when she got an answer back and gave him the meeting place and the time. Again, he told her not to worry, that he'd be listening in. He also said that he would give her soft guidance through her tiny earpiece and that Ineke would not be able to detect it. Obviously, he'd have to go through Jacob, who would be translating. After disconnecting the call, she felt a hint of sweetness, of being cared for in an unfamiliar way, and she dared to hope the feeling might continue.

Since her car was in the shop, she walked to the agreed-upon spot. It took her about an hour. A bench in the park—the one out in the open, not the one almost in the woods—Leonie had insisted. Ineke didn't object and said she'd bring a picnic. The picnic was so out of character, Leonie thought that she wouldn't actually show. But sure enough, after a few minutes wait, there she was in her little car, with a new, longish blonde hairstyle (a wig?), pulling a basket from the back seat. As if providing a picnic was an unaccustomed strain on her system, she swung the basket onto the bench and silently and hurriedly unloaded a thermos, cheese, crackers, paper towel napkins, and a knife.

"How are you?" Leonie decided to ask.

"Fine—why all the fuss? It's dangerous to meet like this."

Ineke wouldn't meet her eye and instead concentrated on cutting cheese squares to fit on the crackers. Wearing black jeans and red kiddie shoes, she was paler than before. Leonie felt the familiar heavy atmosphere and Ineke's furious concentration. It was always as if she were weaving something new out of thin air. Other people—Leonie herself at the moment—figured into Ineke's atmosphere only slightly, and that was the same. But the girl was somehow different—thinner, and behind that sheaf of blonde hair, her movements were grudging and jerky.

"I asked you, what is the big urgency? You must be *lonely*, I guess," Ineke spat, finally lifting her chiseled pale face, its prettiness all but gone, the whites of her eyes showing beneath the iris like crescent moons.

As promised, Jacob spoke quietly—*steady . . . steady*—which prompted Leonie to take a big breath. They sat sipping the spiked cider, pondering the shared secret that Leonie still did not understand.

"No, that's not it. You know it isn't," Leonie finally said, telling herself that Ineke couldn't be as awful as she seemed. That she was still only eighteen years old.

"They've gotten to you," said Ineke.

"Who has gotten to me?"

"The lawyers. They want you to give me up!" said Ineke, dropping the cup down with a clatter.

Leonie took a deep breath. *Creep up on her slowly . . . casually . . .* "You are so pale, Ineke. What have you been living on—cheese and crackers?"

"Don't worry about me. I eat all the time. Dad does a run to the store once a week. I've learned to cook for myself."

"And drink a fair amount—"

"Drinking and cooking is a great combination, no?"

"Do you sleep?" Leonie asked.

"No, I do not sleep. What are we here for?"

"I think you know. All you need to do is think about it. What kind of fool would I be if at this point I didn't want to understand what you are doing . . ."

There was a long silence, while Leonie observed Ineke's sharp elbows through her sweatshirt. She felt for her with a mother's pity, no matter what was coming.

"Did I mention that I'm going to law school? *Utrecht Law*. Full scholarship. That is going to be really important for the outcome of the plan," said Ineke, pulling a pack of Marlboro from her pocket with a trembling hand.

The girl was assuredly up to law school if her life didn't fall apart. As it might very soon. "Our plan? How is it our plan if I don't know what you are talking about?"

Ineke lit the cigarette, her white brow furrowing. "I want you to put your thinking cap on."

"It's on," said Leonie, "and it is telling me that you've been controlling everything from the start, beginning with the heist. And that has got to stop."

"Good," said Jacob/Paul.

"No, that is something that you've dreamed up. All I had to do was talk about the possibilities, a little. Both of your sons were dying to get in on it. And so were you. *Dying* to."

Leonie shook her head. "You seduced them. You think you were sly, but I saw. It's a very lucky thing that Piet didn't crack up his bike that night when you dumped him."

"Steady . . ."

"Your thinking cap is still not on," said Ineke. "It was necessary to separate from him, of course! What about when *I* realized about the license plates that morning, that he had covered them up because of the farmer? So *many things* I worked out—the full moon, the works we should focus on. All good picks . . . and yes, I sold those two Monets in July for a tidy sum. There. That's some good information for you. You should be grateful that I knew enough to sell them for close to what they were worth and make those distributions . . ."

"Yes. Now we are getting somewhere."

". . . well, a good price for the black market, which is different. That's what you want, right? More money?" she asked.

"Sure, yes, I'll take it. But I want to know about the other two. The Picasso and that portrait of the woman. Did you sell them? To whom? If not, where are they?"

Ineke pretended not to hear her.

"Just wait," said Jacob.

"It comes from Dutch shipping history. It comes out of the trade. Do you know your history?"

"What little I was paying attention to in school," Leonie replied, reaching for her bag of tobacco.

"Why do you still smoke that?" asked Ineke. "You can afford better."

"Still pinching the pennies, I guess," said Leonie, her heart beginning to pound. She held herself back from adjusting the wire under her shirt to make sure it was working.

"You must know that through the entire seventeenth century, the Dutch Republic was the biggest shipping power in the world. The bailiffs who watched over everything had to have authority that went further than in other countries; they needed to be able to seize stolen goods on ships without the ships just sailing off with them. If goods were suspected stolen, they were held for a period of time. If no one claimed them, they were possessed by the state, and *that* is connected to the concept of *marché ouvert.*"

"*Marché ouvert* . . ." said Leonie, bracing herself for the spectacular whirl that was going on in the mind of her friend who she had known since she was five, and in whom she had trusted. "Isn't that French?"

"Yes, it means 'open market.' The purpose of laws like these was to extinguish dead issues. If you had been naming yourself as the owner of this or that property, even if you stole it, and nobody *disputes* that, then you're the owner. As long as you make it sometimes available for sale."

"I understand, sort of," said Leonie, licking her cigarette closed.

"And there are discreet ways of carrying that off . . ." said Ineke, jutting out her chin.

"Don't say a word. Wait for her to talk."

"It's a question of time," Ineke eventually continued. "'Forgotten is forgiven.' So said F. Scott Fitzgerald."

"Who is that?"

"American writer," said Ineke, flipping her hand as if imparting this information into a void. "It hardly matters. It's the *meaning* of the line . . ."

"Keep her going. Then you must lay down your aim."

"It sounds true to me," said Leonie, savoring the words. "Forgotten is forgiven. Has a nice ring. At your age, I wouldn't have understood that."

"I just read a lot of books," said Ineke, flicking her long ash to the pavement. "And truly, I can imagine these things. I can imagine myself as old as you."

"As old as *me?"* Leonie kidded her, in the same way that Paul had her.

"Yes, old woman. As old as you. I just go to a place inside my head and assemble around me all the details of such a life. The creaky knees, the trolley for the supermarket, the batwing arms, the long nights. The coupons."

While trying to keep her fingers from shaking, Leonie held a match to her cigarette. "Well, all that is fine, but what I want is to talk about the two paintings that I partially own—the actual, real, two paintings. Being so smart, you must have figured that out."

Ineke didn't hear her or pretended she didn't. "The Netherlands is considered a way station for stolen art in certain circles. Olivier de Weis—you've heard of him?"

"Yes. From you—"

"Also known as The Monkey, he's sitting in the Bijlmerbajes right now. I hear he has a pretty good time—"

"A good time in jail," Leonie said, exhaling. "That's a good laugh."

"Steady . . ."

"He is a powerful man. He's just waiting it out—never talked. He can get anything he wants. He's probably living just like he did at home. What you did cleared the way, Leonie. I was inspired by you," said Ineke.

Leonie was silent at this absurdity. She knew her face was grim.

"You see, if I am free, I can sit on these works. They are safe. Occasionally, I put them in a flea market someplace way out in the country where no one knows anything. But I don't sell them. I just document it."

Leonie shook her head in dismay.

"You don't always put two and two together, old lady—"

"I've done pretty well up till now," said Leonie, asking what sort of inspiration she possibly could have provided.

"Shhhhh . . ."

"First, you left it up to me. Then, burning those thrift store paintings, you took the focus off the search. That was smart."

"I didn't do that for *you,"* said Leonie, hoping to jolt her back to reality. Clearly, she was drifting in and out.

"What does she mean?"

"It just came to me, at the Art Ministry. It came together in a beautiful way . . . You stick with your plea of innocence. There's nothing they can say now. Don't forget that the DNA is inconclusive . . . Remember I told you it would be?"

"Shhhh . . ."

"Then, after about ten years, me taking care of everything, we actually own the paintings. By the law of *marché ouvert*, which, by the way, is an antique cousin of another property rights law: adverse possession. Adverse possession is used all the time in the real estate world. Since I am not legally associated with the theft, I can turn up one day a long time from now. I bought them innocently, see? And there's nothing anyone can say."

"Wow," said Paul.

Leonie waited for an opening and pounced. "I *told* you. You have to take me to where the paintings are. I have to see them."

Again, Ineke ignored her words. "I'm on a new medication. That's why I'm able to keep the job and go to school. You should be happy for me. You've been a little like a mom to me, when I had none."

"You have had an interesting way of showing your appreciation."

"For that I'm sorry. The doctor said the medication can make me irritable."

"I must see them. The paintings. Now. Today."

Ineke pulled open the picnic basket and started loading the

things in quickly. "That's impossible and a bad idea. You would be more vulnerable if you knew."

"If you don't show them to me, forget it—I'm not going on with this farce. Don't try the tears with me. They won't work."

"That will ruin everything," said Ineke, her voice quavering. "I thought we were all in this together."

"Together? *Together*? What a laugh! You were the only one who could have made the call to the police. Yes. I know about that now. I wouldn't even put it past you to leave the dog shit, just to keep me off-balance."

Ineke hopped to her feet, brushing ash and crumbs from her jeans. "How do you know that?"

Leonie was stumped. What should she say?

"You pressed your lawyer to get the police report for you," said Jacob, as fast as translating would allow.

"I . . . I got Benny to get the police report . . . of course, I did! I needed to find out exactly what happened!"

Ineke loomed over her in a scary way. "Yes! I did make the call! It was right around then I realized that we'd have to give way a bit!"

"Give way? *What*? And then the leak about the burning . . . That was you, right?"

"Use your head, you stupid cow! The law and the press, they are like a beast—you have to feed it. Who knows that better than you?"

Leonie stayed rooted to the bench. "Don't think you are going anywhere, Ineke!"

"When you told me about burning the fakes, everything just fell into place. I just kept thinking, of course, *of course* . . . this was meant to be! Then I got into *law school*. Don't ruin it now!"

Leonie saw a glint of metal in Ineke's hand. "Put that away!"

"What is she doing?" asked Jacob.

Instead, Ineke opened the knife and cupped her hand around it, as if hiding her intentions.

"Be careful!"

Leonie leapt to her feet. It was going to be now or never. She must not lose control. "Don't make the mistake of leaving or doing anything stupid. You can move them afterwards. But I want to *see* them."

Ineke's blonde fringe fell over one eye. She looked at Leonie with the cold flat stare of a child. How monstrous she was, with that knife in her hand.

"Don't make it worse," said Leonie. "You've already messed up. We all have."

Her attention was caught by a streak of red. Blood fell into the grass, as Ineke closed her white fist on the knife. "You can't do this," said Ineke, on the verge of tears. "I don't know what I'll do. You can't take this away from me."

"Stop it, Ineke! Stop it! I have a friend, yes! I am no longer alone in this world, and I've left a letter with them that tells everything. Everything! If anything happens to me, you're going down with me."

"What is going on?"

There was a long silence, blood dripping steadily from Ineke's hand. She was so still and pale, Leonie feared she would bleed to death. She looked around wildly, like a trapped bird. "They are here? You've got them here?"

"I will say no more. But you must cooperate now."

"Leonie?"

Ineke whipped around, her eyes glaring from under the wig. Blood from her fist continued to drip as she combed the parking lot and peered into the trees. She looked straight up to the sky with a pained look, as if she might find some kind of answer there.

"Stop it, Ineke. Stop it right now!"

"You know when you feel like you have nothing?" asked Ineke. "I know you know this feeling. That's why you were crazy enough to do it."

"Maybe!" said Leonie, becoming concerned about the amount of blood that was dripping from Ineke's fist.

"Don't lie. You were, and so am I. And that is why we came together, and with Luuk and Piet."

"Stop it, Ineke. It has gone beyond some mystical connection between us, *way beyond that!* There's the real world. There's the law."

"Don't mention the law," said Jacob/Paul quickly.

But Leonie felt that it was right to mention it—to drive a wedge between the exploitive madness of this young woman and herself. To make a permanent remove. To identify, if for no other reason than her own sanity, how she was swept into this bizarre scheme, a scheme that had sprouted tentacles in the past few months while she wasn't looking and exposed a rotten core.

"The law?" asked Ineke, growing paler, a pool of blood in the grass.

"You will show me the paintings now," said Leonie, "or I'll go to the police and tell them the whole story."

Eleven months later

CHAPTER 19
THE INLAND SEA

Sagaponack
September 18th, 2013

Lately, his boyhood self of over sixty years ago in grade school had taken up residence in his mind. "The Boy," he called him. The textural confinement of the experience would come to him—the maddeningly closed classroom door painted gunmetal gray, the black flecks where the paint had chipped. He could see the pages turning, the dry stacks of words and numbers, more on the blackboard and coming out of the teacher's mouth. In springtime, when the window was cracked, he would project himself out into the new air, smelling of daffodils, then further up into the budding trees and then the wide blue sky over the baseball field.

George now stood in his house, at the top of his fusty basement stairs. He was going to be moving soon, he told the boy. Perrin and Kit had bought the house where the Russian had lived. Last October, she had finally left Jack, and she had come out of it very well. She got the land where the house had been and had the studio demolished. Received enough in the settlement to last her and rebuild her own house *and* buy the Russian's house. Since everyone knew there had been a death there, she was able to get it relatively cheap. She closed on it last week. With ceremony and a smattering of bossy pride, she had presented him the keys to that house where his old studio had been. It was dry, it was warm, it had tremendous storage, and the light through those giant plate glass doors to the sea was without equal. It was a dream space, and all his, he told the boy. *Can you believe it?* No response. Asked him again if he could believe it. Nothing. Embellishing for effect, George went on—and no one would care or comment that one of the bedrooms would function like a big closet for his materials! That he'd moved most of the furniture out of the living room and planned a multi-discipline studio with a pottery corner and kiln towards the door, and canvas and paints on the other side! C'mon, it's great! George felt himself to be in a pleasant state of shock while entertaining this annoying shadow self who followed him around while he packed.

While George had respect for these mysteries, he wondered about a lot of things. To begin with—why did Perrin wait so long to make this incredible move? Maybe she was insecure, and then Kit had come along, the supposed art buyer at the Russian's party. Then there was the hurricane, when something snapped between her and Jack. If he remembered correctly, there had been a long build-up to that point. And then along came Kit. He didn't really seem like an experienced art buyer, but that was okay. There was definitely a spark in the air, and that might have been the most important thing. They seemed good together, and she was happy. There was a child, a girl, who was named Iris.

He edged down a few steps and flicked on a light. Together, he and the boy looked at last week's heavy rain still oozing from a crack in the foundation, and the black and green mold crawling up the walls, expiring as it approached the two hopper windows. The canvases he had stored on sawhorses when "Mike" was coming were still there. Good thing too. Underneath, puddles had gathered again. The boy was not impressed with his fancy plans. He scoffed. He was put out. He seemed to be saying that it wasn't really elemental, *was it?* George batted him away. *Let an old dude have a little fun.* He had wrapped each of the paintings in thick plastic sheeting in order to keep the mold from creeping onto the canvases. He stepped down and ripped away the masking tape across the bottom of one of them and checked to see how they had fared.

Had the boy hoped for better? Was that his message? *Not really,* thought George. He was just there sometimes, a cloudy id. He peeled back the plastic, exposing the corner where the mold might have crept. Fortunately, nothing, just the paint he had laid on back then. The boy was a little bit snide, grumbling in the corner. What could one do? From all of these selves came his art. His boyhood self, his youthful self, the early days with Perrin and Iris—all of them unfinished, all of them with their comments. The boy was probably some sort of full-circle nonsense, origin unknown. Hopefully not something about mortality.

The gray legs of a crow landed outside and stalked by. The boy liked that; it was pretty cool. George had never set out to be rich, but neither had he expected to be poor. At the present moment in the cultural conversation, he was credited with originating a movement; he was in all the books about abstract expressionism, at least a few paragraphs or maybe a short chapter. The boy was unimpressed. But what, essentially, had the boy wanted? He had wanted to carve things out of wood, paint pictures, look at the world, feel its pulse, its deep warm heat, its green mysteries, and see what he could see. His favorite class was woodshop. The other kids would do the assignments. *Make a box . . .* George would make a boat, with detailed fittings and a mast out of balsa wood. Or a car with carved headlights. Or an apple, accurately, capturing the personality of the apple—hard to do.

He taped the plastic back nice and tight and put some new strips on, just to be certain. An inland house was more damp than one in the dunes. Salt damp was different from earth damp. Earth damp carried spores, and spores had plans. Salt damp sort of hung around, crystallizing passively. It dried in the sun in patterns, it smelled good, it was clean, and when it dried, it could sometimes just be dusted or scoured off. Nice to return to the dune, thought George, near those two and my grandchild. Let me be happy. For once.

George held that the court of public opinion could never—*must* never—matter to him. To that end, he struggled mightily to express the thing that he felt. Extraneous things—opinions, ego, money, social status—they were all obstacles to seeing clearly. He had tried to shut them out, to stay close to the small, hot fire of his talent. Inside the comforting and distorting atmosphere of success, it was held among his group of friends, artists and writers mainly, that rewards came after a good bit of pain.

Oh no—no! said the boy. *That's dry, that's so dull. Just a lot of analysis and fake humility. Remember looking at the picture books in the library? Well? Weren't we going to do something big? Like the cover?*

I am in the books like you planned, punk. I'm just sort of on the side. We can't care about that—it's stupid. And look at all this, he murmured, motioning to the stacks of work he'd made.

That's a lot to have to drag around.

But even with that, he thought of his reduced status as a kind of limbo that was in its way interesting. He had been returned to a blank state, scratching around in the dirt to see if there was a possibility to make something original. He was as self-doubting as he had been during his art school days. He was stripped down, back where he started, only there was less time. That didn't have to be bad. His artist's eye was empty, all the better to see with. *Right, kid? So shut up.*

He was a cantankerous little fuck.

* * *

In the afternoon, Kit and Perrin went down to the water. Kit set up the red beach tent, so Iris could sleep out of the wind. Perrin was already in. The sea glittered, the breeze whipping up plumes of foam from the waves.

Adjusting his chair, he angled the umbrella again to block the sun, then sat down. He looked around—left, right, and far out in the dark blue water, where Perrin sometimes liked to go. He found her forays far offshore completely unnerving.

He lifted the flap and tied it open, so Iris would have enough air. The sun beating hot on his head, he crawled in. Laying his hand on her back, he noticed that it spanned shoulder to shoulder. He stretched out next to her. Under her tiny striped shirt, her ribs felt as delicate as a bird, rising and falling with urgency, as if transforming the ocean air into creating more of herself. It took energy, this growing. Her flushed face was pressed into the towel, her dark lashes resting upon her cheek, her red mouth open and blowing a bubble of drool. A person! A person where there wasn't a person before! He was in the club. Each day, he spent lovely hours with her strapped to his front, her hand splaying out like a starfish, clutching his ear or his hair. Sweet, beautiful girl. People didn't mention the God-like feeling.

A breeze fluttered the tent flap, the red-hued light browsing here and there upon her sleeping form. Only eleven months before, he had felt like God under the worst possible circumstances, in a moment of extreme insight that he never wanted to have. So he was in that club as well. It crossed his mind sometimes, though less often than before. He knew he'd never forget it. But a baby, new and fresh and innocent, was as close to smudging out that memory as he would ever have. The sound of the ocean wrapped around them and slowed to hold them in its embrace. He leaned in close and smelled her hair, feeling that she was an absolute miracle.

Through the flap, he looked out over a triangle of darkening sea. He wondered about Perrin, who had been out there a while. When she was really intent on getting exercise, she'd wear her goggles and swim cap and swim parallel to the coast for sometimes a mile or two. Then he'd lose track of her. But today she hadn't taken those; she had been in her playful dolphin mode. He loved to watch her dive into the shank of a wave or paddle up to the top as it rolled in, keeping her head above its crest, sometimes screeching in delight if the wave was really big. She swam all through the pregnancy, especially when Iris was feisty, kicking and squirming in the womb, which Perrin called the "inland sea." She claimed it put Iris to sleep. Kit loved to think about that. A sea within a sea as Perrin swam. One world tucked within another, which was the beginning of all life, each responding to the other—a perfect equilibrium. He popped out of the tent to take a look, and there, about fifty yards offshore, he saw her sleek blue form surface and dive under again.

ACKNOWLEDGMENTS

In these distracted days, there's nothing so valuable to a writer as an early reader—someone who will sit with a draft and make notes, or just provide an overview of the experience. For that rare favor, I'd like to thank Maria Matthiessen, Carol Jane Williams, Jessie Pollock, Michele McManus and Blair Seagram sincerely. Many thanks to editor Alexandra Shelley for her insight into my writing, and as well to her Livingroom Workshop, whose talented participants gave me needed feedback and confidence. Thanks also to Amelie van Den Akker and Johanna-Maria Van Rooijs for helping with Dutch inaccuracies, including those impossible spellings! For the unique cover design, my thanks to David Provolo and Blair Seagram. Lastly, I'd like to thank editor and publisher Jon Gosch for seeing the potential of the book and bringing it to market. It's always a pleasure.

ABOUT THE AUTHOR

Rue Matthiessen is based on the East End of Long Island. Nominated for the Pushcart Prize twice, her essays and short fiction have been published in numerous literary journals. Her memoir, *Castles & Ruins*, about growing up in Sagaponack, NY, with parents of ardent literary ambition, was published by Latah Books in February 2024. Recently, Rue was featured in the Bridgehampton Museum's Distinguished Lecturer Series, and Longhouse Talks in East Hampton. See more at ruematthiessen.com.

www.ingramcontent.com/pod-product-compliance
Lightning Source LLC
Chambersburg PA
CBHW020600310726
48979CB00008B/1280/J

* 9 7 8 1 9 5 7 6 0 7 3 3 7 *